SHADOW
— of the —
SACRED ISLANDS

To Tess,

Best wishes!

KEARA BARRON

BALBOA
PRESS

A DIVISION OF HAY HOUSE

Balboa Press
A Division of Hay House
1663 Liberty Drive
Bloomington, IN 47403
www.balboapress.com
1 (877) 407-4847

Because of the dynamic nature of the Internet, any web addresses or links contained in this book may have changed since publication and may no longer be valid. The views expressed in this work are solely those of the author and do not necessarily reflect the views of the publisher, and the publisher hereby disclaims any responsibility for them.

The author of this book does not dispense medical advice or prescribe the use of any technique as a form of treatment for physical, emotional, or medical problems without the advice of a physician, either directly or indirectly. The intent of the author is only to offer information of a general nature to help you in your quest for emotional and spiritual well-being. In the event you use any of the information in this book for yourself, which is your constitutional right, the author and the publisher assume no responsibility for your actions.

Any people depicted in stock imagery provided by Thinkstock are models, and such images are being used for illustrative purposes only.
Certain stock imagery © Thinkstock.

Print information available on the last page.

ISBN: 978-1-5043-4778-5 (sc)
ISBN: 978-1-5043-4777-8 (hc)
ISBN: 978-1-5043-4779-2 (e)

Library of Congress Control Number: 2015920789

Balboa Press rev. date: 03/31/2016

To Connor,
My first reader.

Coast Of Elementum, Lux

Sacred Islands

Lata Sea

City of
Sover

Maze of
Stones

Vast lake

Shrouded
Forest

Forks
Lake
Forks

Elementa

Verdi
Hills

valley
of graves

Lux, city map

Sacred Islands

Gulf of North Lux

Soror

vast
Elementa Lake

Septentrio   Oceanus

Elementum

Furtis
Lake
Furtis

Lux Mountain Range

Spearant Ocean

City of Lux
Parva
Centrum
Lake Vivi

Lux-Grandis

Plains of Lux

Arbor

Planus

City of Stella

Oasis

Terrestial Sea

key
road
river
region border
city

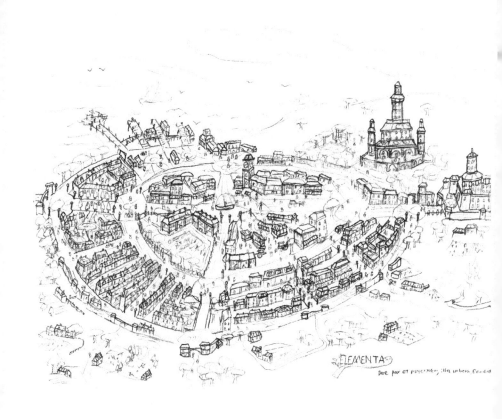

ELEMENTA

Two Back Stories

$\mathcal{T}$he waves repeatedly smashed against the ship and then receded back into the unfathomable depths of the cerulean ocean. I leaned over the rail and studied the water's motion. Sailors called out to me, ordering me to stop so that I wouldn't fall in and drown. I mostly ignored them, but shot some of them the most menacing glare I could manage.

It had been a year and four months since my sister, mother, and I had set out on our voyage across the Spearant Sea. We had left behind the continent of Suri and were starting a new life in the smaller continent that contained one country: Lux. It was such a small place that Lux was a region where several city states swore allegiance to their capital, the City of Lux. I was not impressed. The geographic names of Lux were not meaningful and the continent was only a shred of land in the vast world. Still, the new life we were going to begin would be better than what we had in Suri. My father had died in a terrible accident and my mother was blamed for a crime she did not commit. She was accused for robbing some great temple in our country and being a part of an intricate band of criminals. It was unbelievable that someone as gentle as my mother would be accused of something so horrible. The evidence was not in her favor, for we have a theory that she was framed. After that it seemed like soldiers of where we lived were always watching us. My younger sister called them Watchers. Watchers were swarming around our home and stripped us of most of our money. Those series of events ruined our life and permanently damaged my relationship with my mother. We would always argue and shout at each other. Now we were basically exiled. My mother claims that they gave us a choice for a better life, a second chance, but it seems to me that we were just deported across the globe.

I watched the waves of the water crash and repeat. I held up my hand and twirled it around, imagining the water dancing in a circle. Many people in this world had elemental magic. If only I had magic with water. Ever since I was little I felt as if I had a special connection with the water. I would spend my time swimming in streams, letting the cool water soak into my skin. I felt as if I could feel the water's movements before they happened. Water gave me peace, something I'm not sure anything or anyone else could give me.

A small amount of water from the sea far below me weakly rose and spun ever so slightly in a circular motion, just like my hand. I leaped back from the rail and stumbled onto the deck. Did the water just *rise*? Did I do that? *Impossible. I have no magic of any kind.*

I got up from the deck and up on my feet. I tried to move the water again. A few droplets strayed away from the water and lazily dropped back into the Celestial Sea. I did move it! I had magic! Water magic!

Moving the water made me dizzy. I had never used magic before; I didn't know I had magic. I lost my balance and fell onto the deck again.

* * *

"Elementa? Where is that?" I asked.

"It's northwest of here, past Soror, next to Vast Lake," my father explained.

"You mean that tiny little speck on the maps? Are you sure that's a town?"

"No, it's a city. And I know it's not as big as our city but I'm sure you'll love it there."

"That's what everyone says when people move! What's wrong with our home here, the City of Oceanus? This place is one of a kind, Father! No other city in Lux is by a gulf and we do the most trading with faraway places. Isn't that something to be proud of? And the gardens here! They are spectacular, Father!"

He sighed. He knew that trying to convince me would be useless. I could see it in his eyes, the way those hazel eyes dimmed with defeat. He looked tired.

"I'm sure that there will be gardens in Elementa, too. My job requires us to move and that's inevitable. Could you at least try to enjoy it instead of complaining?"

I scoffed and walked away. He couldn't understand how important Oceanus was to me. I had grown up here, all my life and now our family was whisking away. Were they trying to leave our past in the dust, where it was clouded from sight, letting valuable scraps of my childhood drift away? My parents were letting my scraps of life stir in the dust, left to be trampled on or left to be released into sky. I couldn't let go of my home or my past. My parents were asking too much of me. There wouldn't even be gardens in Elementa like there were here. I could spend all day in those gardens, admiring the blossoms, reaching out to the greenery, and wrapping myself into the wall of vines with tiny purple buds poking out. As a plant mage, I needed those gardens. I needed them and they needed me. We both thrived together. Soon it would all be gone from my life and I would be settled in a new place entirely. Some tiny town called Elementa, a tiny town that no one has heard of.

VOLUME ONE

CHAPTER 1

KORINA

I twirled a small amount of water secretly underneath my desk while Professor Rhydork droned on about ancient history. The Academy could be so dreadfully boring at times. Every student who attended the Academy was training to master their element such as ice and water, stones and metals, or earth and plants and the like. The students had a special talent to control and manipulate a power of nature. Most students were learning to be mages, like me. I was currently in the Academy, learning to be a mage of ice and water. Unfortunately there were a few mandatory classes in the Academy like history. As far as I was concerned, history, geography, math, and language had nothing to do with learning to be a mage. I was forced to mingle with students with elements other than ice and water. That was frustrating for me.

The worst class by far was history. Professor Rhyback had no power of any element and lived a dull life. No excitement and he was the sort of middle aged man that looks like he lives with his mother and her seven cats. My official nickname for him was Rhydork.

I was intrigued by my twirling water. I was hypnotized by its small and pleasant beauty, and the circular motion of my hands that created the water's movement. I was so absorbed in my water that I didn't hear Rhydork creep up on me.

Whap!

The whip of a wooden yard stick snapped on my desk. I jumped, utterly startled. The water fell on the ground, lifeless. I scowled at the floor of the classroom.

"I expect you to pay attention in class, Korina Valletta. Not playing around with your 'water magic'. Next time I catch you messing around I will ban you from your element at all times in this class room and personally send you to the Headmaster of the Academy!" Rhydork sternly looked down on me, glaring. I returned the harsh look.

"You can't ban me from my magic Rhyback! I have the power to control it and my element is something *you* can't ever take away from me," I spat. I narrowed my eyes. Rhydork twitched his nose at me. I could see the annoyance sprouting on his face, his wrinkles growing deeper and bitterer. His eyes flared, anger flashing in the sea of brown.

"*Professor* Rhyback to you. You do not possess the authority to treat me like that, Korina. I am the teacher and when you step into this classroom you listen to *me,*" He said, his voice rising in irritation. Then quietly he added, "Stay after the bell." As he walked away he left a slip of parchment on my desk. I quickly scanned it. I would have to report after classes today as a punishment. I groaned.

All the eyes of the other students resumed their default position to the front of the room as Rhydork began his interrupted lecture once more. I slunk down in my chair. I hated history. Rhydork was stupid and his rules were stupid and his lectures were stupid. I could feel the buzz of my cheeks as they heated like tiny sparks of fire. I needed to calm down. Unfortunately I could never resist a challenge with another person, whether it is someone above me or an equal. Out of spite, I tuned Rhydork out the rest of the class.

I glanced out the window and at the clock tower. Only a few more minutes of the dreadful class and then I could go to one that actually taught me about my element. I looked around the room. Pens bobbed up and down as they darted across papers. Were we supposed to be writing something? Rhydork kept talking and talking, squeezing every ounce out of time as the minutes slowly passed. Then he stopped. *Finally,* I thought.

"I hope you all took good notes on this lecture because we will be having a brief quiz tomorrow about what I spent the whole class talking about," Rhydork announced.

He paused as groans and mumbles spread through the room. "I know, I know. Study hard tonight and you'll do fine! Don't forget to read tonight out of your history scrolls!" Then the city clock tower sung and it was time to go to the next class.

Great. A quiz over a whole lecture that I didn't hear one word of. Oh well, I thought. It won't be the first time I failed a quiz. I got up from my seat, just as I remembered. I wasn't going anywhere. I clutched the slip of paper firmly in my hand, crinkling the paper.

"Korina, your behavior was unacceptable today as usual," Rhydork sighed. "I can't keep having you distract the class and challenge my authority or I will send you to the Headmaster. Don't forget to stay after class today for your consequence. I have declared only an hour, so it's not that bad."

I ripped the slip as I walked out.

Who did Rhydork think he was, anyway? He thought he could suspend me from my abilities whenever he wanted! It wasn't my fault his lectures were dreary and uninteresting! I was sure there were others who had wandered away in their minds during his class. I just happened to be one of his least-favored students, which was not just. I had a hunch that he picked favorites. I snorted in irritation as I stalked through the long dull halls of the Academy.

As I shoved my way through the unmoving knots of people, someone stuck their foot out. Before I had time to react, I lurched forward and flew to the ground, catching myself with my hands. A jolt of sharp pain lunged into my wrists. My face was floating an inch off of the stone floor. My cheeks warmed with rage as I heard teasing laughs waft around me. I pushed myself up to my feet and glared at the circle of people that had enclosed around me.

"What's your problem?!" I sneered at the boy who had purposely tripped me.

He waved his hands in mock fear. "Please don't hurt me!" he turned to his friends and laughed.

I squinted my eyes in fury. "You *should* be scared." More guffaws. "You half-brained toad," I muttered under my breath.

"*What* did you call me?" he demanded. His freckles and scrunched nose were bothersome, only adding to his ugliness.

"I said you were a half-brained toad!" I said loudly, almost a yell. "But that would be an insult to toads!"

"You think you can actually talk to me like that *and* get away with it." He was half-heartedly teasing me, his tone light as a feather and confidence as strong as stone. I knew he was trying to reel me in, dancing for a fight, an argument, anything as long as it entertained him.

"And you think you can go around tripping people for no reason!"

The boy's face flashed with glee and he rapidly swung a fist at me. I ducked, gasping. Did he really just try to punch me? He had the nerve to punch a girl.

The crowd of spectators gleefully shouted as he swung at me. Some were itching for a fight to watch.

"You think you can escape me?" he punched again. I dodged him.

"You're awfully slow, aren't you?" I mocked. The crowd sounded again at the challenge.

"You have a big mouth, don't you?" This time he landed a hard blow. I yelped in pain and touched my hand to my shoulder, where he had hit me.

"What's the matter? I thought I was slow!"

Before I knew what I was doing I whipped a stream of water at his face. It broke in a small explosion as soon as it collided with his head.

"Oh so now we're using elements?" He wiped his hand over his wet and hideous face. He spun a flame into his hands and reared back his arm as if he were going to throw it at me. I felt my eyes widen with fear and I slung another burst of water. It barely dented the harsh flame.

The crowd of onlookers dispersed immediately as two professors approached the scene. "What is going on here?" one sternly demanded. The boy extinguished the flame in a blink of an eye.

"This girl here was threatening me and then she attacked me with her water magic!" he fibbed.

"What!" I protested. "That's not even true and you know it—"

"Quiet, both of you! You will both be punished for this if the story isn't explained. Or do I have to call for the Headmaster? I'm sure the Headmaster wouldn't be too excited, since she is busy with Soror. Apparently they're sending students over." That was twice in the same day a professor had threatened to bring the Headmaster into the conflict. She must be some scary figurehead, I thought.

"I just told you ma'am, this girl was trying to—"

The professor silenced him with a glare. "Listen, I don't care who started it. You are both old enough to act like mature students. No fights in the hallways and no using elements outside of class! Now get to your next class before you're both late!"

I was let off with a warning. That was just luck, I supposed. People in the Academy were so infuriating! The professors were annoying and the students were arrogant and rude. I was constantly being challenged, and constantly being thrown into trouble because of it. I was new to the Academy, after just discovering I possessed magic. I had come from overseas, and the country of Lux was a new life. Most of the people here wielded magic as well, whether they were a mage or wizard or sorcerer or witch or a plain spell caster. Most people in Elementa were mages. The town itself was run by them—giving the city its name for the elements.

The rest of my day at the Academy was a waste of my time. I had managed to squeeze out of trouble but my mind remained blank and unfocused. At the end of the last class I sighed with relief and joy but then remembered I had to go back to Rhydork's class. If it was any other class I would be fine, but consequence in Rhydork's class was a real pain. The old man was even bothersome to look at; he had white hair that only thinly wrapped around his head and round metal rimmed glasses that perched on his nose. His eyes were set back in their sockets and surrounded by a bed of wrinkles that creased his face. He had tried to pull off a cropped beard style, but miserably failed. Instead it looked like he had forgotten to shave wispy white whiskers. He was also a short and thin man, and though he was only middle-aged he looked ancient. I groaned aloud and forced myself to trudge to his classroom.

"Ah, Korina. I was doubting that you would show up," Rhydork said.

I grunted my response.

"Hm." Professor Rhyback pushed his glasses up and twitched his nose. "Please sit down at a desk and remain quiet. Remember: no talking to yourself, sleeping, working on class work, or doodling."

"I'll try to remember that," I grumbled.

"What's that?"

"Nothing."

"Very well then." Rhydork flipped an old hour glass upside down. "Your time has started."

"Don't you know that we have actual clocks?"

"Shh!"

"Why—"

"Shh! No talking!"

I rolled my eyes and crossed my arms over my chest. This would be a long hour.

CHAPTER 2

SAGE

I flicked my short, dark red hair in annoyance as I left the classroom. There wouldn't be a gap in my notes if that trouble maker Korina Valletta hadn't interrupted the class. That's all she could do anyway. Korina probably couldn't even score a high grade on a test and could never stay out of trouble in that class. And now thanks to her inconsiderate and idiotic actions, I was missing a whole section in my notes. To make matters worse, there was a quiz on this material tomorrow. I couldn't miss multiple questions because of Korina! I had no idea who to get the missing section of notes from either. I never missed more than a couple of questions on any history test! If anyone was the smartest fourteen year old in that class, it was me by a long shot. If nobody else was as bright and gifted as I was, how could I get notes that met my high standards?

I angrily sighed and rushed to my next class. Korina was the despised subject in my mind until I settled down. After all, I wasn't going to let that delinquent ruin my day. Especially since I was entering my favorite class of the day. I was in gardening, which isn't at all what it sounds like. In gardening, there were no students like Korina and her ice and water. Instead there were students like me, with the element of plants and earth.

In gardening, each student learned more about how to become a garden mage and how to properly use their magic and extend their power. The professor of my gardening class was Mage Bramble. Mage Bramble was a full garden mage, and probably the best one in the whole Academy. He was also a good teacher, kind with a passion for learning and slightly humorous occasionally.

Outside in the city, the clock tower rang a second time, indicating that it was time for the Academy students to be in their next class.

"Don't be late everyone!" Mage Bramble said. "We have lots to do today as usual and we will be using our plant-like specialties." He waited for everyone to get seated and the whispers to pass.

"Alright, looks like everyone is ready. Get out your garden mage scrolls."

I spent the rest of the class in awe, using my magic to move vines and make them stretch higher. I sharpened leaves and levitated several up in the air, like tiny little daggers ready to charge. Some days we would even work on entwining our magic with combat skills.

"Sage put those leaves down before you lose control and seriously injure someone!" Mage Bramble called out to me.

"Sorry!" I quickly apologized and set the leaves down. They glistened in the artificial light of the classroom. I was ahead of the class, as usual. None of them would know how to fight with leaves. Leaves are delicate and require sensitivity and a careful hand. I didn't think any student knew how to harden them to make them strong instead of flimsy and weak. It required a good amount of focus and dedication. Mage Bramble could do far more impressive magic though. He could probably harden five vines at once, while snapping them with power but control. After all, Mage Bramble was said to have fought in the small scrimmage with the neighboring city state of Fortis.

I looked to the left and watched Mage Bramble assist a slow student. "No, no, no. Your form is a bit sloppy there. You need to have firm motions, but breathe. No, no, you're too stiff there…"

The student could barely levitate a crispy leaf. I rolled my eyes and looked to my right, studying everyone else's progress. The student that Mage Bramble was helping wasn't the only one who had trouble.

After gardening ended the rest of the day wasn't as enjoyable. After classes ended I started to head toward Professor Rhyback's class. Even though he wasn't as exciting as Mage Bramble and quite a bit older, his lectures were still very interesting. It was fascinating to listen and learn about the rich history of our country of Lux. I was going to his class because there was something I kept pondering about in my head. I wanted to ask Professor Rhyback if he knew anything about it.

As I entered his class I felt my spirits drop and excitement vanish. There, sitting in the back of the room was my least favorite person in Elementa. Korina. Probably serving consequence, I thought.

Professor Rhyback sat behind his desk, his nose buried in papers.

"Professor Rhyback?"

He looked up from the papers. "Oh, hello Sage. What can I do for you?"

"I was wondering if you could tell me anything about the Sacred Islands?"

The professor looked surprised and puzzled as he wrinkled his brow. "Where did you hear about the Sacred Islands? No matter. Yes in fact I do, though not very much. I used to do a couple lectures on the Sacred Islands but the Academy cut it out of the curriculum for some reason. Anyway, what do you want to know?"

I heard Korina snort from the back of the room. I briefly spun around to shoot her a glare. How disrespectful of her. She had no appreciation for history, let alone education in its entirety.

"Anything and everything you know, if you don't mind, Professor. I've heard many intriguing rumors about them and wanted to know if they were true. It seems like such a mystical place."

"Well," the professor sniffed and pushed his glasses up, "there are seven of the Sacred Islands. Two main ones and five smaller islands. They used to be populated and a rich civilization, but long ago an enormous volcanic eruption destroyed the towns of the island called Felix Island. It unfortunately killed thousands and affected the neighboring islands. It was like a chain reaction or something unbalanced that area. Other volcanoes erupted, such as Mount Ash on Divite Island. Earthquakes started to split the land. Where the survivors went is unknown. The big island to the left of Felix is Divite Island, with a mountain range and once glorious village and castle. Now it is all sadly abandoned and most likely crumbling in decay by now. Mount Ash and Mount Felix erupted simultaneously, you know. That also caused major damage to the village in Divite. I'm not even sure if anything's left of it, except for maybe a few piles of rock and blankets of ash."

I raised my eyebrows. "What a tragic event, all those people and their homes. It must have been an amazing place."

"Oh it was told to be so. How about you go to the Academy library and check out some books about the Sacred Islands? Then you can come tell me what you have learned."

I smiled. "I will. Thank you for your time and sharing your knowledge."

"Not a bother at all! I enjoy sharing knowledge with my students. Could you stay here a couple of minutes and watch Korina? I have to do something real quick," Rhyback said. He gathered a wad of papers and abruptly left the room. How wonderful. I was alone with Korina.

"Sacred Islands, huh? Never heard of them," She huffed from the back.

"That is certainly not a surprise," I said, rolling my eyes. "They're not very well known anyway. Only a few special ones know about the Sacred Islands."

"Are you calling me dumb? Do you really think that you're superior and so much smarter than me?" She squinted her eyes, scowling at me.

"No, I'm just saying it's not likely for you to know about them. And based on grades at the Academy, yes, I probably am a lot smarter," I replied and crossed my arms.

Korina grumbled. "You think you're all that!" And before I knew what was happening she shot a short dagger of ice, flying straight for my chest. A sharp prick exploded in my chest, turning to a dull and uncomfortable ache. Bitter cold dug its claws into me.

"How dare you abuse your magic on the grounds of the Academy!" I scolded, clutching my chest. I coughed from the impact.

"Like this?" Korina smirked and shot a wave of water at me. I dodged most of it, prepared this time. Bits of icy water splattered on me.

I yanked two potted plants from across the classroom and stretched them up and up until they were like two towering arms. I moved my hands down and the plant arms plunged down on Korina, binding her so that she couldn't move.

Korina struggled and twisted with all her strength. "Let me go!" She groaned and squirmed some more.

I smiled. It was nice to know I had overpowered her easily and took victory over this sad and cocky student.

"That'll teach you not to mess with me. I told you I was smarter, not to mention more skilled." I released her and pushed the plants back into their pots across the room. They shrunk, creeping back into the pots as if nothing had ever happened. Professor Rhyback then entered the room, completely oblivious as he walked with his face in more papers.

"Thank you, Sage. Have a nice day," He said, without even glancing up.

I happily left the room. It was nice to get away from Korina, especially leaving her with bitter defeat for the rest of the day. I walked through the stone hallways of the Academy and made my way to the library. There was something I was thoroughly interested in and worth my time, unlike Korina: the Sacred Islands.

CHAPTER 3

ELIJAH

The final bell of the clock tower rang, announcing that the day was over. I walked over to Teressia Oglesby as everyone rushed out of the classroom. The teacher had left us with a discouraging essay to complete by the end of the week. Language was not a pleasant class and I thoroughly hated essays. I hoped to at least find a topic to write on by the end of the evening when the sun drowned in the dark indigo of the night sky. But I had my doubts. I had been told by Teressia that I was a procrastinator and I could not deny that it always took me hours to find a topic for essays.

"Hey Tres, let's go to the library." There would be plenty of topics to find in the library, right?

"Why would anyone like *you*, Elijah, want to go to the library?" Teressia said with a tentative tone. She sounded tired and seemed like she wanted to go home. Teressia was a little timid and shy but once you got to be her friend you would understand her, and she'd eventually open up. We had known each other since we could barely walk.

"'Cause I really need to find a topic for that stupid essay. I am *not* going to get another late grade in language."

"Fine, I'll go with you. Besides I need to find a topic too," Teressia said. "But let me say, I am impressed with your sudden will to go to the library. People really do change, I suppose."

"Shut up," I said, smiling.

We squeezed between clusters of people in the crowded hallways while students hurried to get home. I stuck out my elbows to push through with confidence, letting everyone know not to push me around. Teressia shrunk her body and hung her head timidly while managing to get through the hallway. I sighed. Tres would never even walk with confidence. She was too modest and humble to ever think too highly of herself.

We approached the old library of the Academy. The library was one of the first additions to the Academy and had scarcely been renovated since. I hauled open the tall, heavy framed glass door. The musty smell of books with tattered pages flew into my nose. There were books and shelves decades old in this library, no doubt some were providing a home for mold and dust. Shelves towered around us in neat and ordered rows with intricate designs on the corners. Desks were spread out in a planned manner between occasional shelves. Cushioned sofas and chairs lined the center of the library and directly behind that was an enormous window that stretched up to the second story tall ceiling. The librarian's desk was planted at the base of the window.

I slung my book bag on one of the library desks. Tres delicately sat her bag down on one seat and pulled out papers and a pen. I plopped into a chair and sighed. Tres arranged her things neatly on the desk then disappeared into the forest of bookshelves that filled the library. I sighed again, tapping my pen on the desk. I had no idea where to begin while Tres obviously knew what she wanted to write about.

I created a tiny flicker of flame on the tip of my finger. I spun it around delicately and weaved it around each finger, passing it back and forth as if weaving a picture. My element was fire and my professors always hinted that I would become a powerful and strong fire mage. I noticed I could do more with flames than any other student but I never admitted it. It was best to keep any opinion of myself hidden and encourage others. Maybe spending so much time with Teressia improved my manners.

As I played with my flame Tres came back with a stack of books. I looked up at her, my flame vanishing.

"What is all of that?" I asked.

"Books. Maybe I should teach you how to use them," Teressia joked.

"How can you already know what you're gonna write about?" I said, jealous and amazed at the same time.

"I just do, Elijah. It's not that hard. I have the element of stone and minerals so I'm researching rocks and stuff. It'll help me in training too."

I chuckled. "That's *lame*," I teased. "No one wants to read about rocks."

Tres slapped me on the shoulder but I knew she was joking when she smiled.

Tres had a book open in no time and was writing furiously. I tapped my foot and drummed my fingers on the table. Tres looked up at me, clearly annoyed. I stopped, smiling.

Tres was obviously tired of me doing nothing. "Elijah, go find a topic. Just go pull out any random book from a shelf."

I got up and walked around aimlessly, not planning to find books. I turned as I heard the heavy library door creak open. A girl my age with somewhat short, dark red wavy hair walked in. She looked around and then headed toward shelves in the back of the library. Why would she be going to that section of the library? With nothing better to do I carefully followed her, hoping to find a topic that way. It was strange, I knew, but I was bored and wanted to avoid my work.

The girl walked deeper into the library with slow hesitant steps. She was looking for something. I followed her into a section where no one else was as she kneeled down to a bottom row of the tall shelf. I then stepped out of hiding.

"What are you looking for?" I said.

She yelped in surprise. "You startled me," she said as she clutched her chest, as if trying to slow her heart beat. "And nothing," she said carefully, watching me with harsh hazel eyes. "Did you follow me?" she asked roughly.

"Um, no why would I, um," I stammered. Of course I followed her but how could I say that openly? It would seem ridiculous. What if this girl told other people? Their opinions of me would surely change for the worse.

"What's your name? You look familiar." She squinted at me, definitely not lightening her harsh look. I was relieved that she seemed uninterested to know whether or not I had followed her.

"Um, Elijah," I said hesitantly. "What about you?"

She studied me, letting moments pass in between us without being uncomfortable. The moments passed us and flew to the books that rested on the shelves, untouched. Was she deciding whether or not to lie about her name?

"Sage," She stated confidently. "Sage Winter. Why did you follow me?" She inquired. Her voice had a confident and cutting edge to it. To my dismay, she did not forget about the me-following-her situation.

"Um…" I was thinking. I definitely did not want Sage to get the wrong impression but was there a way I could play it off without sounding dumb? I decided it was best to tell the truth, even though she might not believe it. I explained that I was bored and was trying to find a topic for the essay. Sage nodded and told me she had the same essay.

"Is that what you were looking for? A book on your topic?" I asked.

"Not exactly," Sage said. She looked at me, probably trying to decide whether or not she should tell me what she was looking for. After a long pause she continued. "Have you…" she hesitated. "Have you heard of the Sacred Islands?"

I thought for a minute. *Sacred Islands. They sound familiar.* Then I realized I had heard my mother mention it to my father once. It was late in the night, and they were whispering in the glowing light emanating from our fireplace. Their voices were hushed and worried and I had figured they were trying to keep something secret from me and my brother. But I had caught scraps of their words that didn't fit together. I had heard the words "Sacred Islands" but at the time I didn't think anything of it.

"Heard of them. Don't know what they are though," I finally replied.

Sage explained to me what her history professor had told her. "I'm looking for a book or two about them but I can't find any and I'm sure I'm in the right place."

I kneeled beside her and rummaged through the books on the shelf. Dust rose and swirled around. I sputtered and coughed. This was the first time these books had even been touched in years.

There was nothing on the Sacred Islands. Sage rolled back on her heels, looking defeated. But I kept searching, scanning the spines of books for any revealing letters that spoke of the islands. A thin slip of old yellow parchment tucked between two books suddenly caught my eye. I carefully pulled the parchment out of the dusty shelf and unfolded it. Sage watched me the whole time.

"What's that?" She peered over my shoulder as I continued to unfold it.

"A map," I breathed, careful not to damage the ancient piece of paper. It was a map of the tip of Lux, showing our city of Elementa, the Shrouded Forest, and our neighboring city of Fortis to the left of us. The Lata Sea took up most of the map, and tucked in the left hand corner were the Sacred Islands.

"I can't believe it. No map I have ever seen of Lux has shown the Sacred Islands. That's odd how there's no book on the Sacred Islands but a lone map stuck in the shelf," Sage mused, studying the map. "This doesn't tell me much about the islands except where they are. Useless."

"It is not! We're looking at something no other student in the Academy has seen. Don't you think that means *something?*" I said.

Sage shrugged. "So? The Sacred Islands aren't a secret. People know about them and some are bound to know where they are."

"Okay, well most people don't. *I* didn't. And since there's nothing here about the Sacred Islands except for this single map, it leads me to think that there used to be books on the Sacred Islands."

"Maybe someone checked them out then."

"Are you kidding? Just look at this shelf! Nobody's touched it for years. The Academy must have removed them and left the map."

Sage sighed. "Well. I guess we'll never know for sure."

"I'm not giving up now. Let's go ask the librarian," I suggested. I didn't care if Sage came or not. If she really wanted to know more about these Sacred Islands she would come with me, but I was not going to give up if she didn't follow. I folded the old map and stuck it into the pocket of my breeches.

"Elijah! That's stealing from the library!" Sage chastised.

"So?" I grinned. "Nobody will ever notice."

Sage reluctantly followed me to the librarian's desk in front of the huge window. The afternoon sunlight filtered through the glass, illuminating the librarian's desk. A trim of gold outlined the librarian's grayish black hair from the sun. She looked up, peering through her thick lenses that sat in the thin wire frame of her glasses.

"May I help you?" she rasped in a scratchy voice.

"Yes. We were looking for books on the Sacred Islands but there doesn't seem to be any. Do you mind showing us where the books on the Sacred Islands are?" I asked politely, speaking for the two of us.

The librarian cleared her throat. "The books on the Sacred Islands were removed from the Academy a while ago after the subject was removed entirely from the history curriculum."

"Why?" I asked. Sage shifted from foot to foot impatiently beside me.

The librarian seemed annoyed. "Because it was decided that the Sacred Islands were not to be a subject that would be studied. They possess many secrets and rumored dangers. The Academy decided it was best that people should not go sticking their noses in places they didn't belong," she said, looking down on us, obviously hinting that we were sticking our noses in places we shouldn't. "So there should be no information on the Sacred Islands in this building. Understand?"

I nodded but Sage didn't. Instead she took a step forward.

"But the islands are abandoned. Why can't we learn about them?" Sage asked.

The librarian exhaled sharply. "I don't know. Ask someone important. No, don't ask anyone at all. Don't speak of it anymore. Now get along. The library will be closing soon."

Sage and I walked away. "It was worth a try," I said.

Sage nodded. "Well I guess it was nice meeting you, Elijah," she said.

"Nice meeting you too. Do you want to meet up anywhere to see if we can find books about the Sacred Islands?"

"I'm not sure, Elijah. But if you find anything let me know. Though I don't think you'll find anything on the islands. Remember? The librarian said they took everything out."

"Out of this building. There's still a library in the City of Elementa."

"If they took information out of here they would probably do the same in Elementa's libraries. Goodbye Elijah."

Sage briskly left the library, the heavy door banging as it swept shut. I turned back and walked to Teressia, who was still writing furiously.

"Did you find a topic?" She asked, without ceasing her writing.

"No."

"Of course you didn't. Even though we've been here for half an hour you've done nothing. That seems like you. Who were you talking to?" Tres looked up, curious.

"Just some girl. I thought she could help me find a topic," I lied.

"Elijah, you must think I'm stupid. I don't know what you were doing but it was probably wasting time. And I know her by the way— Sage. She's supposedly Mage Bramble's most talented student. I've heard him and Mage Isaac talking about students with potential. I wonder why."

"I didn't know you knew her."

"Yeah. She's in my history class too. Her element is plants and earth. You have to be careful around her. She's brilliantly smart and gifted but easily irritated."

I was puzzled. "How do you know so much about her?"

"I have her in several classes. She also lives in the west part of Elementa like we do. I've seen her about."

"Ah." I was bored now. I flicked up my little flame again.

Teressia abruptly slammed a book shut. I was startled and dropped the flame.

"Let's go home Elijah," Tres said.

"No!" I shouted as the flame fell to the floor. I was panicking inside. The whole library was made of paper and I had dropped a tiny little flame that would grow and grow.

"What? You want to stay—" Tres looked down and her expression transformed as she saw the ember burst into more flames on the ground.

The librarian scowled.

CHAPTER 4

TERESSIA

I walked home alone instead of with Elijah. He was ordered to stay and put out the fire he caused in the library. As I had left the library I heard the librarian shouting and yelling 'Elijah Elsbade you are *banned* from here! Don't ever come near my books' and on and on she went. I always told him never to anger the elderly because they could have a heart attack. If our Academy librarian died the next day I wouldn't be surprised. Elijah can lose control over his fire every once in a while. I suppose this time he'll try to blame it on me for closing a book too loudly.

I swung open the door to our small house and hooked my bag around the chair of the table. When you entered the house, the table would be to the left and the living room to the right. The kitchen was through a doorway in front of the table. My mom's room was through the kitchen and to the right, where the only washing room of the house was located. My room was the small second floor.

"Mom?" I called. She was usually sitting in the living room when I got home. No answer. I walked through the kitchen and into her bedroom. She had the curtains drawn over the window so that it was dark. My mother was lying down on the small bed. She turned on her side to face me.

"Hello Tres," She weakly mumbled.

"What's wrong?"

"Oh nothing, nothing. Just a slight headache. It threatens to get worse if I don't lie still."

I nodded and left. My mother got headaches every now and then. When she did it was best to leave her alone and stay quiet. It was up to me to cook dinner when I got hungry. I sighed as I stared at my bag. There was work to be done tonight for my Academy classes. I walked past my bag and out the door.

I didn't feel like dedicating my entire evening to work. My mother was too ill to stay on my back so I walked west, out of the city and to the Shrouded Forest. I decided I would spend my evening doing something fun. I would practice my stone magic at the edge of the forest. The trees would be kind to me since it was spring. They would only blossom instead of dumping snow on me or littering my stones with leaves.

When I arrived at the Shrouded Forest I heard a rustling sound and felt small tremors in the stone. I looked to my right. Sage Winter was there, uprooting a poor tree and spinning vines and brambles around it in the air. How strange she could be, I thought. Why would anyone want to cause discomfort to the innocent creations of nature? There were some instances where Sage would help the plants grow, and other times where it seemed she would be destroying them. I felt a vibration in the ground and heard a loud thump. A tree had fallen out of Sage's grasp and landed on the ground. The vines shrank back and also fell limp beside the tree.

I left the area where Sage was for peace. If I was going to mess around with stones I didn't need any distraction from her. Sage knew she was gifted but she had no idea where her power was limited. I walked south, toward the Elementa River. I spent quite a bit of time reshaping stones, moving them, stacking them. I had broken a large stone into pieces and was levitating them in the air when something felt off. The air around the stones crackled and popped, and the stones fell from my grasp and onto the ground. That's odd, I thought. I knelt to the ground and took a piece of the rock into my hand, running my hand over it, feeling the familiar crevices and lines that told the rock's story. It was jagged and uneven, undisturbed by the harsher elements. I welcomed the feeling of the rock, but something was different. The rock was not itself. It had a different aura, as I would describe it. I couldn't quite place my finger on the change though.

I was still holding the rock when it began to sizzle, small bubbles popping like water bubbling down a stream. I cried out as the heat met my skin and dropped the rock. I clutched my hand, waiting for the burning to subside. I glanced down at it, seeing steam lacing into the air like ghostly fingers of the wind. The grass withered and became a black charred color. I leapt to my feet and backed up, gasping. What was happening? Had I done something wrong with my magic? Had I caused harm to the earth?

The very air seemed disturbed, as if a new feeling was added to it. A feeling of something dark, maybe even sinister. Was that darkness in the air causing all of the abnormality? I glanced around, looking for anything that could be the source of the disturbance. I felt my heart skip a beat as I spotted large black specks piled by the base of a tree. I was considering whether to investigate it or not. What would Elijah have done in this situation? I decided that he would tease me for being scared of nothing and go without fear. I crept to the tree, my palms sweaty. What if it was something dangerous? What if something evil had left black spells there? Or it could be the droppings of an animal. I was being ridiculous.

The black spots were simply rocks. They were scattered around the tree, charred and steaming. I covered my nose, the smell hitting me instantly. It was a heavy scent that was suffocating and revolting. I turned around and ran away from the area.

The whole place was probably poisoned with whatever that was on the rocks. The rocks I had been practicing with had turned almost black like that as well. I slowed down and began walking at a slower pace when I had distanced myself from the area.

After walking for a bit I looked to the left and saw yet *another* person that I recognized. Usually I would see no one near the Shrouded Forest. I recognized her straight black hair that stretched down half of her back. Korina. She was kneeling at the bank of the river.

I didn't know much about Korina other than she was a defiant trouble maker. I had her in my history class as well as Sage. It was amusing to watch her challenge Professor Rhyback. He taught a boring class but he was a kind man. I could never disrespect him. Korina wasn't afraid to though. I stood there watching her, trying to decide if I should go over and introduce myself. We had never talked to each other and it would be nice to get to know her, but what if she didn't like me? What if she treated me like Professor Rhyback? I stood there too long thinking because Korina turned and saw me. I felt shaky and looked around. It was too late to hide.

"What are you looking at!" She shouted from her position by the river. I didn't answer. After all, I wasn't going to yell. I preferred to talk less loudly. It would be awful to hurt someone's ears. So I glanced around and jogged to her.

I was nervous. I was trying to think of what to say first. First impressions were very important. I didn't want Korina to think poorly of me and I needed to have her think of me as a nice person. What if I forgot my manners? What if I came off arrogant? Oh, how that would be awful. What if everything came out in a rush? I just needed to slow down and be calm.

"Um, I just recognized you from the Academy. I wasn't following you! I was just here on my own. Not that I was trying to be here, I mean here at the same time you were. I mean I was here by my own will, I didn't just wander here—"

"Okay, okay enough! I get it." Korina looked up at me. So much for slowing down. "Oh I know you. Teressia, right? You're the shy one in my history class. I guess you saw me blow up at Rhydork—uh, I mean Rhyback."

Rhydork? "Yeah. You're Korina, right?" I said a little timidly. Oh no, I thought. I had said that a little too softly. She already thought I was shy!

"Yup." Korina turned her back on me and stared at the river again. I decided to take a big risk and sat down beside her.

"What are you looking at?" I asked, hoping that I wasn't bothering her.

"You see that? It's a dead fish," Korina answered bluntly.

"I see, but what's special about it?" I asked, trying to be polite. I guess I didn't understand water mages.

"Well that thing floating next to it is also a dead fish. And there's a couple more ahead of them."

"Oh. That's odd," I quietly said. I should probably try to be more confident and a little louder, I thought.

"Yeah. Definitely odd. Why there would be several dead fish in a healthy river makes no sense. I'm gonna see if there's more dead fish. You coming?"

I was surprised that Korina would invite me. Maybe I wasn't annoying to her after all. I nodded and followed her.

As we walked along the river we saw more dead fish until there were so many there was a foul fishy stench in the air. By this time we had gotten deeper into the forest, not just the edges of it. Then the river turned to a darker blue, and as we continued a sickening purple and finally a deep black.

Korina sniffed the air. "The river smells horrible. And I'm not talking about the fish. It smells..." she paused. "It smells like it's poisoned. I could be wrong though. Sometimes I don't pay close attention in class." Korina snapped her wrist upward and the black water obeyed as it lifted into the air. Korina brought it closer to us with a few rapid motions and flicked her hands. The water fell to the ground and Korina let out a short shriek. I jumped.

"Are you okay?" I asked, worried. Korina took in gasps of breath before she spoke, clutching her hand in the other.

"I can't turn this water into ice. When I tried it fell from my grasp. Now my hands hurt and I didn't even touch the blasted water." Korina stopped rubbing her hands and stared at the ground where the water fell. I followed her gaze. The green grass was now a withering black, just as the stones were.

"This water is poisoned. Something's really wrong," Korina said.

I thought of the black stones again. They had to be poisoned, just as I had originally thought. I told Korina.

"We should go," she said. "There's something going on and the two of us are only student mages." We walked down stream again where the water resumed its normal color. Korina flexed her hands again and tried to lift the water. It continued to flow with no disturbance.

"Teressia, I can't control the water," Korina declared. She looked at me with worried black eyes.

"Why not?" I said and immediately wished I hadn't. That was a dumb question.

"I don't know! I used my magic on that stupid poisoned water and now everything is all weird," she huffed. Korina was frustrated.

We walked on, reaching the edge of the forest. Korina looked at me.

"How about we walk to the bay and see if that water is different?" she suggested.

I was skeptical. She had hurt her magic by manipulating the poisoned water and now she wanted to go back and do it again when we were *leaving* the bad stuff. The bay was also a long walk from where we were and it was getting late. My mother would be missing me and I had work from the Academy to get done before morning.

Korina read my thoughts. "I know, I know. It's stupid of me to suggest but if something's wrong we've got to find out and tell someone!"

I sighed, agreeing with her. We exited the forest and headed north toward the bay. We were walking along the edge of the Shrouded Forest when we both saw it at the same time: the unconscious heap that was Sage.

CHAPTER 5

KORINA

*T*eressia and I both rushed over to Sage. She lay in a sprawled position on her side, one arm over her head and the other to her side. Battered plants were strewn around her and the nearby tree was slightly uprooted.

"Maybe she's just takin' a nap," I suggested.

Teressia bent over Sage and felt her forehead. "I don't think so. It seems unlikely that someone would fall over and take a nap in the forest. If she were tired she would simply walk home instead."

I sighed, knowing that Sage was not taking a nap. I had hoped that she was plainly sleeping but that was not the case. Something foul and mysterious was going on. First the blackened stones Teressia had found, then the poisoned water, and now Sage who was lying unconscious. Was it all connected?

Teressia knelt down on her knees and gently shook Sage. When Sage did not respond or show any signs of waking, Teressia stood back up and nudged Sage's limp body with her foot. Sage quietly moaned and twitched. Teressia and I glanced at each other, waiting for anything to happen. Sage opened her eyes in a slit, eyelids heavy and drooping. She moaned again.

"Sage?" I peered at her.

"K-Korina? Why are you here?" she muttered. "Gosh, my head hurts," Sage added after propping back on her elbows.

"We were coming out of the forest when we found you unconscious," Teressia said.

Sage looked at Teressia and then slowly back at me. I could see the disgust in her expression, disappointed that I had to be there. Out of all the people we had to find, why did it have to be Sage? She was cocky and arrogant and we weren't exactly on good terms after what had happened in Rhydork's class. Or at least I wasn't willing to strike up any casual friendly conversation. Yes, I was holding a grudge against Sage. After all, she was somewhat overconfident and a bit of a jerk to me.

"Do you remember anything that happened to you?" Teressia asked, interrupting my thoughts.

Sage looked up, pondering the question for a minute. "Well, I remember I was practicing my plant and earth magic," she began slowly. She paused again. "I was practicing and then I saw something dark on that tree over there," Sage said, nodding to a tree behind us. "I walked over to it and it had this black kind of substance smeared on the trunk of the tree. It looked like the tree was burnt but it wasn't. Then I realized the grass around the tree and in other patches were dead. They were brown and black and withered. It's so unnatural! I mean, there certainly wasn't a small fire or anything. I didn't like how the stems of some of the wildflowers drooped so I tried to use my magic to straighten them up, even though they were dead. I don't know why, I guess it just bothered me or maybe I thought I could bring them back. Anyway, my magic wasn't working at all and then I went and touched the black tree and then..." Sage trailed off.

"And then?" Teressia prompted.

Sage scratched her head. "And then I don't know what really happened; I was unconscious and when I came to, you guys were there."

Teressia nodded. "That's strange. I saw some stones with the same kind of black stuff on them like the tree you described."

"That gives me the shivers. Let's move out of here."

The three of us walked to the wooden bridge that curved over the Elementa River, Teressia explaining the incident with the poisoned water and my abrupt loss of magic.

"Remember we were going down to the shore, Teressia?" I reminded.

"Oh. Yeah," she replied quietly. "But Sage isn't feeling that well. We should at least make sure she gets home safely."

Sage whipped her head around toward us. "No way am I letting you two go out there alone without me. I want to see for myself if there's anything wrong. Besides, I'm not feeling that bad anymore. My headache is gone and I'm fine. I just can't use my magic at the moment. But Korina got hers back so I'm sure it'll come back soon."

I wasn't going to start an argument with Sage. As much as I was tempted to, she was as stubborn as I was and it was better not to waste time. I couldn't say that I enjoyed her company, but at least she wasn't treating me so badly. I was ready to drop the hammer if she did though, regardless if she had passed out earlier.

Ships were dotted along the docks of the bay, their sails gently rustling and swaying in the breeze. The water of the Lata Sea sparkled and gleamed from the sinking sun. Orange light was painted across the sea and the puffy clouds were blotted with sunset pink on their soft underbellies. Small waves rolled and crashed and then slid up the sides of the docks.

I led us to the side of the docks where the Elementa River joined with the Lata Sea and hustled down the steep side of the hill where the land ended and the sea began. Once I lost my footing and fell to the ground, perilously sliding toward the edge where the land dropped off abruptly, high above the shore. I held my breath before letting out a squeak. I clung to the grass with my fists bunched up so that I wouldn't dangle above the water. I prayed that I wouldn't slip any further and fall into the water as the loose soil shifted at my presence. I turned my head to see Teressia with a worried expression, speeding up to help me. Sage seemed to carry a smug look, probably amused. I turned back around and stared at the threatening sea. The waves bounced off the shore, splattering back into the water, but not before spraying my legs. My cheeks warmed with embarrassment.

"I'm fine, I'm fine!" I snapped as Teressia reached me, holding out a hand. I pushed off one of my legs but slammed back onto the ground as the dirt jumped out from beneath me. I resentfully took Teressia's hand and hauled myself up. "Thanks," I grunted.

"Let's go over there where there isn't a drop off into the sea," she suggested.

We followed Teressia to the left of the drop off, closer to the river. The ground leveled out and gave us a flat access to the sea. Black waves with dark purple coloring mixed in lapped at the shore, reaching at our feet. I gagged. The smell was even worse here than at the river. A dead fish slid ashore, a gift from the black waves.

"It seems like it's even worse here at the bay than the river," Teressia remarked.

I nodded. I crouched beside the water, dodging the waves that dared to grasp me. The water wasn't the nice shade of sapphire, or glowing orange from the evening sky. I gazed out toward the horizon in horror, seeing that huge black patches were littered far out into the sea, as if they were bundles of seaweed that would wash in with the waves.

"Something's wrong. Really wrong," Sage stated.

"Really? Way to state the obvious, O Bright One," I retorted.

"Oh shut *up* Korina. As if you're the one that discovered everything! All three of us are figuring this out together, and you're not the head of us like you think you are, so you can get off your high horse!" Sage snapped back.

"You know, we could've left you at home and seen this by ourselves. Your help isn't exactly needed!"

"Stop! There's no use arguing about it. Sometimes it's okay to state the obvious, Korina. Focus on the thing that's important," Teressia intervened.

I gave Sage a final glare, but Teressia was right in the end. There wasn't anything to argue about. Even though I agreed with Tres, I was in no mood to talk to Sage. I was sick of her arrogant attitude and the best thing to do was probably ignore her. Sage rolled her eyes at me and turned her head the opposite direction.

"Who should we report this to?" I asked Tres.

"I don't know. Maybe one of the mages at the Academy? We could tell Mage Isaac, one of my professors."

"Okay, yeah. And Mage Melody. She's one of the best water mages at the Academy."

Teressia nodded. "Let's go then, before it gets too dark." She glanced at the sky. It had darkened even more and the deep blue of night was on the edge of the sky, threatening to take over the last drop of evening sun. The sea had also darkened with the sky. I stared at the waves a final time, trying not to breathe in the revolting smell of the poison. I flexed my hand at the water. It reluctantly raised a few inches and fell from my grasp within seconds. I felt dizzy and stumbled around, feeling sick.

"Korina!" Tres shouted and rushed toward me, Sage following her.

I was surprised to hear "Are you okay?" from Sage. I nodded weakly and then collapsed onto the ground, my head spinning. My eyes became heavy and I was unable to keep them open.

* * *

When I finally awoke, I was being dragged by Sage and Tres. It was even darker, the sun just a faint ember in the distance. Stars were sprinkled across the sky like cinnamon on toast.

"Where are we going?" I feebly murmured.

"To the Academy," Sage answered.

I felt sick again and gagged. Sage jumped, losing her grasp on me and Teressia gave me a sympathetic look.

"Korina? You okay?" she asked.

I shook my head and climbed out of her grip and to the side, doubling over. When I finished I stumbled back, a sour taste perched on my tongue and feeling weak. I knew that I had lost my water magic again.

Tres and Sage grabbed my feet and arms again, this time carrying me. I recognized the buildings we passed as we made our way to the Academy. When we arrived at the entrance, Sage and Tres set me down and tried the door. It was locked of course since it was after hours. Teressia knocked, lifting the iron hoops up and down. Footsteps echoed through the door, feet clacking on the smoothed floor. The wooden doors creaked as one of the mages of the Academy opened it.

"What do you want at this time of the night, children?" she asked, scrunching up her eyes, dangling a lantern in Sage and Tres's faces. She had her dirty blonde hair pulled back into a messy bun, a few locks of hair escaping it. Her face looked tired and old, with stretched wrinkles sitting at the beds of her eyes. Apparently Tres knew her.

"Mage Terra, we need to see Mage Melody. It's urgent. Look, Korina over there is sick and we think Mage Melody can help us," Teressia said.

"Why don't you go to a healer then? I'm not going to disturb Melody. She is in her quarters, children, and probably in bed by now! We mages have a long day at the Academy that starts early, you know. Go home, children!" Mage Terra snapped.

"*Please* ma'am. We need to get our friend to Mage Melody. There's also a question we need to ask her," Sage pleaded.

Our friend? Did she just call me a friend? She must not be feeling well herself.

Mage Terra didn't look pleased. "Can't your question wait 'til morning? You have class, after all."

"No, it can't. Could you please get Mage Melody? And if she's mad you can tell her it's our fault and she can come and yell at us," Sage argued.

"Fine. But if she's unhappy you three will find yourselves in consequence, scraping the floors of my classroom for a week. Is that clear? Now, what should I tell her?" the mage demanded.

"Please inform her that her student Korina is sick and we have something important to discuss with her. Tell her it's urgent. Thank you Mage Terra and we're sorry for any trouble we've caused," Tres politely answered.

"Very well then," Mage Terra snorted. She shut the tall door and left us out in the night. Her heels clicked and clacked on the floor again as she hastily walked away.

I laid on the grass, my stomach feeling queer and my head throbbing. My head was hot but I had chills as the night breeze swept over me. I shivered. Something in that water was poisonous and harmful to people.

Teressia was sitting by Sage and they had their heads bent together, whispering. I gave up on trying to comprehend what they were saying and rested my eyes. It felt like an eternity before the heavy door creaked open again. I raised up. Mage Melody was in the doorway, cloaked in a fancy robe of royal purple and gold silks. Her light brown hair draped over her shoulders.

"I heard that something was urgent? Terra said you children insisted on me coming out here and refused to leave." Her voice was soft, meant for speaking to children, but also firm.

Teressia nodded. "Korina is ill because of something that is unknown to us. We would like to speak to you about it immediately."

Mage Melody looked at me. Her expression transformed with concern as she briskly walked to me. She put her cold hands on each side of my face, carefully examining me. Then she felt my forehead, just as Tres had done to Sage earlier.

"This doesn't look so good. Korina my girl, I hope you don't feel as miserable as you look."

Mage Melody swept me up in her arms and entered the Academy. She turned around to Sage and Teressia, who still stood outside.

"Well, come on now, girls. We'll go to my room, even though it's a few flights up," she said, beckoning them to come forward.

Melody navigated through twists and turns of the huge building. After walking for a couple of minutes Melody led us outside and across a courtyard into another section of the Academy, probably where the quarters of the mages were located. We entered a part of the Academy I had never seen before. Mage Melody carried me up two seemingly long flights of stairs into an elegant corridor with doors unevenly spaced on each side. Then she finally unlocked one with a silver key on a chain that was fastened around her neck.

"Okay, here are my living quarters. Not as fancy as the Headmaster's, I know."

The headmaster must have had luxurious quarters because Melody's was no dump. Marble tiles covered the foyer and spread across the floor into a large living room. Stone columns lined the walls with detailed designs on the top and base of each one. The entire wall across from the entrance was a glass window with deep blue velvet curtains pushed to each side. Moonlight poured in like spilt milk on the floor through the window. I noticed that there was a door on that glass wall that led to a decently sized balcony. Decorative potted plants were both on the balcony and indoors. As we walked further into the living room I saw a comfortable looking sofa in a circular shape with pillows placed on it. Circular chairs were on the each side of the couch. Ahead of that was a small kitchen. It was rare in our city to have such a nice kitchen. Of course, even in this palace you had to light the fireplace to cook. Candles hung from an intricate chandelier and illuminated the place sufficiently.

Mage Melody set me down in one of the white soft chairs. I only took up a third of the enormous chair.

"You two young ladies can sit where you like. I will be back with a hot rag and remedy for Korina and then we can discuss that urgent topic."

Melody gracefully left the room while Sage and Tres awkwardly sat down on the couch. I closed my eyes as my head became light and dizzy once more. Melody was back in a short time with the rag and a bottle. She carefully folded the rag and gently placed it on my head. She studied me once more and then sat down on the sofa on the opposite side of Sage and Tres, facing them. She sat the bottle down beside her and brought her legs up on the couch.

"Okay, now that everything seems to be settled. First of all, I would like to introduce myself. Although you probably know, I am Mage Melody, a water mage, and I teach here at the Academy. Korina here is one of my students. A little defiant and feisty I understand but I believe she is a good student. But I am afraid you two are not in any of my classes. What are your names?" Mage Melody asked.

"I'm Sage. My element deals with the earth and plants."

"Nice to meet you, Sage," Melody replied. "Earth and plants, hm? Do you perhaps have my good friend Bramble as your professor?"

"Yes. He's an excellent teacher."

"He is indeed," Melody smiled. "And you?" She looked at Tres.

"My name is Teressia," she said shyly. "I have the element of stones and any other type of rock."

"Ah I see. And do you perhaps have my closest friend at the Academy, Isaac as a professor?"

"Yes."

"Okay then. Pleasure to meet both of you. Now that we have our introductions out of the way, what is the matter?"

Sage briefly glanced at Tres and began. She carefully explained our experiences with the bay water and her discoveries of the tree and plants. She described how she became unconscious and temporarily lost her magic like I did. Tres filled in the gaps and told Melody of what she saw with the stones and our sights at the river in the forest. Every now and then I nodded off, dipping in and out of sleep while Sage and Tres conversed with Mage Melody. Occasionally Mage Melody asked little questions, such as "was the water fizzing or calm" or "could you describe what the black stuff looked like," but most of the time she sat quietly and patiently, listening. After Sage and Tres had finished, Melody got up and approached me. She looked at me yet again and asked me how I was feeling, and about my experiences with the water and how I became sick.

She opened the bottle. "It must be what I initially thought," Melody said to herself. She dabbed her fingers in the solution and smeared it on my face and left to the kitchen. I watched her open several cabinets and search around before she found the bottle she was looking for. Then she walked back to where I lay and removed the cork. She turned the bottle upside down and squeezed a drop of the liquid into my dry mouth. I still had the faint taste of vomit in my mouth so it was a welcomed relief. The liquid tasted like sour berries and vaguely of honey. It wasn't all that pleasant, though it was like a breath of fresh air after I had gotten sick. After treating me she addressed the three of us.

"What you are describing sounds like dark magic," she paused, allowing time for this to settle in. "One symptom of it is causing magic wielders such as yourselves and other mages and so on to temporarily lose their magic. Of course, you don't really lose your magic, you just aren't able to access it. Some physical forms of dark magic hook on to things of nature such as the trees, plants, stones, and water. When it contaminates the water it causes the organisms in it to become sick and die. That goes for small plants as well, even trees but it takes longer for them. When you are in the presence of one form of dark magic, the one you were describing, it will not affect you like those organisms. It will cause you to become sick in some ways when you try to manipulate it, like how Korina is. However, I am almost certain that it will not kill you."

"Well that's a relief," Sage added sarcastically.

Melody chuckled and continued. "Isaac and I have felt some disturbances around us and your sightings have supported that. Where all of this is coming from we haven't pinpointed yet. As for Korina, I will keep her here overnight and in the morning until she gets better. I need to watch over her and treat her. If the sickness due to dark magic isn't watched or treated, that's when things get serious." Melody left it at that.

"It's late," Melody noticed, looking out the window. She rose and pulled the blue curtains over the glass wall. "You two better get home before your parents start worrying. And could one of you stop by Korina's and tell her parents that she's staying overnight?"

Tres nodded. "I will, but I don't know where she lives."

Melody scribbled down an address on a piece of paper she had folded in a pocket of her robe. "Here." She handed it to Tres. "Because she's one of my students I've had to mail class reports to her parents," Mage Melody explained, which is how she knew my address.

Sage and Teressia left, escorted by Mage Melody. I fell asleep before she returned and didn't move throughout the night. I was still feeling weak and tired. I dozed peacefully, without any troubling dreams.

* * *

Soft voices were barely audible. The curtains were still drawn and no light attempted to crawl through them. I woke in the middle of the early morning, noticing a glow of ember from the fireplace in the kitchen. Flames threw dancing shadows across the room. I noiselessly lifted my head and propped up on my elbows, peering into the kitchen. Three figures were seated on chairs in the middle of the room. I recognized Mage Melody of course but there were two others. One was a middle aged man of average height with somewhat short black hair. The other was a sturdy built, tall woman with fancy garments and long, black wavy hair. The man was addressed as Isaac by the woman and Melody. He must be Mage Isaac, Teressia's teacher, I concluded.

Mage Melody addressed the woman. "Headmaster Ignatia, something must be done though. We can't just wait around for this darkness to engulf us all."

Apparently the woman was the Headmaster of the entire Academy. I was impressed. She spoke with authority and confidence, and not even I would want to challenge her, though she was not unkind.

"I'm not going to let this city nor any other in Northwestern Lux perish. But we cannot be certain of anything, Melody," Ignatia replied sternly. "It is true that there are waves of dark magic coming from that wretched place but why? We don't know and it could be too dangerous to deal with. I'm not sure I am comfortable with your proposal."

This time Mage Isaac spoke. "Ignatia, we won't know until we investigate. And if it is a threat we need to know for certain. Elementa Bay is reeking of the darkness and I don't want it to stay there. It's... unnerving. But more importantly it's also dangerous. Before long everyone will become ill and you know what kind of evil the darkness can create if we don't get rid of it. Elementa will surely be attacked, Ignatia."

The Headmaster stared at Mage Isaac. "I understand your concerns, for I have the same." She sighed. "Very well then. My decision is made. You and Melody will go to the Sacred Islands."

CHAPTER 6

SAGE

$\mathcal{T}$he sun was in the center of the sky, hogging it from any clouds as far as the eye could see. Students piled out of the Academy's doors and diverged into their separate ways. I walked with Teressia, who I now felt a budding friendship with after what had happened last night. I realized I had seen her occasionally at the Academy and around the city.

Korina wasn't in class today but that was expected. She was probably still feeling sick and weak. I was genuinely worried that the poisoned water could do that to her. What if I accidently used my magic on a poisoned tree and that happened to me? It was bad enough missing out on class work, let alone being stuck in some mage's dorm all day.

Tres broke the silence. "Did you notice Elijah wasn't at the Academy today? You know Elijah, right?"

"Of course. I met him in the library." I paused. Should I tell her about what had happened in the Academy library? I decided not to. "Well, to be honest I don't have classes with him so I didn't realize he was missing."

"Maybe he's sick. Let's go check if he's at his house."

Even though I found no interest in Elijah's absence, I followed Teressia through the cobblestone streets of Elementa and through the town square. It wasn't really a square, I thought. It was more circular than anything. In the center of the wide circle there was a water fountain. It was simply stone and had no designs carved into it but it was still pretty. It was one of my favorite places, like the Shrouded Forest.

"Where do you think all of this dark magic is coming from?" Teressia asked.

"I have no idea. It's all over the place, though. In the forest, at the river, and the bay. It seems like it's coming from the Lata Sea. Didn't you see how much black stuff was in it yesterday?"

"Yeah. Maybe. Maybe it's coming from somewhere in Lux. Do you think it's only in our part or in the southern and western and eastern parts as well? Maybe it's coming from Central Lux?"

I shrugged. What if it really was coming from the Lata Sea? If the map that Elijah had was accurate, the Sacred Islands were across the Lata Sea. Could all of this dark magic have appeared after he wanted to know more about the Sacred Islands? Is this all his fault, a warning to stay out of the mystery of the Sacred Islands? Or was it some unknown source of evil that was causing this? Could it be the Academy librarian? She looked pretty mean.

I thought some more, perplexed. Yesterday, when I was at the edge of the woods, it was Korina that had found me. Tres was there too, but Korina? We disliked each other; we were opposites! Out of all the students in the Academy, out of all the people in Elementa, it was Korina. I snorted. It had to be Korina. Was that mere coincidence or fate? Maybe I didn't hate Korina so much. After all, I was really worried about her last night. I had found myself hoping that she would be all right. Was that just common courtesy or was I starting to like Korina? I did have sympathy for her. She must have felt really bad last night and I know how awful it is to lose your magic.

I bumped into Teressia, not paying attention. We had arrived at Elijah's house. We walked up the cobblestone steps, Tres leading. She knocked on the small wooden door and stepped back on the porch. A few seconds passed before the door creaked open. A man peered out, with the same black hair as Elijah, tiny waves running through it, only Elijah's was longer.

"Teressia! How are you? And is this your friend?" He leaned to the side of Tres, staring at me. "I'm Mr. Elsbade, Elijah's father. If you two are looking for Elijah he hasn't come home yet from school."

"What? From school...?" Teressia asked, puzzled. "But Elijah wasn't at the Academy today, Mr. Elsbade," she said slowly.

This time it was Mr. Elsbade's turn to look puzzled. "He wasn't at school? But I saw him leave this morning."

"We were wondering if he was sick so we came by to see how he was, but obviously that's not possible. I'm very sorry Mr. Elsbade. We'll go now and we'll keep an eye out. If we see him we'll come back immediately."

"Thank you ladies. Well, wherever he is, he's in a boat load of trouble. He gets good with a little fire and now he's cocky, thinking he can skip school. His mother and I went through a lot of trouble to get him in that fancy Academy. Well, I guess teenagers will be rebellious, eh? Ha, ha. Well, bye now," Elijah's father slowly shut the door, waving as we turned away, walking down the steps.

"That's not like Elijah to skip school, though. Yes, he's quite popular and everyone adores him but... Elijah wouldn't skip Academy classes," Teressia said, shaking her head. "How about we look for him? What if he's lying unconscious like you were yesterday? He would need us to help him."

I reluctantly agreed. Tres and I began walking again, traveling around the whole city. Elementa was a small city, but too big to be a town. It still took time to navigate through each street. We arrived at the town square again and searched around the market. Striped awnings stretched over carts of fruit, groceries, jewelry, and other small items. People clustered around the carts, examining the products. Some exchanged their money with the gracious sellers and moved on with their shopping. I sat on the edge of the fountain. It was all useless, looking for Elijah. Teressia and I had even searched on the outskirts of town, on the edge of the Shrouded Forest and along the river and docks of the poisoned bay.

"This is ridiculous!" Teressia moaned. "He's nowhere!"

I muttered my agreement and stood beside Tres. "So I guess this is it for the day? See you tomorrow?" I said.

"Wait. How about we go check on Korina back at the Academy. I want to know how she's feeling and she might want to know another person's gone missing. Well we need to report it to Mage Melody anyway. She needs to know."

"Fine," I groaned. We had to walk all the way back to the Academy and ask for Mage Melody again, and would probably go through the same embarrassment as last night, just trying to reach her.

We walked past the same buildings, on the same cobblestone streets yet again before reaching the Academy. My mother would definitely be asking more questions today. She wasn't happy at me for coming home during the night yesterday and her patience was running thin. She would jump on me immediately after I returned home this afternoon, no doubt.

This time the doors of the Academy were unlocked. Students would still be there, stuck in consequence, making up work, or studying in the library.

"So we're here. Do you know where Mage Melody's classroom is?" I questioned.

Tres opened her mouth and then closed it again. "Honestly, no. She teaches water mage students so I don't have her. We could ask Mage Isaac, though."

I followed Teressia to Mage Isaac's classroom. I had never been to the stone element wing of the Academy.

44

As we entered the room, Mage Isaac looked up. He looked like he was middle aged and bore short black hair.

"Teressia, hello. What can I do for you?" He said warmly.

After Tres had explained we were looking for Mage Melody's class, Mage Isaac nodded and rose from his desk chair. He led us out of the stone wing and into the water and ice wing. A light tint of icy blue was spread onto the stone walls. This wing had an entirely different feel from the stone wing and the garden wing, where my element was. I lightly grazed the colored walls of the hallway. It was frosted and a sharp pang of cold zapped my finger, similar to the time Korina shot ice at me a couple of days ago. Or was it yesterday? It seemed so long ago. Streams of water plummeted down into stone tubs at the base of the walls from the top. There was cold ice frosted on the walls, light blue coloring, and mini waterfalls. We were definitely in the water and ice wing. The garden wing had a faint shade of dark green on the walls and think vines were strung along them as well. Each wing had something to characterize its element.

Mage Isaac ushered us into a classroom. "Here we are." He waved to Mage Melody, who looked at us at the sound of Mage Isaac's voice. Mage Isaac briskly left.

"My two girls from last night. How are you? I was just going up to check on Korina if that's why you're here," she said.

I answered for both of us. "Yes, we wanted to see how Korina was doing but we also have another problem that we wanted to report."

Teressia looked like she was going to add something so I quickly cut her off and began again. I didn't want her wasting time with her slow hesitant speech. "You see, one of our other friends has gone missing. We spent the afternoon after school looking for him and we can't find him. He didn't come to the Academy today but his dad said he had left to go this morning." I couldn't believe I had just called Elijah my friend in my rush. More like a fellow student, not a friend.

Mage Melody listened intently. "I would say it sounds like your friend had simply been skipping class but last night leads me to think there are other possible explanations. It is possible he is avoiding a parent after, perhaps, a recent argument and is staying out of the streets? I don't suppose you went in every building?"

"No, we didn't," I informed.

"I see. I will report it to the headmaster if he doesn't turn up, but I don't want to start a fuss over nothing. I'm sure his parents will take care of it. Now, let's go see Korina."

Mage Melody led us to her quarters once more. Korina lay in the same elegant chair as last night, her face looking less pale. She was propped on a couple of crimson pillows, munching pale crackers.

"As you can see, Korina has been doing much better. I've kept her eating and drinking. Those crackers have that special remedy in them that slowly removes the dark magic's effect from her body," Melody explained.

Korina turned toward us, swallowing her crackers. "Hello," she said, sounding much better but a little hoarse. Not her usual self yet.

Mage Melody left the dorm for a couple of minutes, retrieving something for Korina.

"How are you feeling?" Teressia asked.

"Hmm, better." Korina tilted her head and took a tiny nibble off a cracker. "Every now and then I get a little light headed and chilled but I feel much better. It's been awful, you know. Sitting here all day and night, not doing anything but sleeping and eating and feeling as if you're a dried up leaf."

"We were somewhat worried about you," I said, trying not to sound like I cared too extensively.

"Thanks. That's not what I expected to hear from you of all people," Korina said with a slight smile.

I chuckled awkwardly. "Yes, well. So how's your magic?"

"It's getting better. Some of it's back and it doesn't hurt so much to use it. However, not all of my strength has returned so I can't use it to my full potential."

Tres leaned on the back of the couch, facing Korina. I stood next to her with my arms crossed. Korina broke the silence.

"Last night I heard Mage Melody with Mage Isaac and the headmaster. It was still dark outside," Korina began, lowering her voice.

I widened my eyes. "The headmaster of the Academy?"

"Yep. Headmaster Ignatia. The three were whispering in the kitchen." Korina talked about their conversation about the dark magic. "At the end the headmaster said they were going to the Sacred Islands."

"The Sacred Islands? What are those?" Teressia asked, puzzled.

"So the dark magic is connected to the Sacred Islands," I said quietly, staring at the marble floor.

"What are the Sacred Islands?" Teressia repeated.

Korina ignored her. "Sacred Islands. Isn't that what you asked Rhyback about that one day after school?"

She had been in the back of the room that day for consequence. "Yes. That's what caused us to get into that little fight," I said, blushing.

Korina laughed. "I remember that. You got me pretty badly with your plants. We really went after each other, didn't we? Well no matter, it's in the past now."

"Can someone explain to me what the Sacred Islands are?" Teressia said impatiently.

"Oh, right. Sage you'd better. You know the most about them."

I carefully explained what Professor Rhyback told me and finally about the incident in the library. After I finished educating Tres on the Sacred Islands, we told Korina that Elijah was missing.

"Who?" Korina asked, her eyebrows scrunched up.

I groaned with impatience and let Teressia explain who her friend was.

"Elijah wanted to know about the Sacred Islands too. He still has that map he found at the library and wanted to find more information on the islands," I said. Then I had a sudden realization.

"I know where Elijah is," I said.

CHAPTER 7

ELIJAH

I remember running to the Elementa Library so that I wouldn't be late to class that morning. Ever since I had found that map in the Academy library I had been intrigued. I felt like I needed to know more about the Sacred Islands. I only had a few minutes to spare but I believed that if I hurried I would have enough time.

I had pushed open the doors in a frenzy and walked quickly to a shelf that contained the deep history of Northwestern Lux. Several books caught my eye but I had to stay on task. I had slid my finger across every row on that shelf, skimming for something that said Sacred Islands. There was nothing. I had slumped onto the ground for a few seconds, crestfallen. But I couldn't give up just yet. I was too strong willed for that. I fingered the dark brown shelf at the base and sighed. Three circular carvings at the bottom of the shelves had a nice texture so I rested one of my fingers in each carving. The carvings had slid inward like buttons and a drawer popped out of the side of the shelf. I peered into the drawer just as a heavy book plummeted out of it. I quickly caught the book before it slammed onto the floor with a hefty thump. As luck would have it, it was a hidden book on the Sacred Islands. It was quite dusty and old but thick and interesting. I had smiled slyly with delight.

The next thing I remembered was soft footsteps creeping up behind me. As soon as I had spun around to see who it was, my vision was blocked and I was quietly knocked to the ground. Something sour was shoved into my mouth and moments later I felt my consciousness slipping away. I felt peaceful and didn't resist the oncoming sleep.

Sometime later I awakened in front of the same shelf where I had found the hidden book. Only one thing was different. The book was gone. I hauled myself off the ground and leaned my head against the shelf. I was very frustrated. The book was gone and it was probably the only thing in the whole city of Elementa that explained the Sacred Islands. I didn't understand. What was so secretive about these islands? There was once a regular civilization living on them, rich and thriving. Now the islands were sadly abandoned, supposedly because of a volcanic eruption. Why no one returned to the islands didn't make sense to me either. The information on the islands didn't seem so dangerous or bad, so why should it be kept in secret?

I banged my head against the shelf. I had no idea what the time was and I was definitely going to be late for class at the Academy. And if my parents found out they would be livid. I took a deep breath and started to leave the shelf.

"Elijah?"

I turned around at the sound of Tres's voice. "What are you doing here, Tres?"

I noticed Sage behind her. She stepped beside her. "We want to know the same thing, though I already have an idea."

"Is this why you weren't at the Academy? Were you seriously in the *library*, Elijah? That's so unlike you," Tres said.

"I missed the whole day?" I exclaimed, surprised. *Was I really out that long?*

"Uh, yes. What did you think?" Sage said in a demeaning tone. "Did you spend the whole day looking for books on the Sacred Islands? That's ridiculous Elijah. After all that's happened I don't even want to hear the words 'Sacred Islands'."

"Why, what's happened?" I asked.

Teressia crossed her arms. "We'll explain after you do."

"I was looking for books on the Sacred Islands."

"The whole day?" Sage asked, acting as if I were stupid.

"Elijah, you can't possibly think I'm that dumb. What else were you doing?" Tres demanded.

I explained to them my incident. Tres shook her head and rolled her eyes.

"Elijah, you can be so dumb sometimes. Don't go to any more libraries, period."

"Okay, okay you don't have to treat me like a child. Now tell me what Sage meant when she said 'after all that's happened'. What's that supposed to mean?" I asked.

I listened for a long time as Sage and Tres described what had happened as soon as they left the Academy.

"You went to my parents! Why?"

That was the first thing I was concerned about.

"Because you weren't at the Academy and I was worried after what had happened to Korina!" Tres exclaimed.

"I don't even know who that is! And now after a single day two people have decided they need to go to the Sacred Islands when I can't even read about them! It all sounds insane," I cried, frustrated. If only I hadn't set the Academy library aflame I would have been with Tres for the whole thing. That old heap of bones for a librarian just *had* to keep me there, making me clean while yelling at me. She had caused me to miss out on a lot. Everything seemed to happen so quickly.

"Well, now you do know and it's happening, okay? So stop whining," Sage snapped.

"So a couple of mages are going to the Sacred Islands? How does that concern us?" I asked.

Tres shrugged. "Dark magic is poisoning the place and Mage Melody, Mage Isaac, and the headmaster think those islands are the source. If they're taking the time to travel down there to investigate don't you think we're in danger?"

"I guess," I said, unconvinced.

Sage rolled her eyes. "Let's just get out of here. I need to go home and get a decent amount of sleep tonight after my parents are done yelling at me."

I followed the girls out of the library, reluctantly heading toward home. There's no telling what they might do to me now. I parted ways with Sage and Tres and reached the familiar path that led to the door of my house. Holding my breath, I opened the door. As soon as I entered the foyer, my parents were there waiting for me.

"You have some explaining to do," my mother began sternly.

"You'd better start now," my father added.

"What do you mean?" I said, trying to act as if nothing had happened.

"Don't start that nonsense, Elijah," my mother snapped. "You have two seconds to tell us why you weren't at the Academy today."

Before I could begin my father cut me off. "We are disappointed in you, Elijah. We went through a lot to get you into that Academy. If you think you're too good to go we can pull you out and put you into a regular school where no one has any magic."

"But I didn't mean to miss classes!" I protested, wishing I hadn't blurted that out.

"Oh, so you accidently didn't go to school?" my mother challenged.

"That's not what I meant. I went to the library before school started to try and find a book but then I..." I trailed off. I couldn't tell them someone had knocked me out because I had found a secret book that I wasn't supposed to. There was no way that they would believe me. "...I fell asleep," I finished. I knew that wouldn't work. I had hesitated too long anyway.

"You fell asleep, did you? The whole day. In the library? Don't lie, Elijah. Lying is wrong. What were you really doing?" my mother demanded to know.

I tried to add to my story in the library but it was all in vain. After my parents had finished scolding and punishing me, I went upstairs to my room. Unfortunately there were only two bedrooms in the house so I had to share with my younger brother, Isaiah.

"Somebody got in trouble," he teased, grinning.

"Shut up, Isaiah. I'm not in the mood for you."

"Skipping the Academy? That must be pretty bad," Isaiah continued. He was in the other school in Elementa, the regular one since he had no elemental magic.

"Yes, of course," I said, irritated. I flopped down on my bed and turned away from Isaiah and slept.

* * *

I was walking down the halls with Tres. The Academy classes had ended for the day and we were heading home. My elemental professor, Mage Ember approached as Tres and I were almost out of the building.

"Elijah! Sorry to stop you, but could we have a word?" Mage Ember asked.

I looked at Tres apologetically. "Of course."

"Good! Don't worry, it's nothing bad. Well, it could be but you're not in trouble." He led me down the halls of the Academy and to what must be the water and ice wing. The walls were blue and wet with water and ice.

We turned into a class with a mage I recognized. It was Mage Melody, who had often come into Mage Ember's class with questions. There were two others in the room.

"Here he is, Melody! Headmaster Ignatia, how do you do?" He gave a small bow.

"Thank you, Ember. Elijah, welcome. I am Mage Melody and that man is Mage Isaac. This is the headmaster of the Academy."

I said my hellos and walked further into the room.

The headmaster addressed me. "You're probably wondering why you're here, Elijah. You're not in any kind of trouble. You are actually here because of your good character and fire mage skills. I have had several recommendations from your professors that you should go."

"Go where?" I asked.

"To a place called the Sacred Islands. I doubt that you have heard of them, but I am sending my best mages—Melody and Isaac—along with a crew to sail there and investigate. We have some dark magic around and we think it might be coming from one of the islands. Which one is uncertain but it might be one of the two main ones. It is a dangerous quest and we need two other mages in training to go or two full ones. Since you are an advanced fire mage in training I have decided it will be a good experience for you. It will take a lot of courage and I can understand if you decline. The trip requires substantial preparations and detailed plans to be made, so it will be a couple of months before you depart. So, will you go?"

I slowly nodded my head.

CHAPTER 8

KORINA

$\mathcal{T}$he sunlight wove through the giant window, creeping across the marble floor and slithering up the opposite wall. I held my hand up in front of me and slowly rotated it, observing how the light flipped and expanded on my skin. Four days had passed since I had first entered Melody's dorm. By now I was feeling incredibly better and my magic had returned to its full strength. I was sure that the effects of the dark magic had worn off.

Melody abruptly entered her quarters, swinging open the light wooden door. She hunched over slightly as she locked the door.

"Good news for you, Korina. I think it's time you can be heading home now. You should be feeling normal by now. I know it's been a bore to sit in that chair for four days."

"Yes. Thank you, Mage Melody," I said. It had been boring to sit around all day, despite the comfort of the huge plush chair.

Mage Melody nodded with a slight smile, walking over to the kitchen. "How about a quick cup of tea before you go?"

I agreed and watched her sweep out a stream of water from a bucket across the room with a flick of her finger. She lowered the water into two cups and set them over the fireplace.

"Wouldn't it be nice," she grunted, struggling to get a fire going, "if we had two elements. Then I could zap a flame into this blasted thing and have a fire going in no time. But no, everything has to be so difficult."

After a couple of minutes Melody started a fire and kept watch over the cups of boiling water. "Sorry Korina. It might take a few minutes for the tea to be ready. I haven't any prepared."

Once the tea was done I slowly sipped from the cup. "Thank you, Mage Melody," I said a little awkwardly.

She nodded briskly. "Of course, of course. Now if you have any trouble with your magic or any lingering effects of that darkness come to me immediately."

After another thank you I left the dorm, refusing an escort back to the entrance of the Academy. It was good to be on my own feet again and I was sick of being carried and dragged around. I got lost a couple of times, taking the wrong turn at a staircase and walking down an entirely different flight of stairs to a different corridor. I had to retrace my steps several times before I went across the barren courtyard and the familiar halls where the students have classes.

* * *

I flipped over the mush of brown beans with my spoon. After eating nicer food at Mage Melody's quarters, our food looked like garbage. The mages must get a lot of special treatment, I thought.

"Are you feeling okay, Korina?" My mother asked, noticing me playing with my food.

"Oh, I'm fine. Just not that hungry," I quietly answered.

"You sure? You don't seem your usual self."

"I'm fine," I snapped.

My mother was quiet the rest of dinner. I felt bad for once. I shouldn't have snapped at her.

My little sister, Sara, munched on bread with wide eyes. She was so young and didn't understand why I had ever left and why I was back now. She also didn't understand my complicated relationship with my mother, why we never got along and were always yelling at each other. "Why Sissa gone, mama?"

"Sister was sick, Sara."

"Oh." Sara stuck the spoon in her mouth and sucked on it.

I eventually pushed the bowl of bread and beans away and grasped my glass of water. I ate the tiny bit of chicken I had and started upstairs. Tonight we had been lucky and my mother had bought a small chicken from the market today. We weren't poor, just not able to have a wide variety of food. Most of the delicacies and fancy foods were in the heart of Lux, the City of Lux. Elementa was probably poor in the eyes of the people there.

I lay down in my bed, staring at the ceiling. The curtains of the small window flew up and down as the wind crawled in from the open window. I sighed. I wasn't tired at all. It would be one of those long nights as I would struggle to fall asleep. Minutes ticked by as my eyes stayed open and alert. I swung my legs over the side of my bed and walked over to the window. I stared across the fields of grass and at the Valley of Stones and then to the Lux Mountains in the distance, as far as the eye could see. The mountains looked like blue shadows looming on the horizon. Across those mountains was where the City of Lux rested and the other half of Lux. I had always hoped that I would get to travel across those mountains someday and see Lux. There were many wonders, such as the supposedly enormous Impia Forest that stretched for maybe hundreds of miles. There were old tales that fascinated young children, saying that no one who had entered the Impia Forest had come out. Of course, I had never believed in those tales. They were only for scaring mindless toddlers.

I crept down the stairs and soundlessly exited the back door. I went to the front of the house and sat on the porch, staring at the bay. I squinted my eyes, searching for the Sacred Islands perched on the Lata Sea. I spotted a tiny speck in the night sea. Could it be the Sacred Islands? *Of course it's not the Sacred Islands. Don't be ridiculous, Korina. Those things aren't visible from the shore. It's probably just a boat or something I'm imagining.*

I gazed upon the dark waters of the bay. Even in the night the poison was visible. It seemed worse than four days ago.

Each day the darkness grows, I thought. Each day it worsens.

I got up, stretched, and went back inside. I needed to at least attempt to fall asleep.

Back in my bed, I resumed lying on my back. Somehow, after much time had passed, I fell asleep.

* * *

Swabs of white light dipped into the blank space. It was most definitely a dream. A dreamscape opened up, replacing the white light. I was on the bay of Elementa and then suddenly racing across the water at a speed that made everything a blur of colors. It was a mixing bowl of blazes of color for every characteristic of nature: murky greens, blues, puffy whites, browns, cobblestone grays and peaches. The speed slowed and it became night. Shadows cloaked a black castle nestled in the night. The stone castle was embedded in a cliff side, and loomed before me, stretching into the night sky. The air around me seemed heavy, and a strange and unnerving feeling emanated from the castle. I began traveling again as I flew backwards into a sea. I slowed down and my vision hovered over the water. Slithery worm like bodies slid up and down out of the surface of the water. There were hard green and blue scales that shimmered on them. A wide head popped out of the water and the dream zoomed in. The creature snarled, flashing long white fangs. Yellow eyes gleamed and watched harshly. In a quick second the menacing creatures vanished from the dream and

I continued my travel. I was back at the bay where the dream had started. The dreamscape disappeared and was replaced by the white light.

Don't let them leave without you.

My eyes opened slowly and I jerked up. I bounced softly on the soft cushioned bed. There had been a voice at the end of the dream. What did it say? I couldn't remember anymore. Did it say something about leaving? Something about people?

Don't let them leave without you. That's what my dream had said. What did all those images mean? No, the images meant nothing, I decided. It was simply just a dream that had emerged from the depths of my mind.

I raised a hand to my head, running it through my black hair. It was matted and tangled into a thousand knots. I rested my head on the pillow and shut my eyes, falling asleep in no time.

* * *

Sara stood at the side of the bed, leaning over me.

"Back away, Sara. You're too close," I mumbled.

"It's time get up, Sissa. Get up."

"Go away Sara." I turned away from her and pulled the blanket up over my head.

"Get up!" She whined.

"Go away Sara. I mean it."

"Sissa! You gonna be late for schoo!"

I flipped the blanket off. "I thought it was Saturday."

Sara shook her head slowly and walked downstairs with her thumb in her mouth. I sprang up and threw on a shirt and pants and then slid on the pale blue robe for the Academy. A stain had planted itself on the sleeve of it.

I decided to skip breakfast and ran out the door, jogging through the city and to the Academy. I was going to be late today—again. Why couldn't it be Saturday? As I ran through the square I almost ran into a kid around my age, with slightly wavy black hair. A small lock hung down in his face. This kid seemed familiar.

"Watch it!" I snapped.

"You ran into me!" He protested. "Don't go blaming me."

"Just get out of my way, okay? I'm already late." People were so annoying. They get in your way and stay there, always at the worst of times.

"Well, so am I! I have to get to the Academy in two minutes."

"You go to the Academy too?" I said. I noticed he had on an Academy robe. It was a deep shade of red so he must have had the element of fire.

"Mhm. No time for talking right now. Got to run."

I slid past him and started to run again. I heard footsteps thumping behind me. It was the same boy who I had ran into. That was no surprise; we were going to the same place. He kept running behind me, right on my heels. I felt the irritation rise in the pit of my stomach. I stopped abruptly and spun around, facing him. He skidded to a stop on his toes, tipping forward.

"Could you get *off* my heels?! Go past me or something!"

"Didn't know I was bothering you so much," he smirked.

Who does this kid think he is? No one messes with me and he's about to find out why.

"Look. You better wipe off that stupid grin off your pitiful face and get away from me. I don't want to be even later to class than I already am, especially because of some arrogant slice of rat meat that I ran into on the streets!" It was a weak order, but I didn't have time to think and I was going easy on him. I felt like being nice today.

"Whoa, calm down. I'll just go in front of you. You're a little slow anyway."

"You know what? I'm tired of people!" I reared back and shot a splinter of ice at him, aiming for his chest. Before it hit, he flicked out a flame at it and it instantly melted in the air.

He looked up at me. "Did you really just do that?" He seemed to be laughing. I angrily snorted. It had worked on Sage, but she had been slower.

"Just leave me alone."

"Leave you alone? You're the one who shot ice at *me*."

I started to walk faster, leaving the boy behind me. I heard the footsteps again. He was right on my heels. I nearly stopped again, but as I turned my head he shot past and continued running ahead of me.

"Jerk," I muttered under my breath.

I despised the people with the element of fire. They always thought they could overpower all the other elements. At least Sage had accepted that her measly green plants weren't the most important thing in the world, even if she did act arrogantly.

I walked quickly the rest of the way instead of jogging. What was the point? I was already even later, thanks to that annoying kid and the fact that I didn't want to be in my first class. It was with Rhydork and I did not feel like interacting with him.

* * *

I slowly opened the door to the class, trying not to draw too much attention. It still creaked and Rhydork stopped in mid-sentence, staring at me.

"Thank you for joining us, Korina," he said sarcastically and adding, "fifteen minutes late," under his breath.

I slumped into my desk at the back of the room.

CHAPTER 9

TERESSIA

*A*fter the last set of classes for the week, I started home. I was walking alone again, because Elijah was late to several classes and was forced to stay at the Academy after regular hours. I decided to go to a store with metal works and tools instead of going home. One store carried tools that many stone mages used when practicing their magic and I had saved a few silver coins.

I walked south of the Academy and found the store by its metal sign that dangled above the entry.

Different metals that waited to be welded were lined behind the counter of the store. A variety of weapons sat upon several shelves and other objects of metals were located across from them. I walked to the back of the small store, toward the tools. There were lots of hammers of all sorts and other tools I did not recognize.

"Can I help ya find something?" A hefty voice startled me. I spun around to face a stout man with a round belly. He was almost completely bald on his head and had a trimmed beard on the edges of his face. His work apron was stained with grease and sweat beaded on his reddened face. He had been bending some metal, no doubt.

"Um, I was looking for something," I began quietly.

"Well, what were ya looking for?" The smith bellowed before I could continue.

"Um, maybe some type of tool or hammer."

"Ya seem a bit young for such a tool. Maybe not, eh? Does yer mother order you to go fixin' things and tell yer brother to go cookin' the meals?" He mocked, laughing at his own joke.

"I, uh, don't have a brother, sir."

The smith chuckled. "No brother, eh? Ya can't do nothin' 'round yer property with no young man! Ha ha!"

My face became hot. Talking to the smith was very awkward and I preferred to just get on my way.

"Well lemme help ya find that tool, miss."

I followed the smith down an aisle of tools. He paused at a section of hammers. "What kind o' tool are ya lookin' for? A hammer or maybe a metal mage's rod? They're fer mages that do that fancy magic with metal but ya can still use it fer other purposes."

"What's a mage's rod?"

The smith picked up a tool with a long slim body made of wood and a metal cube on the top. It was about the size of a regular hammer. "There are different types of these rods but this here is the most common."

"You said metal mages use it, right? What for?" I asked

"Well they use it to hammer on the metal, reshape it, other stuff. Stone mages use it too, just as well. Ya can do just about anything with it, as long as yer creative."

I nodded and took it from his hand. The smith walked back up to the counter in the front of the store, leaving me staring at the tools. The mage's rod was just what I wanted. I set it back on the shelf and looked at the other rods. Some had different colored metal tops and some were different shapes. Some had cubes and some had triangular shapes. Some even had detailed symbols carved on them. A rod with dark, richly colored wood caught my eye. There was hard sturdy stone instead of slick metal that had been melted and reshaped before. It was a stone in a cube shape, but not perfect, with several jagged edges and extra sides. A ring of dark purple colored stone surrounded the stone at the base, wrapping around the cube in a ring shape. I picked the mage's rod up and watched the stone twinkle in the dim light of the store. The wood was soft and carved nicely. As my fingers brushed it I felt an inscription. I turned the tool on its side, seeing letters take form in the wood.

"Don't let them leave without you," I read aloud. What did that mean? Why would the tool maker put those words there on the handle?

As I studied the words harder, the engraved letters began to fade right before my eyes. Soon there was no letters, just smooth wood. I slid my hand along the polished wood, feeling no inscriptions. Did it just disappear? I shrugged to myself and carried the mage's rod to the counter.

"Did ya find something?" the smith asked.

"Yes sir." I placed the rod on the counter.

The smith picked it up, studying it. "Ah, this is quite a nice one. One of the better rods I own. This will cost ya eight silver coins."

"Eight silver coins?" I asked in disbelief. "That seems so expensive," I muttered quietly to myself.

"I know it, miss. But I don't decide on the prices. Ha ha, actually I do, but I can't help it, youngin'. I have to feed my family and when the products cost more to make, they cost more to buy, and therefore I have to price them higher to make profit."

"I understand." I reached into my pocket, fishing out five silver coins. I felt disappointment rise in myself. How could I have been so stupid? I should've brought extra.

"Looks like yer a bit short, ha, ha," the man said, then paused for a bit, becoming serious. "How about I take these five coins and it's yers, then come back whenever ya can and pay me back, let's say two silver coins?"

"Really? Thank you so much sir! But that would only be seven silver coins. That would be cheating you, sir."

The smith flapped his hand. "Don't worry about it, young miss."

I paid the money and took the mage's rod. "I will come back as soon as I can, sir."

I admired the rod in my pale hands as I exited the store. The purple stone gleamed and shimmered brightly in the sunlight. I felt a rush of excitement; I was anxious to use the rod. I turned south and was going to walk the two miles to the Valley of Stones but I felt a sort of tug to go east, toward the Vast Lake. I paused on the cobblestone streets of town and sprinted out of the way as I was nearly trampled by a carriage being pulled by two horses.

"Watch it, kid!" The driver shouted from the carriage.

I ran to the side of the street and turned east where two streets met. I ran until I was out of Elementa and on the peaceful grass just outside of the city. The Valley of Stones was just ahead of me, but the Vast Lake was to the left. The Valley of Stones would be the perfect place to practice my magic with stones and try out my new tool, but something was pulling me away from the valley. I turned to the left and walked to a cluster of trees that were in front of the lake. I gazed out ahead of me, watching the blue water of the Vast Lake roll peacefully in the breeze. The water sparkled with blinding light from the sun. I continued walking toward the trees.

The cluster of trees were much too small to be a forest, but still took up quite a bit of space. Unfortunately I was still in my long dark purple dress and gray robe from the Academy. I slid off the robe and neatly folded it and then placed it on the grass. The dress would most likely get caught in thorns, but it was old anyway and just a casual one. I didn't want to take any chance of tearing the Academy robe though. Elijah had torn a hole in his dark red robe before, and had to wear it to the Academy in that condition. After class he was sent in to the head fire mage and left me to walk home alone for the first time.

Now I walked home alone all the time. As Elijah's confidence grew, so did his carelessness.

I entered the cluster of trees, unsure of what I would find. I was hoping to find a group of stones somewhere so that I could use my mage's rod. There was soil everywhere but I wasn't sure how I could use the rod on that.

Every time I took a step through the trees, the end of my dress would catch on bushes and thorns, just as I expected. The trees blocked the sunlight and it was dark and dreary. Plants were so bothersome sometimes. They changed the mood of things too much. Once I got tired of the reaching thorns and bushes and other plants and parted the ground with my magic, pushing aside the plants and creating a clear path. Then I returned the ground to its original form and left the plants drooping.

Ahead of me loomed the mouth of a lone cave in the shadows of the trees. I felt the familiar rush of excitement again. Stones and rocks and earth and minerals! No bushes or thorns or weeds or flowers, except maybe the occasional moss. I dashed to the cave, flexing my fingers, preparing them to feel the nice cold touch of stone. Even though the cave was darker than the trees, I was still happy to get away from the mass of plants. When I entered the cave, the light immediately vanished. It was almost pitch dark, except for the light that snuck in from the roof of the cave.

I raised my hands and tightly curled my fingers, then slowly flattened them out again. The stone in front of me melted into a flat stretch of hard stone. I raised my mage's rod, unsure of how to use it. I twirled it around in the air like a child playing with a toy. The stone rose and spun itself, became liquid for a split second, and then took the shape of a coiled rope. I brought the hammer-like tool down lower in the air and the stone collapsed into an irregular pile instead of a neat coiled shape. The mage's rod was just an extension to my movements. Maybe it could do more than that if I just handled it differently. I practiced more movements with the rod and then became bored with the front area of the cave and decided to give the rocks I was messing with a break. I walked further into the cave, following the complex twists and turns down the winding tunnels.

A gleam caught my eye. Green and purple crystals grew from the sides of the cave in pointed pentagon shapes. I bent down and examined the lovely minerals. Light bounced off of them at different angles, creating bright dancing dots around the crystals. Maybe I should bring some back as a token. Maybe I could give one to Elijah and it would ward away his bad habits.

This time I brought down the tool and physically hit the crystals with considerable force. I dented the green crystal, but did not break or remove it from its spot. Using my magic, I tried to break a piece off and reshape them, but the minerals were stubborn. They decided they did not want to leave their cozy spots in the dark cave and wouldn't budge. I hit the crystal again with the mage's rod. An image appeared in the crystal, a reflection. I thrust my face closer to the crystal, observing the reflection. It wasn't my own.

A menacing face of some creature glared back at me, with black beady eyes. It snarled in the reflection and revealed two rows of short and sharp pearly teeth. I let out a yelp and jumped back. My palms sweated and my head became dizzy with rising panic. Was I not alone? I forced myself to turn my head to face whatever monster awaited. I was relieved to find empty darkness behind me. No breath or growl sounded in the cave. My shoulders relaxed a little but my legs still trembled. I shakily sighed and rose to my feet. I would leave the crystals alone. They were threatening me in their own way, putting images of horror into my mind. The rocks and minerals of this cave were not kind, I decided. It was time to leave this menacing place.

I was about to leave when I realized I had no idea where to go. There were four ways that I could go and I didn't know which one I had come in. I picked one of the center ones and followed down the winding path. The jagged roof of the cave became lower as I continued through the passage way. I came to a dead end, stooped over and unable to stand straight up without bumping my head. I shuffled back and came to the chamber where the crystals grew.

I randomly chose a different path and eventually came to another chambor where the path forked. I picked the one on the right and continued, unsure of where it would lead me. I was shaky and worried that I would never escape from the wretched cave. Why did I have to be so careless? Why didn't I just go to the Valley of Stones? I should've turned around as soon as I came to the cluster of trees. Nothing good ever came from plants anyway.

I followed the path I had chosen and came to another dead end. I retraced my steps back to the chamber with the fork and sat down on a boulder in the center of the area.

Okay Teressia. Don't panic. I'll get out of this cave somehow. It could be worse. I could be thirsty and hungry.

I craned my neck and looked for a way out when suddenly I had an epiphany. I'm an earth mage! I could just use my magic to make a hole and escape! It would probably be best to tear a hole in the roof so that I wouldn't be stuck in yet another chamber.

As I rose to my feet I brushed against something that felt like carvings on the boulder I was sitting on. I turned and looked down, facing the inscription. I squinted in vain. It was too dark to see if it was words or just natural markings on the rock. I set the mage's rod on the boulder, searching for a spot to climb. A faint glow came from the cube shaped stone on top of the rod. I picked the tool up again and held it above the etching in the boulder. There were words engraved into the boulder, just like the rod I was holding. As I read the words, I discovered it was the same. Don't let them leave without you.

I jerked the mage's rod away from the boulder in astonishment and shock and scrambled to a wall. I began to climb and after some sweat and exertion, reached the roof of the chamber. I used my magic to create a hole that was just big enough for my body to squeeze through and clambered out into the sunlight and drank in the warmth. I was perched on top of what seemed like a regular boulder that stretched for many yards, still surrounded by those few trees. I slung my legs over the side of the walls of the cave and slid down to the ground.

The mage's rod had worked I supposed. After being trapped in that horrible cave I was done with stones for the day. I would be sure to practice with the rod another time and in a different setting. But whatever I was going to do later, it would be much later. I was ready to escape from the tiresome cluster of trees and collapse in my bed.

Chapter 10

Elijah

$\mathcal{I}$ supposed it was bad that I had been late to several classes today, but it didn't bother me too much. I could always just impress my professors and regain their respect for me. None of them would dare send me, one of their favorite students, to consequence or any other punishment. Today I was in a little trouble though, for Mage Ember ordered me to stay after classes had ended for the day.

"Now Elijah, if you want to go to the Sacred Islands, you have to keep up responsibility," Mage Ember had said.

"Of course, of course. It won't happen again, Mage Ember," I had reassured.

Mage Ember had led me to a classroom in the ice and water wing again. Mage Melody and Mage Isaac were there, talking to the Headmaster.

"Ah, here is Mage Ember with him now. Welcome, Elijah," Headmaster Ignatia said. "I've gotten a report from Mage Ember that you were carelessly late to four out of six of your classes today. We need to fix that," she said sternly.

"It was just today, Headmaster. I assure you, it won't happen again. You see, I was just a little tired today from last night—"

"I don't want excuses!" The Headmaster roared. She straightened out her fancy silk robe and cleared her throat. "Elijah, you are very lucky that you have even been considered for going on this expedition. I was about to send six of my best mages but I was convinced otherwise." Headmaster Ignatia shot a cold glare at Mage Isaac. "And I can change my mind in a second. If your cocky behavior doesn't change right now I can dump a pile of work on your plate every week and it will not be pretty. If that doesn't work out you'll wish that you never entered the doors of the Academy. I expect more from you Elijah and I can cancel your trip to the Sacred Islands if you don't meet my expectations. Is that clear?"

I nodded my head. I had only been late one day and now the Headmaster was already jumping on my "behavior". Nevertheless, I did *not* want to get on her bad side again.

"Melody, Isaac, come with me." With a sweep of her robe the three left the room. Headmaster Ignatia paused at the doorway and said "We will be back momentarily."

"So you got a little taste of the Headmaster's wrath, eh?" Mage Ember chuckled. "You're lucky she held back."

Held back? "Uh, yes. Lucky."

I had only been a couple minutes late to my first class and that was because I woke up late. I would've been on time if some girl didn't run into me and start yelling at me. I had handled her pretty well, especially with my clever move of flame. The look on her face was priceless when I ruined her little trick. I smiled to myself. Mage Ember noticed my grin. "What are you smiling about, boy?"

"Nothing, Mage Ember. I have a question about this trip to the islands," I said, changing the subject.

"What's that?"

"What are we supposed to find? And why are students picked to go?"

"Well, the mages insist that traces of dark magic are here in Elementa and that it's coming from one of those islands. The Headmaster believes all you will find is an abandoned stone or something that was full of darkness and was just left there unattended or something like that. The point is, no one thinks there is anything dangerous there."

"And what do you think?" I prompted.

"Me? Well, personally I think anything is possible. I don't find it likely that it's something serious which is why a couple of you mages-in-training are going. It's only for experience. But they want two students that are serious about it and responsible and skilled. It's quite an honor for you to have been chosen."

"Are you one of the mages that are going?" I asked.

"Oh, heavens, no! I'm to stay here. Headmaster Ignatia wants to send only the best two and keep as many instructors here as possible."

"But you're one of the best mages in the Academy," I flattered.

"Why thank you, Elijah. I don't know what you want from me, but that was still a nice thing to say."

I smiled at Mage Ember. It was always a good thing to get on a professor's good side. "So what's all the worry about the dark magic? It doesn't seem like there's much harm at all," I said.

Mage Ember shrugged. "Maybe it's just an excuse to visit the Sacred Islands. No one has set foot on them since that terrible volcanic eruption so long ago and Elementa might get a lot of attention for going there. Maybe the great City of Lux will pay more attention to us then. Elementa is such a small city state you know. The capital doesn't care much for us, only the bigger cities that have more importance. They sure seem to favor the City of Oceanus. After all, that city does most of the trading with neighboring continents. Or maybe not, since they have recently raised the tariffs on the trade. It's going to be very difficult to export goods now."

"Ah. But does the Headmaster think that there is possible harm to Elementa, or for that matter any of the city states in Lux?"

"I don't know what the Headmaster thinks. But if she thought it was very perilous she would definitely not be sending you there. If Headmaster Ignatia thought the whole region of Lux was in danger, she'd travel all the way to the capital—the City of Lux—to report it."

"Has it been decided who will be the other student to go on the expedition?"

Mage Ember stroked his chin. "All the mages talk about it when we have our meetings. But, uh, no. We haven't decided on the other student. There's one other thing I need to tell you. Headmaster Ignatia has received a student all the way from Soror. He has been sent here because there are signs of magic within him but he can't manipulate any element. The professors at Soror wanted our very own mages to help him develop his magic, if he has any. It doesn't seem like he's to be a mage. Seems like he's more of a wizard, maybe he has the potential to become a sorcerer. We don't have many of those anymore. We're being overrun by mages, ha."

"What's this kid have to do with me?" I asked. Would I have to compete against him for the Headmaster to decide who will go to the Sacred Islands?

"Well, Headmaster Ignatia has decided it would help us find out if he has magical powers if he were to go on the expedition to the Sacred Islands. It seems a bit rash in my opinion. Some city sends you over, a possible prodigy, and then right off the bat you ship them to some faraway place."

"What?" I cried in disbelief. "He's going to the Sacred Islands with us? But we don't even know what he's like! He could be a troublemaker, a thief, or have no magic at all and just slow us down during the trip."

"Now, now Elijah. If Soror sent him over I'm sure he's fine. The people from that city are usually well mannered, unlike those barbarians in Fortis. Those people will do anything to start a riot!"

I laughed. "My great grandfather is from Fortis, you know."

"Oh, no offense! I certainly meant none," Mage Ember said at once, regretting his comment about Fortis.

Headmaster Ignatia walked in the classroom, Mage Melody and Isaac behind her. Another person was also there, trailing behind. It was a boy almost my age, maybe a couple years older, taller, and with straight brown hair, shorter than mine but certainly not cropped. It swept effortlessly across his forehead without any waves in the way.

"All right, we're back with some decisions made. Elijah, this is August Primerano. He is from Soror and will be going to the Sacred Islands with you. I expect that Mage Ember told you about him?" Headmaster Ignatia said.

"Yes, Headmaster."

"Good. We need to prepare both of you for this journey. Follow me, you two." The Headmaster started to briskly walk out of the room, and then abruptly came to a halt. "Wait, what am I thinking?" She laughed suddenly, a rich booming laugh. I had never heard the fierce Headmaster laugh before. "You two need to introduce yourselves. If you're going to be spending the next few months together, you need to start building a friendship now."

"I'm Elijah," I said somewhat gruffly.

"Nice to meet you. I'm August, but you already knew that," he said. August's voice was a bit deeper than mine, more mature. He was definitely older than I was by a few years. His features were sharp and chiseled, revealing his age. He seemed confident, but maybe a little timid. He wasn't shy or timid like Tres though. *Tres. I had left her to walk home alone again today. Did she think that I was becoming arrogant? She had once told me that if I wasn't careful, my head would become bigger than my brain.*

August's voice interrupted my thoughts. "So are you training to be a wizard?"

"Uh, no. I'm training to be a fire mage. What about you?"

"I haven't figured that out yet. That's why I'm here in Elementa."

"Really? Someone as old as you hasn't discovered if they have any magic?" I said, pretending not to know he didn't have any magical knowledge. At least that was one thing I had over him.

Headmaster Ignatia broke into our conversation. "Sometimes it takes longer for one person than it does for others, Elijah," she snapped, shooting me a warning glare. I stopped immediately. "Let's go now. You two will get plenty of time to talk before I send you away on this trip. For now we're going to train. Follow me."

August and I followed behind the Headmaster, Mage Melody and Isaac trailing behind us. We stopped once we entered an outdoor courtyard in the Academy.

"August, you sit over there and watch," she ordered, pointing to a lone bench on the side. "Elijah, you will train with Melody and Isaac. First we will begin by evaluating you. Melody and Isaac will throw several shots at you, and I want to see how you react."

I nodded and steadied myself, checking my stance and balancing on my toes. I raised my arms and held them bent, close to my chest. Mage Melody stood a few yards in front of me, and quickly jumped into her stance. "Ready?" she called.

She first darted to the side, causing me to pause for a second before I regained my composure and followed her quick movements. Then without warning, she shot a strong blast of water that was so wide I wouldn't be able to dodge it. I quickly made a wide sweeping motion with both of my arms, creating a wall of fire that would block the water. The wave of water reached the fire as soon as I created it, instantly extinguishing it. Most of the water had evaporated but spurts still splashed onto me with no effect. If I hadn't counteracted the wave, it would have knocked me off my feet.

As soon I had blocked the first wave of water, Melody dashed closer to me and rapidly sent five or six daggers of ice straight at my face. I threw flames at each one, recalling my trick I used on the girl that morning. Unfortunately Mage Melody's ice was stronger and didn't melt completely. I dodged out of the way of the remaining daggers. Mage Melody did not let up though. She quickly advanced, shooting more icicles at me. I jumped onto my hands, still on the ground with stomach facing up. I spun around as fast as I could, shooting out a ring of fire around me with my feet. Mage Melody leaped backwards, then dropped onto the ground and rolled, retreating. I took the opportunity and sprang to my feet, back into my stance but breathing hard. Mage Melody shot three thick streams of water straight into the air and entwined them together in a water braid with swift wide motions of her arms. She then turned the jets of water horizontally, the water spinning furiously and threatening to come at me. She released the water with a pushing motion, sending the streams of water flying at me. I dropped onto the ground before most of it could hit me, but Mage Melody had anticipated my reaction and skillfully redirected the water right at me. I was pushed back at the strong force of the attack.

"Stop!" Headmaster Ignatia ordered. "I've seen enough. Thank you, Melody. Well done, Elijah. I'm almost impressed. Usually students don't last that long with Melody, even though she's always holding back. I'm proud to have such accomplished mages-in-training at the Academy."

"Thank you, Headmaster Ignatia," I said.

"Elijah, that was good but you'll have to become much better by the time you leave for the Sacred Islands. Who knows when you'll need to use your combat skills. Okay, Isaac, it's your turn," the Headmaster beckoned. "Elijah, do you know what element Mage Isaac commands?"

"Um, earth?" I guessed.

"Right. Be prepared for that. Remember, earth mages are also called stone mages. I hope you can figure out that that means he doesn't move just chunks of dirt."

Isaac started in the same spot Melody had, but took a different approach. Right away he pulled up a wall of hard earth from the ground and pushed it toward me. I spun to my right and shot flames at Mage Isaac. He easily extinguished them by raising another wall of earth, this time balancing on the top of it. He surfed through the ground, using motions of his arms to move the wall of earth. While Mage Isaac glided along he flung discs of earth at me. Instead of dodging them I sent blasts of fire at them, stopping the discs and causing them to fall to the ground. I was proud of my precise aim.

Mage Isaac thrust the wall back into the earth, then stomped the ground. It puzzled me for a second, until I was knocked off my feet by some unknown force. Mage Isaac had sent a small quake to knock me down when he had stomped the ground. Mage Isaac took advantage of my fall as he ran toward me, jumping up and landing hard on the ground but gracefully on his feet. I bounced off the ground, wincing as a piece of ground shot up and into my back.

"Don't hurt the boy!" Headmaster Ignatia called from the side.

I sprung up and created a sphere of fire with rapid motions. I spun it quickly and then shot it a little to the side of Mage Isaac, hoping he would move there in an attempt to dodge it. Isaac did as I expected, sliding to the side where the fireball was to land. Surprised, he awkwardly threw up his hands, thrusting a stone in front of him.

"Good!" the Headmaster praised.

The fireball smashed into the stone, causing Mage Isaac to stagger back. I advanced, running to the side and shooting flames at him. Isaac dodged them and shot two small walls of earth toward me. I avoided the first, but Mage Isaac changed the path of the second one and caused it to smash into me. I fell backwards, onto the ground again.

"That's enough!" Headmaster Ignatia ordered. "Good, good. You showed a little more improvement this time around, Elijah. You learn quickly." Ignatia smiled slightly. "Okay, now my evaluation is done. Go home, Elijah. Stay after class again tomorrow and we will continue your training." Her smile quickly vanished when she turned and approached August, who still sat on the bench watching indifferently with a look of boredom written on his face.

I exited the grounds of the Academy and headed home, thoroughly exhausted. I felt sorry for Tres. I would have to explain to her that she would be walking home alone again.

CHAPTER 11

SAGE

I stood at the entrance of the Shrouded Forest. After my last visit there, I was starting to worry about it. Not only was the forest the place where I trained, it was full of glorious life. The forest was a home to many species of plants and trees and if it were poisoned with dark magic, it would soon be dead. I had thought that after a few days the forest would be looking better, the effects of the dark magic vanishing. Every once in a while I would be wrong, I would miscalculate. This was one of those times.

The edge of the forest was looking even worse. The grass had turned golden and was flecked with black spots. Bushes and shrubs and brambles and flowers and weeds were shriveled and dead. Even the trees on the outer edges were losing their leaves, becoming bare in the middle of spring. I slowly ambled further into the Shrouded Forest, studying the plant life around me. I wanted to know if plants were dying further into the forest or only on the edges. The amount of dead plants decreased as I got deeper, just as I had assumed.

Most of the trees were fine, but some were an unsettling shade of bleak gray, the tips of their branches charred with black grit, reeking of the dark magic. I wrinkled my nose and tried to stay away from those trees, for it gave me the shivers. From stones to trees to water, the dark magic had contaminated every creation of nature. Not everything was poisoned, but quite a few things were. Most of all, I was worried about the plants. I had always took them for granted, manipulating them without mercy, but now I pitied them. I felt genuine concern for the plants and was worried deeply.

I came to a small clearing in the forest. Three or four lone branches reached over my head, but no undergrowth or trees were in the small space. There were several splotches of dark ugly magic, and those spots were yellowed grass. I placed my hands on my knees and bent over to study the splotches. Something was different about these. These were dark purple and black and… sticky maybe? I reached down and felt it, instantly regretting it. I yanked my hand back in disgust. The spots were piles of goo, slimy and revolting. I smelled my finger where I had touched the stuff. I threw my hand away from me and coughed. It reeked as much as the dead plants, maybe even worse. I rubbed my fingers together, trying to get rid of the stuff.

As I looked around the clearing, I noticed more droplets of the slime. It was like a trail, as if someone dribbled it around as they walked. Was someone spreading this around? Was that where the dark magic was coming from? Maybe I could figure it out, and catch the criminal with my mage skills. I followed the trail of droplets, exiting the clearing and reentering the mass of trees.

As I tracked the trail, I kept my face down, watching it and following closely. After following it for a few minutes the goo disappeared, the trail coming to an end. I looked around, searching for where it might begin again.

Then I felt a zap of cold plop onto my shoulder. I turned my neck and stared at my shoulder, trying to see what had landed on it.

I froze, holding my breath. It was the "goo" of dark magic, slimy and gleaming mischievously. My heart thudding rapidly, I looked upward. Perched in a branch above me, sat a creature made of the nasty slime, a horrifying blob that had arms and legs. Yellow eyes glared menacingly at me from above. The monster snarled, its mouth a gaping black hole. I screamed as loud as I could and ran, my legs feeling as heavy as lead. I heard plants rustle as the creature plopped down from the branch. I blundered through the forest, trying not to trip on a reaching root. I glanced behind me in fear, seeing the creature pursue me swiftly. It opened its mouth and shrieked at me, piercing right through my ears. It stretched its arms out and revealed what looked like sharp claws. I screamed again and picked up my speed. Branches whipped my face, stinging my soft skin, and thorns cut my ankles as I ran in my skirt and leggings.

At last I burst out from the Shrouded Forest, shrieking in cold terror. I glanced behind me again, expecting the creature to be there, about to jump me. Then I felt a hard impact as I slammed into a body. I screamed again, thinking it was the creature.

"Ack! What's wrong with you! Why can't you watch where you're going, you—Sage? Is that you?"

I was relieved that it was Korina, even though I somewhat despised her. I was breathless and couldn't muster any words. I collapsed at Korina's feet, utterly shaken. I panted, still breathing hard.

"My water, Sage! What's wrong with you? You look like you've just seen a ghost *and* spent the last hour running from it."

"I... think I... did," I gasped between breaths.

"What do you mean?" Korina asked, scrunching up her black eyebrows.

After I had finally caught my breath, I explained what I had seen, and how it had chased me through the forest.

"Now that I think of it, it looked vaguely like an animal. Maybe it was some sort of bird that had become poisoned with the dark magic and changed shape," I suggested.

Korina nodded. "Maybe," she muttered. "It seems a bit strange. We should tell Mage Melody. Let's get out of this area before one of those things comes chasing us."

Korina and I headed toward the Academy, not saying much to each other on the way. As we were passing the square market on the way, Korina spotted Mage Melody shopping at a fruit stand.

"Oh, there she is! Now we won't have to walk all the way to that blasted Academy," Korina muttered.

I followed Korina to the stand where Mage Melody stood.

"I would like to take this one and here's another one. Let me get the money out," she said to a seller, rummaging through her purse.

"Let's just wait here, Korina, until she's finished," I whispered. We were standing a few feet behind Mage Melody and the stand of fruit.

"Okay, whatever you say," Korina murmured, keeping her eyes on Mage Melody. As soon as she pulled out ten copper coins, a young boy darted past and quickly snatched it out of her hands.

"Hey! Child you get back here!" she called, but it was too late. "Oh well, it looks like he needs it more than I do."

As soon as she said that, I had realized Korina had left my side. I looked up, seeing Korina sprinting after the thief.

"Korina! Stop!" I yelled, but Korina either didn't hear or didn't respond. She was probably ignoring me.

Korina easily caught up to the boy and shot a splash of icy water in his face, snatching the copper coins back.

"What do you think this is? Law-free day? You don't steal from people, you idiot!" she harshly scolded.

The boy was rubbing the water off of his dirty, golden skinned face. "Don't tell me what to do, street girl!"

"Wow, street girl? I'm *so* insulted. And if you're breaking the law I *will* tell you what to do and if you don't listen to me, I'll toss you over to the guards."

The boy stared at her fiercely, brown eyes cold, but I saw the gulp in his throat.

"Whatever," he said, rolling his eyes.

"Why don't you get out of here and go bother someone else?" Korina said, and shot another spurt of water, this time on his neck, making sure it traveled down his shirt. He shivered and spat at the ground.

"I was leavin' but you had to stop me!" he protested, and then left the square.

Korina walked back over to me and then approached Mage Melody and handed her the coins.

"Oh, thank you," she said, looking at her hand. Then she looked up, recognizing Korina. "Korina? Was that you over there, chewing that boy out? You'd better be careful. Someday someone's gonna seriously hurt you for doing that. You're lucky that was just a mindless child."

"I know my limits, Mage Melody."

Mage Melody exchanged the coins for the fruit and approached me, following Korina.

"So what brings you girls over to the market, Saturday shopping?" Melody asked, smiling.

"Well, actually, Sage and I were on our way to the Academy to find you. Sage saw something weird in Shrouded Forest," Korina responded.

The mage's smile vanished. "What did you see, Sage?"

I described my encounter with the strange slime creature.

"It's worse than we thought," she murmured, more to herself than us. "You say it smelt like the dark magic in the forest, and you're sure it was made of the same stuff, just slimy?"

"Yes! I touched it, it touched me! I was drowning in that horrible stench and running for my life! I know what I saw, and I know I wasn't imagining it," I said firmly.

Mage Melody solemnly nodded. "Do you two know what that creature was?"

Korina and I shook our heads.

"I didn't think so. That creature made of slime was made of dark magic, you see."

"Doesn't look like any black magic I've ever seen," Korina interrupted.

"No, no, no. *Dark* magic. There's quite a difference. Dark magic is mostly bad, evil, poisoning. *Black* magic is just a type of magic that wizards, witches, and the like can use. Black magic is not evil, it is good. Like light or white magic, it can be evil, all depending on how it is used."

"You were explaining the creature," I prompted.

"Ah, yes! That creature used to be an animal. From what you described, maybe a bird. Anyway, the darkness is so strong in that forest that it mutated the animals. It makes them bigger, and slightly changes their shape. The animals' minds have been poisoned, and their one desire is to destroy, or to injure things. That means stay out of Shrouded Forest. Don't even go near it. The mutations will not venture out of the forest, but as each day passes they will grow stronger and grow in numbers until they are confident enough to attack the city."

"Elementa's in danger!" I cried.

"Yes, it is. We didn't think it was this bad. I need to report this to the Headmaster. Remember girls, stay clear of the forest!"

* * *

Almost a week had passed since I had last been to the Shrouded Forest. I assumed it was becoming poisoned even worse as each day passed.

Now I was in the Academy, worrying about the dark magic and unfocused on my work.

"Sage, it's not like you to miss four questions on a test," one of my professors had remarked.

I was even unfocused in the hall as I was leaving the Academy. I jumped as someone grabbed my arm.

"Sorry, Sage. I didn't mean to startle you," the man said. I looked up, seeing Mage Bramble.

"Oh, that's quite all right, Mage Bramble. What is it? Am I in trouble?"

"No, not at all. The Headmaster wants to see you though," he replied.

"The Headmaster? Are you sure I'm not in trouble?" I asked in disbelief. The Headmaster did not waste her time with students unless it was serious. Why would she want to see me?

I followed Mage Bramble into the ice and water wing of the Academy and into a classroom. Mage Bramble ushered me in, stepping behind me. A tall woman with thick black hair stood talking to Mage Melody and another man. She wore a fancy silk robe that stretched to the ground. It was a deep blue with specks of gold in it, like stars in a night sky. It was trimmed with the same gold on the cuffs of the sleeve and trim. A velvet royal purple lined the gold trim. She turned toward us, fixing a firm gaze with gray eyes on me.

"Is this the girl, Bramble?" she asked.

"Yes, Headmaster Ignatia. This is Sage," he politely answered.

"Good. Sage, I am the Headmaster of the Academy. Don't worry, you're not in trouble," she said, seeming bored. "Most students think that if they see me it's a bad sign, and it is usually is. But that's not the case today, Sage."

"Um, nice to meet you," I said softly.

"Don't be shy! Be confident in your speech, stand up straight!" the Headmaster boomed. I immediately obeyed, straightening my slumping back.

"Now you're probably wondering why you're here. Have you heard of the Sacred Islands?" Without giving me a chance to respond, Ignatia continued. She described the dark magic and how they think it's coming from one of the islands. "Just last Saturday, Melody told me it was worse than we thought and there are mutations in Shrouded Forest."

"I know about that. I was the one that was chased by a mutation," I said.

The Headmaster raised her eyebrows. "Really, now? I'm sorry that you had to go through that. You're lucky that you escaped with your life," she said darkly. In a brighter and louder tone, she continued,

"Now, you and the other student, along with Melody and Isaac will go to the Sacred Islands soon. Oh, and that kid from Soror."

"What kid?" I asked.

"Isaac, explain to her about August," the Headmaster ordered.

I listened closely as he quickly told me about August Primerano, who didn't know if he had magic or not.

"If you don't mind me asking, who is the other student that's going?" I said.

"You'll find out soon enough once you begin your training. That is, if you want to go. Do you?" Headmaster Ignatia inquired.

"Oh, I uh, don't know," I stammered. "It might take some time for me to think it over. If it's anything like my encounter last week, I don't think it's safe for me to go."

"Did you even think about using your magic to stop it?" Headmaster Ignatia questioned, already knowing the answer.

"Well, no."

"Exactly! Anyway, I'm glad you didn't. That thing would surely have overpowered you. But if you undergo the training you'll be so strong you'll be able to defend yourself. Does that change your mind? I'm not trying to force you into going, Sage. It's up to you. We need someone with courage, discipline, brains, and combat skills. We can whip you up into an advanced mage in no time. Well, mage in training."

"Thanks for the offer but I don't know. It seems dangerous."

"It will be. But if I thought it was too dangerous I would not dare send you there. I need an answer by tomorrow."

"Okay." I paused for a minute, thinking it over in my mind. At last I had decided. "I'm sorry but I don't think this trip is for me."

The Headmaster inhaled and exhaled sharply. "Very well. Thank you for your honesty."

* * *

As I struggled to fall asleep that night, my mind kept wandering back to the Sacred Islands. I knew I had always been intrigued by them, but was denied access to information about them. And now I was given the chance to go to them and I had brushed it away in fear. What would Elijah do? He would've gone, for I had gotten him interested in the islands as well. And with all that special training with the Headmaster herself, I could advance further ahead than any of the other students. I would be very skilled. And two students were picked to go out of the entire Academy. That had to mean I was the best student out of them all! I would have to go to Mage Melody the next day and tell her that I changed my mind about going.

CHAPTER 12

TERESSIA

*A*nother week had passed and each day I walked home alone after the Academy. Elijah stayed after classes every day, coming up with several excuses. Some days he would say "I have to stay for tutoring," or "I promised this professor I would help out," and once he even said "the librarian said I wouldn't be banned anymore if I helped shelf books." Every day he would lie to me, hiding things. I wasn't dumb; I knew that Elijah stayed after class for the same thing each day.

Today I was done with his excuses. I was determined to find out the truth about his whereabouts. I decided to secretly follow Elijah after the last class of the day ended, after he had said "Sorry Tres, I'm failing trigonometry so I'm required to stay late again." I had nodded, pretended I understood and believed him.

I slunk through the crowd of people that rushed to escape the Academy for the day. I kept sight of Elijah's dark red robe through the gaps in the clusters of students. Elijah abruptly turned into a hallway I had never been down. The number of people had thinned out and this area was almost empty. I stood close to the wall, edging toward the corridor Elijah had entered.

As soon as I got there, I almost collided with another person, a student I had never seen before.

"Sorry, I didn't see you," I said softly.

"Nothing wrong with that." His voice was slightly deeper than Elijah's, and he looked older than the two of us. His hair was a light shimmering brown, and his face told me he was definitely a couple of years older, along with his height. Instead of any of the colors I was used to, he wore a cream colored robe. He wasn't training to be a mage.

"If you don't mind me asking, are you training to be a wizard?" I said. Had I asked too much of a personal question? What if the student suddenly thought I was nosy?

"No. At the moment I don't know what I'm training to be. That's why I'm here. I was sent from Soror because my teachers believe I possess magic, and they want the mages and other magic wielders here to figure out if that's true."

"Oh. That's interesting. No wonder I haven't seen you around. My name's Teressia." I decided to introduce myself, but I should not have been so hasty. What if he wasn't in the right mood for introducing himself? It could have been a bad time.

"August. Pleasure to meet you. I'm looking for the library. Could you show me where it is?"

"Uh, sure. This way." I turned around, back to the front of the Academy, away from where Elijah had gone. I sighed. I guess it was supposed to remain a secret about what Elijah did every day.

We reached the sober doors of the library. "In here," I gestured.

"Thank you. I know I'm asking for a lot but will you show me around? I'm looking for a certain type of book."

"Okay," I said. I hauled open the door and stepped into the library, August behind me. "What type of book are you looking for?"

I spent the next few minutes leading August around, showing him where history and mage books were. When he had pulled a few off the shelves we both walked to the center of the library to a desk.

"Thank you," August said, opening a book.

I faintly smiled as a response.

"Do you know how Lux came to be?" He asked, eyes gleaming.

"Not exactly." I sat down across from August.

"Well long ago, in the beginning age, there was one big continent of land. In a great earthquake that lasted for days, it split into four continents, Lux being the center and the smallest. Later, when centuries passed and civilizations began to develop, the empires on the neighboring continents that are now Osen and Tringuli, wanted this tiny little continent. They thought it was the center of our region of the planet and believed it would be abundant in resources, rich with metals, gold, and jewels. They also believed that whoever had this tiny continent would overpower the others. So the two sent their forces, the greatest armies they could manage and met on Lux to begin the Battle of the Ages. A few months into the war, a blinding light swept over the land and the armies were forced to stop fighting. The light was rumored to chase them away, saving the continent. The continent was so small it was made into one country, and the country was called Lux, in honor of the light. People from all over the world ventured out bravely to live in Lux. The first city built was the City of Lux, our current capital. Each year after it was originally completed, there were more additions to the city until it became the size it is now. As the centuries passed, more city states developed. And here we are today."

"I never knew all of that," I said.

August laughed, startling me. "How could you not? That's the most famous history lesson there is in Soror. I bet you haven't heard of how Vast Lake was made, have you?"

I shook my head.

August opened his mouth to begin, but then closed it. "I have to go. Some other time, yes?"

I turned around, seeing Elijah at the entrance of the library. I hastily scrambled out of my chair and followed August. "Elijah? What are you doing?" I demanded.

"What are *you* doing here, Tres?" he said, shocked to see me.

"I asked you first," I replied, placing my hands on my hips impatiently.

"Um, well, I told you I had to stay for extra class lessons—"

"Oh, don't start! You think I'm so dumb, that I'll believe all your excuses. Why are you hiding things from me?"

"I'm not hiding anything!" Elijah lied.

I glared at Elijah, tired of his lies. I exhaled sharply and stormed out of the library, throwing open the library doors and marching out of the Academy angrily. I wanted to get away from all the people, all of their lies and questions. I needed to calm down somewhere before I said something that I would regret. I started to run, and stopped once I had exited Elementa and came before the Shrouded Forest. I sat down and leaned against a tree that marked the beginning of the forest but I did not dare enter it. After last week, I was done with woods.

I sniffed, wrinkling my nose. Something smelt awful. A rustling coming behind me, from the forest, had me on my feet. I faced the forest, carefully watching for any movement. The rustling continued, getting closer. Finally the shrub closest to me shook, something inside of it. I pulled out my mage's rod from my bag and raised it, ready to use it. I trembled slightly, afraid of what could emerge.

A small brown blur dashed out of the bush in a frenzy. I relaxed as I watched the rabbit bound away. Then I realized that the rabbit had to be fleeing from something. I slowly took steps backwards, wondering why I was not running like the rabbit. I heard more rustling in the forest. The rustling became louder and louder until it reached the border of the forest.

Three monsters erupted from the undergrowth leaping toward me. They were large, shaped like deer but were made of thick, hardened, dark black and purple puddles. Their yellow eyes were fixed on me and they all howled, an unnerving screeching sound. I didn't scream, but began gasping and pivoted to the other direction and began running. I swerved, realizing I couldn't lead these monsters into Elementa.

I heard the sickening thuds of the monsters pursuing me, not slowing. I was lucky that they were slow, or else I would probably be dead. As I ran I managed to order the earth to rise in small walls with my magic. It only slowed the creatures down, for they smashed through the walls. I ran south, panting heavily. I had forgotten about the Elementa River. It unavoidably loomed in front of me, the water rushing along in a swift current. There was no bridge here and the monsters were closing the distance between me and them.

Without thinking I thrust my mage's rod in an upward motion, creating stepping stones that I could jump across. As I hopped from one to another, I used my hammer-like tool to create more ahead of me. Once I had finally reached the other side, heart pounding and my brow dripping with sweat, I turned around. The monsters were using my stepping stones to clamber across the river. I brought the mage's rod down, making one of the stepping stones vanish. The monster in the lead tumbled into the water, shrieking. As it flew down the river, splatters of the slime that made up the body began to dissolve. It kept screeching as it rode on the current. The other two creatures advanced, and I didn't have time to make the stones vanish.

I turned west without thinking and ran along the river, which separated me and the forest. The creatures were still chasing me but I couldn't continue running much longer.

"Help!" I hollered to no one. What was I thinking? There was no one around between Elementa and Fortis. Fortis. I had forgotten about Fortis. I was leading the creatures right into the neighboring city!

I heard shouting behind me, human shouting.

"Hey!" the voice called. The monsters stopped, looking behind them for the body that belonged to the voice. It was August.

I dashed to the side and plunged into the fast moving river. I was swept along with the strong current, bumping into rocks. I smashed into a boulder and felt a sharp stab race up my leg. Struggling against the current, I pushed out my mage's rod, trying to stop. I used the boulder to push up against, throwing my head above the water, and gasped for air and crawled on top of the flat boulder. My leg ached from the impact with the rock. I created more stepping stones with the rod, hopping from one to the next on one foot. I traveled downstream, not daring to cross the river again. That would put me closer to the forest and I did not want to meet up with one of those creatures again.

Eventually the pain of my injured leg became unbearable and I crossed over to the bank opposite the forest and crawled out of the river. I lay on the grass, panting and sputtering. After a few moments, August appeared and collapsed next to me, panting as well.

"Thank you," I gasped.

"No," he began, but didn't have enough air to continue. "No, I made it worse. They went in the direction of Fortis. I tried to stop them but they ran right past me, going to the city."

He sat up next to me, resting.

"Let's get out of here," I said.

"Good idea."

Despite the pain in my leg, we jogged back toward Elementa, running into Korina and Sage before we reached the city.

"Did you two go near Shrouded Forest?" Sage asked, a worried expression coming onto her face.

"Um, perhaps," I answered.

Korina turned around and groaned. "Don't go near there! Stay *away* from the forest!"

"I think we found out why," August said.

Korina spun around and faced us. "Did you get chased? Hm? By those slimy mutations?"

"Mutations?" I said.

"Yes, they're called mutations. Did you get chased by one?" Korina demanded impatiently.

"Three. One fell in the river though," I replied.

"Three? I was chased by only one last week," Sage added.

"Yes, three. August distracted the other two and they ran toward Fortis."

"You mean they left the forest? They went to a city?" Sage asked worriedly.

I nodded. "You look surprised."

"If they left the forest it means they're becoming stronger and more confident. If they're going to attack Fortis then we can expect the same."

"I tried to stop them, but they kept on running to Fortis," August said.

Korina cleared her throat deliberately. "Could we get out of here, please? I don't feel like being chased. I just ate."

As soon as the four of us turned around, Elijah came trotting up.

"I heard someone was in danger. Mage Melody and Mage Isaac are coming, they're behind me," he said.

"You!" Korina said, wrinkling her brow.

Elijah turned toward her. "Hey, you're that girl that—"

"—that you got in the way of! What are *you* doing here?" Korina finished.

"Okay, enough you two! Let's start walking," Sage said.

"Elijah, Korina. Korina, Elijah," I said as we began to walk. "I'm glad you two have finally met."

Korina grunted, staring ahead.

"So Elijah," I said, "would you like to tell me where you've been every day, now that you're finally in the same place I am?"

"You mean you haven't told her?" Sage and August asked.

"Told her what?" Korina said.

"Well…" Elijah began.

"No, no more 'well.' Tell me!" I ordered, embarrassed to be doing so in front of several people.

"I've been training after classes with Sage and August."

"Why?" I asked.

"The three of us are going to the Sacred Islands with Mage Melody and Mage Isaac."

CHAPTER 13

KORINA

"*W*hat! The Sacred Islands? You expect me to believe that?" I spat. This Elijah must have been lying. I did not like him very much. The first time I noticed him, he got on my bad side and that had made a lasting impression on my opinion of him.

"Whatever are you going to the Sacred Islands for?" Tres asked, the loudest I had ever heard her speak.

"Where do you think all of this dark magic is coming from? The skilled mages of the Academy believe strongly that it's coming from the Sacred Islands. They can feel it coming from Divite Island. So they're sending the two best mages, along with two students and August to go investigate."

"Why would they pick you and Sage? How is that fair to me or Tres or any other student of the Academy?" I exclaimed.

Elijah looked at me innocently. "It's not, I'm afraid. I'm sure it was a hard decision to make by the professors and the Headmaster."

I groaned. "Whatever! Don't think you're all important and of value now, Elijah. I already don't like you."

"It doesn't matter if you like me or not, we're not going to be spending time together in the next few months because I'll be gone. I didn't even know you existed until this year; I've never seen you in the Academy before."

"It's because this is my first year living here. I came from Suri, from all the way across the Spearant Ocean. Whatever, it doesn't matter," I retorted.

"Can you stop arguing? Please!" Tres pleaded.

"Yeah, we're tired of hearing you bicker," snorted Sage.

"I'm not arguing," Elijah protested.

"It takes two to tango, Elijah!" I said.

"We're not doing a tango, though!" Elijah argued.

"Just shut up!" I ordered. I was tired of hearing Elijah's voice.

"Could you both be quiet before you attract a whole herd of those mutations?" Sage said.

I noticed August, the new kid that I had just recently met, was not saying anything. "August? You seem quiet about this."

He looked up, as if he was in deep thought. "Oh, I usually don't pick fights with people. It's not my place to say anything."

Tres smiled shyly. It obviously made her feel good to know someone that was as quiet as she was. It didn't matter to me, I was someone who would speak their mind without a second thought.

As the four of us squabbled, Mage Melody and Isaac approached us.

"We heard that Teressia was being pursued by one of those mutations. Is everyone all right? Is anybody hurt?" Mage Melody asked.

Everyone shook their heads, affirming that we were fine, only a little shaken.

"Where did the mutations go?" Mage Isaac inquired.

"I tried to stop them, but they kept running toward Fortis," August explained.

"Toward Fortis?" Mage Melody cried. She and Mage Isaac worriedly glanced at each other.

"Wonderful. We can expect a declaration of war from them in the morning. They'll claim we sent monsters over there to harm them. Those people will do anything to start a war, even in this time of peace," Mage Isaac complained. Turning to Melody he said, "We need to go back to the Academy. The Headmaster needs to know what has happened, how the mutations have been growing stronger. She can report it to the Headman of Elementa and the council."

"Remember, stay away from Shrouded Forest, and don't even go near Elementa River. In fact, just stay within the city," Mage Melody warned.

The five of us trudged away from the river and forest, toward Elementa.

"So why did you keep your expedition a secret, Elijah?" Tres asked quietly.

"Yeah, Elijah. Why don't you explain yourself?" I demanded, louder than Tres.

"It's simple," he replied, "I didn't think the Headmaster wanted everyone to know. That means don't go around blabbing to people, especially you, Korina."

"Why me?" I exclaimed. "You barely even know me!"

Elijah shrugged. "You just seem like that kind of person."

I rolled my eyes.

"Okay, okay that's enough. Don't start another argument," Sage said.

"I'm not starting another conflict, don't worry—"

"Shh!" Sage silenced. "Listen."

A rustling kept us quiet. The five of us turned around, facing the forest. Across the bridge over the river, and from the forest came rustling, a disturbance in the undergrowth. Something was moving closer, almost out of the Shrouded Forest.

"It's the same rustling as when those three mutations came out of the forest," Teressia whispered.

More rustling sounded, stretching on the whole side of the beginning of the forest. If it were mutations that were coming, it was a bunch of them.

We stood there, unable to move. I wanted to run, to hide in the safe streets of the city, but I couldn't move my legs. I was planted there, waiting for something to emerge from the forest. Soon, the bushes and clusters of plants that were visible from our position, were trembling.

I counted seven mutations that sprang out of the forest, snarling and releasing horrible shrieking screams. Then more mutations burst on each side of the original seven. I lost count as more mutations swarmed out of the forest, until there were at least fifty of them. By this time, the five of us were running as fast as we could back to the city.

As I glanced over my shoulder, I could see the mutations advancing, sauntering toward the city. I wasn't sure why they weren't running, but that gave us more time to get away and the more time, the better.

"We're leading them to the city!" Teressia protested.

"We have nowhere else to go!" I said.

When we reached the city, we still ran. We were panting hard, but continued to sprint across town to the Academy, Elijah in the lead.

Elijah and I yanked open the tall doors of the Academy, the five us bursting into the foyer.

"Where now?" I asked, to one in particular.

"We need to find the Headmaster," Elijah said.

Footsteps echoed through the halls. A familiar mage entered the foyer. Of course. It was Mage... what was her name? Mage Terra. The same one we had ran into just a little over a week ago, when I was sick and was with Sage and Tres.

"You three again! And you brought your little friends. What do you want this time?" Mage Terra inquired, a bit harshly.

"We need to see the Headmaster immediately," Sage stated.

"So now you want to see the queen herself? Forget about it, children! Classes are over, go home! I'm not going to argue with you this time. You were pushing your luck the first time, and I'm not going to submit to you again."

"Children!" Cried a familiar voice. We turned to see Mage Melody. "What's wrong?"

"Mutations! Tons of them are coming!" Sage said.

"We need to warn Headmaster Ignatia," Elijah added.

"Of course! Follow me," Melody said.

"But Melody! Surely you're not going to bother with these children?" Mage Terra called.

"It's urgent, Terra," she responded briskly.

We followed Mage Melody for a long time, the furthest I had ever been into the Academy. We climbed a flight of stairs and stopped at the door of an office. Mage Melody knocked rapidly.

A tall woman appeared at the door, her black wavy hair falling to her chest. I recognized the Headmaster from the night I was in Mage Melody's quarters.

"What is it, Melody?" She asked firmly.

"Tell her, children."

Elijah decided to speak for us, explaining the swarming mutations. Headmaster Ignatia's eyes widened.

"I must go now. I will report this pending attack to the Headman of Elementa at the temple. We don't have much time. Melody, gather the mages. You will all fight with the guards, if Headman Gileon decides to use them to protect the city. If he's feeling stubborn and unreasonable, we will have to face the mutations alone."

Headmaster Ignatia rushed past us, clearing a path for herself. Mage Melody trailed behind her, walking at a fast pace. The five of us followed her, not wanting to be left alone in the Academy.

The five of us parted when we exited the Academy. August stayed with Mage Melody in the Academy, where he apparently stayed when he came from Soror. Elijah and Teressia started walking together down the streets, probably going home. I was left with Sage.

"What do we do now?" I asked.

Sage shrugged. "Hide? Take refuge in your home, maybe?" she suggested. "I don't know, but I don't feel like being killed by mutants today. I'm going home."

I felt like I couldn't go home by myself. I walked north of the Academy, toward the Temple of Elementa. I could wait outside until Headmaster Ignatia returned. Then I could find out news of what the Headman had decided to do. There wasn't much time, I thought. The mutations would probably be at the edges of the city by now.

I leaned up against the dark green walls of the temple. I waited for a couple of minutes before Headmaster Ignatia burst out, along with the Headman of Elementa.

"Headmaster!" I called.

She turned quickly at my voice. "What? Korina, is that you? Is that one of my students?" She squinted, for the light of the day was sinking away.

"Yes, it's Korina. What's going to happen?"

"The guards of the city will fight the mutations along with me and my mages. Melody is bringing them out right now. There's no time, everyone is leaving now."

I trailed behind the Headmaster of the Academy and Headman Gileon to the edge of the city. As we walked through the town square, tons of guards were assembled. I kept following, even though I knew they wouldn't want me to.

I ran with the guards and mages to the west edge of the city, the edge that faced Shrouded Forest. The Headmaster was ushering people ahead and saw me.

"Korina! What are you doing? Go back inside the city! This isn't safe!" She demanded sternly.

"I can help, I can fight! I promise, I can do this!" I said.

"I don't want to explain to your parents that you died because I let you fight mutations. Go back, now!"

"No!" I refused.

"I'm not arguing with you! Go now!" Headmaster Ignatia ordered.

Without waiting for a reply, Headmaster Ignatia swooped away, exiting the city with the guards and mages.

I followed, refusing to leave. *I will fight.*

I bravely exited Elementa and jumped into the mass of guards. One of them planted a heavy helm on my head. I didn't know whether they mistook me for one of them or just allowed me to stay.

The mutations were almost there at the city, their mouths gaping open, howling into the evening. The small force of guards and mages advanced until they met with the line of mutations.

I dodged a heavy swipe from a claw dripping with slime. Kneeling low on the ground, I swept a wave of water and drowned three mutations. They dropped into the grass, melting into a puddle of dark magic.

A sharp pain erupted in my back. I turned around, a snarling mutation in my face. My back was stinging, and my plain blouse stuck to my body because of the wound. My brown bodice was probably ripped. I spread my palm out and jetted a thick sheet of ice that expanded in size as it planted itself on the mutation's face. I darted away, waiting for the next mutation.

All around me guards used their sharp weapons to slash at the mutations. Mages used their fire to melt the mutations, their water to soak them, their vicious plants to bind them, or their stones to injure them or bury them. The mutations were deadly, but easy to defeat. Many were wounded, and some lay on the ground limp.

I was covered in scratches and dried blood clumped on my forehead. My right ankle was sprained and throbbed with every beat of my heart. I was slow, but kept fighting. Before a mutation got too close to me, I blasted them away with water. Eventually I became dizzy, exhausted from using so much magic. I was not used to using so much at a time, and I was feeling weak. One mutation snuck up behind me again, and knocked me to the ground. I was saved by a guard and clambered to my feet again.

After what seemed like hours, the number of mutations had decreased, the remaining retreating back to the forest. The assembled guards receded into Elementa, carrying the wounded and counting the dead. I spotted Headmaster Ignatia in the mass of people, standing tall and giving orders. There were a few scratches and bruises throughout her body, but otherwise she was uninjured. I limped toward her.

"Hurry! Get the wounded and fall back into the city! You, find the general! Go now!" The Headmaster directed. "Good gracious, Korina! What are you doing? I told you to go back into the city! You're lucky you're not dead!"

"I'm sorry, but I couldn't sit around doing nothing while these noble people risked their lives for the safety of the city."

"No matter, it's over for now. Find the medical personnel and they'll fix you up. And if I catch you disobeying my orders again, you'll be punished at the Academy. I'll have you scrubbing the kitchen for a month."

"But isn't everything fine now? We won the battle," I said.

Headmaster Ignatia cackled. "Don't be a fool, Korina. Those surviving mutations that scampered back into the forest will surely let the others know of this recent battle. They start off weak at first, then grow in numbers and observe how we fight. It's funny how mindless animals that exist to survive are manipulated by magic and become a powerful enemy. But do not believe that we won the battle. It's only getting started, Korina. Just watch, we'll be snoozing in our beds during the night and they'll attack the city. The guards won't be assembled, there won't be any time to fight them off."

"Will that really happen?" I asked in dread.

Headmaster Ignatia nodded. "It will some night. I hope this doesn't mean the Sacred Islands are too dangerous. I expect Elijah or Sage spilled the truth on the expedition, hm?"

"Yes, they did. I was bound to find out eventually though."

"Maybe not. Go off now." The Headmaster ushered me away.

CHAPTER 14

ELIJAH

A couple of days had passed since the attack from the mutations and since Fortis had declared war on Elementa. The guards and soldiers of Elementa were constantly swarming the city and patrolling the city's borders, every hour of the day and night. All the citizens walked in dazes of fear, anticipating another attack from the mutations and another battle from Fortis to come soon. My parents tried to act as if everything were normal for the sake of my brother, Isaiah. Isaiah was still worried, for his school had canceled class because of the mutations. The Academy had decided that it was still safe, as long as the mutations were not in the city. I still had to get up early for class so I retired to my bed. Soon, the whole family was asleep.

I couldn't force myself to sleep. My mind was flooding with thoughts of the upcoming expedition and the anxiety of the mutations.

A loud knock boomed from the front door. I padded across the floor and down the stairs, joining my parents as they moved toward the door.

My father opened the door to a guard. "Sorry to disturb you, Elsbade, but we need you to join us as a soldier. We'll provide clothes, armor, and weapons for you. Please come now."

"Right now?" my father cried. "Why? What for?"

"Fortis is coming, sir. The Headman has ordered us to gather the men who participated in the skirmish with them before, and any other boy who is of age. That means your son is to come as well."

"Elijah? Elijah can't go, sir! He's never fought, he's not trained for this!" My father protested.

"Please, soldier. He's underage. Don't take my son," my mother pleaded softly.

"The Headmaster says Elijah has been training every day after school and is prepared. If not for her opinion, we wouldn't take him, ma'am."

"I suppose we have no choice?" said my father.

The soldier shook his head. We followed him out the door, the rate of my heartbeat rapidly increasing. Would I live through the night, or would I be killed by some rotten Fortis soldier?

Once we were assembled with the other soldiers, we were given clothes to slip over our night ones, and armor over that. A helmet was placed on my head, and I was given a sword and shield. I secretly dropped the sword on the ground and kept the shield. I had no idea how to use a sword, so it wouldn't do me much good. I would fight with my fire.

The commander of the Elementa guards led us to the western border, the one that faced the Shrouded Forest. We assembled in neat rows, waiting for the Fortis soldiers to come. I was placed in between two strangers in the second row, so I had a view of the Shrouded Forest and Elementa River. The night droned on, the soft breezing rustling the grass, the stars dancing in the sky. The Elementa soldiers stared blankly ahead, waiting. No soldiers came.

I whispered to a guard beside me, "How are we sure that Fortis is coming?"

Without looking toward me, the guard leaned toward me and said, "We heard their war horn sound. Without a doubt, it was them."

After more waiting, shouts and screams of terror and pain sounded from the forest. Cries of men echoed into the night. Howls made by mutations followed. The soldier next to me shook his head.

"They must've taken the river through the forest. The brainless dim-wits. Those mutations probably attacked them easily, jumping into their boats and slaying their men."

Two boats floated out of the forest on the Elementa River. Lifeless men with scratches and injuries lay in the boats. More small boats followed, the wood torn and damaged. The boats traveled quietly, making their way to Elementa Bay.

"You two! Go get those boats from the bay. We don't want rotting man meat to dirty up our waters," our commander ordered.

Another boat made its way out of Shrouded Forest. Instead of dead men, there were blobs in an unmistakable man shape. The mutations had mutated the people into one of them.

"It's impossible..." the soldier next to me whispered to himself.

The human mutations leaped out of the boat, landing on the ground. They started charging toward us, and out of the forest tons of mutations followed. It was like the first time they attacked, this time more mutations that were better skilled. My mouth became bone dry and my stomach flipped over. Death was surely waiting for me this night.

"They're human mutations and forest animal mutations!" The commander warned. "Hold your ground and prepare to fight! Someone run to the Academy and get Headmaster Ignatia and the mages!"

I watched a lucky soldier flee from the pending battle to retrieve the reinforcements from the Academy. I swallowed hard, trying to get rid of the dehydrated feeling in my mouth. It stayed dry.

The mutations reached us quickly, some springing into the air and landing heavily on guards, quickly bringing them down. With no trouble, the mutations swiped a heavy blow to the guards' neck and the guards were through. The mutations had grown stronger than the last time, seemingly learning the combat moves the guards used and easily countering them.

I looked straight up as I heard a growl. A mutation was above me, about to land on top of my head. I dropped to the ground and rolled, shooting a blast of fire at the mutation. The creature dodged the fire and charged at me while I was still on the ground. I thrust my shield out in front of me and the mutation banged into it. Then it reached over my shield, and brought an arm out, preparing to land a blow. A guard slashed the mutation in the side while its yellow eyes were fixed on me. The creature slumped to the ground, and I quickly hopped to my feet.

Two mutations advanced on me as soon as I was up. They were coming toward me from each side. I flung out my arms and hurled spheres of fire from both hands. The mutations melted into a pile of slime as soon as the fire came into contact with their bodies.

I jumped up reflexively as another mutation appeared. I landed on where its shoulders would've been if it have any. I attempted to burn it with another blast of fire, but it shook me off, throwing me to the ground. It slammed into me and brought its arm back. I ducked and threw the shield out. With my feet, I sent the creature flying.

I quickly looked around me. More and more mutations appeared, maliciously attacking the Elementa soldiers. The mages had not arrived and we were struggling.

I slammed to the ground, a force knocking me off my feet from behind. A mutation was on my back, and clawed at my exposed neck. I shrieked in agony; my neck was *burning.* The claws of the mutation seemed as if they were made of acid. I felt the weight disappear from my back. Another guard had saved me and the creature lay dead beside me, staining the grass. I got up and felt my neck. I winced in pain at the touch. My neck was sticky and wet, still burning as if it were on fire.

I blasted out a comet of fire from my palms as two mutations ran toward me. I was too quick for them, and part of their bodies dissolved quickly. Three more mutations surrounded me, and I swiftly spun, creating a ring of fire.

As soon as I had done so, my vision was dotted by swarming black specks. I became light headed, my neck still on fire. I collapsed to the ground, unable to stand. I prayed that the mutations would think I was dead, and leave me alone. My vision blackened and I became oblivious to my surroundings, and felt as if I had fallen asleep.

As I regained consciousness, I felt a sharp poking in my side.

"This one's dead!" A voice shouted from my side. "Just look at the back of his neck! It's all torn up into a bloody mess."

"Yep, he's definitely dead," another voice agreed.

I parted my lips as much as I could, without much success. I tried to call out, to say, "I'm not dead!" but it came out as a small mutter.

"What'd ya say?" one of the voices asked.

"I didn't say nothin'."

"Well, I heard something!" the voice protested.

"You were scratched on the ear, what can ya expect?"

"No! I heard something!"

I tried to say something again, tried to be louder. "Not dead," I managed in a quiet murmur.

"Hey! This one's alive after all!"

I was lifted by two men. I yelled out in severe pain, though it was only a quiet cry.

"Hang in there, little guy," one of the men said.

I was carried for a few minutes, and then placed onto a soft cot. I slept for a while, exhausted. When I awoke, my neck felt better but still stung. I reached back and felt a thick bandage on my neck wound, wet from blood. Some type of ointment must have been smeared underneath the bandage.

I was in a dimly lit tent. A woman entered. "Good! You're awake! Don't worry, young man. I've gotten all that poison out from that wound and it should heal in a few weeks, leaving a small scar."

A few weeks? No, it has to heal now! *I can't go to the Sacred Islands in pain and with an injury!*

"It hurts," I muttered.

"I know, I know. Here, let me give you some medicine." The woman gave me a glass of water and a couple of soft cubes of medicine. "If all of those mages hadn't shown up, every one of you would be dead. Those mutations have grown in strength and number. And who would have guessed that humans would mutate! If that wound of yours was bigger and had stretched down your spine, why! I'm sure you would've mutated as well! It's only a shame that so many were killed. There were more dead than living..." the lady ranted on while she worked on remedies, her back turned to me.

I slid into sleep again. When I awoke, light crept into the sky. The sun was rising and it was dawn. The woman that had treated me was gone and I was alone. I exited the tent and looked around. The tent was pitched on the edge of the city, wisely away from the border. A small Fortis patrol was talking to the Headman of Elementa and some guards.

"What have you done to our people? They lay dead and most have transformed into monsters! What sorcery have you performed? I demand that you answer me!" The Fortis commander cried in anger.

"We have done nothing to your people! This war you have declared is because of nothing! Didn't you listen to us when we tried to warn you? We told you darkness was upon us and you ignored us! Look at what it's led to! These dark mutations have killed and mutated your own men!" The Headman shouted.

"Don't pass the blame to something that does not exist! War is upon you, Elementa! Expect Fortis forces to come and destroy you all!"

The angry Fortis patrol stormed away, this time traveling around the forest instead of through it.

"The fools!" The Headman grumbled.

I returned to the tent and sat on the cot, my chin resting in my hands. The back of my neck was hot from the bundle of bandages.

Headmaster Ignatia threw the flap of the tent to the side and entered.

"Elijah, I have news. I'm tired of waiting. I can't have all of this mutation nonsense continue for much longer. We're running out of guards in the city and Fortis is blaming us for the mutations. I've decided that you will depart for the Sacred Islands at the end of the next week. Do you think your neck will be better in time? If not, you will stay here."

"I'm sure it'll be better, but not healed," I answered.

"Of course it won't. I'll have a supply of medicine prepared for the voyage." Headmaster Ignatia started to leave, then turned back around. "I almost forgot," she said. "Korina will be going with the group."

"Why?" I asked. She was always a jerk to me and it wouldn't be very pleasant with her around.

"Because of the way she fought in the first battle of the mutations. I was amazed that a child like her wasn't killed. I've decided it would be unwise of me to prevent someone as skilled as she is from going. I'll have her train with you, Sage, and August as well. Rest and take care of that neck." Headmaster Ignatia left without another word.

I sighed, wishing Korina wasn't going. I had no idea she even fought in the first battle. I was also worried that my neck would be a burden for the expedition. There was no way that I was going to stay in Elementa though. Going to the Sacred Islands had to be safer than staying here with the mutations and Fortis. I lay down on the cot.

As soon as I gently rested my head on the small pillow, I quickly rose up again. My father had fought in the battle, and I hadn't seen him since. Was he unharmed? Was he injured? Could he even be dead? I shook my head at the thought. He *couldn't* be dead, I wouldn't think like that. I got up from the cot, left the tent, and walked up to a guard that was passing the tent.

"Excuse me! Do you know where Dein Elsbade is?"

"Don't know 'em," the guard said curtly and kept walking.

I ventured away from the tent until I found a different guard and asked the same thing as before.

"Elsbade? He's in one of the recovery tents over that little hill." The guard pointed to a small rise. I clambered over it, seeing a dozen of tents that looked like mine. The tents took up a small side street, where not very many buildings were.

As soon as I saw a nurse dressed in a white apron I rushed to her. "Which tent is Dein Elsbade in?" I asked.

"How should I know? I've been in too many to remember who's in which. Now run along child, I have important work to do." The nurse brushed me aside as if I were a little kid.

I walked up to another nurse that just exited a tent. "Excuse me, I know you're busy, but do you know where Dein Elsbade is? He's my father and I just want to know if he's alright."

"I understand. I think I remember where he is. Follow me."

I followed the short nurse through a maze of tents until she paused. "Nope, it wasn't this one," she said.

She paused in front of two more tents before she said anything else.

"I'm positive it's this one. Wait here." The nurse disappeared behind the flap of the red tent. I heard a quiet exchange of murmurs and she returned. "He's ready to see you."

The tent was brighter than it had been in mine, now that it was morning.

"Elijah! I'm so thankful you're alive! How are you?" my father asked brightly, despite the cast on his foot and the rings of bandages rising up his arm. I ran to him and threw my arms around his neck.

"I've been better. How about yourself?"

"They say my foot is broken, and it does hurt a little, but other than that I feel great!"

I smiled. My father was in a cot meant for the injured, the people that were suffering, but he was in bright spirits. "You shouldn't be in here. None of us should. We should be home, eating breakfast," I said.

"I know." My dad lowered his head, his voice becoming slightly sadder. "We should, but those blasted Fortis people have to go around starting a war from for nothing. Are you still going to go to the Secret Islands with that neck wound?"

"It's the Sacred Islands, and yes, I feel like I have to."

"You don't, though. Tell me again, when are you leaving?"

"At the end of the week. Headmaster Ignatia said she's tired of waiting."

"She would say that," my father chuckled. "That's awfully soon. Are you sure your neck will be up to it? You can always stay here, you know."

"It'll be fine. Well I'd better let you get some rest. Mom will be thrilled that we're both alive."

"You better go tell her then."

I left the tent, relieved that my father was alive. I headed for home, thinking about the voyage ahead and everything I needed to pack for the journey.

CHAPTER 15

SAGE

$\mathcal{T}$wo battles had occurred in three days. The mutations had grown stronger and wiser and the people of Fortis were livid, declaring war on us for the second time. Even though the mutations could attack the city at any moment, Headmaster Ignatia kept the Academy open. On the day that the second battle occurred, the Academy had closed because most of the mages had just battled. Last week she had also decided that we were leaving for the Sacred Islands sooner than planned. We would now depart at the end of the week, which was either tomorrow or the next day—it was up to the Headmaster.

After classes ended I went to the courtyard to train as usual. August was sparring with Mage Isaac while Mage Melody talked with the Headmaster. Elijah sat on the bench, kicking at the ground and looking bored. I was surprised to see the face of Korina.

I rushed up to Elijah and whispered harshly, "What is *she* doing here?"

"The Headmaster said Korina fought well in the first battle," he replied flatly.

"I didn't know she fought in that."

"Neither did I."

"What happened to your neck?" I asked, noticing the wad of bandages on the back of it.

"Mutation got me yesterday. The Headmaster and the mages are making me rest and aren't letting me train like usual. They're going easy on me just because of this stupid injury."

"Sounds painful. How did it happen? Is it really bad?" I asked.

"Mhm. The nurse said that there was poison in it. It burned as if it were lit on fire when it first happened and it still stings a little bit. I even have to take medicine."

"Yikes. I would've hated to fight in that battle," I replied.

"I didn't really have a choice. My father and I were drafted in the middle of the night, the soldiers telling us that Fortis was coming. They traveled by boat on the river, and went through Shrouded Forest."

"Idiots," I muttered. "So the Fortis soldiers mutated?"

"The ones that weren't killed," Elijah answered bluntly.

"I didn't think that was possible," I whispered.

"It is. I saw them. They jumped off the boats on two legs, looking vaguely like a human shape but were mutations. It was horrendous. I thought I was going to die."

The Headmaster ended our conversation. "Sage! You'll spar with Korina. Elijah, you can go home."

"But I just got here!" Elijah protested.

"I want that neck to heal! If it you don't take care of it, you won't be going to the Sacred Islands," Headmaster Ignatia firmly stated.

Elijah groaned. "I just want it to be gone already!"

"I'm sorry but it's not like we have a magical—wait. Melody!"

"Yes, Headmaster Ignatia?"

"Did you ever finish that solution?"

"Yes, but I haven't tested it yet."

"Go get it. Now," the Headmaster ordered.

"Yes, of course." Mage Melody rose and hurriedly darted away.

"Elijah, sit right there," Headmaster Ignatia commanded.

Elijah remained where he was on the bench.

"August, I want you to continue sparring with Mage Isaac. Try using that technique I taught you. I'm still hoping that it will reveal any magic that you might have."

August nodded. He stood in a combat stance like he was a mage and put his hands together. Closing his eyes, he inhaled deeply and exhaled slowly. Then he opened his eyes and slightly bent his knees. Mage Isaac ran toward him, bending his knees as he was about to jump.

August read his movements and dropped down on one foot and spun the other foot at Mage Isaac's as he was rising into the air. August's foot knocked Mage Isaac off balance and he tumbled to the ground, performing a quick somersault to save himself. August darted in front of Mage Isaac as he rose up and tried to throw Isaac off balance again. Mage Isaac was prepared and shifted his leg to the side, and attempted to jab August in the stomach. August quickly blocked the attack with his forearm and attempted to use the same jab. Isaac blocked the attack with his forearm as well. The attacks went on for a little bit until August ducked and slid his fist through Isaac's defense. Mage Isaac jumped back and August advanced.

I was distracted from the sparring as Mage Melody returned with a glass bottle filled with turquoise colored liquid. She sat down on the bench next to Elijah and removed the cork.

"Undo the bandage," Melody said.

Elijah reached behind him, and slowly began unwrapping the white gauze material from around his neck. I looked away, not wanting to see the wound.

I stepped in front of Elijah so that I wouldn't see the back of his neck. Mage Melody scrunched up her face in silent disgust and dabbed her finger in the clear bottle.

"This is a solution that I mixed myself. I haven't tested it on anything so I don't know what's going to happen," Melody said.

Elijah jerked away. "What is it?" he asked.

"It's a healing remedy. It's supposed to heal any wound in three days or less. As soon as I apply it, it should begin to speed up the healing process, causing the cuts in your skin to knit together at once."

"How does that work?" Elijah wondered.

"It has magical ingredients mixed in with herbs and other medicine cubes. Once it comes into contact with your skin, it reacts with the skin and speeds up its growth. Once it is sufficiently healed, the skin will return to its normal condition and the growing will stop. If your body doesn't like the stuff there are possible side effects, but I don't know what they are yet."

"Okay," Elijah said slowly, and reluctantly let Melody apply the remedy. At first Elijah cringed and squeezed his eyes shut, crying out and gasping in pain. Then he relaxed and exhaled.

"How does it feel?" Mage Melody asked.

"Better." Elijah let his shoulders slump.

"It already looks better," Melody said, but still wrinkled her nose at the sight. She took out a wad of bandage from her robe and began placing it on the wound.

"It doesn't sting anymore," Elijah remarked.

"Good," Melody said brightly.

"Can you bend your neck faster now?" Headmaster Ignatia asked in a stern tone.

Elijah rotated his neck slowly at first, then sped up. "It doesn't hurt anymore. Wow, this is amazing."

Mage Melody smiled but Headmaster Ignatia's expression remained grave. "Elijah, I want you to spar with Sage. If Melody's solution worked you should be ready. Whoever wins gets to take a break on training and go home for the day, unless I am disappointed by your performance."

August and Mage Isaac ceased their fight and walked to the side. Sweat rolled down his face and his breeches were blemished with grit.

Despite how hot he was, August slid on his cream colored Academy robe.

I removed myself from the bench and faced Elijah on the field. We started out in the usual places, several yards in front of each other. As soon as we were ordered to begin, Elijah ran straight toward me, blasting a wave of fire. I dove to the side just as the flames were about to reach me. Elijah continued to fire jets of flame toward me. I kept moving to the left, until he shot a fireball to my left, causing me to move to my right. Soon he was firing on both sides of me. I lifted my arms up, flicking my wrists as I did so. Vines rapidly stretched from the ground and plunged onto Elijah. Using my arms I commanded the vines to wrap themselves around the boy.

Elijah struggled for a few moments. I seized the opportunity and grew a web of thorn bushes around Elijah, like a prison made of plants. I added crimson roses as a joke.

Elijah did something I couldn't see, for he caused the vines that bound him to turn into a flaming red, then black. The vines disintegrated and fell to the ground as ashes. Elijah then sent a ring of fire flying out around him, burning the web of thorns. I grew more as the ones surrounding him burned away. Elijah became impatient and blasted an eruption of flame out, not stopping the fire until all of the thorns were destroyed.

He kicked his leg in the air, sending a stream of flame at me. I pulled up two small trees from the earth. It took a lot of my strength and wasn't a fast process, but the wide trunks blocked the fire. I then pulled several leaves off of the trees and hardened them as I had done in gardening class so long ago. I sent the daggers of leaves flying toward Elijah, and he conjured a swarm of small embers and attempted to burn the leaves. They were hard though, and flew straight threw the embers. Elijah realized he was in danger and dropped to the ground. Two leaves struck him.

"Ow!" Elijah cried, and rubbed his shoulder where the leaves had hit him.

I grinned and sent three vines stretching after him. Elijah spun around, releasing scalpels of flame onto the vines. The vines fell to the ground. I hadn't made them strong enough.

Elijah advanced, leaping into the air and landing square on his feet, sending a wave of fire toward me. I tried to jump, but was too late and was slightly singed. I was fortunate Elijah had decided not to make the fire very hot.

The blast sent me to the ground, sliding on my rear in the dust.

"Enough!" Headmaster Ignatia shouted, ending the spar. "Good job, you two. Elijah wins. What did you learn, Sage?"

"To move faster and anticipate the opponent's next move," I offered.

"Mm," the Headmaster grunted. "Did you think to sharpen the grass below his feet?"

"No," I admitted. I made a mental note to use that trick.

"That's what I thought. Now you have an idea on how to use tricks to distract your opponent."

Elijah widened his eyes in surprise. "Sharp grass?"

The Headmaster chuckled. "Whatever you can think of to win. What would you have done differently, Elijah?"

"I think I would've fired higher and then aimed at her feet so they would be forced to get hit."

"What if you used your feet more? You were a bit slow and very repetitive. An accomplished mage would've learned the way you fight and countered every move, then he would've exploited your weaknesses. Use a variety of motions and shots."

Elijah nodded seriously.

"Okay, I'll allow you to go home now," Ignatia said. Then she looked to her side at the two mages and August and Korina. "All of you come here," she commanded.

Every one gathered around the Headmaster. "Have you all heard of the war?"

We all nodded. "The war with Fortis, you mean?" Melody questioned.

"No," Ignatia said. "The City of Oceanus and Soror have joined forces. They have declared war on the capitol, the City of Lux. The two city states claim that the capital is not giving them their share of the profit from traded goods. They also complain that the capital is raising taxes and trying to cheat them out of their resources. Soror requested our help in the war, and like an idiot Headman Gileon agreed to join. I tried to persuade him not to at that meeting, but somehow he thought it would benefit us. We don't even trade with other countries!" Headmaster Ignatia snorted. "That foolish man needs to be impeached. If I was the headwoman of this town, we would be better off. But no! We have to spare our greatest soldiers and guards for a war we have no business in! In the meantime, we have mutations attacking and Fortis declaring war on us. And that imbecile wants to ship off our defense and leave us vulnerable! If he asks me for the mages of the Academy, he's plain stupid. Oh wait—he already is." Ignatia looked at us. "Don't repeat any of this to anyone. I didn't say anything about Gileon."

Mage Melody and Mage Isaac chuckled. "Don't worry, we agree with you," Mage Isaac said.

"When is Elementa joining the war with Soror and Oceanus?" Mage Melody queried.

"I don't know," Headmaster Ignatia said softly. "Don't worry about the war for now. In two days from now, at the crack of dawn, I want all of you at the docks. You depart for the Sacred Islands then. Elijah, you are dismissed. The rest of you, pair up and practice together. I'll teach you some techniques, August."

I was worried for the City of Oceanus. It was where I was born and where I had lived my entire life until I had moved to Elementa this year.

The two mages paired up together. I was left with Korina.

"So how'd you get in on this expedition?" I asked.

"I'm just amazing," Korina replied.

"Ha, sure!" I mocked. "Really, how did you get invited?"

"I fought in the first battle with the mutations."

"So? Elijah fought in the second, and that was more difficult. You saw what happened to his neck."

Korina shrugged. "I guess the Headmaster just thought I was skilled enough to come."

The two of us sparred together, going easy on each other. We both burst out hysterically laughing as Korina tripped over a sheet of ice she made herself. I even offered to give her a hand. She pulled me down onto the ground and we laughed again. When Headmaster Ignatia shot a stern glance at us, we became serious and hopped on our feet. When the Headmaster looked away we both began giggling again.

When the training session was over, I went home tired but in a good mood. I felt that Korina and I had finally gotten along for once. I was almost to the porch of my house when I ran into Teressia. She was rushing past in a worried manner.

"Teressia, what's wrong?"

"It said 'Don't let them leave without you.' What's that supposed to mean? Is it referring to your trip to the Sacred Islands? Elijah said Korina is going. I'm the only one out of the four of us that's wasn't invited!"

"I have no idea what you're talking about and there's no 'us four.' We just happened to clash into each other's lives briefly and now we're carrying on. It just so happens that the three of us are going on the same voyage. But it could've been anyone else."

"Exactly!" Teressia cried. "It *could* have been anyone else. But you three were chosen! And we've been through a lot together recently! Like in the library—you and Elijah! And remember we helped Korina when she was sick? And when we went to the city library together to see if Elijah was there and—"

"Enough! That is all over. It's just a coincidence, Teressia. I'm sorry."

"But it said I was supposed to come!" Teressia cried.

"What are you talking about?" I exclaimed, puzzled.

"There was an inscription!" Teressia said, rummaging through her bag that was slung over her shoulder. "On this!" She held out a hammer-looking tool. It had a gray stone on the top of it, and a small purple ring made of stone at the base that surrounded the gray stone.

"What is that?" I said.

"It's a mage's rod. And when I first handled it, there was an inscription on it saying 'Don't let them leave without you,'" Teressia continued. "Does that mean I'm supposed to go to the Sacred Islands? What else could it be talking about?"

"I don't know. But obviously you're not meant to go. We're leaving in two days at the crack of dawn and everyone's been training recently."

"You're leaving in two days?!" Tres exclaimed.

I nodded. "Sorry, Tres. At least we got to know each other in the past few weeks. Maybe we'll become friends when I return from the expedition."

"Of course. I'm sorry, I didn't mean to annoy you," Teressia apologized, blushing.

"You didn't," I lied. Teressia left and I entered my home.

* * *

The next day after classes we didn't train. Headmaster Ignatia ordered us to go home and rest and prepare for tomorrow.

As I was returning to my home, I spotted the Headmaster outside of the Academy, talking to the Headman of Elementa.

"Are you out of your mind, Gileon? You will surely send them all to their deaths!" Headmaster Ignatia shouted.

"Ignatia, please calm down. They will not die, they will be successful."

"Did you see what happened in the last battle against the mutations? Or did you sit in your office, stuffing your face with expensive chocolates?"

Headman Gileon seemed taken aback. "No, of course not! I saw what happened."

"Then you would know that you are sending these guards to their deaths!" Ignatia repeated.

"I am not. My mind is made up, Ignatia. Do not try to stop me." Gileon turned his back on her and marched to a large patrol of guards. I hurried over to the Headmaster.

"Headmaster, what's wrong?"

"That idiot Gileon is sending those guards into Shrouded Forest. Into the forest, where the whole nest of mutations lie in wait. They will all die and the mutations will come into the city and attack us all because of his dumb decision! Not to mention Fortis is still on our backs." Headmaster Ignatia sighed angrily. "I tried to stop him, but he's so stubborn. He always thinks what he believes is right."

We both watched Headman Gileon send the patrol into the Shrouded Forest. The short Headman waddled back into the city, returning to the Temple of Elementa where his office was. Headmaster Ignatia and I sat on the grass, just outside Elementa and waited for the patrol of guards to return. For once, the Headmaster of the Academy was soft, and didn't have a stern and commanding tone.

"So, Sage, are you ready for the expedition tomorrow?" she asked.

"I think so," I replied. "I'm awfully excited about it. It'll be nice to get away from the mutations and fighting."

Ignatia chuckled. "Hopefully you won't have to do much fighting." *What does she mean by that?*

We both looked up in the direction of Shrouded Forest as we heard yells and shouts. We knew what that meant.

Out of the small patrol of maybe twenty guards, three returned, running out of the forest for their lives. They stopped, panting, as they reached the Headmaster and me.

"Headmaster!" one gasped. "Those creatures mutated the guards before our own eyes!"

"We barely escaped with our own lives!" another added.

Headmaster Ignatia nodded. "I predicted that would happen. But no, Headman Gileon insisted that you would defeat the mutations and make it safer for Elementa. Instead we lost more soldiers and added to the population of mutations. Go to the temple and report back to Gileon at once."

The three soldiers staggered into the city, exhausted from their ordeal. Ignatia rose to her feet, brushing grass off of her dress. I did the same to my long green skirt.

"It's evening. Go home and prepare for the trip tomorrow, Sage. It'll be a long sail across the Lata Sea. I'll meet you at the docks in the morning."

* * *

I had risen when it was still dark outside, barely able to keep my eyes open. I spent a long time giving hugs and repeatedly telling my family goodbye. Finally, I checked my large bag over and over, then slung it over my shoulder and left the house. It would be a long time until I returned to it again.

When I reached the docks everyone was already there. Mage Melody and Mage Isaac chatted with Headmaster Ignatia. Teressia was there, bidding farewell to Elijah. August and Korina talked quietly with their bags at their feet. I was on time, noting that the sun was just beginning to rise. A ship with crew members loading crates and bags loomed in front of everyone.

Ignatia noticed me as I walked across the dock. "Good. We're all here." She paused as she was about to speak. A horn had sounded across the land. "That's the Fortis war horn," she informed.

I began to panic on the inside. Fortis was coming for war! What if they sunk our ship, and we weren't able to go to the Sacred Islands as planned?

"Are they coming for battle?" Elijah asked.

Headmaster Ignatia answered, "Yes. I can't stay for much longer; I have to gather the mages and fight with the guards. I'm glad it's Saturday, otherwise I would have to lock down the Academy and protect the students."

August suddenly gasped. "I forgot something very important!" He patted the pockets in his breeches. "I'll be right back!"

Ignatia tried to stop him. "August, no! It isn't safe!"

August ran past, ignoring her. Ignatia shook her head with worry.

I looked out across the water, spotting Fortis ships. There were cannons on the side, ready to be used. "War ships!" I shouted.

The Headmaster looked at the bay. "You must leave now! If you don't get across the bay those ships will almost certainly sink yours! Farewell my brave students, and be safe! Remember everything you've learned." Headmaster Ignatia actually bent down and hugged us all, even the two mages. She looked at Teressia.

"How am I supposed to get home safely?" Teressia asked, her gray eyes filled with worry and fear.

After thinking for a minute, Ignatia replied, "Go with them. You're ready. I don't know why I didn't invite you in the first place." Ignatia hugged Teressia as well.

"But my mother doesn't know," Tres protested.

"I'll tell her as soon as Fortis leaves."

"What about August?" Elijah asked.

"Blast it!" Ignatia cried. "You'll have to go without him." She ran down the docks, and headed toward the Academy to assemble the mages.

The six of us clambered onto the ship and the crew members welcomed us. They were all dressed in white suits.

"This here is the *Naviganti*. She'll keep us safe as we journey across the Lata Sea," the captain explained.

We glided out into the bay. The Fortis ships moved toward us, men shouting to fire their cannons at us.

"Why do they even want to attack us?" Korina asked.

"Because they're not sensible and we're at war," Elijah answered.

The *Naviganti* slid past the Fortis ships. A couple of cannons fired, their projectiles nearly hitting us. I screamed.

"Don't worry! I'll make sure they won't hit us!" the captain called as he struggled to steer the ship out of harm's way.

We barely made it out of Elementa Bay without being hit. We were on our way to the Sacred Islands, leaving Elementa in war. I looked behind us, seeing the city awaken into chaos. Fortis soldiers were in the city, and Elementa's soldiers scrambled about, trying to protect the city.

CHAPTER 16

AUGUST

I was sprinting as fast as I could toward the Academy, my beige colored robe flapping behind me. I had forgotten my special dagger, a dagger my parents had given to me long ago. It had a gold painted handle with a clear crystal set in the middle of it. I always kept the silver blade sharpened and never went anywhere without it.

Fortis soldiers were going to be in the city at any moment. If I wanted to snatch the dagger from my room in the Academy and run back to the port safely, I had to hurry. I dashed across the cobblestone streets, my feet thudding on the faded stone. I was almost at the Academy, one corner to turn and I would be there. I didn't get any farther.

An Elementa guard halted me and I was forced to skid to a quick stop.

"Where do you think you're going, boy?" he asked.

"To the—"

"It was a rhetorical question, you witty tongued scamp."

"I wasn't being witty—"

"Hush! We're being assembled. Don't you know Fortis is already at our borders and their ships are in our waters? Put this on." The guard handed me a helm. "And where's your armor? Let's go, there isn't much time."

"No, there must be some mistake! I'm not a soldier!" I protested.

"That's what all the young ones say. They just want to get out of fighting. I know it's scary at first, but there's still a chance you'll live."

The guard beckoned me to follow him and turned around. I took a couple steps toward him, deliberately thumping my feet on the stone road so that he would believe that I was following him. Instead I quietly began to walk in the other direction, toward the Academy.

When I turned the corner, out of sight from the guard, I began sprinting again to the Academy. I came to a stop when I reached the tall double doors. I pulled the iron handles, but the doors didn't budge. The Academy was locked.

I knocked furiously on the wood until my knuckles hurt. Finally a man with a white and gray beard answered the door. He wore a dark navy robe with silver lining, signifying that he was a wizard.

"What do you want? There's no class today," the wizard said.

"I'm August, the student from Soror."

"What are you doing here!" he exclaimed. "You're going to miss your boat; you're supposed to be leaving for those islands right now! Don't you know there are war ships in our bay?"

"What?" I cried. What if our sailing ship didn't make it out of the port?

"That's right. And the mages are coming out to fight Fortis. You'd best be on your way."

"Excuse me," I said, squeezing past him. "I forgot something."

I ran down the familiar corridors and up two flights of stairs before I reached my room. I slipped the key out of the pocket in my breeches and fumbled it into the lock. Once I flung open the door, I jerked open the drawer in my nightstand and grabbed the dagger. I stuffed it in its scabbard on my belt and dashed out of my dorm.

It took me a few more moments to race back to the docks again. By the time I had pounded across the dock where the ship had been, it was gone. The anchor had been pulled up and the *Naviganti* was sailing across the bay. Two Fortis war ships had fired at the ship. I heard a faint scream sound from it.

I ran until I was at the very edge of the dock where the ship had been.

"Wait!" I shouted, jumping and waving my arms. I knew it was useless. Nobody would be able to hear me, and even if they did there was no way the ship would be turned around. If it did, it would surely be hit by Fortis war ships and would be sunk. The sailors would not jeopardize the lives of others just to come back for a boy who missed the boat.

I dismissed the idea of swimming out to the ship. I would be in danger of drowning or being killed by Fortis cannon fire. I stood on the dock, not knowing what to do.

"Hey you!" someone called out to me.

I turned around to see an Elementa guard running up to me.

"What do you think you're doing, standing out here? You're gonna get killed by some Fortis rat. Follow me and I'll lead you to where everyone else is taking cover."

I followed without objecting. There was nothing else for me to do since the ship to the Sacred Islands had already begun sailing out into the Lata Sea.

I crouched down and darted along the buildings, trusting the shadows to keep me unseen. All around me were invading Fortis soldiers, blundering through shops and threatening the citizens who had not found safety. They even brought small portable cannons, and fired at the stone buildings. Bricks and stones tumbled down, creating dents in the streets. I couldn't hear myself speak with all the screams.

As I followed the Elementa guard, I saw Headmaster Ignatia in clothes I had never seen before. She didn't wear her usual dress, but leggings and a protective tunic. She shouted out orders to mages and guards. She quickly organized a band of guards into a patrol.

"I want this patrol to go to the south border of the city, now! You two find any women and children and get them to safety! Those Fortis worms are merciless!" Ignatia shouted.

I slunk around the corner of a crumbling building, running into the guard that had abruptly stopped.

"We're almost there," he said.

I followed him into the back of an empty shop, where he opened a hatch on the floor behind a counter. He stood there holding the door open for me, then gave me a quick shove. I tumbled into the darkness, the guard closing the door as soon as I entered.

I skidded onto a dirt floor. Eyes watched me as I rose to my feet. Many children and women were hiding in the cellar. The other citizens of the city were either fighting or hiding somewhere else. People were crouched against the walls and huddled into corners, silent with worry.

I chose a spot without a word and sat, hearing shouts and cannons from above. Several times dirt plummeted from the ceiling, revealing that Fortis soldiers were passing our hiding place. I became tired of waiting in suspense and nodded off into sleep.

The movement of others woke me. The people taking refuge were climbing up and out of the cellar. I lazily got to my feet and converged into the crowd. Finally it was my turn to clamber out of the hatch and into the blinding light. The shop we had taken refuge in was crumbling, unsafe to be in. The city was in worse condition than I had last seen it. Fortis and Elementa soldiers were strewn on the ground, littering the streets. It would take a long time to clean up Elementa.

As I exited the shop, I was surprised to see Fortis soldiers. Why had we revealed ourselves before they left? Was the battle still in motion? I followed the crowd of people gathering in the square.

I instantly recognized the flags that had the black crescent moons on them with the symbol meaning sister in the old language right beside them. A patrol from Soror was here.

The living Fortis and Elementa soldiers were also gathered in the square, the Soror people in front of them. I recognized the second commander of the Soror soldiers.

"People of Elementa, your Headman has decided that you are to join the war between us and Oceanus against the capital. It is time you send your forces to our city, Soror. Tomorrow we will return to Elementa and collect your soldiers that Headman Gileon has decided to send. After preparing in Soror, we will then march to the base of the Lux Mountain Range, across the Vast Fields. I don't know what is occurring between you and Fortis but it needs to end now," the Soror commander announced.

The Fortis commander stepped out of the crowd, near the Soror patrol. "Who are you to tell us to end our war? You cannot walk in as you please and disrupt our fight. You have no business in this. Why are you here?" he roared.

The Soror commander remained calm and composed. "I just explained why we are here, Commander Haxis. We are in a war, a war that is greater than your little skirmish. It could potentially lead all of the city states of Lux into it against the capital. Civil war is upon us, for the City of Lux is abusing its power. The city states deserve justice."

"A war between the capital and city states?" The Fortis commander, Commander Haxis, guffawed. "You will all lose as quickly as lightning falls from the sky. Very well. If Elementa is joining a civil war, Fortis will join the civil war too—on the capital's side. We shall carry on the war against Elementa, only now our victory will be assured." The Fortis commander then gathered up his troops and left.

The Soror patrol left after the Fortis troops departed. The Elementa citizens dispersed into the city, some helping to clean up the rubble or bury fallen men, others returning to their homes to see what was left of them. Headman Gileon appeared right after the battle and commotion ended. He spoke with the commander of the Elementa soldiers.

Headmaster Ignatia was close by, watching Gileon intently and listening to his conversation. When the commander left, leaving

Gileon alone, Ignatia quietly marched up to him. Grabbing the collar of his tunic, she yanked him back. Gileon gasped and turned around, looking up at Ignatia. She towered over Gileon with a stern face. Gileon was a short man and was no match for the Headmaster of the Academy.

"Where were you in all of this?" she demanded, throwing her arms in the direction of crumbling buildings. "Did you waddle up to your little haven in the temple, abandoning your people in the time they needed you most?"

"You know I don't fight, Ignatia. I—"

"—sit around in your cushioned chair while our men are dying!" Ignatia finished. "And now Fortis has decided they will join the war on the capital's side. Our buildings are falling apart, our streets are damaged, and dead men are lying on the ground! And you know what you're going to do about it? Nothing. You'll sit in your office and expect the commander and me to take care of it. I'm going to get an election started, Gileon. Then I'm going to get voted Headwoman of Elementa and I'll toss you out to the mutations in the forest, just like you did to those guards. I'll appoint a Headmaster for the Academy so that the magic wielders of this city will be organized as well. I'll do whatever I can to keep people like *you* out of office!"

"Ignatia, don't be irrational—"

"I'm not the one being irrational, Gileon," she spat. Headmaster Ignatia released Gileon's tunic and stalked away. Gileon remained where he was, stunned and smoothing out his tunic. He then walked away, gathering the guards and speaking to them about the civil war.

* * *

A night had passed since the battle with Fortis. The citizens of Elementa were scurrying around, repairing their homes and shops. The mass of soldiers were gathered at the East border, about to depart for Soror.

I watched the commander of the soldiers speak to them from a distance. He picked out a few soldiers from among those going to war and ordered them to stay in the city. A lot of the soldiers were husbands and fathers, and sadly their wives and children would have to live without them for a while.

I glanced to my left, seeing movement out of the corner of my eye. I peered into the shadows, seeing someone crouched down as I was. It was Headmaster Ignatia. *Is this how she knows everything that's going on around the city?*

Soon the patrol from Soror came, leading the soldiers of Elementa away to their city—my home. I wished that I could go with them and return to my home. I doubted that I had any magic anyway. I turned to look at Ignatia to check if she was still there. When I saw that she was, I crept up to her.

"August?" she asked, surprised to see me.

"I don't think I have any magic, Headmaster," I began randomly.

Ignatia chortled. "You haven't been here that long and you're already giving up? Why? Are you frustrated that you missed the boat?"

"Well, of course. But it's not that. I haven't progressed at all, only in combat skills and I'm starting to miss Soror."

"Ah, you're homesick. You were sent here to me by a friend of mine who believes in you. I'm not going to let them down, August. I myself believe you possess magic. But you haven't been here long enough to discover it. That's why I wanted to send you to the Sacred Islands. That would've sped the process up, I believe." Ignatia paused for a moment. "Don't give up, August."

I shrugged. "Maybe I could go back to Soror with the soldiers. It wouldn't take me long to catch up."

"I just said not to give up!" Ignatia boomed sternly. In a quieter voice she continued, "You have to believe in yourself too, you know. I'm not letting you walk out of this city. I need you to help me and the mages protect the city from mutations. That's final." Without another word Ignatia left.

I returned to the Academy and spent the rest of the day in my dorm, reading a book that I had checked out from the Academy about magic. I looked out the window for a long time, a yearning feeling in my stomach. Then I finally ate and left my room as the sun was setting.

I sat down in front of the main entrance of the Academy, watching the sun sink below the horizon. I sat with my chin rested in my hands, thinking. I looked up, alarmed by the thought of what lurked in the night as I heard the familiar screeches and howls in the distance.

CHAPTER 17

TERESSIA

*A*s we were leaving the bay, the *Naviganti* seemed to glide over the water at a slow pace. There wasn't much wind, which powered the vessel. I craned my neck upward, gazing at the trapezoidal sails that were slightly buffeted. At the bow of the ship, there were three triangular sails. Thin lines ran all over the sails in a mess, and ladder-like ropes stretched up the masts. In my eyes, it was all a complicated tangle of ropes with unknown functions.

The sailors worked around us, constantly walking across the deck. Mage Melody and Mage Isaac conversed with a sailor. The captain was at the stern of the ship at the wheel. Korina sat on the deck, leaning against the center mast, while Elijah was sauntering at the bow of the ship, examining everything. Sage leaned against the rail of the ship at the stern, near the captain. Our bags were tossed on the deck in a pile, except for the two mages'.

"Fortis ships are following us!" Sage cried in a panicked voice.

The captain glanced over his shoulder and the two mages ended their conversation with the sailor and rushed to the stern. Korina jumped to her feet and followed, and Elijah watched from the bow. I approached the stern with everyone else.

"We'll shake 'em off!" the captain assured. He shouted out orders to the rest of the crew. "Mared! Grab the mainmast and the main topsail sheet—they're luffing just a tad and we need to pick up the pace."

I raced up beside Sage and peered over the rail. Two Fortis ships were right behind us. A cannon went off in our direction. The Fortis ship was firing at us. Something heavy dropped right behind the stern of the ship, plopping into the water. A bang sounded and black smoke puffed out from behind us. Sage screamed again and backed away from the rail.

"Don't worry, they're not going to hit us!" the captain called, just as another cannonball was shot at us.

"Get away from the stern!" Mage Melody ordered us.

The cannonball grazed the hull of the ship, causing the ship to rock. I stumbled around, not used to the motion, and instinctively, dropped to the deck to steady myself. After I was balanced I rose to my feet and staggered to the bow, climbing up a few steps to get to a higher deck.

Sailors rushed by us to tend to the hull and disappeared into a hatch on the floor of the deck. Korina, who was still at the stern, asked the captain where they were going.

"They're going to the bulkhead to repair the hull and check on the rudder," he answered.

"Rudder?" Korina questioned.

"We're standing right above it. Right now we're on the quarterdeck, and I'm at the helm which is where the ship is steered. The rudder is the flat piece of wood on the hull that is near the stern for steering the ship."

Korina nodded like she understood.

"Korina! Get away from the stern before you get hurt! Get off of the quarterdeck!" Mage Melody shouted. She was standing at the center of the lower deck with Mage Isaac.

I stood next to Elijah. "What if they sink the ship?" I asked.

He shook his head. "They won't."

Behind us, the Fortis ships advanced and came closer. One of them fired two cannons. The cannonballs plummeted into the sea, right behind the stern again. The ship swayed as the cannonballs exploded under the water.

More cannons fired and a rally of cannonballs plunged toward us. Sage screamed as one crashed into the rail of the ship. I was blown off my feet and rolled along the deck.

Sailors rushed with tools to the rail to repair it. The black smoke was still billowing at the rail. There was an opening in the rail where it had hit, and the deck was smashed.

The two Fortis ships gained speed and were coming up on each side of the *Naviganti*. One of the sailors on the Fortis ships shouted at us.

"Stop your ship! No one leaves the bay!" the Fortis sailor called.

"Last time I checked this was Elementa Bay, not Fortis Bay!" the captain replied.

Unfortunately the Fortis ships did not slow and continued to pursue us. Once again, they fired their cannons. A cannonball from each side of the ship flew toward us, hitting the masts and the sails.

"Repair the masts and replace the sails!" the captain ordered.

The remaining crew that wasn't working on the hull or rail sprinted with supplies to the bases of the masts and began to climb the ropes that stretched up to the sails. They spent a long time up there as the Fortis ships continued to fire. The sailors came down after a break in the firing and said they had done the best they could, which would have to do for now.

I thanked the wind as it picked up, slamming into the sails of the *Naviganti*. The sailors grasped the lines of different sails, tugging at them to change the sails for the wind condition.

The *Naviganti* sped up and left the Fortis ships behind. I sighed with relief. Sage was also relieved, crouched on the deck below Elijah and me.

Sailors opened the hatch on the deck and clambered out.

"The bulkhead's patched up. It was damaged and water was flooding into the hold. We'll have to go to the outside of the hull to look at the rudder," one informed. While he was still speaking, a number of sailors approached carrying a small dinghy. They hooked it to the side of the stern and then lowered it.

The captain nodded with satisfaction. "Good." He let a sailor take over steering the ship and left the helm, walking off of what he called the quarterdeck.

He approached the two mages and Sage at the center of the deck. Mage Melody beckoned Korina, Elijah, and me to come.

"Wasn't that an exciting way start to our voyage?" the captain grinned.

"I'd like to get to the islands alive," Sage retorted sharply.

The captain chuckled. "I will ensure that you do. I hope that you will all make yourselves comfortable on the *Naviganti*. She will be your home for the next two months or so. I am Captain Serulean. You all must be wondering where you'll be staying. I'll lead you to your cabins, so find your bags."

We all grabbed our luggage and followed the captain to the hatch where the sailors had gone to repair the hull. We carefully shuffled down the steps into a dimly lit area below the deck.

"This area below the main deck is called the hold. We usually put cargo here, but since the *Naviganti* is a small ship, we've constructed temporary cabins," Serulean explained.

Even though it was dark, I saw Sage raise her eyebrows. She must've thought temporary cabins meant we were going to stay in a shabby corner. I was worried myself about the quality of our quarters.

"There are three cabins on this side, one below the forecastle and the other two cabins are on the side of that one," Serulean pointed. "The other three are across to the other side nearest to the stern, right next to the bulkhead. I know it's not very extravagant but it's the best we can do. The kitchen is accessible through a hatch on the forecastle but you can eat wherever you like. The kitchen is only for cooking—there isn't enough room to eat there. But please, unpack and make yourselves comfortable."

I chose the cabin directly below the forecastle, whatever that was. I pushed aside the curtain that was acting as the door. The cabin was very small, with only a bed and chair inside. The rest of the space was wooden boards that made up the floor. I supposed that having one small cabin was better than having a bigger space and having to share with someone.

Even though the cabins were hastily put together by the crew, each room still had wooden walls. I guessed that it was like a stall that separated cargo. All you had to do was add a curtain and bed and it would become a cabin. I sat on the narrow mattress that served as my bed.

I placed my bag on the bed. Since I wasn't supposed to go on the trip, it only possessed a few copper coins, an extra skirt and blouse that I had forgotten to remove, and my mage's rod. I was thankful that I had forgotten to take the laundry out of it. Now I wouldn't have to wear the same dress every day. I would sleep in my day clothes since I didn't have any sleeping gowns.

After lying on the bed to test its comfort, I left the cabin. There was nothing to do in the tiny space. I pushed the thin curtain aside and went to see who my neighbors were. I knocked on the fabric that hung over the entrance to the cabin that was directly below the forecastle.

Elijah's face peered out from the side of it. "Yes?" He said, blinking.

"Just wanted to see who my neighbors are. How is your space?"

Elijah pushed the curtain back, revealing a space as small as mine. "I feel like a caged bird," he joked.

I smiled slightly, looking around. There was a thick wooden pole in the center of the space. "What's with the pole?" I asked.

"I think it's the base of one of the masts."

"It's taking up a fourth of your room," I said.

Elijah grinned. "I know, but if the ship is rocking I'll have something to hold on to." "Very resourceful of you," I mocked.

"You're just jealous that you don't have a fat wooden pole in the middle of your cabin." "Oh yes, you got me. I'm so ever jealous," I said sarcastically, rolling my eyes. I left Elijah and went back into the main area of the hold. I stopped and listened to the waves that crashed against the hull. Now that I thought about it, I realized that the hold must be underwater.

I pushed opened the hatch, letting light spill into the hold. I clambered up the steps and onto the deck. It was noticeably darker outside even though it was only midday. Gray clouds were starting to gather in the sky.

I scrambled onto the wooden deck and walked over to a rail. The waves of the sea seemed to be anxious as they pounded the sides of the ship. It seemed as if the waves had gotten bigger since this morning.

"A storm is coming," Serulean said, startling me.

"I think you're right," I replied.

"Can you tell the wind has picked up?" the captain closed his eyes, letting the wind rush over his face. "Ah, the salty smell of the sea. I'll never tire of it."

"What's a forecastle?" I asked.

Captain Serulean opened his eyes. "The forecastle is that deck on the bow of the ship, the deck where you have to climb up a few steps to access. That's also where the foremast is."

"Oh. And the masts have names?"

Serulean chortled. "Of course they have names! This ship is one of the smaller sailing ships, so it only has two masts. The one in the center of this main deck is called the mainmast."

"I never knew ships got this complicated," I said. "I thought you just had to move the sails in the right direction of the wind."

"No, things are never that simple. There's many parts to this ship. I can tell you a little about some of them if you'd like."

"Yes, please," I answered. "I'd like that."

"We're standing on the main deck, which is in between the stern and bow. It is the biggest deck as you can see. On the stern, that upper deck is the quarterdeck." Serulean pointed to the quarterdeck. "The helm is located on the quarterdeck, which is where the wheel is for steering the ship. Since this ship is a bilander, there are two masts. Each mast has two sails. The mainsail is attached to the mainmast, which is noticeably trapezoidal. The smaller sail above that one is called the main topsail. The foremast is located on the forecastle, which I explained to you just a few moments ago. The big sail is called the foresail, and the smaller one above that is called the fore topsail. All these lines that run everywhere are called sheets, and they allow us to control the sails. For instance, if the wind is blowing at a fast speed, less area of the sails are needed. Without switching out sails for smaller ones, we can use sheets to take away some of the area on the sails which is called reefing."

"You and your crew must have a lot of work to do," I remarked. "What're those black squares halfway up the mast?"

"Some people call those the crow's nest. Those rope-like things to get up to the crow's nest or any sail are called shrouds. Shrouds are there to support the masts."

"What about those three triangular sails at the, er, bow?"

"Those sails are also attached to the foremast. The first one is called the fore stay sail, the middle one is the jib, and the outermost one is the flying jib. The bottom 'corner' of each of them are attached to the bow sprit. The bow sprit is that long pole that sticks out from the bow."

"There is so much to a ship," I observed.

Captain Serulean nodded in agreement. "There is much to learn. I have been working on these types of ships since I was a young boy, and I still make mistakes every now and then."

After conversing with the captain, I walked to the mainmast and studied it more closely, recognizing the sails. The mainsail and foresail was still trapezoidal, just as the captain had said and just as I had noticed earlier.

Above the topsails were the dark ominous clouds. The wind was stronger and it was chillier. My sleeves only stretched halfway down my arms, and most of my forearm was dotted with chilled bumps.

The crew was working sheets, reducing the amount of area on each sail. Remembering my lesson on the ship, I realized the sailors were reefing.

Mage Isaac popped the hatch open. He looked at the sky and observed the change in weather.

"Looks like a storm's approaching, right Teressia?"

"I would say so," I murmured.

Korina and Elijah appeared out of the floor of the deck as well.

"It's gotten so much darker," Elijah said. He rubbed his arms where his dark red tunic did not cover.

Korina strolled over to the rail steadily, despite the uneasy rocking of the ship. She peered over the side of the ship and watched the waves below.

"Yes, a storm is coming."

Sage flipped open the hatch and climbed onto the main deck. The only one left in the hold was Mage Melody.

"What's happening?" Sage asked.

"Storm's coming," Korina answered from the rail.

Sage's eyes widened. "A storm? Is it going to be a bad one? Will it sink the ship?"

"The ship will be fine," Captain Serulean shouted over the wind from the helm. "You may want to stay in your cabins if you don't want to get wet. And there's also a slight chance a wave can knock you overboard."

"Overboard?" Sage cried, her voice going shrill.

Korina rolled her eyes and turned back to stare at the waves. Elijah walked over to where I stood leaning against the mainmast.

"Are you scared?" He teased, his eyes gleaming.

"Not like Sage. But I feel strangely calm," I replied.

Korina walked up to us. "Why would you be scared in the first place? Isn't it great to be surrounded by this much water? I'm excited for this voyage." She hopped around the mainmast.

Sage looked uneasy and anxious. "I'm going to go back to my cabin."

The wind picked up, spraying water across the ship from the growing waves. The captain barked orders from the helm.

"The wind's picking up! Furl the jib and reef the mainsail! Too much area on the sails could capsize the boat!"

The sailors scurried around to get their job done while Captain Serulean struggled to steer the ship in the harsh wind. The clouds became impatient and released a drizzle of water. The light sprinkle grew stronger, until a heavy rain was pouring down. It sounded like little beads of thunder as the rain hit the deck, and the waves were growing.

Elijah and I scuttled to the hatch on the main deck. The wind whipped into the ship, fighting us.

"It's like the wind doesn't want us to get in there!" Elijah shouted over the storm. Even though I was right next to him we had to yell at each other to hear.

A crew member approached us, his white suit drenched. "You've waited too late to go in there," he yelled. "The wind will fight you and you could flood the hold with water. It's best not to get any water down there or in the bulkhead!"

I groaned. We would have to wait on the deck throughout the storm. I would be surprised if I didn't catch a cold. I searched for a place to hang on to. I gave up on a safe spot and crawled to the mainmast, Elijah following.

Korina gazed around her in excitement and awe as a giant wave reared up over the ship and crashed down into the deck. I clutched the mainmast and hugged it tightly so I wouldn't be swept away. I felt the ship sway to the left, leaning over.

"The ship's heeling!" The captain warned.

"What does that even mean?" Elijah asked from beside me.

I struggled to keep water out of my mouth and blinked my eyes constantly. "I don't know!"

The sliver of blue sky had vanished and the sky had transformed into a menacing black and gray sheet. The storm continued and the rain did not lighten. Waves stretched above the decks of the ship and plummeted onto them. As each wave crashed onto the main deck, Elijah and I embraced the mainmast with all our strength. Water was flooding the ship, pooling around me. My dress was soaked from the seawater and rain.

I watched a dark treacherous wave loom over the side and plunge toward us. I reached for the mainmast but the wave swept me away from it, and carried me to the opposite side of the deck. I was submerged in water and flailed, trying to reach for something to grab onto. I couldn't even see and was hoping that I wasn't near the rail. I prayed that I wouldn't fly overboard and into the sea.

The wave washed over me and I banged into something hard. My forehead hurt and my leg was aching. I looked up to see I was pushed onto the rail. I pushed off it with my arms, but another wave from behind forced me into it once more. I banged my head on the rail again, but this time the wave carried me with it, flipping me over.

I screamed helplessly, dangling over the side of the rail. I was only holding on by my arms and my legs were flailing over the side of the ship. I looked down, into the black waves. I became shaky and gasped in short breaths. I felt sick to my stomach. If I let go of the rail, I would plummet into the sea.

A wave from below saved me. It flipped me back over onto the deck and threw me across the main deck. As I banged into the mainmast, I saw a flash of movement in the pouring rain. It was hard to see anything because of the rain and darkness of the sky.

It was Elijah, who was still hugging the mainmast. "Welcome back!" He shouted at me.

Water continually washed over our heads, forcing us to hold our breaths. The deck was flooded, and Elijah and I were sitting waist deep in water. I coughed and sputtered for air just as more waves washed over us.

By the time the rain lightened and the waves waned, I was drenched and frightened. I wish I had followed in Sage's footsteps and went to my cabin. Instead I had almost been thrown into the sea.

Eventually the wind died down and the rain became a light drizzle once more. I felt sick to my stomach after gulping down sea water and from fear. My mouth was bone dry and I coughed, gagging. I splashed around in the water on the deck, crawling over to a rail. I used it to haul myself to my feet and hacked up water from my stomach. The water turned into vomit as I was doubled over the side of the ship. When I finished I slumped to the floor and heaved.

I knew that Elijah was fine, but I had no idea where Korina and Mage Isaac were. I hoped that they were fine and didn't get swept overboard. I crawled across the main deck and back to the base of the mainmast. Elijah sat leaning against it, his soaked breeches and tunic sticking to his skin. He held his head in his hands.

"That turned out worse than I thought," he mumbled.

"It could've been worse," I said. "The boat could've capsized. Or the storm could have been much longer."

I staggered to my feet and let my legs readjust to the rocking motion of the ship. I spotted Korina near the stern, looking up at the quarterdeck and talking to somebody. I walked over to her.

Korina was casually chatting with the captain. "And you had the worst of it, I suppose," she said grinning. "You could've been washed away. Wow, what a storm." Korina turned around to face me as I approached her. She was in the best mood I had ever seen her. "Teressia! Wasn't that storm fun? Your forehead is bleeding and bruised and you look pale. Are you okay?" Korina had a few bruises herself and a scratch on her cheek, not to mention she was soaked as well, her clothes plastered to her skin.

"Maybe," I rasped. "Where were you in all of this?"

"Oh, I was here, holding onto the steps that lead up to the quarterdeck so that I wouldn't be washed away. I used my magic when I could so I wouldn't be completely drowned. Where were you?"

"Hugging the mainmast with Elijah. I got caught up in a wave once."

"That's scary. What happened? Did it hurt?"

"Yes! I smashed into a rail and flipped over the side! I was almost tossed into the sea!"

"You almost went overboard?" Korina cried in disbelief. "Yikes. I wonder how Sage is doing."

Just as Korina finished her sentence, the hatched flipped over. Water spilled into the hold. Mage Melody appeared, damp from the water.

"My, my. How bad was the storm?" she asked, wobbling around until she gained her balance.

"Not too bad," Captain Serulean answered. "Not the worst one I've been in and certainly no hurricane. Didn't last too long, either." The captain was also soaked and had a few bruises.

"I'm glad I was in my cabin. The ship was rocking around quite a bit. And there's all of this water," Mage Melody observed, watching sailors scoop it up in buckets and toss it overboard. "I was being tossed around in my cabin. I just hope I feel better in time for dinner."

I dismissed myself, still woozy, and climbed down into my cabin. I was exhausted from being slung around and getting seasick. Even though I was drenched in seawater, I collapsed onto my bed and fell asleep.

CHAPTER 18

ELIJAH

*T*he storm had left me unsteady and dazed. I was bruised from being smashed into the mast several times by the waves that crashed over me. I had barely spent any time on the *Naviganti* and I was already drenched in seawater and attacked by war ships. It seemed that the odds were against our party that was voyaging to the Sacred Islands.

After the storm had abated, I had remained sitting where I was during the storm, leaning on the mainmast. My head was aching and my stomach was not in the best state after the swinging motion of the ship. Cold water swirled around me, but I was too fatigued to climb to my feet.

After sitting down for a few minutes I forced myself to my feet. I stood in the same place for a second while my head spun and my vision cleared. Then I wobbled over to the hatch and descended into the hold. I lazily pushed my curtain back and entered my cabin and slid off my wet tunic and flopped onto the bed. I did not feel like moving. My head was still throbbing and my stomach was still queasy.

I closed my eyes and tried to rest. I was exhausted, but couldn't fall into a peaceful nap. I laid in silence, listening for the waves. Instead I heard moans from the cabin to the right of me. I lifted my head and strained my ears. It sounded like Sage in a whiny mood. I left the mattress and listened through the thin wooden wall. Sage was probably seasick.

I heard retching and moved away from the wall. I hoped there was a bucket in Sage's cabin. I returned to the bed and thought about the islands, trying to get my mind to wander away from the salty aroma of the sea. Since summer was approaching, the temperature was rising and the smell of the salty water was stronger than usual.

I must've fallen asleep at last. I dreamed that the *Naviganti* was trapped in another storm and I was struggling to breathe in the flood of water. In the middle of the storm, a whirlpool gaped in the sea, threatening to suck the ship down into it. The sailors were shouting orders at each other. Sage was screaming as a hand reached out of the whirlpool and snatched her away into the sea. Korina was laughing and used her magic to make the waves grow higher. Teressia was calling my name as she dangled over the side of the rail as she did in the real storm. I was lying on the deck, unable to get up and save Teressia. I shouted as Teressia lost her grip and plunged into the water. The sailors could do nothing as the ship spun round and round and was lost in the whirlpool.

I awoke, panting. I reached to my neck, feeling drops of sweat. The back of my neck stung. I remembered the wound that the mutation had caused. Mage Melody's magical remedy had helped tremendously, but the wound was not fully healed and the storm made it hurt. My shoulders were also aching from bruises. My whole body was sore. And did I hear the captain mention that it wasn't even a hurricane? I shuddered at the thought of it.

My tunic was still a little damp. I slid it over my head and sat down in the only chair in the cabin. I heard tapping on the curtain and went to see who it was. Mage Isaac was there with an arm wrapped in a bandage and bruises scattered on his arms and face.

"Oh, Elijah it looks like you survived the storm."

"Barely. Is there something wrong?" I inquired.

"No, not at all. Thank goodness everything's all right for now. Dinner has been cooked by the some of the crew. Would you like a serving?"

I glanced at my stomach, which was still unsettled. "I don't think I'll be hungry tonight," I replied.

"Very well. Are you feeling okay after that nasty storm?"

"Well, my head hurts and my stomach's uneasy and I have a few bruises, but I'll surive." I didn't mention the pain from my neck wound.

"Good. I'm sure you'll adapt in no time. Were you outside during the storm?"

"Yes. I assume you were as well?"

"Unfortunately. A sailor told me I couldn't go into the hold when it started to rain. Ha, I started to panic. I ended up taking shelter outside of the kitchen on the forecastle. Were you in a safe spot? Never mind—that was a foolish question. It wasn't really safe anywhere out on the deck."

"I stayed at the mainmast with Teressia. I think she had the worse time out of all of us."

Mage Isaac nodded. "Yes, I heard that she was almost thrown overboard by a wave. I'm going to check on Sage next door. You should try to get some rest." Mage Isaac shuffled to his right and tapped on Sage's curtain.

I opened the hatch to a small crack that I could peer out of. Voices carried from the decks and the sailors were tending to the sails. The wind had died down and it was evening. The sun wasn't in sight, but it wasn't completely dark outside. I closed the hatch and returned to my cabin and plopped onto my bed once again to rest. I let my thoughts wander wherever they pleased and dozed off once more.

I awoke in the middle of the night, my cabin pitch black. I created a small flame on the tip of my index finger. Poking my head out of the curtain, I listened for voices. I heard soft snores from across the hold, either from Mage Isaac's cabin or Korina's. I assumed it was Korina's. I began to recede back into my cabin but stopped when I heard soft murmurs. I brushed the curtain aside and tiptoed around the hold. There were no whispers or movement. *Am I hearing things?*

I began to question my consciousness until I heard the same whispers. I snuck up the steps and raised the hatch to a crack. I spotted two sailors chatting next to the mainmast, in the shadows of the sails. The moonlight softly illuminated the deck with a white glow.

I opened the hatch farther and listened intently. I could barely make out the voices and the dim moonlight prevented me from recognizing the two sailors.

"What if we get capsized or run out of food and water? What if we get attacked?" one of the crew members asked.

"The odds are we won't. But if we do, it'll be a better way to die. Do you know what's upon us?"

"Yes, yes, yes. But surely it won't be much of a threat?"

"Fool! You do not know what's coming after all. Not even the Headmaster of the Academy foresaw it. She doesn't have the ability to scry into the future after all. If we even survive the dangers of this cursed sea, we'll surely be brought to our deaths at the Sacred Islands. Why would anyone send people there? Do they not know that the volcanic eruptions weren't the cause for scaring everyone away?" the other sailor hissed.

"Do we really have to take a dinghy, though? Why can't we just turn the ship around tonight? I'm sure the captain won't notice."

"Are you really stupid enough to believe that? If he doesn't feel it in the night, or hear us—the captain's cabin is right below the quarterdeck—he'll notice the compass. He'll see that the sun is rising and setting at a different perspective, he'll *sense* the change."

The other sailor grumbled. "I suppose you're right. So we escape in two nights?"

"Two nights," the crew member confirmed.

I watched them walk toward the bow where the crew's quarters were. I noiselessly shut the hatch and shuffled to my cabin, my flame resting on my fingertip so that I could see. I froze, hearing movement in the cabin next to mine.

Teressia's head appeared. "Elijah?" she squinted at me. "Is that you?"

"Er, yes, uh, no. You're dreaming!" I stammered.

I could see Tres's brow furrow. "Really, Elijah? You think I'm going to believe that? What *are* you doing in the middle of the night?"

"Uh, privy."

"There's a chamber pot in your cabin."

"I didn't want it to stink the whole night."

"Then where did you—never mind. I don't want to know," Teressia said. She disappeared behind the curtain.

I entered my cabin and extinguished the flame. Resting on my bed, I wondered about the conversation I had heard. Were the two sailors going to abandon the ship? What dangers were they scared of? Should I report their plans to the captain?

I pulled the quilt over me, feeling the chill of the night. I fell asleep once more as I snuggled into the warmth of the quilt and thin sheet.

Even though there was no porthole in my cabin, faint light spilt in. I climbed out of bed, feeling much better than yesterday. My neck wound from the mutation was the only injury I was concerned about. The back of my neck throbbed and stung slightly. Maybe I should tell Mage Melody about its sudden pain.

The hatch was the culprit for the light. I swung it open and stepped out onto the deck. The skies were clear and the waves were small. I was exposed to the fierce wind on the main deck. The *Naviganti* would be traveling at a quick pace today.

My stomach rumbled. My appetite was back and wanted to make its presence known. I approached a sailor and asked if breakfast was ready.

"Yes," he answered. "Go on to the kitchen and ask for some grub."

Unsure of where the kitchen was, I climbed onto the forecastle. I spotted the first real door I had seen on the ship. I swung it open and a cramped kitchen was revealed. There was a wood-burning stove wherein someone had built a hot fire to cook the food. Cabinets and a couple of rows of counters lined the wall. A sailor saw me at the entrance.

"Here for breakfast?" he asked. Without waiting for a reply he handed me a bundle wrapped in cloth. I took it without question and ambled back to the main deck. With nowhere to sit, I took up my usual spot by the mainmast and sat down. This time the deck was dry.

I unwrapped the cloth to reveal a biscuit, a thin slice of ham, and part of a potato. It was a small portion but a decent meal for a ship. Most of the food was dried so I was pleased. I greedily gobbled down the food and leaned back. The wind whipped on my face, a pleasant feeling. It carried the smell of the water but I had gotten used to it. It was a serene day.

I noticed the two mages eating their breakfast together on the quarterdeck with a map stretched out in front of them. Mage Isaac was pointing at a spot on the map while Mage Melody nodded and spoke.

Korina was just exiting the kitchen with her bundle of food. She placed it in a pouch that was attached to a belt around her leggings. I watched her as she strolled over to the foremast and began to climb the shrouds (Teressia had educated me on the parts of the ship).

What is she doing? I wondered. I had to crane my neck upward to keep Korina in sight. After a few minutes she was halfway up the mast and then disappeared, my view blocked by the foresail. I watched for her to reappear but she never did. I shrugged to myself and closed my eyes, feeling the warmth of the sun.

A thud next to me caused me to open my eyes. A sailor had plopped down from the shrouds.

"Where did you come from?" I asked, puzzled.

"The crow's nest. Lookout post. Whatever you want to call it. My shift is done up there."

Maybe that's where Korina disappeared to eat. "Is there one on the foremast as well?" I questioned.

"Of course," the sailor replied as he walked away.

I approached a web of rope and looked up. The mainmast stretched high into the sky. Korina had to be brave to climb up there. I spotted the black ring around the mast and decided that was the crow's nest. I placed my hands on the shroud and considered climbing up to the crow's nest. I swallowed my fear and began to ascend the ropes.

My arms began to burn before I got very far. I constantly paused to catch my breath and give my arms and legs a break. I tried to avoid looking down, but occasionally I did. It was unnerving to see the deck so far below me. I prayed that I wouldn't lose my balance and tumble to my death.

The crow's nest became larger as I neared it. I scrambled to the side of it and hauled myself into it. I sat down, panting. When I caught my breath I stood up and examined my surroundings. The crow's nest wasn't very big and it had a bell fastened to it. One end of a thin rope was tied to the bell's clapper and the other end stretched over to the crow's nest on the foremast.

I leaned over the edge of the lookout. I was far above the main deck. The people below me were only small flickers of movement. The Lata Sea stretched around the *Naviganti* for miles and miles. It seemed like everything was visible from here. Only the main topsail was above me. The mainsail stretched around me but did not block my view. The wind blew stronger at this height.

I looked at the foremast, trying to see if I could spot Korina. I saw her long black hair flying in the wind. I rang the bell.

Korina turned around and faced my crow's nest. I waved, feeling dumb. Did she roll her eyes at me? She turned back around and flipped her hand at me. I chuckled at her motion. Korina was still herself today. Suddenly she threw something from her crow's nest. I watched the cloth from her breakfast fly in the wind, rushing over the ship and over the sea. Korina had evidently finished eating her food.

I was in awe of the view so I remained in the crow's nest for a while. I turned to face the bow of the ship and immediately spotted what appeared to be a labyrinth of tall gray objects sticking out of the water. *What are those things?*

As the ship came perilously close to the gray objects, I recognized them as huge rock formations. Did the crew not know we were heading straight toward ship-sinking stones?

"Korina!" I shouted over the wind.

She spun around to face me. "What!" she responded. Even against the wind I could hear the sharp edge in her voice.

"Do you… see… that!" I called in between gusts of wind.

"What?!"

"Rocks!" I yelled and pointed ahead of us.

"We're… to… run… rocks!" Korina replied. I couldn't hear the whole sentence. I nodded as an answer and crawled carefully out of the crow's nest. I glanced at Korina. She was doing the same.

When we finally reached the deck, we both raced over to the helm. Captain Serulean wasn't there, but to our amazement, the helmsman was fast asleep with his back against the wheel.

"Where's the captain?" Korina demanded. Korina's voice startled the helmsman into consciousness. "What did you say, miss?" he mumbled.

"I said, where's the captain!" Korina exclaimed loudly.

"I suppose he's in his cabin," the helmsman replied.

"Which is where?" Korina asked.

"Right below us."

The two of us hopped off the quarterdeck and knocked on the door to the captain's cabin.

"Come in!" Serulean called from inside. I followed Korina into the room.

"Yes?"

"There's a bunch of rocks sticking out of the water, straight ahead of us," Korina informed. "And we found the helmsman asleep at the wheel."

"Are you being truthful?" the captain worriedly asked. We nodded our heads in response.

"Are they dark pointed formations clustered together that rise out of the sea?"

"Yes," I answered.

"Curse the water!" Serulean shouted in frustration. "We're heading straight toward the Maze of Stones. We'll surely sink if we don't go around them."

We followed Captain Serulean out of his cabin. He found the helmsman fast asleep again.

"What are you doing, man? Are you trying to get us all killed?" he asked in panicked anger.

Korina snickered.

"Korina, that's not even funny!" I whispered sharply.

The helmsmen awoke and shook his head. "What's wrong?" he muttered.

"We're about to face the Maze of Stones head on if we don't change course! I hope for your sake we can avoid these formations!"

"The Maze of Stones? Surely they're farther along in the sea?"

Serulean shook his head. "No, Jeril. They're right ahead. We're upon them now."

The wind suddenly picked up and the sailors tugged at the sheets to readjust the sails. The *Naviganti* began to travel slightly faster. The captain shoved Jeril aside and muttered under his breath as he began to steer the ship.

"Go warn the others," Serulean ordered. Jeril ran across the main deck.

I ran toward the bow and raced up the steps of the forecastle. The Maze of Stones was straight ahead, now almost on top of the ship. I stumbled to the side as the ship turned. The crew was shouting at each other in worried voices. *Was the Maze of Stones one of the dangers those two sailors were discussing?* I remembered the conversation I heard and rushed to the stern again to talk to the captain.

"Captain Serulean, I need to talk to you," I panted.

"Not now, boy. We're going to sink if I don't steer this thing away and on top of that, I've just gotten a report of a missing dinghy."

"It has something to do with that! I know why it's missing!" It seemed that the two sailors had decided to depart from the *Naviganti* earlier than planned.

I had caught the captain's attention. "Why is it missing?"

I reported the conversation between the two sailors. The captain mumbled angrily under his breath. "Mared!" He shouted.

A sailor came to the helm. "Yes, Captain?"

"Go do a quick roll check. We might have two deserters."

Mared left as quickly as he came to carry out Serulean's order.

I stared ahead, in awe of the rock formations that seemed close enough to touch.

"We're not going to have enough room to turn her!" the captain shouted.

"What does that mean?" I asked, knowing the answer.

"We're going to have to go through the Maze of Stones," Captain Serulean replied darkly.

I shuddered. "Will it be as bad as the storm?"

"I'm afraid it will be worse than the storm. We'll be lucky if we get out of this without sinking. Better start praying, boy," the captain answered.

I walked across the main deck and toward the hatch. I had learned my lesson from before and wanted to get into the hold before disaster struck. The hatch popped open as I reached it. Sage stuck her head out.

"What's going on? I hear shouting and running from my cabin." Sage looked pale.

"We're going to die," I said curtly and pushed my way past Sage.

"What?" she cried.

I ignored her and marched to my cabin. Teressia emerged from her cabin. "Is something wrong?" she inquired.

"Aye. The boat's gonna sink and we're gonna be dead or stranded on giant rocks." The carelessness of the crew had put me in an edgy mood. How could they be so absentminded like this? We would have to pay for their mistake with our lives!

"Elijah." Tres grabbed my arm as I tried to rush past. She looked straight into my eyes, her cold gray ones glaring at me.

"Don't look at me like that," I said, shrugging out of her grasp.

"Elijah, think about what you're doing. Sage didn't deserve to be treated like that and neither did I. Get a grip on yourself. What's happening?"

"A big cluster of rock formations called the Maze of Stones are right ahead. The captain can't steer us away from it, so we have to go right through it. He doesn't think we'll get through it without sinking."

Teressia squeezed her eyes shut and opened them, taking a deep breath while doing so. "I hope we don't."

She briskly walked past me and out of the hatch. I decided to follow her.

When we got onto the deck, we were entering the Maze of Stones. Tres gasped in shock at the rocks. Sage was staring at them in horror, unable to move. Tres approached her.

"Are you okay?"

"No, no I'm not okay. This trip has been nothing but dangerous! Why can't we just sail to the islands without any harm? I don't do well in disasters!" she cried. A tear slid down her cheek. "I'm going to panic again." She started to take short breaths. "I feel sick." Sage ran to the rail and leaned over. I looked away.

Korina came trotting up from the bow, completely calm. "Why is Sage puking over the side of the ship?"

"She's scared," Tres answered.

"Oh. Well, she has a good reason to be. Everybody seems to think we're going to sink."

The three of us fell on the deck as the ship hit something. After I stopped rolling I looked at the bow. The ship had slammed into a rock. It towered above us, stretching as high as the masts. Sage screamed from the rail. "We're gonna die!" she shouted.

Sailors rushed down into the hold to check the damage.

The four of us got up and ran to the forecastle. Water was spilling into the hull. The bow dipped down.

"We're sinking!" Sage cried.

"It'll be fine, I'm sure," Tres soothed.

"Yeah, the sailors are already down there repairing the damage," I added.

Sage looked unconvinced. "But there's already water down there. I want to see for myself."

"No!" Korina lunged forward and grabbed Sage. "You'll only scare yourself. Besides, if you go into the hold, you'll be the first one to sink."

That had changed Sage's mind. "Fine. I just need to sit down."

We followed Sage, falling down twice as the ship grazed another rock. All around us were towers of rocks. They loomed high into the sky, creating an ominous atmosphere. The captain struggled to weave the *Naviganti* through the rocks, grazing multiple formations. The sailors that had disappeared into the hold were forced to stay there while the rest of them were constantly tugging on the sheets. Sweat formed on their red faces as they struggled to keep the sails in the right positions.

The four of us sat in the middle of the main deck. The bow frequently dipped downward, which led me to think that the hull was probably being torn into pieces. Sage held back screams and yelped instead.

Soon the ship was surrounded by formations, with no path to weave through. The wind still blew, and pushed the *Naviganti* against a formation. Serulean exited the helm and ordered the crew to reef the sails.

"How much?" one sailor asked.

"All of it," the captain answered.

"All of it? You want all of the sails to be furled?"

"Yes. The wind will keep pushing us and we have no way out of these blasted rocks."

"But if we furl the sails we'll just be stuck here," a sailor protested.

"I know, I know. Just until I think of something," Serulean replied.

The ship looked completely different with the sails rolled up. We sat in the middle of rock formations, unable to move.

"We're stuck," Sage mumbled. "We'll never get out of here."

"Well, it doesn't help when someone has a negative attitude," Korina retorted.

"It's the truth!" Sage said.

"We can still get out of here," Teressia assured.

Mage Melody appeared from the hatch. The bottom of her dress was wet. "Is everyone okay?" she checked. The four of us nodded. "Good. Don't worry—there was only a slight leak in the hull. The sailors are repairing it right now. Why are the sails drawn up? What's going on?"

I explained to Mage Melody that we had nowhere to sail. She looked around, noticing it was true.

"I hope we can find a way out of here," Mage Melody said. She left the four of us and found Mage Isaac.

"This is so boring!" Korina complained.

"Boring? We're stuck in the middle of all these stones and you think this is boring?" Sage said.

"Stones…" Tres murmured. "I wish I had a better view of where we're at. I have an idea that might get us out of here."

"The crow's nest!" I remembered.

Everyone looked at me with a puzzled look, except Korina who was grinning.

"The what?" Sage asked.

"You want a better view? Follow me," I exclaimed.

"I'm coming," Korina declared. "It'll be nice to go to the crow's nest again."

I led them to the shrouds at the base of the foremast. I began to climb, Teressia following and Korina right behind her. Sage stood at the bottom.

"There is no way I'm going up there. It's way too high for my liking," Sage stated.

"If the ship sinks we'll be the last to drown," Korina persuaded.

"We'll still drown and I'll have a chance to get to a dinghy on the deck. Besides, we're not going to sink if we remain stationary."

"Whatever," Korina replied. We continued to ascend the shrouds to the crow's nest. I glanced behind me, seeing Sage change her mind. I smiled to myself. She didn't want to be left alone.

My arms were burning when we finally reached the crow's nest. We all climbed into the lookout. A scream sounded from below us. Sage's legs were dangling in midair, her arms keeping her from falling.

"I'm okay!" she reassured as she regained her footing. She joined us in the lookout.

"Glad you could come," Korina smirked.

Sage grunted her response. "Okay I'm here and alive." She peered over the edge of the crow's nest and whimpered. "That's quite a long way down."

"Okay Tres, here's your view," I said.

"Perfect," Tres replied.

Stone formations reached as high as the crow's nest and some even higher, but we could see further than on the decks. Ahead of us, outside the circle we were trapped in, was a small path with formations on either side. The small passage took a sharp turn to the left and the formations closed in on the open space of water. The path would be too small for the *Naviganti* to squeeze through and it only came to a dead end anyway. Tres was staring out in front of the bow, mouthing words that were inaudible and pointing her finger through the maze of rock formations. I followed her gaze and noticed that for probably a mile or two, there were only rocks. How could we ever get out of this mess?

"I got it!" Tres suddenly exclaimed, causing the other three of us to jump.

"What do you got, genius?' Korina sarcastically questioned.

"Mage Isaac and I can use our magic to clear a way for the *Naviganti* to sail through," Tres excitedly explained.

"Not to be a storm cloud in your clear sky but those rocks are *huge*. Even with Mage Isaac, how are you two going to be able to move those things?" Korina asked.

"I don't know, but we'll have to think of something. We'll be stranded here if we don't. Let's face it, Serulean is a good captain and all, but he has no idea what to do and we're not going anywhere for who knows how long," Tres said. We all murmured in agreement. "Let's get back onto the deck. Korina, you stay here so you can keep watch on the rocks."

"Isn't that the sailors' job?"

"Do you want to tell one to get up here then?" Tres challenged.

"Sure," Korina answered, which was not the response Tres was hoping for.

"Fine, we'll have to get the captain to spare one or two sailors when we get on the deck."

The four of us descended the shrouds, taking longer than usual since Sage was in the lead. When we got to the deck, Korina left to find the captain. Sage and I followed Teressia to Mage Isaac.

"You want to what?" Mage Isaac said in disbelief, after Tres had explained her plan. "Teressia that would take a lot of work and magic. I'm not sure if the two of us can manage."

"But we have to try!" Tres protested. "There's no other way out of here!"

"I suppose you're right. The least we can do is try," Mage Isaac finally agreed.

"I'll be right back," Tres said, and abruptly ran to the hatch and vanished into the hold. A couple of minutes later she reappeared with a tool that looked like a hammer in her hand.

"Where did you get a mage's rod?" Mage Isaac marveled.

"The smith's shop back in Elementa," Tres answered.

"This is a very nice one," Mage Isaac observed. "How much did it cost you?"

"Seven silver coins," Tres replied. Mage Isaac whistled. Seven silver coins was a lot of money to pay for a mage's rod.

Mage Isaac left to inform the captain of their plans. When he returned, crew members were scurrying to the sheets and unfurling the sails. "We need to hurry. If we mess up, the ship could be seriously damaged," Mage Isaac warned.

I stayed with Sage while Mage Isaac and Teressia went to the forecastle. Mage Isaac lifted his arms straight out in front of him while Tres raised her mage's rod. They both swung their arms to the right at the same time, causing the nearest rock formation to crack. Mage Isaac and Tres repeated the same motion, their faces becoming red and creased with concentration. After a few minutes the single rock formation broke in half, crashing into the sea with a big splash. They did the same to the rock formation to the left.

The ship began to move again and quickly picked up speed in the strong wind that had come up. Now it was moving too fast for Mage Isaac and Tres. The crew members had to readjust the sails to slow the ship. Even at the slowest pace the two were struggling. The Naviganti brushed up against rock formations and a terrible scraping sound shook the boat. On the bow, Mage Isaac dropped down on his knees, heaving.

"I can't use my magic anymore. Something's in the air," he informed.

Sage, Korina, and I ran to the rail and inspected the water. The familiar black was mixed in with the blue-green sea water.

Korina gagged. "It's poisoned with the same dark magic." She gagged again and sat down on the deck. "I feel dizzy."

"There's no way out of here!" Serulean shouted. "Furl the sails! We're not going anywhere."

"No!" Tres called. "We can't give up! If we do we'll be stuck here! I have to keep trying before all of my magic fades like Mage Isaac's. The rock formations are poisoned with the dark magic as well, but I have to keep trying." She lifted her mage's rod with determination and brought it down heavily. The rock in front of the ship cracked in several places. Tres repeated the motion until the rock snapped into pieces and tumbled into the sea.

The crew members reluctantly followed the captain's orders. In a few moments the sails were completely furled and the ship stopped moving. Sailors rushed to get into the hatch.

"It's flooding in the hold! We're going to sink!" a sailor cried.

"Then get the water out! We can't let her go down!" Serulean ordered.

Teressia collapsed on the forecastle, unable to use her magic and too exhausted to stand up. Sage and I were knocked off our feet and tumbled down onto the deck next to Korina. The stern dipped down and we rolled backward.

"We're sinking!" the same sailor shouted.

"I know that!" Serulean shouted from the helm, which was dipping down further and further. "We're not going to go down! Keep getting water out and try to patch the bulkhead. No one abandons their posts!"

"We're going to die," Sage whispered next to me.

"No we're not," I argued. "There's still a chance they can fix the ship and even if it does sink, there'll be lifeboats.

"I feel sick," Korina moaned. "This dark magic is all around us."

I clutched the rail with the two girls as the bow rose and the stern sunk. Water was already pooling onto the quarter deck.

Please don't sink, please don't sink.

CHAPTER 19

KORINA

I rolled toward the stern as it dipped further down into the water. My stomach flipped and my head spun. The dark magic in the sea had made me feel sick. I was unable to get to my feet and I helplessly tumbled along the deck. Sage and Elijah grabbed onto the base of the rail and were forced to let their feet hang loosely toward the stern. I flung an arm out in attempt to stop myself, but I had no strength in me and continued to slide across the deck. I eventually stopped once I had hit the base of the quarterdeck. Seawater spilled onto my head from the sinking quarterdeck. I lifted my arm and tried to use my magic but it refused to obey. Evidently the dark magic had overpowered my own elemental magic.

A group of sailors emerged from the hold, soaking wet. "It's all useless, Captain! There's too much water. We've patched the bulkhead but it won't last long," one informed.

"Nonsense! We must try harder!" Serulean protested.

A sailor grabbed him by the arm as Serulean rushed to the hold. "It's flooded in there. The ship is going to sink. We must get to the dinghy before it's too late."

"Don't give up, Mared. Continue to get the water out." Serulean continued into the hold with a bucket, and stood at the steps as he scooped up the water. The sailors joined him with their shoulders slumped. The crew had given up.

Water was pooling around me. I managed to rise to my knees and crawl upward, in the direction of the bow. I stopped when I reached Elijah and Sage, who were trying to reach the forecastle.

"Wait," I panted.

"Korina! Are you okay?" Elijah asked, looking over his shoulder.

"No, but I'll live. What about Sage? Is she in a panic? And Teressia, is she still on the forecastle?"

"I'm fine!" Sage spat from above me. "And yes, I'm in a panic—the ship is sinking! I knew this would happen!"

"Teressia is still unconscious on the forecastle. We're trying to crawl there for high ground. Mage Isaac is there too," Elijah stated.

Mage Melody appeared to the left of us. "We need to get to the dinghy. Follow me, children."

"What about Teressia and Mage Isaac?" Elijah asked.

"They'll be fine. Mage Isaac has regained his strength, but he is unable to use his magic. He'll take care of Teressia," Melody explained.

We crawled to the right and trailed after Mage Melody. I slipped and slid down the deck and the water lapped at my leggings.

"Help!" I cried.

Melody shuffled to me and held out a hand, using the other to balance herself. I mustered up the strength to throw an arm to her outstretched hand. She pulled me upward but lost her grip on me as the ship swayed with a moan.

I gasped as I hit the water. Without my magic I couldn't stop myself. I could only hold my breath as I tumbled into the flooded part of the ship, stopping when I slammed into the quarterdeck for the second time. I floated up to the surface of the water and sputtered. I felt my body shoot forward as a blast of water pushed from behind me. Mage Melody had used her magic to save me. As I returned to her side, she gasped and clutched her chest.

"The dark magic has poisoned my magic as well. Come on, Korina. We have to keep going."

I crawled to the rail of the ship where the dingy was and Mage Melody helped me climb into it. I expected it to drop into the sea but we didn't move.

"What's going on?" I murmured.

"The ship has stopped sinking," Mage Melody informed. I raised my head up and saw that she was right. Sage and Elijah were next to me, watching the *Naviganti* as well. Cheers came from the deck despite the partial flooding of the ship. Serulean poked his head over the side at us.

"We stopped it! She's going to make it!" Serulean grinned and disappeared.

"How about we stay in here for a few minutes," Mage Melody suggested.

I closed my eyes and rested while the crew worked on the ship. I dozed off for a few minutes until I felt a shift of movement. The ship creaked and groaned and the stern rose. The bow slowly crashed into the water with a big splash. The ship was balanced once more.

"How did they do it?" Elijah wondered aloud.

We climbed out of the small boat and onto the main deck. Water sloshed to our ankles. The deck was flooded but at least the hold wasn't anymore. The sailors were dumping out the water with the buckets. Some were in the hold doing the same thing. Captain Serulean was smiling and helping.

I followed Elijah and Sage to the forecastle where Mage Isaac and Tres were. They had not attempted to reach the dinghy but had stayed there the whole time. Tres was on the floor unconscious.

"It's up to Teressia to get us out of here," Isaac declared. "My magic is gone for now. We'll have to get her to rest and then maybe she can continue to clear a way for us." Mage Isaac left us to watch Tres and joined Mage Melody.

After Teressia woke up she was still weak. "Oh my head," she groaned. "Did the ship sink? Are we on a dinghy?"

"No, but it almost did," Sage explained.

"Never mind that. How are you feeling?" Elijah questioned.

Tres propped herself up on her elbows. "Iffy. I need to keep trying though. We have to get out of here."

"You need to rest," Elijah ordered.

"If she thinks she can do it, let her," I argued. I would admit that Elijah didn't turn out to be as bad as I thought he was, but we still weren't exactly friends.

"No, she needs to regain her strength. You of all people should know that," Elijah objected.

"You don't know that! I'm fine right now," I lied.

"How many times are you two going to get into an argument?" Sage complained. "Stop bickering!"

"I'm not bickering with her!" Elijah protested. "I just think that Tres needs to rest before using a lot of magic again."

"She doesn't need you to decide what she can and cannot do!" I spat.

"I'm not deciding what she needs to do!" Elijah cried.

"Yes you are!"

"Shut up!" Sage said.

"Don't tell me to shut up!" I argued.

"Well, we're tired of hearing you, so please do," Elijah remarked.

"And we're tired of hearing you too," I retorted.

"Both of you need to be quiet!" Sage said.

"Who asked you?"

"She's right, we're not helping."

"She doesn't have the right to—"

"All of you *shut up*!" Teressia interrupted from the floor. "I would like to use my magic right away but I can't. I need to rest or I'll feel worse. But as soon as I do, I will return to the rock formations." She got up and disappeared into the hold.

I snorted at Elijah and Sage and left to my cabin as well. There was still water in the hold, but I went to my cabin anyway. Most of it was drenched in water from the opening in the bulkhead. I sat on my bed, crossed. Elijah and Sage were so bossy. I hated it when people told me what to do. Tres was probably fine and just tired. She was going to destroy those rocks and get us out of here. I just knew it.

After I cooled down I returned to the main deck. Sage, Elijah, and Tres were already on the forecastle. I joined them as Teressia lifted her tool and attempted to clear the rock formation.

She chose one formation in front of us and implanted several cracks in it. Then she rose her mage's rod and brought it down in the air with force. The formation creaked as smaller stones rolled off of it. The cracks widened and spread down the rock like fingers. With a final move, Tres sliced the tower of rock in half. It crashed into the water, sending a ripple through the sea and waves bouncing. Tres gasped.

"Are you okay?" I asked.

"Yes. It's just a lot of work."

Tres continued, the process becoming slower and slower. She took frequent breaks to replenish her strength. A path big enough for the ship was made but ended too soon. Teressia was too far away to continue making the path.

"Now what?" Sage said.

"We have to get closer," Tres replied. She went to inform the captain and returned with a defeated expression. "He's not moving the ship. We're going to stay in one spot. He says that after what happened last time it's not a good idea to keep going."

"Does he have any other ideas?" I spat. "No, he doesn't. I'm going to go reason with him."

"Korina—" Elijah started.

"What? Are you going to stop me?"

Elijah said nothing more. I marched to the captain, who was standing on the main deck.

"How are we going to get out of here?" I questioned angrily.

"I don't know yet, Korina. I'm going to meet with the crew tonight and decide what to do. We'll be moving in the morning."

"That's the thing though—there's no other way out. There's not enough room to travel or else we'll collide with more rocks. The only way out is Teressia's way. If you don't let her continue clearing away rocks we'll be stuck here unless we travel by the dinghy!"

Captain Serulean sighed. "Last time I let her and Mage Isaac try their idea the ship almost sank. I can't let that happen again."

"But if you just moved the ship up a little and then stopped it we would be fine. She already cleared part of the way."

"I'm sorry, Korina. It's not going to happen."

I exhaled sharply. "Why aren't you listening? *There's no other way out!*"

"Korina," Serulean warned. "That's quite enough."

I returned to the forecastle. "He won't listen. There's no way we're getting out of the Maze of Stones."

Teressia squeezed her eyes shut. "We can't be stuck here," she whispered.

"Well, we are. If the ship doesn't move you can't use your magic on the rocks," I said.

"If only I could stretch my magic out further. Mage Isaac can but he can't use his magic right now."

"Serulean said that he's not moving the ship until morning when they've thought of a way out. But there isn't any other way out. There's nothing else we can do today. We might as well go back to our cabins and rest."

"My cabin smells like seawater," Sage complained. "I don't want to go back in there until it dries more and the stench goes away."

"If you haven't noticed, we're in the middle of the sea. It's going to smell like seawater anyway," I sneered.

"Please don't go picking fights, Korina," Tres pleaded.

I exhaled angrily. Maybe I should try to be nicer to everyone, at least while we were in danger. On the other hand, it wasn't my fault everyone was so annoying.

"What if we told the crew to unfurl the sails?" Elijah suddenly suggested. He had been silent for a few moments, apparently thinking.

"They probably won't carry out orders unless it's from the captain," Tres murmured.

"It's worth a try though. I'm tired of these creepy rocks everywhere. I feel so small and trapped," Sage said.

"Yeah and ordering people around is fun," I added.

"I'll go start," Elijah said. "You three go too."

The three of us split and approached different sailors until all of them were dealt with. Some questioned me, but I easily persuaded them. A couple refused to carry out the orders and some even began to unfurl the sails without a second thought.

Soon the sails were all unfolded. The *Naviganti* edged forward toward the rocks. The captain was unaware, for he was resting in the captain's cabin. Teressia did her best to quickly demolish the formations. She worked faster than the last time, forming a routine of repeated motions. It took a long time, but the *Naviganti* finally exited the Maze of Stones. By the time we escaped the towers of rock, it was dark outside.

Teressia was completely worn out. By the time she destroyed the last formation she was shaking. As soon as the ship was free of the rocks she collapsed onto the forecastle. We knelt beside her and quickly made sure she was okay. Mage Isaac was proud of her and Mage Melody had a special tea made for her. Teressia was then carried into her cabin and I did not see her for the rest of the night.

Eventually Captain Serulean emerged from his cabin. When he saw that the sails were unfurled and we were moving, he was not happy.

"What is going on?" he demanded angrily.

"We heard that you wanted the sails to be—"

"I wanted no such thing! Who told you this?"

"Those four kids did, Captain."

"Really? And you actually listened to those children? Next time you do nothing unless I personally tell you to, unless I am on my deathbed!"

The three of us began to sneak to the hold, hoping that Serulean wouldn't spot us. He saw us immediately.

"And where do you think you're going?" he questioned.

We froze in our tracks and faced him.

"I have a feeling Korina was behind all of this," the captain assumed.

"Actually, sir, it was my idea to tell the crew members to unfurl the sails," Elijah admitted.

"Ah, I see. But you all were guilty of it. I thank you for your honesty. But next time don't you dare impersonate me. If you do it again I'll force you to walk the plank! Now I do admit that I was being a bit irrational; I couldn't figure out a way to get out of this mess and my pride caused me to ignore your ideas. I see that it worked and got us out of here. Thank you."

The crew was rejoicing that night. They disappeared into the kitchen to celebrate while our little party went into our cabins for sleep.

The next morning the sky was partly cloudy. I hoped that we wouldn't have to go through another storm. For me it was fun, but for the others it was torture. I didn't want to have to see Sage seasick again or Tres thrown overboard or Elijah injured.

After I retrieved breakfast from the kitchen I climbed into the crow's nest to eat as I usually did. It was peaceful in that little post and I didn't want to be bothered by anyone. The day before, Elijah had spoiled my breakfast by discovering the other crow's nest and attempting to communicate with me.

I slowly ate the food and then tossed the old cloth that it was wrapped in into the wind. When I returned to the deck, everyone, excluding the crew, was clustered around Serulean. I joined them and listened.

"I know the first couple of days have been a little rough. Let me assure you, it would be very rare for things to continue this way so do not be anxious. From here on out, it should be smooth sailing. The only thing I want to warn you about is a whirlpool. It appears from spring to summer and lies somewhere northwest of the Maze of Stones. I will make sure we avoid it, unlike the Maze of Stones. If there is some reason that we are unable to avoid it, I want you to be ready. Every ship that has foolishly gone near the whirlpool has been sucked into it and destroyed. I fear that the force of it may be too strong to escape. I will make sure our path avoids this whirlpool. That is all," Serulean explained.

I walked away with Teressia, Elijah, and Sage. Even though I didn't consider them to be my friends, they were the only people my age on the ship.

"Great. Yet another perilous event we will have to suffer through. If we don't die, anyway," Sage complained.

"Hey, the captain said we're going to stay clear of the whirlpool," Elijah said. He looked paler than usual after Serulean had informed us of the whirlpool.

"Maybe, maybe not," Sage grumbled.

* * *

The next few days the four of us regularly climbed to a crow's nest together. After the incident with the Maze of Stones, we didn't exactly trust the crew members to keep us out of danger.

The four of us were up in the crow's nest chatting as we usually did.

"And that's why I call him Rhydork," I explained.

"Rhydork? That's kind of mean," Sage remarked.

I shrugged. "He picks favorites and I'm not one of them. We don't like each other."

"Yeah, maybe he has a nickname for you too," Elijah suggested. "Maybe it's 'Kor-witch-a'."

"Elijah, that is the dumbest thing I have ever heard of," Tres replied.

Elijah blushed at his juvenile suggestion and we all laughed. Sage's sudden gasp grabbed our attention.

"What's wrong?" Elijah asked.

"Look over there, a little to the left of the bow." We followed Sage's pointing finger to a disturbance in the water in the distance. White foam was visible and waves danced around the edge.

"It's the whirlpool," Elijah breathed.

CHAPTER 20

AUGUST

*T*wo nights ago, the night I had heard the screeches of mutations in the forest, the mutations had attacked the city. Many innocent citizens were injured and others even killed. The damage was even worse since all of the guards had left for Soror. The mages and the small patrol of guards that didn't go had struggled to protect the city. Most of the civilian men were forced to fight as well. Headmaster Ignatia's prediction had come true: the mutations had become more intelligent and attacked the city at night.

Yesterday was spent tending to the injured and repairing or cleaning up the city. The night the mutations had attacked, a storm had occurred. It had rolled in from the northwest, where the group of four students and two mages had sailed to on the Lata Sea. I hoped that the ship had not sunk or capsized and that everyone was uninjured.

It was a menacing storm, and had left trees blown over from the gale force winds.

I laid on my bed, bones aching. Everything was sore from working in the city yesterday. At least I didn't have classes today, though Headmaster Ignatia did not take a break from combat training on weekends. She was persistent and would not stop grilling me until she determined if I had magic or not.

I rolled out of bed and dressed. I arched my back and stretched my arms, then headed down to the courtyard where I trained. There, Headmaster Ignatia was waiting for me with her hands on her hips.

"You're late," she snapped briskly.

"I know, I'm sorry. It was hard to get out of bed."

"Was it also hard to miss the boat?"

I blushed and looked to the ground. "I didn't mean to."

"No?" Ignatia snapped loudly, causing me to jump. "Just like you didn't mean to be late this morning or to be mistaken for a soldier when fighting against Fortis? Get rid of the excuses and we'll have a better relationship."

I spent the whole morning training, my muscles screaming the whole time. When noon finally came, I was dismissed from the courtyard. I rushed to the city kitchen, only to remember it was a weekend and there was no lunch. I decided to go to the square market to buy food.

I paid eleven copper coins to get fruit, a slice of meat, and a roll. After I ate my meal I wandered around Elementa aimlessly. People were still bustling about, repairing all the damage from two days ago.

I sat down under a tree in the Elementa garden, on the north side of town and right next to the Temple of Elementa. It was a peaceful place and one of the only spots in town with so much greenery. The only other spot with growing fruits and vegetables was the small yard next to the city kitchen.

As I sat against the tree, worrying thoughts broke into my mind. There had been several attacks from mutations, and they were still growing stronger and more intelligent by the hour. If the mutations attacked again, we could be caught off-guard just as one of the previous nights. We needed to know *when* they were going to attack next. I decided that I would go investigate the Shrouded Forest to find out. I had to go alone, for if I told anyone they would stop me. I knew it was an unwise idea and that I would most likely be injured, but I had to do it for the safety of the city.

I left the Elementa garden and traveled across the city, stopping at the west border. Peering out across the small field and to the forest, I looked for any signs of mutations. I heard no sounds and continued. I was a little nervous as I was crossing the curved bridge across the river. I paused to take a deep breath and summon my courage, remembering the breathing techniques that Ignatia had taught me.

I decided that it would not be a good idea to enter Shrouded Forest. There could be a group of mutations waiting for me, hiding in the trees and undergrowth. They could attack me before I even knew they were there. I turned to the left of the sick forest where I had saved Teressia from mutations before. The forest seemed to whisper; it seemed to be sick with disease and drooping with sinister thoughts. Instead of a peaceful greenwood, it was browning and almost seemed to have purple splotches mixed in.

I carefully crept around the edge of Shrouded Forest, freezing in my tracks when I heard a branch snap among the trees. The leaves that were littered on the forest floor crackled and crunched. I could hear my own breath becoming louder and heavier. I relaxed as the sounds ceased. Everything seemed calm. I assumed that there would be no attacks from the mutations this afternoon.

I turned around and began to walk back to Elementa, but a tremble in the bushes had me spinning around to see a mutation in mid leap. I panicked and stood still like a startled rabbit. The mutation plunged onto me and I slammed onto the ground. I yelled in agony as the mutation's paws (was it even a paw?) slid over my arms. It stopped suddenly as another mutation growled from nearby. It growled a response.

"F-i-i-i-ne," it seemed to hiss. Did it really talk or was I just hearing things from that sober growl?

I got up and was immediately knocked to the ground again as the two mutations pounced on me. The surface of their bodies stung me and there was bleeding gashes where they had contacted my skin. I clenched my teeth in pain.

The two mutations growled at each other for a minute until three more mutations joined. I didn't dare get up, in fear that they would attack me again. I was outnumbered badly. I laid in the grass and wondered why I wasn't dead yet.

At last the mutations approached me. They stretched their slimy arms toward me and I rolled back. I leaped to my feet, fearing that the creatures would burn me with their acid bodies.

The mutations advanced and lunged toward me, apparently angered by my action. One snuck under my feet as another leaped in the air toward me. I shouted as they contacted my body. The other three crept closer, all four legs on the ground. All five mutations surrounded me and screeched, revealing black mouths with black and violet strings of slime stretching from top to bottom. I darted to the side as two sprang at me. The five regrouped and charged. Shouting, I thrust my hands in front of me with my palms exposed. I closed my eyes so I wouldn't see them rip me open.

The mutations shrieked and I opened my eyes. A blinding light was shooting out of my hands, slowly altering the form and nature of the mutations. I reflexively slammed my hands over my ears. One mutation had transformed into a deer. The deer sprinted into the forest, realizing it was in danger.

Was that magic I did?

I was full of pride, then heavy with fear as the other four mutations charged at me. Their eyes were cold yellow shards of stone, glaring in fury at me. I turned my palms at them again, expecting the light to return. Only a small beam escaped my hand and I felt faint. The mutations pounced on me and I helplessly fell to the ground. One mutation swiped at my head and struck me just above my ear; I slammed onto the ground and lost consciousness.

When I awoke, my head was pounding and my hair was sticky with blood. I was in some sort of nest, with branches and twigs poking into me. I was also in a shady place, where sunlight barely penetrated the canopy of leaves above me. I lifted my head up to examine my surroundings. *I must be in the forest.*

I laid my head back down as I heard mutations growl. I listened hard, and it seemed as if they were talking in our language. They spoke in hissing whispers, their words pronounced slowly.

"Why would you brrrring thisss blood-bagg innnto our nessst?" one hissed.

"Weee should killll it nooow," another sneered.

"Silence!" a voice boomed. It was unmistakably a mutation, but did not whisper slowly like the others. The mutations whimpered and shrank back into the branches. I realized that we were in a large tree. The voice continued to speak and I searched for its body. "I ordered them to bring the blood-bag into our nest. I sense it is not like the others. I want to try to converse with it before we kill it. If we release the blood-bag, it will retreat to its nest and warn the others about us."

So this is the leader.

"Iss it awaake?" a mutation asked.

"Nooo! Can't you ssseee itsss ffllaappss overr itsss ssseeing-holesss?"

I felt the air become heavier around me, as if it was infected. "Get away from it!" the leader ordered. The air returned to normal, but was still poisoned by the dark magic.

"Wwheen willll it beee awwaake?"

"Soon," the leader stated. "I will get it up now."

I felt a hard prod in my side. I blinked and rose, pretending that I had just woke up. A dark tall mutation towered above me. It was on two legs and must've been nine feet tall. Blades of armor stuck out of its sides and its eyes were a deep green instead of yellow. It must've been a mutated Fortis soldier, whose mind had been taken over by a dark spirit. It leaned toward me and my stomach turned cold. This mutation was demoralizing.

"Who are you blood-bag? Why do I get a different feel inside of me when I'm near you? I do not feel this way when I am around the others of your rotten kind. Speak!"

"I, uh, I don't know," I stammered quietly.

"Are you telling me that you don't know what you are?" the leader boomed.

"No, not at all, I just don't know—"

"Enough of your blubbering! Are you some sort of spy? You will tell me everything about your nest and what you are plotting, blood-bag."

"I'm not a spy, I promise! I was just taking a walk."

"A walk, hm? While we are invading your nest and dwelling in this dark web of leaves? I do not think that even a blood-bag would be so foolish."

"I, uh um, am sorta foolish, Your... Viciousness."

"What is this viciousness that you speak of?"

"Well, it um, means cruel, malicious, fierce, frightening."

"Hm. I do make you blood-bags run cold with fear, don't I? Hm. I like this viciousness." The leader turned around and addressed the mutations. "You will all address me as 'Your Viciousness'." He turned back to me. "You have three clicks to start talking before I kill you."

"What are clicks?"

"You blood-bags really are dense. It is a measure of time. What you call 'seconds' is almost equivalent to clicks. Now begin talking! I want to know your plots."

"Well, uh, we don't really have plots. Everyone in the city—er nest—is just trying to live peacefully but we keep getting hurt because of your attacks," I explained.

"That is wet-mush! Just a few—what you call 'days'—ago, a pack of blood-bags snuck into our nest with their sharplings. You were trying to kill us! But you blood-bags are dumb and slow. We killed your pack of blood-bags and ate them. Am I correct or are you lying?"

"That was only because our leader was afraid that you were a threat," I assured.

The leader bent down and sniffed the air around me. "You know what I smell, blood-bag? I smell fear. You reek of it. Tell me what your plots are and I may spare your life. Or not. I make no promises."

"We have no plots! Only to fight when you attack—but only as protection for the people," I answered. My heart thudded against my chest. I was surprised that I couldn't smell my own fear.

"People? You mean blood-bags? I do not know the word 'people.' And I know how you blood-bags fight. It's the same every time. That's how we wipe you out. And sometimes you use your magic blood-bags, blood-bags that move the wet-mush or green stuff or red-burns. Those are harder to defeat but we still overcome them. And every day we smell your fear, waves of it coming from your nest. The Master will be pleased to know you are all weak and have no plots. You are helpless."

"Master?" I whispered under my breath. Aloud I asked, "Well, you know us blood-bags are scared and weak. What about your plots?"

"Our plots?" the leader spat. "How dare you, blood-bag! Scared but feisty I see. You are foolish to think that we would reveal our plots to you."

I shrugged nonchalantly. "It just seemed fair. I tell you my plots and you tell me yours. Maybe we could work out a deal. If you tell me your plots, I'll tell you one of our secrets."

"You dare hold information from me! I will kill you if you don't speak at once!"

"But if you kill me you won't know the secret," I reasoned.

The human mutation grunted. "Very clever of you, blood-bag. But don't think I won't kill you. Our plots are simple, but complex in the minds of blood-bags. I will simplify our plots for you. The Master is very powerful. He has forces and spreads his dark magic everywhere. In the beginning stage, he spreads it to this land. You blood-bags call it Lux. Lux becomes poisoned and weaker. The Master uses us to gain control of it. When you are weak enough, the Master comes and destroys the last of you. Then the land belongs to the Master."

"This is only the beginning stage? Does he plan to take over the world?"

"Clever you are, blood-bag. Not like others of your kind."

"And who is the Master? Where is he?"

"You are foolish to think I would tell you plainly. But I will reveal his identity and abode in a riddle. Take a breadth and he is there. Take a craft and you are there. In a turret he lies. If you disturb him, it will be your demise." The human mutation paused. "Think quickly, blood-bag, because your time has run out! Now you will die!"

The mutation lunged at me. I rolled out of the way and leaped over the nest of twigs that I was laying in. Now I was plummeting toward the ground. I reached out and grabbed anything I could get a hold of. My hands caught on a fork of branches on a tree and I slammed into the trunk. Above me, the leader was swiftly leaping down the branches with waves of mutations behind him. I let go and dropped to a branch below me. I threw my arms toward the mutations and shot a beam of light in their direction. Screeches filled the air and I plugged my ears as I dropped to the ground and sprinted away as fast as I could.

I had no idea where I was going. I was probably in the middle of the forest and there was no telling how long it would take me to get out. I glanced behind me, seeing the slimy creatures pursuing me far back in the trees. I was ahead of them for now.

I didn't stop sprinting even after I escaped the arms of the forest. I realized I had exited Shrouded Forest on its west side, facing Fortis. There was a river to my left that flowed back into the forest and a road that crossed over the river by way of a wooden bridge not too far from where I was. I veered toward the bridge, trying desperately to maintain my speed, and finally crossed over the river. Once on the other side I turned around, running to the east, aiming to skirt around the south side of the forest. To my dismay, I encountered yet another branch of the river flowing north toward Elementa that prevented me from getting away from the forest.

As the mutations erupted from the forest, I dove into the river. The current was strong and it carried me toward the sea, away from the Lux Mountain Range. I made it to the other side with difficulty and hauled myself out of the water. By this time, the mutations had reached the other side of the river. Some even jumped into it and yowled as they dissolved.

"Ssstayy out offff theee wwwwet-musshhh!" the mutations cried.

I continued running and collapsed as soon as I reached the city. The mutations had receded back into the forest. I hoped they didn't come out of it on Elementa's side to attack.

Once I caught my breath I returned to the Academy. I stopped to speak with the Headmaster once she saw me.

"August, is that you?" she asked firmly.

"Yes," I replied, staring at the stone floor.

"What in the name of Lux happened to you?" she demanded. "Your forehead is a bloody mess, you have scrapes that are as long as your arms *on* your arms, and you can barely stand. What *did* you get into?" Ignatia exhaled sharply with her eyes squinted. Then she widened them. "You didn't." She squeezed her eyes shut and tilted her head.

"I'm sorry, I know you're—"

"Sorry doesn't help!" she spat loudly. "Sorry doesn't help you when you're dead, it doesn't help you when the city's attacked for the twentieth time, and it doesn't help you when other people are killed! You know better than to go into the forest, August!"

"I didn't go into the forest—I was trying to help Elementa. I just thought that I might be able to find out if they were planning to attack so I could warn the city and we could be prepared this time."

"You know better!" she repeated harshly. "What happened then? Did you get attacked, chased?"

"Yes. They attacked me when I was outside the forest and then they took me deep into the woods, in front of their leader."

"In front of their leader?" Ignatia lost the menacing, scolding tone. "Why? Did it say anything? What happened?"

I reported our conversation. "Headmaster, this means that the whole of Lux is in danger! We could all die!"

"I know, August," she said sharply. "Take a breadth and he is there. Take a craft and you are there. In a turret he lies. If you disturb him, it will be your demise. Hm."

I stood there quietly while Ignatia thought. Then her expression turned grave and she became pale.

She grimaced and covered her face with her hands. In a whisper she rasped, "I just sent them to their deaths." Ignatia abruptly rushed into a hall, leaving me alone.

I retired to my dorm and cleaned my wounds. I went to bed early and thought while I struggled to fall asleep. Ignatia had obviously solved the riddle. What did it mean, though?

Take a breadth and he is there. Shouldn't it be breath? No, it must be breadth on purpose. What does breadth mean? Is it the same as breath?

I grabbed a book I had checked out from the Academy library: the dictionary. It was a new edition, and ever since someone had invented it, dictionaries had become more and more popular and convenient.

I flipped through the pages of the dictionary until I found the word breadth.

Breadth is an excessive extent, something large. The riddle deals with distances. So it must mean the Master is far away. How very helpful.

Take a craft and you are there. Craft, meaning something that was made? What craft? It could also mean a vessel. So it must mean a boat. The breadth must mean sea and craft is a ship.

In a turret he lies. What's a turret? I've heard of it before. I thought hard. I remembered reading it somewhere. *Of course! A turret is a tower! So the Master is in a tower?*

And what was Ignatia talking about, sending them to their deaths? Of course. Why hadn't I realized it sooner?

The four students and Mage Isaac and Mage Melody were in more peril than we had ever imagined.

CHAPTER 21

SAGE

*T*he four of us rushed down the shrouds and onto the main deck. The whirlpool was far off in the distance but we needed to report our sighting of it to the captain immediately.

By the time we reached the helm we were panting.

"Goodness, children. I'd say you all saw a ghost out on the water," Captain Serulean remarked.

"The whirlpool… it's… we're… coming… closer," Elijah gasped in between breaths.

"Oh, for crying out loud!" Korina exclaimed. "He means to say the whirlpool is right ahead of us in the distance." She paused to catch her breath. "You might want to change course before it's too late."

Serulean nodded. "That would be a wise idea. I will tell the crew right away. Miles!" he called to one of the sailors.

A sailor paused as he was tugging on a sheet. He approached the base of the quarter deck. "Yes, Captain?"

"Take over for me, will ya?" The two traded places, and Miles took on the wheel of the ship. "Whirlpool is coming up fast and we need change course. I'll go tell the crew."

While the sailors gathered around the captain, the four of us left the quarterdeck and went to the bow. There we sat on the steps of the forecastle. I turned around and peered over the rail, gazing at the whirlpool. If we hadn't seen it from above, I would have never known it was even there. I began to tremble and my stomach turned sour.

"I'm really worried," I admitted. "What if we get pulled into the whirlpool? We'll go down, down, down. Never to escape. I don't want to die!"

"Relax, garden freak. We're changing course," Korina said.

"But what if the strong current sweeps us away and we can't change course?" I fretted.

"Not gonna happen. We're turning right now, look." Korina stood up and gestured to the side. The ship swayed and turned slowly.

"Yeah, it's all going to be fine," Teressia soothed gently.

Elijah smiled as he gazed out over the sea. "And don't worry, if we don't get eaten by the whirlpool, we'll get swallowed by a whale."

Teressia shot him a glare. "Elijah, that's not funny and you know it."

"Ugh, my stomach," I groaned. After Elijah mentioned "whale" I became even more nauseous. I shivered as a breeze ran by.

"You're just scared," Korina muttered, more to herself than to me.

"I'm not scared," I lied. "Just a little nervous."

"You need to get your mind off the whirlpool. How about we get the captain to tell us a story about one of his trips at sea," Tres suggested.

"It's probably going to be about more hurricanes and such. It's just going to make me feel worse."

"Then we'll ask him to infant-proof the story," Korina mocked. Her smile vanished when Tres shot her a glare. "I'm just kidding. He can tell us a friendly story."

The captain was on the main deck, monitoring the crew and the sails. He looked our way as he saw us coming. "Hello, children. What's the matter this time?"

"We were wondering if you had any exciting stories from times you were at sea," Teressia said.

Serulean chuckled. "I have many stories. What type are you in the mood for?"

Teressia was about to say something but Korina cut her off. "Do you know anything about where we're going?"

The captain's smile faded. "You mean the Sacred Islands?"

"Yes. You must know something about the Sacred Islands if we're traveling there."

"Well, Korina, it's not very hard for someone as experienced as me to look at a map and plan a route." Serulean scratched his salt and pepper beard. "But you're right, I do know some things about that mysterious place."

"Really?" Korina said, brightening up. "How? I thought people were forbidden to learn about them."

"Well," Captain Serulean sighed, "eh, maybe it's not a good idea."

Elijah looked up at the sky dramatically and then to the captain. "You've been to the Sacred Islands, haven't you?"

Serulean sighed again. "Yes. I don't know how you guessed, boy, but I have."

"I've always wanted to know more about the islands. When I asked one of my professors, he didn't know much. Could you tell us about them?" I asked.

"If you have time, of course," Tres added politely.

"What do they look like?" Korina said.

"Okay, calm down. One voice at a time. When I was a younger lad, I ventured to the Sacred Islands on a voyage. No one had ever dared to go to the islands, and our voyage was kept a secret. We told everyone we were voyaging to Osen for a special occasion. If anybody had known we were actually traveling to the islands, we would've been stopped. Did you mention somethin' 'bout their appearance,

Korina?" After she nodded he continued, "Well, they are something. You'll never see any land like 'em. Divite Island has a glorious and symmetrical mountain range, set behind a magnificent shore. There are sands on that shore, unlike our bay back in Elementa. The sands are as soft as velvet and as white as a glass of pallid wine. Those grains sparkle like diamonds and feel like silk when they stream through your hands. The village on the center mountain, which was also the tallest, was stunning. It was in ruins of course, and covered in heaps of ash. You'd never seen so much ash in your entire life. The buildings were half gone and in ruins. Even in ruins, the architecture was stupendous. That city must've been carved out of marble. Shame it had to be destroyed. And the other big island, Felix Island, was the main attraction. There were so many land features on that one island. It was a living wonder. Forests, mountains, basins, hills, you name it. There were even three lakes, all as big as Vast Lake or even bigger, right next to each other. In the back of the island, lay the infamous Mount Felix. It was treacherous looking and gave me chills."

"And we'll get to see it with our very own eyes!" Korina squeaked. She cleared her throat when she realized we were staring at her.

"Do you know anything about the actual history?" Teressia curiously asked.

"Of course. Way back in the early ages, foreigners discovered the islands. They claimed the islands were rich in resources, just as Lux is, and these foreigners began to colonize the islands. It is unknown whether they came from one area nearby, such as from Osen or Tringuli or even the Celestial Islands; or if the foreigners were from all around the world."

"Why did so many people go to the Sacred Islands?" Elijah asked.

Serulean shrugged. "I suppose they heard of them somehow and decided it would be the ideal place to live. Some might've gone there to start a new life, a second chance if you will. Some left thinking that it would be a better place to live than where they were. Less people, more room. Well, after everyone had settled in and their civilizations were established and developed, the Sacred Islands became an appealing place to live. A new way of life was formed." Serulean swallowed and scratched his chin. He thought for a few moments, trying to think of what to explain next. His eye brows knitted together and he continued, "I seem to remember learning that the people of these islands were excellent seafarers. They devised a route of trade and cleverly traded with several different city states without anyone realizing it. It was a clever tactic if you ask me, pricing their goods exorbitantly higher since they had no competition. The islands began to become very wealthy due to their method of trading, especially Divite Island. That name actually means wealthy, prosperous."

"So they basically cheated people?" Korina questioned, her eyes squinted. She tucked a lock of black hair behind her ear as it fell in her face.

Serulean chortled. "You could say that. They were smart, yes they were." The captain looked upward, studying the clouds in the azure sky. His eyes were a light shade of blue themselves, and matched the sky. His face was weather beaten and sunburned, revealing all the long hours he had spent out at sea. "You know," he began softly, "the islands were a spectacular place. After they had become more famous, there were rumors that Divite Village was carved out of marble, paved with gold streets, and that silver rain fell from the sky. Those were only rumors, though. Everyone was dazzled by the success of the city. Some just went to Divite to see if the legends were true."

"Were they?" Korina asked breathlessly.

"Some were indeed, lass. For example, there were rumors of creatures that walked the islands. Some were indigenous only to those islands, never seen anywhere else. How that is possible is beyond my knowledge," the captain mused, shaking his head. "Though, some were rumored to be evil creatures. The ones I mentioned were more like animals. These evil creatures hadn't been seen too often, and several people had only claimed to have seen them. There are no records of these creatures and no drawn pictures. They were said to be dark, evil, but not very powerful. It was claimed that these creatures lived peacefully alongside humans. They would sometimes wander into the towns, but mostly slink around in the shadows and wooded areas."

"Do you think they were real or just people begging for attention?" I asked doubtfully.

Captain Serulean shot me a sideways look. "I believe they could've existed," he said in a low voice. "What do you believe?" His blue eyes squinted at me, in a questioning way but not threatening. There was a flicker of challenge in them, as if he was daring me to reveal my beliefs.

I returned the gaze to Serulean and he was the first one to look away. His eyes widened into their normal shape and he continued his lecture in a nonchalant tone. "After the people living on the islands were just getting used to their life, fame, and wealth, disaster struck fiercely. The volcanoes on Divite began to smoke. Mount Ash was the volcano that began to erupt first, and did the most damage. Mount Felix, the enormous volcano on Felix, erupted at the same time. Mount Ash and Mount Felix caused incomprehensible damage when they blew their tops off. The caldera on each is said to be gone, so wide now that you wouldn't be able to discern the existence of either among the features of the land. Two other mountains joined in on Divite, and so four volcanoes destroyed Divite Village and all other towns, including those on Felix. It affected the smaller islands nearby as well. For instance, the shores and pools on Gaudium Island were super heated and began to crumble. The eruptions went on for two days straight. Over half of the populations were killed and the rest were injured in some way. Every single soul on those islands fled. People said that the Sacred Islands' inhabitants vowed to never return to those cursed islands. I wonder why they would say that. You'd think that after things settled down they would return. I don't find it very likely that those volcanoes would explode with such fury every year. But there are also tales of a greater evil there that caused everyone to leave and have no desire to return. Not that the volcanic activity wasn't a factor. As I said before, I saw the aftermath of the volcanic eruptions with my very own eyes. I'm no historian, but it doesn't take a learned man to tell what happened there. Divite still lays in ash to this very day." Serulean stared at the deck below his feet.

"That's a bad tragedy," Elijah said gently.

"Mighty sad, yes it is," Serulean agreed. "Those islands were said to have amazing people on them. Magic wielders of all kinds used to live there. Some say that's where the mages came from, but I believe mages existed long before that. But I do believe in one thing—those people were mighty bright. Those mages figured out a way to manipulate light, just as you kids do to water, fire, greenery, and so on. After that was invented, mages were born with that ability. Isn't that something? And the descendants of those mages are living all around this world right now. Sometimes I wonder if the light mages still exist.

"Light mages? You believe in that?" Korina challenged.

Serulean looked at her with a surprised expression. His gray brow came together once more, causing his forehead to wrinkle into several rows. "Why, yes of course! You don't?"

"It seems very unlikely," I added.

"Exactly. I've never heard of it and I don't think anything like that is possible," Korina stubbornly stated.

"Just because you've never heard of something doesn't mean it doesn't exist," Serulean said.

Korina glanced away from the captain and rolled her eyes. Korina obviously didn't believe in light mages. I hadn't even considered if they existed, myself. The captain did have a point, though. I had never heard of the Sacred Islands until this season but the islands had always existed. The Sacred Islands were a wonder, a place full of undiscovered secrets. The people that lived there were supposedly intelligent and clever beings. If they were so amazing, maybe it really was possible for the mages that lived there to manipulate light.

Was light even an element? Could somebody use it during a battle? How would they control it, and would it even be effective? What are the powers of light? I wondered to myself, tuning out the squabbling of Korina and Elijah. Those two were probably arguing again. I ceased my wandering thoughts and returned to the setting of the ship.

"Now, now, kids. Stop arguing about it," Serulean ordered.

Korina had a look of protest on her face. "*I'm* not the one that's making a big deal out of it!"

"Yes you were," Elijah muttered under his breath.

"Shut up," Korina sneered. "I'm just saying that if they really do exist, they would still be here and I for one haven't seen any light mages."

"They could live on the other side of the continent!" Elijah exclaimed with frustration, throwing up his arms.

"Really? Because Elementa is on the shore that's closest to the Sacred Islands!"

"There could've been one left and they could've traveled somewhere far away. You don't know that there aren't anymore of them, Korina. You probably haven't even been out of Elementa since you got here." Elijah glared at Korina, who was glaring back with her usual squinted eyes.

"I'm just saying it doesn't seem very likely," she huffed.

"Enough!" Serulean shouted. "It doesn't matter, okay? Now, there could be some light mages but they certainly don't live here anymore. Let's get off this subject." The captain looked at Tres. "You've been awfully quiet during all of this."

"I'm just waiting to hear more about the islands. There's no use in getting in another argument," she answered, shooting a quick look at Elijah and Korina.

"Yes, yes. The islands. We got off topic. Now, is there anything else you'd like to know about them?"

"You say you've been there," I started. "And you told us what you saw. Is there anything else that you might've left out?"

Captain Serulean rested his chin in his hand. "I might have, yes." He removed his sailor cap and scratched his head, which only had a thin layer of gray hair underneath. "Let me back up. Before I set out on the voyage to the islands, I met an old man back in Elementa."

"And?" Korina prompted impatiently.

"Well, you see, this was an *old* man. He was the kind of man that was hunched over and relied on a walking staff to get around. His face had as many wrinkles as his hands and his head was basically bald. I recall that he approached me when I was on the docks. He asked me if we were going to the Sacred Islands. I was mighty puzzled, for we didn't tell anyone of our destination. I asked the man if he was joking, pretending that I had no intention of going there. I don't know how, but that old geezer had everything figured out. He made it clear that he didn't want me to lie to him because he knew the truth."

"Strange. What's with that old man?" Korina inquired.

"Maybe he'd tell us if you'd stop interrupting," Elijah said.

Korina shot him a menacing glare but kept quiet for once. I was thankful that she had decided to keep her mouth shut. Elijah and Korina had gotten into so many arguments lately. We were all tired of hearing them quarrel.

"This man claimed to have lived on Divite Island. He looked old enough but I still doubted him. I said to him, 'really now? Mister, I don't believe that's possible' and he said 'don't go doubting what a truthful old man says, especially if he was a town crier for most of his life. I can prove it to you.' And he went on talking but I can't remember our conversation now. Just the same, he got me believing and I still believe he was truthful to this day."

"So you just believed something that an old man off the street told you?" Korina asked with her eyebrows raised.

"Just let him continue," Elijah ordered.

"If you had met him, even you would believe it, Korina." Korina snorted in disagreement but Serulean continued. "The old man told me all of the things that I would see and he was right about every one of them. He scared me though when he mentioned that I had a good of chance of not returning. Anyway, the man gave me an object, a little token. It was a smooth stone that's about the size of a regular copper coin, but a little thicker. On the stone was a symbol. I never figured out what the symbol meant but I believe it has some significance. When I asked the man what it meant and why he gave it to me, he refused to tell me. He said 'there are many questions in this world that cannot be answered by others. To find the real truth, we must seek the answers ourselves.' I never forgot those words he said to me on that overcast day."

"Do you still have the stone?" Teressia wondered out loud.

"Yes, I do." Serulean reached into his pocket and revealed a small, light gray rock. It was an oval shape, curved perfectly. On one side was a symbol in an ancient rune. Teressia stared at it with admiration. It was a stone and she was a stone mage. Teressia saw more meaning in it than I could. If it was a fossilized leaf I would have been intrigued, but to me it was just a regular rock.

"It's beautiful," Tres whispered.

"It's just a plain 'o rock, Tres," Korina remarked.

"Maybe to you it is but I see its beauty."

"Isn't it something, though? Look how smooth the edges are. I have a hunch that it's marble. I'm still trying to figure out what it means. The old man claimed to have witnessed the eruptions. Maybe it's connected to that disaster. Or maybe it's connected to why everyone left. I believe that something else scared everyone away. Or maybe it's just a plain old rock like Korina said," Serulean chuckled.

"You believe that something else scared the people away?" I asked.

"Yes." The captain looked away from us and out across the sea. He was looking at the whirlpool, probably trying to figure out how much time we had before we would need to veer off to the side of it. His gaze returned to our circle. In a serious tone he said, "When we left Divite Island that day, it was cloudy, overcast. The wind was blowing strong and the morning fog was still lingering. But I think I saw something. I could've sworn I saw something in those clouds that day." He paused and shook his head.

"What?" Elijah asked.

"I don't know, maybe it was just a shadow of a cloud or my eyes playing tricks on me. I thought I saw some huge shadowy figure flying through the clouds. It was an enormous shadow. It was probably nothing."

A loud thump sounded on the deck. Sailors started to chatter, some laughing. I felt the vibration from the thump on the floor of the deck. I looked behind me to see a sailor sprawled on the deck. He lay on his back and groaned. Some sailors around him laughed and teased him.

"Did you have a nice fall?" one mocked. The crew laughed.

Serulean rose to his feet. "What's going on over here, eh? What's all the chattering about?"

"Old Colt here took a tumble off the shrouds, Captain," a sailor explained.

"He fell off the shrouds? How far up was he?" Serulean questioned.

"Not far up at all, Serulean. He got up about there," a crew member pointed.

Serulean approached the fallen sailor. "Help us all, Colt. What did you do?"

The sailor, Colt, rubbed his eyes and looked up at Serulean. "Father?"

"I'm not you father, boy! Somebody get him up!"

I tore my gaze away from the scene and back to our circle. Korina was laughing at the incident, Elijah was smiling, and Tres watched blankly. I yanked their attention away. "Do you guys think that Serulean really saw something?"

Korina snorted. "Of course not. It was just a cloud."

"Maybe he did see something. Or maybe he didn't," Elijah said.

"It could've been a bird," Tres suggested.

"He said it was huge, remember?" I said.

"Then it was probably a cloud," Korina repeated.

I shrugged. I believed that Serulean had really saw something. It could've been one of those creatures that lived only on the islands. Or maybe it had something to do with all of the dark magic.

Elijah, Korina, and Tres rose to their feet and left me. The three of them walked across the deck, casually talking. I glanced to the side of the ship and gazed at the whirlpool. It seemed to get closer every second. I trembled, suddenly feeling a little sick.

Two sailors caught my attention. They stood on the main deck, talking in hushed voices.

"You remember long ago when we went with Serulean to the Sacred Islands? The air was thick and heavy and full of ash. Hard to breathe. Everything was ominous and unnerving."

"Yes, I vaguely remember. What of it?"

"I don't like that place. There were too many whispers in the air, cries of unknown animals and mysterious creatures. Gives me the shivers. I don't like it, Jade. I could've sworn I saw a ghostly figure there."

"There are no ghosts. They don't exist. Anyway, what can we do about it? We're committed to this voyage and I will keep my word that I gave to the captain, Devin."

"I'm just saying, what if it's not that bad of an idea? You know those two, Natan and Solice, they left. They abandoned the ship. Why would they have done that? Because they were worried and scared."

"There's nothing to worry about, Devin. We've been to this place before."

"It's different this time. We're going for a different purpose. If you change your mind, you know where to find me. Think about it, Jade."

The two sailors separated. *Should I go tell the captain about their conversation?* I decided Serulean needed to know. Two crew members had abandoned the *Naviganti* already; he didn't need to lose two more.

I started across the main deck. I felt the speed of the ship pick up, and it lurched forward abruptly. I stumbled backward, losing my balance. Elijah happened to be behind me and I fell into him.

"'Ey! Watch what you're doing!" he spat. Elijah flailed his arms to try to regain his balance but failed. He tumbled into Korina, who was beside him.

"Get off, you scum!" Korina sneered, and shot a spurt of water toward Elijah. Elijah ducked and the water flew behind him. A sailor was standing a few yards behind Elijah, near the rail of the ship, with a cloth of food in his hand. The water struck the sailor in the neck.

The sailor jumped, startled by the water. The cloth of food in his hand tumbled away as he jumped, flying over the side of the ship. He turned toward the three of us although Korina and Elijah were too busy arguing to notice.

"Why don't you watch where you're falling!" Korina hissed.

"Why don't you get out of my way?" The arguing overlapped and I couldn't understand what the two of them were saying until Elijah brought me into the quarrel.

"*She's* the one who ran into me!" Elijah pointed.

"Hey! It's not my fault the ship lurched forward!" I protested.

The sailor approached us. "That was my lunch!" he whined.

"Well isn't that too bad?" Korina sympathized in mockery.

The four of us continued our squabbling, shouting loudly at each other. I was pretty sure none of us could understand the others, for we were all yelling at the same time.

Captain Serulean broke up the argument. "Hey! Cut it out! Shame on you, Jeril. You know better than to argue like a little kid! I already have to deal with Colt and I am not in the mood for this foolishness."

Teressia snuck up behind us. I was mindful of her presence, but she had to try several times before she could get a word in to us. "Guys—guys." She sighed. "Guys!" Teressia worriedly looked to the bow of the ship.

"What is it, girl?" Serulean asked.

"We're in a current. The helmsman says that we can't get out of it."

"Sure we can," Serulean said.

Teressia shook her head. "No, we can't. It's too late. We're here."

CHAPTER 22

KORINA

I followed Serulean as he sprinted toward the bow of the ship. Ahead of us were threads of spiraling currents, and in the center a gaping black hole. The ship was sucked into the outer currents of the vortex, drawing us closer to the menacing coils of water.

I studied the faces of Teressia, Elijah, and Sage, who had all followed as well. Sage had turned pale and was shaking. Tres stared at the whirlpool vacantly, not taking her eyes off of it. Elijah calmly looked around the sea, seemingly unmoved by the impending danger.

Serulean scrunched his brow together, which he did frequently. "I don't understand," he said. "We turned away from this onto a different course and we still got sucked toward it. I'm afraid luck isn't on our side on this voyage."

"We're going to die," Sage proclaimed. She shivered and squeezed her eyes shut.

"What makes you think that?" Serulean queried.

"We're heading straight toward a whirlpool! We're going to get sucked into it and sink!" Sage exclaimed.

"Can you stop worrying for once?" I demanded. Every time we were faced with an obstacle, Sage would insist that we weren't going to make it. She had no faith in the crew's skills or any of her peers. "We're not going to die! Did we die in those rocks? No! Did we sink when Fortis attacked us? No! Stop saying we're going to die!"

"Korina," Serulean sharply warned. "She's just nervous. That's natural. But Sage, I assure you everything is going to be fine." Addressing all of us he announced, "You kids think that that thing is going to suck us into the bottom of the ocean. That's a fantasy that everyone believes. The worse that can happen is that the ship gets severely damaged and sinks, or gets trapped in the vortex." Serulean started to say more but stopped himself. "I suppose that is bad enough but those possibilities aren't very likely."

"Sink? Trapped? That doesn't seem so unlikely to me!" Sage fretted.

"Relax, Sage," Elijah said. "If the captain says it's not likely to happen, he's right."

"I sure hope I am," Serulean remarked, laughing despite the possible jeopardy. "Based on my experience, the vast majority of whirlpools aren't that powerful. Unfortunately, this one looks like it could be a threat. Whirlpools like this one are called maelstroms."

"Maelstroms?" I asked distrustfully.

"Strong whirlpools," Serulean replied. "If the whirlpool has a downdraft, then it's called a vortex."

"Is this one a vortex?" Elijah wondered.

"Looks like it. I haven't seen any other whirlpool like this one. I'd guess the speed of the current is pretty fast."

"How did it even form?" Elijah asked.

I groaned impatiently. *Stop asking questions and let the man do his job so we won't drown, idiot.*

"Whirlpools are created by the meeting of opposing currents. In an ocean, or sea in our case, they are usually created because of tides. I have to go help Miles and the crew steer us out of here." Serulean dashed across the main deck toward the quarterdeck. Serulean approached the helmsman and swapped places with him. Serulean now steering the ship.

Sage began to speak behind me with a stressed tone. "What if we don't get out of this current? I mean, we shouldn't be in it in the first place."

"Didn't you listen to anything the captain just said?" I snapped. "He said we're going to get out of it and the worse that can happen is a little damage to the ship."

"And it sinks and we die," Sage muttered.

"Stop saying we're going to die!" I demanded. "That's all you can say when we get in any danger!"

"It's a possibility!" Sage defended.

"Stop!" Tres interrupted. "Korina, you need to figure out how to stop arguing with everyone. It's getting old."

"I'll say," Sage mumbled.

Elijah had his back turned to us, leaning up against the rail that faced directly in front of the ship. He was ignoring our babbling and focusing on the vortex. Teressia noticed his silence as I looked at him. She walked over to his side and leaned on the rail as well.

"Anything wrong?" she asked quietly. I could barely hear her; she must have wanted Sage and me to stay out of the conversation.

I silenced Sage with a quick wave of my hand as she began to speak. Elijah answered, "Nothing. I just hope the crew really can get us out of here before it's too late." He kept his face fixed on the vortex. "And it doesn't help when those two are arguing," he added, dropping his voice.

"Hey," I said sharply. "I can hear you, you know. And it's not going to make a difference whether I argue or not."

"Whatever. Like Tres said, it's getting old."

201

The ship lunged forward and we stumbled backward, but for once didn't fall down. The current was speeding up and the crew members rotated the sails in vain. The wind wouldn't get us out of this mess.

"You can feel the ship moving faster," Elijah observed.

The vortex grew in size as we neared it. Shouts were exchanged all over the decks as sailors sprinted around. Serulean was still at the helm, fighting the current with the wheel.

"Don't fight the current, Captain!" a sailor called.

"You're right Miles. Fighting the current is just going to make it worse!" Serulean replied, raising his voice over the wind.

I left the quarterdeck and ran to the helm, tripping every time the speed of the ship changed.

"How are we going to get out of here? The vortex is literally right there!"

"Well Korina, all we can do is try our best. It doesn't look like we'll be able to avoid this maelstrom. Our only chance is to ride the current and hopefully be carried out of it."

"But it spirals downward," I pointed out. My stomach twirled inside of me as my fear grew. What if we really didn't get out of here? *No. We will. I'm not going to be doubtful like Sage.*

"That is true, yes. But we'll see what happens," Serulean said.

"See what happens?" Sage's voice exclaimed from behind me. "You can't just relax and wait for us to drown! You have to do something!"

"Do you have any suggestions?" Serulean challenged. "I know you're panicking, Sage, but there's nothing else we can do."

"Ugh! This is just like the Maze of Stones!" Sage cried as she turned away from the helm.

"Go into the hold, then! Find those two mages or whatever but don't scare yourself by staying up on deck!" Serulean called to Sage. To a sailor he said, "Miles, get over here and steer the ship. I need to take care of some things."

I figured there was nothing better to do than to wait around. I began to go down the steps of the quarterdeck, but flew off them as the ship suddenly veered to the right. I slammed onto the main deck, face first. I groaned after the heavy landing. My foot ached after the impact of my fall; it wasn't fully healed from when I fought against the mutations in the first attack on Elementa.

The next thing I saw was Teressia at my side. "Are you all right?"

"I'm fine," I grunted. I took her hand as she helped me to my feet. I winced as I put weight on my foot.

"What's wrong?" she asked in a concerned tone.

"My ankle is hurt, I think. I'll be fine though," I assured.

The two of us staggered to the side as the ship turned sharply. I peered over the side of the ship from where I stood, seeing that we were on the outer edges of the vortex. I sighed. "It's not as petrifying as I thought it would be."

"What happens when we get into the center of it though?"

I stared at Teressia with realization. "Will we get pulled downward?"

"Captain Serulean said that whirlpools usually aren't very strong. Maybe we'll be okay."

Water splashed up onto the deck as we circled around. The ship swayed to the left and to the right, brusquely rocking. Teressia and I stayed on the floor of the deck, unable to stand.

As we continued to flow along the current, the swaying got sharper and harder to withstand. My head spun and was on the verge of having an intense headache. Tres said something but I couldn't understand her with the wind and water whipping about.

"What?!" I shouted.

"We're not going to get out of here!" she said.

"Yes we will!"

"How?!"

I couldn't answer that question. I fell silent as the ship continued to be battered by the merciless sea. Objects and boxes that were freely lying around on the deck were thrown about. I rolled to the left as a box flew at me.

I could feel the side of the ship that was closest to the center of the vortex dip down into the sea. Water spilled over the side of the ship and spread onto the deck. Sailors scrambled to the water with buckets and hurriedly scooped water off of the deck as quickly as they could.

The hatch to the hold flipped open. Mage Melody's head popped out and she paused to observe our surroundings. With a calm expression she climbed out of the hold.

"Sage said we were in a whirlpool. I suppose she was right," she said.

I nodded from where I was crouched on the deck. Mage Melody crawled toward me and Tres without losing her balance.

"And we don't have a way to get out of this vortex either. Serulean doesn't have a plan as usual," I said.

"What?" Melody asked in shock. "He doesn't have a way to get us out?"

"Nope," Tres affirmed.

I yelped as I helplessly flipped onto my side and slid down the deck. I flung my arms out, trying to grab something to hold onto but there was nothing. My back eventually slammed onto the mainmast. I glanced behind me, seeing a pool of water on the far side of the main deck. I shifted my body and gripped the mainmast so that I wouldn't slide away again.

The ship was helplessly turning around and around. Serulean had decided to let it be carried along by the current but the crew hadn't given up. As soon as the *Naviganti* made the slightest movement they tugged at the sheets, forcing the sails to rotate.

A wave of water splashed over the side of the ship, and I felt the seawater rush onto me. It was soothing in a way, the feeling of water as smooth as sheets flowing over me. The water was refreshing and gave me energy.

I pushed off of the mainmast and clambered up the main deck toward Melody and Teressia. I had an idea that might get us out of the vortex.

"Korina! Are you alright?" Melody asked frantically.

"Yes, but I think I know a way we can get out of this thing."

Melody and Tres exchanged looks. "How?" they asked.

"Mage Melody and I can use our magic to move the water and help us escape."

Melody looked doubtful. "And how do you suppose we do that?"

"I don't know," I admitted. "But we can easily come up with a way."

"Okay," Melody finally said. "But we can't push ourselves too hard. By the way, where's Elijah?"

Tres and I looked at each other. "The last time we saw him was on the forecastle," Tres answered slowly.

"The forecastle? I'm sure I would have seen him if he had gone into the hold. Well I suppose he's somewhere on one of these decks. I hope he hasn't been flung overboard."

Mage Melody and I struggled to get to our feet. Tres disappeared into the hold, not wanting to be slung around the deck like me. Mage Melody and I went to the side of the ship to study how we could change the direction of the water.

"We should tell the captain what we're doing," Melody suggested. I nodded in agreement, but in truth didn't care if Serulean knew or not.

I stayed at the rail as Melody went to the helm. She returned quickly and surveyed the vortex that we were trapped in. While she was doing so, I was distracted by a distant cry.

"Did you hear that?" I asked.

"What?"

I shook my head. I followed Melody's gaze, realizing that we didn't have much time until we were going to be at the center of the vortex.

"How about we both raise this section of the water and move it along, and then cut it across that side, or whichever side we're at when we lift it," Melody suggested, pointing as she described her idea.

I nodded and rose my arms as Melody did the same to hers. Together we raised a whole section of the water, and the *Naviganti* shifted. I had to regain my balance before I could continue.

Mage Melody and I fluidly moved our arms about in a circular motion, commanding the water to flow away from the vortex and carry us out. We were hovering near the center of the vortex when Melody gasped.

"What's wrong?" I said quickly.

"I can't—I'm losing my grip—" Melody gasped again and her arms dropped to her sides. Then she fell to the deck and I couldn't keep my hold on the water. The ship plunged toward the vortex once more, and with a huge splash was sucked into the current. The ship bounced on the waves and I dropped to the deck, and rolled several times before I slung my arms out and got up again. Instead of helping us escape, we had brought the ship closer to the center. I could feel the ship sink deeper into the sea, and more water flooded onto the deck.

"I can't do this alone," I panted. It was too much magic for me to work and I was already tired.

Melody stood up on her feet, then bent over. "I feel sick. I'm sorry Korina but there must be dark magic around. I can't use my magic, just like what happened to Mage Isaac when he was helping Tres."

It was up to me to get the ship out of the vortex. I now knew how Tres felt when she was clearing a path out of those rock formations. I lifted my arms once more and attempted to create a wave. Only a small portion of the water obeyed for a second, then dropped out of my grasp. I panted and bent over on my knees.

"Come on, Korina. You can do this. Summon your magic and strength in your core, let it flow through you like water and surge through your arms. Let them be extensions, a connection to the water—not a commanding gesture. Think hard and focus Korina, but let your mind be calm and clear. Don't think about how it's too much work, or too much of a strain. Move with the water, Korina," Melody instructed.

I tried to do what Melody had said, but kept dropping the water. When I had finally focused and cleared my mind, I was distracted by the same shout I had heard earlier.

I growled to myself. "What was that stupid noise?"

"I heard it too," Melody said. "It sounds like it came from above." I followed her gaze up the mainmast, and into the crow's nest. A small figure was clutching onto the side of it.

"That's Elijah!" I realized. Why the in the name of Lux was Elijah up there at a time like this? The idiot had no sense.

"Why is he up there?" Melody asked, echoing my thoughts.

"Because he's stupid," I muttered under my breath. I ignored Elijah and turned to the sea. Taking a deep breath, I gathered my energy and readied myself, following Melody's instructions. With a focused mind, I strained to move the water.

The *Naviganti* lurched forward, but glided over the vortex. When we were at the outer edges of the whirlpool, I dropped the wave of water. I fell to my knees and struggled to breathe, exhausted. Melody patted my back and told me I had done well.

Even though I had gotten the ship out of the center of the vortex, we were still following its current. I managed a groan when I realized we were about to be trapped in its spiraling currents again.

Mage Melody had realized this too, saying, "Get up Korina. You still have to finish and get us out of here. Remember, clear your mind."

I dizzily straightened up and leaned over the side of the ship. I weakly lifted my arms, but they dropped to my sides. I had no strength left. I couldn't get us out of here. We would be stuck in the vortex and it would be my fault. Sage was right, we would drown. I slumped tiredly to the floor.

"Get up Korina," Melody ordered. "You can't give up. You're telling yourself that you're done but you're not." Melody continued but I couldn't understand. Her words faded into nothing as I closed my eyelids, eyelids that were as heavy as lead.

CHAPTER 23

ELIJAH

I had foolishly climbed up to the crow's nest when we entered the whirlpool, thinking that I would be safer up there. Instead I was grasping the side of the lookout as tightly as I could while the waves battered and jarred the ship from side to side. It was a wonder the ship had not been severly damaged.

I had watched Korina and Mage Melody move the ship out of the whirlpool, but it was threatening to reenter the violent torrent of water. Apparently Mage Melody was unable to use her magic and stood by Korina, guiding her. Korina had done her best to help us escape, but now she was slouched on the deck, unmoving. She *had* to get up and use her magic to get us out. I was dizzy from the ship's continuous circular path.

Taking a deep breath, I hesitantly climbed out of the crow's nest and onto the shrouds. I squeezed the rope tightly as the ship swerved.

My foot lost its hold and dangled in the air, causing my heart to skip a beat. My body leaned in the direction of my foot and I fought to stay upright. As the ship finally slowed down, I found my steadiness once more. Then I slowly descended the shrouds, careful not to lose my footing. It took me longer than usual until my feet felt the familiar hardness of the deck.

I ambled toward Korina, who was still sitting on her rump. Mage Melody was bent over beside her, trying to wake her.

"Finish what you've started, Korina. Get up. You can't give in," she said.

Korina remained silent as Mage Melody continued to shake her. Then she slid on the deck until she was lying on it, no longer sitting.

Mage Melody noticed me. "It's no use," she sighed. "We'll just have to let her rest for a few moments. We can't wait too long though." She looked over the side of the ship and examined the movement of the whirlpool.

"Will she be able to get us out of here?" I asked.

"I hope so. I'm not able to use my magic and apparently Captain Serulean has no plans. I just hope it won't be too much of a strain." Mage Melody pulled up the sleeves of her dark blue dress. "I'm afraid summer is finally here." She murmured words in the ancient language that I couldn't understand. "*Sola-ni*," were the words that I caught.

"What does that mean?" I said.

"It means the season of the sun. I wish we could go back to *Aya-traht*, season of blossom. Meaning, sprouting, blossoming, and an actual flower."

"You mean spring?"

"Yes, spring." She shifted her gaze onto Korina. The young water mage-in-training was seemingly sleeping.

"You know the ancient language?" I prompted.

"The?" Mage Melody chuckled softly. "There are many ancient languages, Elijah. I know the tongue of *Elin Kieht*. It is the old language that existed in the region of Elementum, our region."

"I think I've heard of that. But I thought it was extinct."

"No language is extinct until you lose your own knowledge of it, your own connection to it. You have to remember not to limit your capabilities and your knowledge, Elijah. That's what Ignatia always tells me. She's the one that taught me the language when I first came to the Academy." Mage Melody smiled as she reflected on her memories.

"I didn't know Ignatia knew the language," I said.

"Oh, yes. She knows much more than you think she does."

We both leaned to one side as the ship made a sharp turn. Korina remained motionless on the deck.

"I've had quite enough of this," Mage Melody declared. She bent over and hooked her arms under Korina's, dragging her up onto her feet. Korina's knees buckled and Mage Melody hauled her up again. "Get up, Korina! That's enough!"

Korina moaned and fluttered her eyes. "No, Sara. Stop." She closed her eyes again.

Mage Melody persisted and shook Korina. "I am not Sara. You are on the *Naviganti*, going to the Sacred Islands and we are going to be sucked into a vortex if you don't wake up!"

"What?" Korina stiffened and supported herself. This time her eyes were broad and she was conscious of her environment. "Sorry! I became so tired." She rubbed her face and tugged on her bodice, straightening it out. Instead of her usual riding breeches, Korina wore a skirt that only stretched just below her knees. It had obviously been cut that short, for it was considered improper to wear such clothing. If we were at the Academy, she would have been sent home for wearing that skirt. I wondered how she got by with it even on the ship.

"I'll say," Mage Melody snapped. "If you don't get busy right now, that vortex is going to eat us up!"

Korina hopped to the edge of the ship and took a deep breath. She then stretched her arms out and swiftly motioned to the sea. The water minded her commands and a huge wave formed. The wave rushed under the *Naviganti* and pushed us in the opposite direction.

"Korina Valletta, no!" Mage Melody shrieked.

"What?" Korina frantically yelped. She looked behind her at Mage Melody and lost concentration on her magic. The ship crashed into a fierce current of water and spun halfway around. I flipped onto the deck, barely catching myself with my arms.

"You need to follow the current!" Mage Melody shouted. "And never lose focus in the middle of a big conjuring of magic! You could seriously injure yourself and your magic!"

The ship moaned and leaned toward one side. The babbling of the sailors rose as they scurried up and down the decks.

"You're going to capsize us!" Melody cried.

The masts were already pointing to the side as the ship no longer remained completely upright. Water lapped at the side of the ship and all the sailors not working the sails raced to the other side to balance the weight. I wondered if that was really enough.

Korina turned back to the sea and resumed working her magic. The *Naviganti* slowly became upright again as she created a wave on the side of the ship that was leaning over into the sea. The wave flew up past the side of the ship and pushed it upright once more.

Korina created another wave, this time in the other direction, guiding it along with the current. The *Naviganti* was smoothly pushed out of the whirlpool with the wave. When Korina pushed the ship a safe distance away from the whirlpool, she immediately dropped the wave she had conjured. She gasped for breath, exhausted by the amount of magic she had just used.

The ship was slung to the side when it was released by the wave. The outer currents of the whirlpool were attempting to draw us into the swirling vortex again. This time, however, the crew was at the sheets of the sails and Captain Serulean was able to steer the ship away.

We finally pulled free of the whirlpool and returned to our original course. Korina retired to her cabin, struggling even to walk. Sage never came out of the hold for the rest of the evening and Mage Melody ate dinner with Mage Isaac on the deck. I sat against the mainmast, eating my own dinner.

By this time it was night, and the stars shed their shyness and flickered proudly in the sky. The moon illuminated the sea and cast a white shadow upon the ship. The moon's identical twin danced in the sea, happily riding the black waves. The sails of the ship rustled in the gentle sea breeze. But something seemed wrong about the sails.

I spotted Serulean disappearing into the captain's cabin and quickly stopped him.

"Is the ship okay after today?"

"Do you want the truth or the feeling of safety?" Serulean questioned grimly.

"The truth."

Captain Serulean gave a heavy sigh. "Unfortunately, she's damaged. The sails are torn in some places and—well simply disconnected from some of the sheets if you understand. That means traveling will go a little slower until we can switch out the sails and sew the torn ones back together. Also, the side of the hull is a bit beaten up and a bulkhead has been compromised. The night shift will have to keep an eye on it and make immediate repairs if it gets any worse. I'm sure the hull is fine, though. A few boards are probably busted, that's all."

"Will everything be all right?"

"I sure do hope so." Without another word he disappeared into his cabin.

* * *

The next week was the smoothest sailing we had experienced yet. The sailors had repaired the sails and the hull, and we were traveling at a nice speed. We had encountered another storm, but it was mild and we were smart enough to stay in the hold. Teressia was the first one to be ushered into the hold as soon as the clouds began to gather. Sage had become agitated again, thinking that the storm could possibly capsize the ship. She was also tucked away in the hold.

As we continued to shorten the distance between us and the Sacred Islands, the dark magic became heavier. Mage Melody and Mage Isaac discovered they couldn't use their magic at times. The Lata Sea was mucky from the reeking dark magic, and some even clung to the sides of the ship. Some sailors were forced to scrub it off, and they weren't pleased by doing so. One of the crew members, Jeril, had complained about the smell and fell out of the dinghy that was lowered to the side of the ship. A piece of wood had to be thrown to him so that he could float back and board the *Naviganti* again.

Today had been a pleasant day, with clear skies and a strong breeze. The sun was the only thing that had spoiled the weather. It had beaten down on our backs the entire day and heated the decks. Korina, who usually walked around with no shoes, was forced to wear her plain leather boots.

The hot sun had kept me in my cabin all day, and I was bored. I had not thought to bring a book along with me and I had nothing to do but sleep. When night came, I was wide awake and hungry for dinner.

When I came onto the main deck, I was surprised to see the crew gathered and our party scattered about. It seemed that everyone was weary of the heat and pleased with the cool temperature of the night.

I fetched my dinner from the kitchen and searched for a place to eat. The three girls were huddled together, munching on their food and laughing. I decided not to spoil their company and settled outside the kitchen on the forecastle.

After I finished my meal, I stretched my legs. I didn't want to retreat to my cabin after spending the whole day there. I would walk around the deck, with nothing better to do.

I realized the ceiling of the kitchen was the floor of the forecastle deck. The entrance to the kitchen was beside the steps that led up onto the forecastle, where the bow was. I walked around the sides of the enclosed kitchen, wondering if there was anything behind it. I found another door on one of the side walls. *Does this also lead to the kitchen?* From looking inside the kitchen, it seemed too small to stretch this far back.

I hesitantly opened the door. It easily swung open, revealing hammocks that hung low from the ceiling and a couple of wooden chairs. Of course, it was the sailors' quarters.

The quarters were dark, except for a blue-white glow in a corner of the room. Someone was murmuring quiet words. They were hunched over, sitting in a chair around the light. I wondered why they didn't light an oil lamp.

The door that I had opened shut with a soft bang.

"Who's there?" the sailor demanded. "Jeril, if that's you again, I swear I'll throw you overboard."

I darted behind a fairly large wooden chest. Peering around the corner of it, I could see the sailor on his feet, looking around the room. Suddenly, the door swung open widely and another sailor entered the quarters.

"Devin? Is that you?"

The sailor threw a blanket over the white light and raised a lit oil lamp. *There's no way he could light one that fast. He must have fire magic.*

"Yes, it's me," he said. "Who are you?"

"It's me, Mared," replied the sailor who had just entered the quarters. "Why are you in here alone? Everybody else is outside having a good time."

"Oh I just, uh, I'm just in here doing some work," Devin stammered.

"Ah," Mared nodded. "Working out the shifts for tomorrow?"

"Yes, exactly." Devin was lying.

"Don't work too hard," Mared joked. He left the quarters.

Devin set the oil lamp on the floor and uncovered the light. I squinted, trying to figure out what was making the odd light. I couldn't see what he was doing, for Devin was sitting directly in front of the object. Whatever he was doing, he obviously wanted it to be kept hidden.

I silently and slowly inched forward, peeking out from the side of the chest as much as I could without entirely exposing myself. I could hear Devin whispering into the light, and then noticed that the glow changed brightness and flickered, causing shadows to dance across the walls. It was as if something was *moving* inside whatever generated the light. In a split second the healing injury on my neck burned like flames. I bit my lip to hold back a screech of pain.

A voice answered Devin's whispering, a voice that was unmistakably different from his, deeper and firmer, yet still a quiet murmuring from where I eavesdropped. As Devin shifted into a different sitting position, the object that he bent over was revealed. In the center of a desk, lay a perfectly shaped sphere. Inside it was a dark mist, and a figure. I recognized it as a crystal ball, a circular object that people would use to scry or communicate with.

Devin abruptly flinched and then shielded his eyes as the crystal flashed wildly. I looked away as well. When the blinding flash receded, Devin spoke in urgency. I caught a few words, which mostly consisted of "sorry." The voice boomed at him, causing a humming vibration to pulse through the floor. Devin replied, "I'm telling you the location, Master. You can send them now if you'd like and I'm sure it'll work out as planned." The voice responded to him and began to fade. Devin started to say one last sentence, but the figure vanished. The crystal ball dimmed and became white then clear. Devin rose and tossed a blanket over the sphere. The immense pain on the back of my neck slowly subsided.

I rapidly shrank back behind the chest, wedging myself in between the wall and the wooden piece of furniture. I misjudged my distance and hit the wall, and a thud sounded. Devin heard and whipped around in my direction. I held my breath, fearing that he would hear it.

"Who's there?" he sharply spat.

I continued to hold my breath, gripping my arm as Devin slowly stalked around the room, searching for anyone. He skulked in my direction, taking slow deliberate steps as he gazed around. His head moved up and down, and he peered into corners and behind the scarce pieces of furniture. When he reached the chest I pinched myself, hastily pleading in my head that he would stop. I crouched down lower as Devin's hand appeared on the chest. I could see his head rising above me as he began to push the chest aside. I squeezed my eyes shut and waited for him to begin shouting and scolding me.

I opened my eyes as the chest stopped moving. The door of the quarters had swung open and captured Devin's attention.

"Hey, Devin! You in here? Ah, there you are. Come out and join us; the captain wants you," a voice called.

"Oh, uh, I shall come then, Miles," Devin answered.

"What were you doing in here, anyway?"

"Ah, nothing."

The door closed and the room became pitch black. It was deathly quiet, and I was sure that both sailors had left. I left my hiding spot and sprouted a flame on my fingertip so that I could see. I would search Devin's things before I left the crew's quarters. He seemed suspicious.

I started toward the desk where the crystal ball lay. I gradually edged toward it, making sure I wouldn't trip over anything. I paused when I heard a creak from the floorboards, my heart jumping into my throat. I felt a bead of sweat roll down the side of my forehead. Was someone in the room? Was someone waiting for me to run into them so they could catch me? When I didn't hear another sound, I began moving again. My breath was unsteady and my skin felt sticky. What would happen if someone caught me? How would I explain myself?

I slowly inched forward, fear bottled up in my chest. No, it was in my mind. All in my mind. I trudged forward in the dark room, my small flame producing the only light. My footsteps were heavy and gradual but cautious. I felt as if someone was watching me. I gasped in horror as a rough hand seized my forehead. A panicked shout escaped me and I jumped back throwing my arms up. The flame went out and it became dark once more. I swung my arms wildly, hoping to hit whoever was there. The dark seemed to eat me up; it seemed to swallow me. It knew that I feared it, and whatever was in it. I hurriedly conjured a new flame, throwing it in the direction of the hand. I gasped for breath while hastily searching for the person that touched me. My shoulders slumped in relief as I saw the ropes of a hammock hanging down in front of me.

Pushing the hammock aside, I came to the desk. I reached out a shaky hand and swiped away the blanket. Remembering the oil lamp, I blindly groped the floor for it. When I had the lamp lit, I set it on the table and examined the crystal. It had thin etches that ran all over it, like scratches on glass. They intersected and crossed each other, and faded away in some areas. A mixture of clear and clouded regions randomly stretched across its surface, and its color was a faint shade of white. I ran a finger over a smooth portion of the cold crystal, examining it. There was no residue from its last usage. I covered the crystal with the blanket once more.

The hammock next to the table was obviously Devin's. Another navy colored blanket was tossed over some objects that were placed on a small shelf. Devin is very secretive, I thought to myself. I bent over and yanked the blanket off, seeing three small wooden boxes. On the edges were gold painted metal plates that served as decorative pieces. Teressia would know at once what kind of metal it was, and if it was really gold or just painted gold.

Unfortunately each box had a lock that ran across the top. I picked up one of the boxes and studied the lock that sealed it shut. As I did so, my neck screamed in pain. I instinctively dropped the box and clutched the back of my neck. The box fell with a clang onto the wooden planks of the floor. The pain of the wound eased. I then quickly bent over and picked up the box again, and the pain returned. This time I gritted my teeth and gently set the box on the shelf. Whatever was in that box made my injury received from the mutation blaze with intense pain.

I sat perched on my knees in front of the shelf. I felt like I needed to open the boxes that belonged to Devin. It was as if he was hiding something huge—the way he snuck around the crew's quarters, used the crystal ball in secret, and now locked up mysterious contents in finely crafted boxes. The fact that spiked my curiosity and alarmed me the most was the stinging in my neck when I contacted the boxes, and when Devin was bent over the crystal ball.

I slid my hands around on the planks of the floor, cringing when a splinter bit into my rough palm. I should've known better, I thought. I picked out the splinter and dropped my hands to the floor once more. My hands felt a small, cold thin object. The object felt like a splash of ice-water on a harsh winter's night. I picked up the object and squinted at it, bringing it closer to my face. It was a slender piece of metal, about the size of a nail. An idea hit me like a blow to the face. *Maybe it's a key to the boxes.*

I gingerly and delicately slid the metal into the key hole. I heard a soft click and felt the lock release its tight hold.

The door swung open behind me. I slid the metal into a pocket in my breeches and whipped around to see Mage Melody and Mage Isaac standing in front of a couple of sailors.

"Elijah Elsbade, what are you doing?" Mage Melody demanded crossly. She had the same menacing edge to her tone just as Korina often did.

"Yes, please explain yourself," Mage Isaac said, a little more coolly.

"Um, well, you see—"

Mage Melody raised her thin eyebrows. Her arms were sternly folded over her chest, a gesture that signified impatience, irritancy, and seriousness.

I felt my shoulders slump. I shamefully clambered to my feet and faced the two mages that waited for an explanation. "I was just exploring the ship," I began. "And happened to find the crew's quarters by accident—"

"Accident, hm?" Mage Melody interrupted. I had never seen her so angry, let alone chastising anyone. She spoke with a harsh and firm tone like Korina and scolded like Headmaster Ignatia. I couldn't imagine her being anything but calm and kind.

"Yes... but then I decided to walk around and I saw some interesting knick-knacks. I just wanted a better look, that's all."

"You weren't planning to steal any of 'em, were you, boy?" a sailor challenged.

Mage Melody cut me off before I could reply. "You look mighty suspicious, Elijah. Get out of here and stay out. I'll confine you to your cabin for the rest of the night and the morning if you don't listen. I have half a mind to already. You're lucky I'm not the Headmaster, who wouldn't think twice about restricting you to your cabin for a week."

I obeyed and disgracefully exited the quarters with the two mages on my heels. Korina, Sage, and Tres sat in a line in front of the forecastle, watching me with my head hung in shame and the two adults flanking my side. Korina seemed to slyly smile in amusement, while Sage rolled her eyes and Tres stared blankly.

When I was left alone Korina spoke to me. "Did someone get in trouble?"

"Yes, Elijah what happened?" Tres joined.

"Nothing," I said flatly. I tried to brush the situation aside, but Korina kept persisting.

"Aw, come on. Why don't you tell us? I'm sure it can't be *that* bad."

"I don't want to talk about it, okay?" I snapped. I decided that I had had enough of her and started toward the hold. I needed sleep anyway. The moon had already climbed high in the sky, foretelling the end of the night.

Behind my back I heard Korina. "What's the matter, crab?"

I ignored her and entered the hold. Inside my cabin my mattress welcomed me. The sheets swallowed me up and the quilt hugged me, luring me into the dream world.

* * *

I was peaceful, laying delicately on a bed of clouds. My eyes were not closed tightly, but lay comfortably shut. I think I had dreamt, but couldn't remember. I was suddenly disturbed, and had the feeling that someone was watching me.

I fluttered my eyes open and listened. At the entrance to my cabin I heard whispers and movement. Then a soft voice called to me. "Elijah? Are you awake?"

I grunted in reply. I raised up and rubbed my eyes. I saw nothing but pitch black, and created a tiny flame. It revealed three shadowy figures. The slim figure and short body of Sage, the tall and slender

Tres, and the filled-out stature of Korina. Tres was barely taller than Korina, but I towered over them all. Even in the dark, Tres and Sage's pale skin glowed. Korina's was the opposite; she had a golden shade of skin, more like mine. My skin tone was bronzed heavier than even hers.

"What do you three *girls* want?" Didn't they understand that I didn't care about their gossip? Couldn't whatever they had to say wait until morning? This trip would be a lot easier if there was at least one other guy my age. If only August had come, I sighed to myself. Having three girls aboard the ship caused a lot of drama. My thoughts wandered into various subjects that weren't relevant, such as how girls could become so annoying. Why did they always think so highly of themselves? Why did they draw attention to themselves?

Teressia interrupted my thoughts. "We wanted to say we're sorry—Korina wants to say she's sorry."

"For what?" Korina snorted.

Sage must have stomped deliberately on her foot, for Korina grumbled an "ow."

"Okay, I'm sorry for talking to you like that earlier," she said. In the light produced by the flame I could see Korina roll her eyes.

"That wasn't very sincere," Sage mumbled.

"Couldn't that have waited until tomorrow?" I asked in annoyance.

"There was something else we wanted to tell you, well rather ask," Tres announced.

"Couldn't that have waited until tomorrow?"

"No!" Korina suddenly snapped. Her patience was running thin as usual.

"Okay," I sighed tiredly. "What is it?" Maybe I could grab a few more ounces of sleep if they would hurry up.

"What were you doing in the crew's quarters, Elijah?" asked Sage. "We have decided that you weren't in there just because you were bored. Why were you in there?"

"Was there something odd in there?" Tres added.

"Not particularly..." I lied. Should I keep it a secret or should I trust the girls? I knew that Tres was fine, but Sage and Korina? Sage would probably try to persuade me that it didn't happen, and Korina might blab to everyone on the ship. Maybe it was best to keep it to myself.

"You're lying." Korina saw right through me.

"You are, aren't you, Elijah?" Tres challenged. Her dark gray eyes glinted knowingly in her small round face in the dim light.

Sage persisted as well as the other two. "What are you hiding, Elijah? Just tell us for goodness' sake! You might as well trust us—we're going to be stuck together on the same ship for a few more weeks, not to mention the return journey."

I remained silent for a few moments, thinking. Should I deny it again or tell them? Maybe Sage had a point, but that didn't mean I liked her. She seemed okay in the library when we first met, but now she came off as someone who was cocky and superior to everyone else. And then there was Korina.

"Well?" Tres prompted.

"Yes, we would like to know before the sun rises," said Korina.

"Fine. Yes, I saw something."

Sage dipped her head expectantly. "Would you like to tell us what you saw?"

"Oh, uh, yes. It was all dark in there but someone was alone in the room. It was one of the sailors, Devin is his name. He was using a crystal ball."

"A crystal ball?" Sage said disbelievingly. "No one uses those things, and certainly no one on this ship. In modern days it's all mirrors and looking-glasses."

"No, I'm positive it was a crystal ball."

"It doesn't matter *what* it was, just tell us if you saw anything!" Korina demanded impatiently.

I carefully explained what I had witnessed, all the way until I had discovered the locked boxes. I left out the part where I had found the key.

"He could have anything in there. Maybe it was just personal items," Sage suggested.

"But it made my neck hurt. Ordinary things don't do that."

"I thought your neck was healed," Tres said softly.

I shook my head. "Not quite, though Mage Melody's remedy did help. Can I go to sleep now?"

"No, we need to discuss what we think you saw," Tres declared.

Korina yawned. "Can we make it fast then?"

"What more is there to discuss? I already told you everything I saw and there's nothing more to it."

"Maybe there is," Sage said. "We know he's hiding something, but what? And maybe it has to do with dark magic since it made your neck hurt. The neck wound itself was infected with dark magic by that mutation, right?" I nodded my head in response. Sage continued, "Then maybe Devin is working for an evil force. Or maybe he's the reason we've had so much bad luck on this voyage."

Korina snorted. "Yes, of course. He just created the vortex and caused us to get stuck in the Maze of Stones. Even though he's on the ship as well, he's trying to kill us all."

"Whatever," Sage sighed. "You know what I mean. Or maybe you don't."

"How about we report this to the captain in the morning?" Tres suggested. "I'm going to my cabin."

We agreed with Tres's plan and the three girls left. *Finally, peace.* I dove back into the sheets and buried myself into sleep. It felt as if I had only awakened a minute later when I felt the ship rock and creak. Footsteps thudded above me on the forecastle, probably coming from the crew's quarters. Questioning voices were tossed back and forth. What was going on with the ship?

I sat up and rubbed my eyes. I didn't think I could go back to sleep with all the commotion on the decks. What if something bad was happening? I was worrying too much to feel safe. Maybe I should go up on the deck and see what's going on, I thought.

As soon as I swung my legs onto the floor, I heard the voices rise in volume, until they were panicked shouts. Something heavily crashed onto the main deck with a loud *boom!* More frightened yells. Did I hear a howl on the decks?

My curtain was hastily flapped open by Mage Isaac. "Elijah? Stay in here, okay? Do *not* leave this cabin unless an adult tells you to, or unless this ship is sinking! If you hear anyone coming, hide and don't make a sound."

"Why? What's—"

Mage Isaac disappeared behind the curtain, gone. I pushed the drape aside and peered out. Mage Isaac was dashing up out of the hold. *What is going on?*

I froze as I heard howls and screeches from the deck. They sounded very close to where I stood in the hold. Men screamed and yelled. It sounded as if the mutations were attacking Elementa. I decided to find out what was happening.

I slowly opened the hatch of the hold, trying to be as quiet as possible. I didn't open the hatch any more than a small slit, a slit wide enough to observe the deck. Were we being attacked by pirates?

I think I stopped breathing for a moment. In front of my eyes, lit up by the light of the moon, was a swarm of flying, vicious attacking animals. Only they weren't animals. They were mutations.

CHAPTER 24

AUGUST

*E*lementa had been lucky over the past week. Surprisingly, mutations hadn't attacked the city since their last appearance. I was astonished that the mutations hadn't decided to invade the city in my honor, because of how I had been carelessly caught and dragged to the nest of the slimy monsters. Maybe it was a bad thing that the mutations were minding their own business, I thought to myself. What if they were becoming more intelligent and stronger while they kept to the sick shadows of Shrouded Forest? I dismissed the thought. Elementa wasn't in the best state to handle the creatures of the dark magic. Especially Ignatia, who was ill with worry and anxiety about the party that had been sent to the Sacred Islands. After I had recounted the riddle to her, she instantly unraveled its meaning and then isolated herself in the Academy, rarely exiting her quarters or her office. Ignatia had been acting strangely, or at least not her usual self. She cancelled all of my combat lessons and told me we would work later.

I sat up in my bed and rubbed my eyes. Last night was unwilling to let me get a speck of sleep and the morning's light ordered me to rise. The glass window in my dorm vomited sunlight across the room in spite of the sheer gold curtains that covered the window. At night the curtains would become solid, but in the day they would be as clear as a crystal goblet.

I tiredly threw off the sheets and attempted to shrug off sleep as I clambered out of bed. There was no use in trying to get a few more minutes of rest. Besides, Headmaster Ignatia did not tolerate people who overslept. Even though I probably wouldn't have any training or lessons today, it was time to get out of my dorm. Maybe I should talk to Headmaster Ignatia today, I thought. I hadn't told her about the strange magic I had used against the mutations a week ago. Maybe today was the time to tell her.

I quickly dressed and stepped out into the empty hall outside of my room. The floor was crafted from a smooth stone, and seemed to reflect the barren and cold absence of people. The walls of the corridor had decorative white columns on them, with elaborate designs engraved into them. The Academy had spared no expense on minute details of décor.

After descending an ornate staircase I was on the first floor of the Academy. I sought out the kitchen in almost no time; after living in the Academy for awhile, I had memorized most of its floor plan. I retrieved breakfast from the kitchen and ate in silence. Since it was a weekend the Academy seemed more relaxed. Fewer people roamed the halls in haste. Most residents of the extravagant building were either out in the city or in their quarters.

I decided to find Ignatia. She needed to know I had found my magic and I was worried about her. The idea that the people venturing to the Sacred Islands were being sent to their doom stressed me, but not as much as Ignatia. Surely she wasn't blaming this disaster on herself?

I rapped on the elaborately carved, dark mahogany door of the Headmaster's office. I heard an anxious voice plead for me to wait a moment and then Ignatia appeared.

Ignatia's appearance startled me. Dark circles swept under her eyes and her hair was disheveled. Dark curls stuck out in various places and her usual golden skin color was pale instead, especially her face. Ignatia's regularly neat robe was littered with wrinkles. She looked as if she had not slept in days.

"Yes, August?" she asked expectantly. Her tone had lost its firm confidence and authority. It seemed wiry and softer today. My concern for the Headmaster grew since I had last seen her.

"Are you feeling all right, Headmaster Ignatia?" I worriedly questioned.

She brushed a black lock of hair from her forehead and knitted her slender eyebrows together. "Whatever do you mean, child?" There was an apprehensive edge to her voice.

"You seem… different today."

"Different? How so?"

"Tired, Headmaster. Have you gotten enough sleep lately?"

"You sound like that blasted healer, August!" Ignatia exclaimed, her old self slightly seeping back into her speech. "No, I haven't been sleeping well. That's not why you came, is it?"

"No, mistress. When I reported my run-in with the mutations last week, I left out an event."

Ignatia shut her eyes and brought a palm to her forehead, rubbing it. "Not about the mutations again. I've heard enough about those dung creatures to last me for a lifetime."

I grinned at her choice of words. "It's not necessarily about the mutations, Headmaster."

"Whatever you say. I suppose I better let you come in and tell me about it then." Ignatia opened the door wider and brought a hand to my back, sweeping me into her office.

The room was not brightly lit; the window had thick navy curtains drawn tightly. Dim lights hung on the walls and a large desk stretched across the floor that lay directly in front of the door. The desk matched the dark wood on the door of the office. Behind the desk was an expansive bookcase, crammed with books and parchments and scrolls. A dark red rug extended like a path that led further into the room. It traveled past the window, which was to the right of the bookcase, and ended at curtain that was drawn back. Behind the curtain was a corner of the room with a lower ceiling, an alcove, an area where two cushioned chairs sat lazily. On the far opposite side of that area (which was as far as the office went on the right) was a dark hallway, to the left of the bookcase. The hall was as short as it was narrow, but it was too dark to make out anything in the space to which it led.

Ignatia went behind the desk and sat down in a large chair. She motioned to me to sit down across from her in one of two chairs. Ignatia folded her hands on the desk that separated us. "Now what did you want to tell me?"

"When I was attacked by mutations, I fought back—"

"I would assume so, if you had any brains."

"—yes, but something happened. I was trying to defend myself when all of the sudden I shot light out from my palms. I think it was some sort of magic, Headmaster Ignatia."

She raised her eyebrows and turned her head by the slightest amount. "Really, now? Light, you say? Are you sure, August?"

"Very. There's no other way to describe it."

"Then it seems as if you do have magic of your own, light magic. To be honest, I expected something different than magery, but it seems as if I was wrong. And that doesn't happen very often," she added under her breath.

"Excuse me, but I have never heard of any kind of magery that deals with light. Are you sure that's the kind of magic I have?"

"Yes, August. There are few that possess the magic that I assume you have. And few know that it exists. It's called exactly what you would've guessed: a light mage. Mages that manipulate the element of light."

"Headmaster Ignatia, are you sure that such a thing exists?"

Ignatia scowled at me and tilted her head in impatience. She got out of the chair and turned her back to me as she rummaged through shelves of the bookcase. When she had pulled out the book she was searching for, she plopped in front of me on the deck, and sat down. Flipping it open, she pointed to the text. She kept her finger on the words and grabbed a pair of glasses that lay on the desk, on a stack of papers. When she had perched the reading glasses on her nose, she read. "Light mages were said to have originated from the Sacred Islands. The magic wielders of the Sacred Islands were known for creating new techniques and styles of magic. They were advanced in these ways and even developed a new element that mages could wield. After the inhabitants had dispersed from the islands, descendants of light mages could scarcely be found in areas such as the region northwest of Lux, Northern Osen, and even in the Celestial Islands." Ignatia looked up at me with raised eyebrows. Taking off her glasses she asked, "Now do you believe me?"

I nodded. "But are you sure *I'm* a light mage?"

Ignatia sighed in exasperation. "Yes, August!" she said in an irritated tone. She sounded like herself with that tone.

"But you haven't even seen me use my magic."

"August!" she warned. "I will see you tomorrow when I feel better. Right now I can't stop thinking about my two mages and the four students I sent to the Sacred Islands. I don't know how to get word to them to let them know that the expedition needs to be abandoned."

"Abandoned?"

"August, if I let them step foot on Divite Island, they'll most likely die! I don't know what kind of evil rests there, but it's more powerful than I imagined. I mean, have you seen what has been taking place around us? Mutations have formed *speech!* They have grown in both strength and numbers, and a great distance separates them from the Sacred Islands."

I followed Ignatia's logic. "You should try to stop thinking about that for a day," I suggested.

"No, August. I need to find a way to communicate with the *Naviganti* before it's too late. Maybe there's a looking-glass on the ship."

"Looking glass?"

"Do you not know anything, August? What do they teach people in Soror," Ignatia murmured to herself. "It's like a mirror or a crystal ball that people use to see one another. Do you understand?"

"I think?"

Ignatia sighed. "If the captain has one of those on the ship, I can talk with them. I just have to send my magic through one of the looking-glasses here."

"I thought you were a mage?"

Ignatia smiled mischievously. "I am. But I keep people wondering."

"So you are a mage? What kind?"

"Anyway," Ignatia said, ignoring my question, "I need to find a way to stop the ship."

"You think the expedition is too dangerous now?"

"Definitely. In fact—"

A knock thumped on the door behind me.

"Looks like we have company," Ignatia remarked as she headed to the door. The Headman of Elementa was revealed, Headman Gileon. He was very short and slightly plump. He wore fancy garments—a cloak that was draped over his shoulders, gold rings on his fingers, and a blue tunic over a plain silk shirt.

"What do *you* want?" Ignatia spat.

Gileon looked like he was sweating. "Ignatia, I need to talk to you. Alone," he added, throwing a glance my way.

"It cannot wait?"

"No, Ignatia. I need to speak with you now." There was an urgent tone embedded in his words.

"Fine. I will drop what *I'm* doing to speak with *you*." Ignatia looked at me with an apologizing expression. "Do you mind, August?"

I left the office. Gileon was obviously worried about a matter that was to be kept secret. I knew I was supposed to leave the area completely; this would not be a brief discussion and Ignatia would search for me later in the day if she wished to continue our conversation. Instead I quietly pressed my ear to the door and strained to hear. I eventually heard Gileon's stressed voice.

"...in debt with Fortis. That's one of the reasons they declared war, Ignatia. But you mustn't tell a soul, or else the city council will impeach me from the Headman position."

Ignatia's angry voice vibrated through the door. "Impeach you from—! You are the worst—gah! What were you thinking, Gileon? You don't have a single brain cell in that fat little head of yours, do you? Debt! And you didn't tell any members of the council! What did you think—that the debt would just magically vanish into thin air?"

"I know, it was stupid of me—"

"Stupid doesn't begin to describe it!"

"I know—"

"No, I don't think you do know."

"Okay, okay. Yes, I didn't—"

"Perhaps impeachment is not such a bad idea—a fitting end for a corrupt and incompetent politician."

"Impeachment isn't my main concern right now, Ignatia. The Headman of Fortis swore that he would have me hanged if I don't have it paid within two weeks! They're building a gallows right now!" Gileon cried with despair and panic. I imagined him on his knees in front of Ignatia.

"Hm. Maybe that wouldn't be so bad either. No, I mustn't think like that, it's wrong. Well what do you want me to do about it?"

"I don't have enough money for this. I was wondering if the Academy could—"

"Don't you dare! Don't you dare expect the Academy to take out its own money to clean up *your* mess!"

"Please consider, Ignatia—"

"Do you have any other matters you'd like to discuss?"

"No, not particularly—"

"Then rid me of your pitiful presence!"

"Well, there is one more thing before I leave. I'm afraid without the Academy's help I won't be able to pay in time. I don't want to be executed, so I have decided to join Elementa's troops in the war with Lux. Of course, I won't fight but I can lead the troops and discuss battle plans with the commanders."

"So your solution is to abandon ship? You're just going to leave the city because of your inability to pay off a debt? You are a sad man, Gileon. How you were elected Headman is beyond me!" Ignatia exclaimed, her voice gradually rising.

"Yes, yes. But while I'm away, I've decided to leave Elementa in your hands. I'm trusting you to govern the city and keep it safe with all of this mutation business going on."

"I have to manage the Academy and look after its students, plus oversee the mages in defense of Elementa while the troops are at war. And now you want me to take charge of the city too? Leave, Gileon. I will come to the temple and speak with you when I have cooled off."

"But Ignatia—"

"I said leave!"

More protests sounded from Gileon as he neared the door. I jumped away and searched for a place to hide. There were two doors next to the office. I ran to one and yanked on the handle. The door didn't budge, for it was locked. The handle of Ignatia's office door turned. I held my breath and tried the next door. It easily swung open, revealing a closet. I hopped into it and shut the door noiselessly as Gileon exited Ignatia's office. I stood with my hand on the knob, waiting. I stepped back, knocking something over with a loud clatter. I scolded myself and swung around. A stack of brooms was scattered on the floor. I bent over and began to pick them up. As my hand came into contact with one, I felt a shiver go up my arm. It was as if I had used some of my magic, apparently my "light" magic. Were these brooms magical? *Of course, stupid. This is the Academy. They must be witches' brooms. Or am I just plain stupid? This is just a custodian's closet.*

I leaned the brooms against the wall as they were before I had knocked them over. I turned my head, looking at the back of the closest. There was a stack of mops, just like the brooms. I carefully made my way to the mops and picked one up. *It's so dark in here I can barely see.*

I brought my other hand that wasn't grasping the mop in front of me. Closing my eyes, I cleared my mind and pretended that I was about to fight in a combat practice. I thought of light, a glow, a lantern. I opened my eyes to see a tiny orb of light in my palm. I smiled at myself. I had worked my own magic, this time on purpose. The orb of light jumped from my hand. I yelped and reached for it, but I couldn't grasp the light. My hand passed through it as if it was air. The light bounced onto the mop and then to the floor.

The mop felt like it squirmed in my hand as my gaze followed the leaping light. I gasped in surprise and stared at the mop. It was *moving*, as if it had life. The mop jumped out of my hand like the light did and danced to the floor. It seemed as if it was searching for something, for it rotated and then bounded to the back of the closest. It dipped its handle down to the other mops, as if it was waking them. The pile of mops stirred, until all of them danced around like the first one. The mops were full of magic, and my light had activated them.

The mops pushed past me and clustered at the door, waiting for it to open. I made my way to the door, in front of the mops and held my hands out.

"No, stay here," I ordered them. I opened the closet door slightly and peered out to make sure no one was there. The next thing I knew, I was knocked to the ground and trampled by mops, which caused the door to swing all the way open. The mops marched out into the hall, being led by the small orb of light.

"No! Stop!" I pleaded in a whisper. The mops ignored me. "Come back!" I cried.

I held my breath as the mops turned a corner, leaving me alone. When would they stop? When would they go back to sleep? And where would a bunch of cleaning instruments go, for that matter? Not to mention my magic on the loose in the form of a ball of light.

I hurried back to the closest to shut the door. Before I did, I fixed my vision on a broom. If the mops had magic in them, surely the broom did. I tried to resist the urge to take a broom but failed. What was the big deal anyway? I would just try it out for one night and then immediately return it. I tried to ignore the voice that warned me that this was a bad idea. The voice seemed to say, *just think about how well your encounter with the mops went. Do you want that to happen again?*

I shut the closet door and rushed to my dorm. I tucked the broom under my bed and then left my dorm, deciding that I should go outside of the Academy. What if I ran into the wandering mops? How would I explain that? And how mad would Ignatia be if she found out I was the cause of it?

I was entering the student area of the Academy, heading for the main entrance when I heard women chattering in puzzled voices.

"Where did the mops come from this time?"

"Why are they marching around the Academy?"

"Who is responsible for this monstrosity?"

"Someone find Headmaster Ignatia, or at least the head custodian!"

I hurried away and out of the Academy.

* * *

I was in my room, closing the curtains for the night when a knocking came at my door. I answered, surprised to see Ignatia.

"I have something to ask you," she said irritably.

"Um, yes?" I tried to sound innocent and clueless.

"Today I got reports of marching mops roaming around the Academy. In fact, I had to deactivate them myself because some people are too mindless to think. But do you know the strangest thing of all about it?"

"What?"

"A little sphere of light was leading them around. Do you know anyone in the Academy that can do that sort of conjuring?"

"Uh—"

"What were you thinking? And where did you find those mops? No, forget the mops right now. Why did you try using magic on your own? You haven't received any instruction yet! What if you had decided to make something bigger, hm? Judging by today's events, it most certainly would have escaped and caused destruction to this building! And you could've fainted from exhaustion!"

I hung my head in shame, staring at Ignatia's feet. "I'm sorry. I shouldn't have—"

"No, you shouldn't have. And about the mops—don't mess with those blasted mops unless I grant you permission! Those things don't listen to *anyone*! Imagine if they had found buckets of water! That would have been quite messy. The irony in that last sentence alone is ridiculous," Ignatia sighed, releasing her anger. "Tomorrow I want you at the courtyard at eight—regular time. I've been putting off your lessons all week. And I'll make sure to start teaching you how to use your magic—but don't expect too much. You will only be learning the basics. As you saw today, magic can easily get out of control. Goodnight, August."

"Get some rest, Headmaster." I closed the door and knelt beside my bed, groping for the broom. Once I had found it, I slid on my Academy robe over my plain shirt and breeches and quickly dashed down the halls.

I stood outside one of the sides of the Academy, careful to make sure it wasn't the side where Ignatia's quarters were located. I positioned the broom and slung a leg over it, trying to figure out how the broom worked.

I tapped the broom twice. I hit it with a larger amount of force. Nothing. I inhaled slowly and then exhaled. Nothing. I thought the broom might be similar to the mops, so I tried to conjure light, despite Ignatia's warnings. I remembered my motions from earlier and repeated them, hoping to conjure another orb of light. Nothing.

"Why isn't this working!" I exclaimed aloud, banging my fist on the broom. A stream of light flickered out of my hand, flowing into the broom. It wobbled and then began to rise.

I lost my balance as the broom slowly ascended. I leaned to the side and gripped as hard as I could, feeling a force push me to the side. I yanked my hands to the side and the direction of the broom changed. I regained my balance, but then lost it and hung on the other side.

I almost fell a couple of more times. When the broom finally stopped ascending, I was really high off of the ground. I looked down, and to my horror the ground distorted beneath me. I was far above the highest tower of the Academy. I leaned forward unsteadily and slowly, and dipped the broom down. I slid forward, and almost plummeted off the broom.

It took a few minutes of flying in circles until I gained balance and control. Then I directed the broom toward Soror, where my family was. *I could go back to Soror. Ignatia wouldn't want me to though. But I could go home right now, back to Mother and Father and the rest of my family.*

I started to urge the broom to Soror when a flicker of light in the direction of the Lux Mountain Range grabbed my eyes. I then saw hundreds of lights, bobbing dimly in the distance. The lights stretched for seemingly miles, in a huge bunch that dominated the land in front of the base of the mountains. A realization hit me like the stifling summer air. Those lights were an army, and the army was marching this way.

CHAPTER 25

TERESSIA

*A*fter Mage Melody had burst into my cabin and ordered me to stay there, I became worried. Crashes and thumps vibrated the deck above me. It sounded as if a riot was taking place on the main deck. Yowls and shrieks could also be heard, and they sounded inhuman.

Mage Melody had told me to hide quietly in my cabin if I heard anyone coming, and only to come out if I was sure the person was someone I knew. I became anxious and wondered what could be happening. We were in the middle of the sea, so what could be attacking us? Was it another ship? Did sailors from another ship board ours?

I sat on my mattress, taking shallow breaths. I suddenly felt trapped, as if the walls of the cabin were shrinking, growing closer. I closed my eyes and tried to think of earth and stones. In reality, I was surrounded by water, enclosed in a sea. The hold itself was underwater, I was underwater...

My eyes popped open as a loud *bang* boomed directly above me. I jumped, startled by the noise. *I can't stand this. I can't just sit here and be eaten by fear while I wait.* No, there was no escaping fear and anxiety right now.

Soft footsteps in the hold alarmed me. I flung myself off the mattress and dove behind it, between the mattress and a wall. The footsteps stopped, and the person didn't seem to keep walking, but stood there unmoving. I held my breath until I couldn't, then slowly got to my feet. I decided to swallow my fear and face whoever was out in the hold.

I gripped the curtain with pale sweaty palms. When I mustered the courage, I shakily pushed it back by a small amount. In the hold stood Korina, lacing up the last section of her bodice. Under that she wore a basic white blouse and loose trousers with leather boots that stretched halfway up her shins. In her belt pouch a silver dagger winked.

"Korina!" I whispered.

She looked up and looked around until her eyes found me. "What?" she asked in a petulant tone.

"What are you doing? Didn't Mage Melody tell you to stay in your cabin?" I continued to whisper in a hushed voice.

"Well yeah, but you can't seriously expect me to stay in that worm's hole."

"But something dangerous is going on up there!"

Korina shrugged nonchalantly. "Well—"

A soft thud caused both of us to freeze. I jumped and Korina whipped her head in the direction of the hatch. Elijah clambered down the steps.

"You scared the life out of me, Elijah!" Korina scolded angrily. "What in the name of Lux are you doing?"

"We're being attacked by winged mutations!" he exclaimed.

I felt my mouth open in fear and my breathing ceased for a moment. "What?" I attempted to say, but my throat dried out and no sound escaped.

"That's impossible. Mutations don't have wings and they're all the way back in Elementa."

Elijah shook his head in disagreement. "No, Korina. See for yourself."

She obeyed and trudged to the hatch, opening it slightly. Screeches flowed into the hold as Korina stared with unblinking eyes. "If you were ever right about anything, this is it."

"I don't think I can just stay here in the hold while men are being slaughtered," Elijah said.

"Me either. I have magic that I can use and I intend to do just that."

"I'm not going to let you get all the credit. I'll help," Elijah said.

To my disbelief, Korina and Elijah started toward the hatch. "What are you two doing? Didn't you hear Mage Melody? She said to stay in the hold!" I protested.

"You want to stop us?" Korina challenged. She continued to the hatch and flipped it completely open. She and Elijah disappeared into the storm. The hatch closed behind them with a clunk.

I sighed helplessly. What if Korina and Elijah got hurt up there? It would be my fault for just letting them leave the hold while I idly stood by. How would I explain this to Mage Melody and Mage Isaac? Screams erupted once more from above. *I hope that's not Elijah or Korina.*

Then I remembered Sage. She must still be in her cabin, hopefully not as dumb as Korina and Elijah to wander out on deck. I flinched as more heavy footsteps and crashes roamed above me on the ship's deck. I decided to check on Sage and get out of the exposed area in the hold. As I did so, worry flooded in from the edges of my mind. I prayed that Korina and Elijah wouldn't get themselves killed.

I hesitantly knocked on the thick curtain of Sage's cabin. No answer came. "Sage?" I called. Still no answer.

I swept back the curtain and stuck my head in the room. It would be rude to barge into the cabin uninvited, so I was careful to keep my feet outside. I surveyed the cabin, searching for any sign of Sage. A shift in the sheets on the mattress caught my attention.

"Sage? Is that you?" I tentatively drew closer to the mattress that was tucked into a corner of her cabin. On the floor behind the mattress was a bundle of sheets. Half the bundle was on the mattress and the other half was covering a body. I bent over the mattress, steadying myself by resting my hands on the edge of the bed.

A hand appeared out of the sheets. It struggled to push back the sheets and then Sage's head appeared.

"Tres?" She stared up at me with wide hazel eyes, revealing faint freckles dotted across her nose. Wisps of her dark ginger hair stuck out of the linens that she hid under. "I thought you were someone else."

"No, it's just me," I said gently. I pushed back a lock of brown hair that fell into my face.

Sage gave a shaky sigh and threw the sheets off of herself. "You had me worried for a second, Tres. Mage Melody told me to hide if anyone came and I thought… thought that you could be someone bad. I've been hearing lots of noises up there." Sage glanced up at the ceiling.

"Yeah." I sat on the mattress and brought my knees to my chest. "Me too."

Sage seemed petrified by the unknown trouble. Her face was paler than usual, like when she became seasick. I could see her body shake as if she had chills. Sage was definitely nervous, just as she always was every time the *Naviganti* became endangered. Maybe it was because there was no greenery or trees to comfort and soothe her. Korina was the opposite, and seemed more relaxed and happier out on the sea. Since her element was water she could use her magic whenever she felt like it, only having to lean over the side of the ship. Korina had already used a lot of her magic to help us escape from the whirlpool but Sage had not used hers since we set foot on the *Naviganti*. I had used my magic once, when the ship became trapped in the Maze of Stones. And then there was Elijah, who had a different kind of magic than the three of us. Korina, Sage, and I could only use our magic when our element was present. Elijah could create a flame whenever he felt like doing so. He could also control flames that were not created by him.

Sage sat beside me on the mattress. "I guess all we can do is wait."

"Yes," I agreed.

"I can't help but wonder what's going on. Why would Mage Melody be so worried about it? It makes me nervous. Ugh, I feel like I'm going to be sick to my stomach."

"Please don't get sick."

Sage looked at me and made a face. "I wouldn't if I had the choice."

The two of us sat in silence for moments in time that became lost. I stared at the floor of the cabin with thoughts racing through my head while Sage kept a tight empty gaze on nothing. Her breath was uneven at times. Then she stood up and turned toward me.

"I can't do this anymore. I can't keep listening to all of this ruckus and not do anything. Korina and Elijah might even be dead and we wouldn't even know it! We don't even know what's *happening!*"

"What are you suggesting?" I asked, knowing the answer.

"We should really go up there. I know I'm scared and you probably are too, but I'm going to go mad if we don't get out of this hold."

"But Mage Melody told us not to leave the hold! She made that very clear, so don't you think—"

"Are you going to let someone tell you what you can and can't do? Goodness, I sound like Korina," Sage added under her breath. "We're mages! Mages that were chosen out of many to go on this expedition. I think we can handle whatever's happening."

I took a deep breath. "I don't know that we can, Sage. You don't know what's happening, but I do."

"Then what is it?"

"Winged mutations."

Sage startled me with a laugh. "*Winged* mutations? Out in the middle of the sea? In the middle of *nowhere*?"

"Sage, I'm not kidding. I was with Elijah and Korina when they cracked open the hatch and Korina saw the mutations with her own eyes."

"Then we're going to go see some winged mutations. At least I am. You coming?"

"I don't think so. How are you going to fight? There aren't any plants for miles."

Sage's face darkened with realization. "I suppose you're right," she mumbled. "I'll find some way then. At least you can pull up rocks from the seafloor."

"It takes a lot of strength and more magic to reach them since the rocks are so far down, Sage. I don't know if I could."

"Whatever. I need to stop thinking about things and start doing them instead. Starting now." Sage left the cabin without another word. I hurried after her.

"Sage, wait!" I cried.

Sage turned around as she climbed the first step up to the hatch. "Coming?"

"I guess so. I can't let you go out there alone. You need someone to watch your back. Plus I'll cover if Mage Melody scolds you."

"Why, thanks. Don't know what I'd do without you."

I followed Sage up to the hatch. As soon as we flipped it open, I felt like retreating into the hold. The black and darkly colored monsters invaded the evening sky, all of them with ominous wings that had a large span. Other mutations flung themselves against the mainmast and foremast, ripping sails to shreds, snapping sheets, and destroying other parts. The hull of the ship thumped as a group of mutations repeatedly rammed into it, probably creating a mess of damage. Some mutations swooped down from the sky with outstretched claws, like an eagle descending on its prey. They plunged onto the deck and picked up crew members, then released the humans as they gained height. The humans were flung back onto the deck, paralyzed. To my horror, some bodies even lay on the deck, motionless in a pool of blood.

Sage stiffened with fear beside me. "Maybe we should turn back." We ducked as a shrieking mutation flew past. Its claws were outstretched, directed at our faces.

"Sage, shut the door!" I shrieked. Together we slammed the hatch, but it didn't close all the way. The mutation slid its talons underneath the opening and writhed them in the air, trying to claw at Sage and me. Its sharp talons scraped against wood while it growled menacingly.

Sage began to scream beside me. The mutation sensed her fear and pushed harder. It stretched and slashed at us, and I jumped back as I dodged an attack. I lost my balance and fell backwards, plummeting down the steps. Sage screeched in pain as I tumbled hard onto my back. The growling ceased as the mutation left.

I rose up and rubbed my bruised back. I looked up at Sage, who held her hand out in front of herself, shrieking.

"Sage! Sage, what's wrong?" I scrambled to my feet and hopped back onto the steps, careful to avoid the poisonous splatters of slime that the mutation had left behind.

Sage stopped her shrill screaming and began to yell continuously.

"Sage, what's wrong?" I demanded more firmly.

Sage took in gasps of air and held her hand in front of me. Four thick lines of dark purpled wrapped around her palm and the backside of her hand where the mutation's talons had clawed her. The skin around it seemed to have shrunken a bit and transformed into a bloody red. I gasped and looked away, horrified at the sight.

"We need to stay in the hold. Come on, let's get to your cabin."

Sage shook her head and wiped away the runaway tears. "No," she sputtered. "I won't."

"You can't go up there with an injury like this."

"No... I... have to..." she gasped in between breaths. She let out a sharp yell of pain.

"Let's at least wrap it before you bleed to death." I led her into my cabin where my bag was. I took out a strip of cloth and carefully wound it around Sage's disgusting hand. Black poison seeped out of the broad cut. Sage fought me, trying to hit me with her good hand as

I wrapped the other one. I would've tried to get her to stay in the hold, but I knew it would be useless. Sage was intent on getting out there, even with a serious injury.

Sage hobbled up to the hatch, and I followed.

"We need to be careful," I said before we opened the hatch. "These things are more threatening than anything we've ever seen before, and we need to watch the skies. I don't think either of us want to be carried into the air and dropped like some of those sailors."

Sage nodded her response, not saying a word. I took a deep breath and slowly opened the hatch, hoping not to attract any attention from unwanted beasts. When I could see out the hatch, I looked to the sides and up to make sure no mutations were in sight. Then Sage and I stealthily crept out of the hatch.

"We should try to stay together," I whispered.

Sage nodded her response again. I glanced at her hand, cringing when I saw the red soaking through the bandage.

I clasped my hands over my ears as a larger mutation stood powerfully like a lion on the rail of the ship and roared. The other mutations then shrilly yowled in reply. When the noise finally stopped, the large mutation, which seemed like their leader, sprung off the rail and charged toward a sailor who began to run. The other mutations resumed their fighting.

Sage and I bent over to avoid being noticed, and darted across the main deck to hide behind the barrels of water placed in front of the kitchen.

"What are we even going to do, besides get ourselves killed?" I asked in a whisper.

"I don't know! I'm starting to think we should've stayed in the hold. The least we can do is—ah!" Sage winced in pain, then continued. "The best we can do is fight the mutations. But I don't know how since I don't have any plants to fight with."

"You should've brought a bag of seeds."

"And what good would that have done?" Another gasp of pain. "I can't speed up the process of growing!"

"Sorry, thought you could."

"Well, I can't," Sage snapped.

"Okay, okay, sorry. How about we get out of here and try to find Korina and Elijah, and I'll try to use my magic to reach the rocks on the seafloor. You try to figure something out too, Sage. I know you're smart."

"Figure something out?" Sage grumbled. "Yeah, sure. I guess that won't be too hard even though we've seen nothing green since Elementa and my hand hurts so much it could fall off!"

I didn't respond but left the shelter of the barrels. I looked up, seeing a mutation perched on the fore boom of the foresail. The creature gazed intently at me with bright green eyes. *Didn't mutations have yellow eyes?*

I froze, unmoving. I feared that if I moved, the mutation would dive toward me and thrust me up into the air, clawing me along the way. Sage appeared at my side.

"Tres, let's go. What are you staring at—" Sage followed my gaze as I put a hand up to stop her from moving.

"Don't move," I whispered in warning.

Sage obeyed and fixed her gaze on the mutation.

"Don't stare at it either. It could see that and—" The mutation gave a loud piercing screech and Sage and I instinctively covered our ears. I looked up just in time to see the creature plunging toward us.

"Run, Sage!" I cried. Sage didn't waste a moment and sprinted away. I inched away, at the same time calling on my magic to reach the rocks at the bottom of the sea.

Please work, please work. I let my magic flow down the sides of the ship and seep into the sea. I felt the presence of large stone formations and boulders at the bottom of the sea. In my mind, I visualized my magic fastening around the boulders and yanking them toward the surface. They didn't budge. I felt my strength dwindling as I used large quantities of my magic just to reach the stones. Then I gripped them as hard as I could and pulled fiercely. I felt the stones shift. *Come on, I'm your friend! Please listen to me!* I pleaded in my mind. Suddenly the stones broke free from the sea floor and began to rise higher and higher.

The mutation was as quick as a flash of light, darting in my direction. I ran away from it, to the side of the ship where I could concentrate on the stones. The rock formations that I had called on were still rising to the surface. The mutation charged at me, then leaped in the air. Its slimy wings fluttered and flapped until it glided a few feet off the ground. I screamed, knowing that wherever I fled, I would have no time to escape the monster. It would surely kill me in a single blow.

The rocks saved me. As the mutation was about to pounce on me, the rocks shot out of the water. I used my magic to sling the heavy objects over the side of the ship toward the mutation. The creature was instantly crushed as a huge boulder, one about the size of the crow's nest, slammed into the mutation. The boulder crashed onto the main deck, creating a large dent that threatened to become a gaping hole. I raced away from the side of the ship, a bit shaken.

I had lost Sage when the mutation attacked. At my urging, she had fled without a second thought and was now hiding somewhere on the deck, hopefully alive. I frantically searched for her, tossing my head in each direction and dodging mutations. The mutations continued to decimate the crew and their numbers were quickly dwindling. If the attack didn't stop soon, there would be no live sailors.

Instead of finding Sage I spotted Korina blasting waves of water at a mutation in the air. The mutation dodged each of Korina's attacks, with impressive strength and speed. Raindrops of sweat firmly planted themselves on Korina's forehead as she swung her arms in a graceful motion to direct the water. Finally she ran out of stamina, and the water dropped. The mutation seized the opportunity and instantly plunged toward Korina.

I sprinted toward Korina, who was cowering near the quarterdeck. She stood motionless like a startled rabbit but stood firmly in defiance of her impending defeat. Korina had lost her strength and had decided to give up. I knew that it was Korina's way of thinking—to stop when she felt tired.

As the mutation raced toward Korina, I remembered the bolder lying on the deck, the one I'd raised from the seafloor and used to crush one of those hideous creatures before. In a flash, I gripped the boulder with my magic as hard as I could and yanked on it with all the force I could muster. It immediately sprang up, hovering above the deck for a split second until I rapidly slung my arms to the side in a whipping motion. The stone soared across the deck and struck the mutation, knocking it backwards and injuring its wings. Unfortunately my aim wasn't as accurate as it had been before, and the mutation staggered to its four legs, then took slow steps toward me, growling.

"Korina! Move!" I shouted. Korina was still standing in the same spot, staring at the mutation with wide eyes. She looked up at me and then briskly swept her arms over her shoulders and back, commanding a wave of water. The sea rose and flooded over the side of the ship, crashing onto the main deck. The mutation took one glance at the water and fluttered its wings. It shrieked in pain as the crushed wing flopped limply to its side. The water reached the creature and carried it away.

"Thanks," I breathed as Korina joined my side.

"Yeah, yeah. How many are there, anyway?" She counted silently, her lips moving as she gazed around the ship. "Sixteen. There's only sixteen of them and look how much damage has been done."

"Some of them have been killed," I remarked.

Korina nodded absently and grabbed my wrist. "Let's go find Elijah. Last I saw him, he was limping toward the kitchen with a hand on his neck. He probably went there to hide, no doubt. Oh, and Mage Melody. She screamed at us for disobeying her, but I don't think she was too upset when we saved her from being eaten alive." Korina rolled her eyes. "I hate mutations."

"They've gotten smarter, haven't they?"

"Yeah."

Korina and I opened the kitchen door and shut it quietly behind us.

"Elijah? Elijah!" Korina impatiently called.

A couple of pots that were hanging over a counter abruptly fell with a loud clatter. A person grumbled and then winced at a sudden burst of pain. Korina and I approached the source of the noise to find Elijah on the floor with his ankle bent at an awkward angle. When he painfully placed his hands on his ankle, they were smeared in blood.

"What did you *do* to yourself?" Korina snapped. She surveyed his hands and sighed sharply. Korina had no sympathy.

"Nothing, nothing."

"Elijah!"

"A mutation caught me off guard, okay! I was helping Mage Isaac—he lost his magic again when the mutations came—and then I was attacked. I spun around and retaliated with flame, but I was too late and the blasted monster pounced on my foot. I fell back but Mage Isaac chased it off. I'm just lucky the thing didn't shred me with its claws."

"Why are your hands so bloody then?" I asked softly, my eyes on his hands.

"Out of nowhere, my neck started screaming with pain. When I touched it, it burned like acid and my hands came back bloody. It kept bleeding and bleeding… I can't go back out there. My neck is going to be the end of me and I can't walk on this ankle. Probably broken anyway."

"Let me see your neck," Korina ordered.

Elijah turned away and raised his hand to wipe his black hair aside. I looked away, seeing a mass of red before his hair was out of the way. I heard Korina gag.

"Is it that bad?" Elijah asked.

"What did you *do*?"

"I thought it was healed," I said softly. "I asked you this last night when you told us about that sailor. Didn't Mage Melody fix everything?"

"She did," Elijah gasped, gripping his neck suddenly. His hands came back covered with another coat of blood.

"Ugh, stop doing that," Korina grumbled.

"She did, but when the mutations came, the pain returned. It's like the poison or dark magic was never cleaned out and now it resurfaces when anything with dark magic appears. Like with Devin."

"We don't know if Devin had dark magic," I pointed out.

"I think he did," Elijah shrugged. He gasped like Sage did when she favored her hand. "My ankle, my neck, my ankle, my neck. Gosh, I feel like someone took a knife and butchered my neck and took a hammer and smashed by ankle. I'm not going to live to see the Sacred Islands."

"Don't talk like—"

"Shut up," Korina said at the same time.

Elijah shut his eyes and leaned against a cabinet. "Oh, just leave me here to suffer. Or come and get me when the mutations leave. *If* they leave."

"Stop feeling sorry for yourself. Come on Tres. We need to find the helpless kitten—er Sage, I mean."

By the time we finally trudged out of the kitchen, a dark cloud had settled overhead and was casting a shadow over the ship. With terrible realization, I learned that it wasn't a cloud. It was a swarm of mutations.

Korina pushed me back into the kitchen. "Get back. They've come because they think everyone's dead, or they're reinforcements. People don't need reinforcements if they're winning, so that leaves the first option."

We watched through the tiny opening in the kitchen door. The mutations kicked and prodded the lifeless bodies that were strewn about the deck. Then the leader spoke in a gruff voice.

"Most blood-bags dead. We leave them with broken ship. They never reach main nest. Let's fly—leave injured and weak and report to Master."

A mutation spoke to the leader. "What about the other blood-bag, one that works for Master?"

"We take him. Master decides to let him live or not."

"I don't like him."

"Your thinking don't count. We don't kill right away—remember brothers in forest nest, ones that hiss like animals and can't speak? They smart for once." The mutation looked up and growled. With a howl it sprang up and the other mutations followed. The flock of mutations left and the sky brightened.

A cluster of three mutations lingered on the deck. In front of them stood a sailor.

Korina squinted, something she did often. Whether she was annoyed by someone or just trying to see better, squinting was one of Korina's defining characteristics. "I know that sailor..." she paused, thinking. "It's *Devin*." There was a hint of anger in her tone.

"Was that the one Elijah saw?"

Korina nodded, her eyes fixed on Devin. "Elijah was right. He is in on this."

The mutations growled a few words to Devin, then lifted him with their talons and followed the rest of the mutations into the sky. The mutations were traveling in the direction of the Sacred Islands.

"Do you see that?" I asked.

"What?"

"I'll bet you ten silver coins that those mutations are from the Sacred Islands."

"I don't have that kind of money on me, Tres. Besides, I agree with you. I bet they are from those islands."

Korina and I went onto the main deck. There were several bodies that I recognized, all of them sailors. I didn't see Captain Serulean or any of the mages. I didn't see Sage either, which could be good or bad.

Virtually on cue, Captain Serulean emerged from his cabin. He had bandages on his arm and a band around his head. At least he hadn't abandoned his crew.

"I saw that sea rat, Devin," he spat. "What a traitor. And he hid the whole time while we risked our lives out here." Tears replaced Serulean's anger. "Look at all of them. Mared, Colt, and Miles. They're all here on this blasted deck. Here and gone. Here then gone in a second. Just this morning I talked to Mared and laughed with Colt. Only minutes ago, Miles was joking with Jeril. At least Jeril is still here. Out of twelve of us, only six remain."

Six crew members emerged from the captain's cabin with their heads bent. A lump formed in my throat as I looked around at the fallen sailors. I couldn't shake the feeling that they should be alive and standing, talking, and barking orders at each other.

Korina stared with grave eyes. She understood the tragedy, but said nothing, probably out of respect for the fallen. No tears came to her eyes. She kept a glazed look fixed on the deck floor, studying nothing but the sad wood of the deck. The poor wood—it had witnessed too much today, and had too much blood spilled on it. Life had seeped away on this very wood.

"Where is Mage Melody and Mage Isaac?" I asked.

Serulean tore his depressed gaze away from the lifeless sailors and looked at me. "Why, I don't know. Check the hold." He ambled into his cabin, shoulders slumped. He looked defeated. His cheery tone was drained and replaced with an empty one.

Korina followed me in silence. We opened the hold, just as we had earlier. But earlier, lives had not been lost. She and Elijah had bravely entered the fight against the mutations, as had Sage and I. And Elijah—he was still in the kitchen, assuring himself that his injuries would be the end of him.

We found the mages in the hold. Mage Melody was wrapping bandaging around Mage Isaac. There was a medical kit beside them on the floor.

"Korina, Teressia!" Mage Melody looked up. "Are either of you hurt?"

We shook our heads.

"Good. Sage is in her cabin. We found her huddled beside the water barrels. Except for her hand she was uninjured, thank goodness. Though, she was terrified to death. The poor thing, she was shaking all over, wasn't she Isaac?"

"Yes, Melody."

"And all of a sudden Isaac and I lost our magic. This keeps happening to us, of all things. I don't understand it. You four have yours but then something happens, and when we need it, we lose it." Melody sighed and shook her head.

"I need some ice, Melody. My head is bruised and you have a cut on your forehead that you need to tend to," Mage Isaac informed.

"Ah, fine. I'm glad we're not dead. Those monsters have gotten stronger. And where's Elijah? Is he okay? We told you kids to stay in your cabins! You could've been killed like those poor sailors."

Korina led Mage Isaac into the kitchen where he picked up Elijah off the floor and carried him back to the hold. Mage Melody tended to his injuries while I went back to my cabin.

I had witnessed deaths today. I had seen the damage to the ship: the torn sails with holes in them, holes in the deck, holes in the side of the ship, the injured hull. But those things were material, and could be repaired with some effort and hard work. I knew what was really lost. Futures and essences and gifts. Cheer was diminished, and would take a long time to come back. I laid down on the mattress. Lives had been lost, lives had been lost, lives had been lost. They were gone— no, that's impossible—I would see those sailors the next morning, making repairs. But I knew better. They were gone and they would never be coming back. *But I'm only fourteen.* I shouldn't have to cope with something like this yet. I argued with myself. Before I drifted into a restless sleep, I wondered, was this voyage was worth it, losing lives to get to some abandoned chunk of land?

CHAPTER 26

SAGE

I sat huddled on my mattress, chewing on a nail. I had the sheets from my mattress lazily draped across my lap. I shivered, images of black flashing mutations dancing across my mind. I was unmoving, feeling empty as I gazed blankly ahead. I didn't feel like leaving my bed or talking. I stared at my shaky hands, hands that seemingly carried a vibrating storm within them. More images of the mutations' attack on the ship jumped into my mind: piles of lifeless bodies strewn around the deck, some with a pool of blood bedside them. The images became surreal—more and more bodies heaped on the deck until there was a sea of them, the stench of death—

I cleared my mind of the horrific vision. My eyes narrowed from their widened state and I began to chew on my nail again. Had these events emotionally scarred me? No, not *me*. Many people had been known to go mad, crazy, or insane because of traumatizing events like the one I had witnessed. But I had never considered that I might be affected by something like this—not me, Sage Winter. I had always considered myself intelligent, emotionally mature, ahead of everyone in all the ways that count. Was it possible that I could be emotionally altered? No, I have conscious, rational thoughts, I told myself. But at the same time... at the same time, I felt so barren and changed. What was happening to me?

I laid on my back, chest facing upward on the mattress. My eyes seldom blinked and I stared at the ceiling for the longest time. I had no thoughts that I could recall. Did my eyes glaze over? I was soon lost in a wintery flurry of sleep. Snowflakes swirled around me, biting at my nose. I was being crowded by nipping shreds of dancing dots... cold flakes of ice that soon turned red.

It became a crimson storm, engulfing me and carrying me away, high into the air. My feet flailed about, touching nothing. I think I might've shrieked, cried out for help, but I couldn't be sure of anything. The flurries became sticky liquid, fusing to my skin. I was flung down onto a gritty blanket of red snow. I heaved myself to my feet, but couldn't get balanced. An invisible force yanked me down again. I was being suffocated by a sandy substance. I crawled to the side, cringing when my hand landed on something soft and spongy. I jerked my hand back, seeing a broken limb lying in front of me. I gasped for air, for it seemed like the oxygen had been sucked out of my lungs.

My vision was drawn to the horizon, where the red sand or snow—I couldn't tell which—stretched endlessly, and detached limbs littered the ground. I gagged and sputtered until I sprang upright on the mattress. I realized that I was wet and hot. I swiped a hand across a sweaty forehead, then stuck my hands under my arms.

I took deep breaths, trying to comprehend what I had just experienced. My mind had haunted me with a merciless dream. Was this the sort of dream I could expect every night? Would it ever stop?

I winced, feeling a spike of silver pain prick my hand like needles. Aching followed the sharp burst of pain. My bandaged hand yelled with hurt. I examined it, staring at the white wrap. I should count myself lucky that the wound on my hand was the only injury I had received. But I couldn't be thankful, happy that it was the only wound. Instead I felt cursed. I shed the thought immediately. I've always been blessed, I told myself. How could you think you've been cursed? You could be dead at this moment! Just like those sailors who gave their lives to save yours, I scolded myself.

The bandage that wrapped my grotesque hand had blemishes of crimson soaking through. I decided to go to Mage Melody to get new bandages.

Mage Melody was in her cabin, reading a book in dim candle light. The candle was protected by a clear globe made of glass, with an open top so that the flame could gulp down the air it needed to survive. Mage Melody looked up. "Sage, darling. Are you all right?" She glanced down at my hand. "Is it hurting?"

"It's always hurting," I complained. "I just came for new bandaging. This one is kind of..." I trailed off, holding my hand in front of my face, indicating that it needed to be replaced. Mage Melody understood, nodding her head. She then went to a chest at the foot of her mattress and dug around in it until she found a roll of bandage.

"Ah, here we are. I'll leave it to you to wrap your hand and dispose of the old one. Sometimes I can't stand seeing bad injuries." Mage Melody made a face. I grinned as I took the wrap, then thanked her and left.

After supper, I threw away the old bandaging and somehow managed to keep the food in my stomach. Then I crawled into bed, feeling bags weigh down my eyes. Outside the cool celestial cover of the sky was calm and silent. Tiny white dots sat all over the night sky, unmoving. The midnight vault of the galaxy made it seem as if nothing bad had happened the previous evening. It just... remained still and idle. Night. Night was empty just as I was feeling empty. Or maybe it wasn't that the night sky was empty, but I was making it feel empty. Maybe in reality the night sky was alive and full of color and life. It was a dance floor for eager stars, and the moon was the hostess until the sun took over, bringing day with it. It was a space that flourished with prosperity, and blazed with energy—but all I saw were vacant beings that didn't twinkle or glitter like everyone claimed.

I left the comfort of my mattress and the hold, fearing what sleep might bring and anxious to study the sky. I sat down on the deck, crossing my legs. I craned my neck until my face was straight up and I stared at the heavens. I squinted, trying to make the moon seem bigger so that I could study its fine details. It remained still just as the stars. I looked at them too, trying to catch their movement. I saw nothing.

I must have been staring vacantly for a few moments until I had drifted away from the world. A firm hand shook my shoulder, reeling me back to the ship like a fish in a net. I closed my mouth, which apparently had been wide open in my absence of mind.

"Sage?" the voice asked.

I blinked and stiffly looked to the side. My neck ached from looking up so long. "Who...?" I felt dazed. Then I recognized Elijah. His wavy hair was trimmed on the sides, making it look straight, yet not too short. The real length of his hair was spread nicely over his neck and the front was hanging low, right above his eyes, slightly covering distinctive eyebrows. It was shiny and smooth, and reflected the moonlight in a silver halo that lined the top of his head. I blinked again, trying to get the captivating image of that halo out of my vision. I had never thought of how nice his hair looked... I shook my head. I was definitely tired. *If I'm starting to think Elijah doesn't look half bad, I need to go to bed before I start thinking Korina is sensible.*

"How long have you been out here?" Elijah shivered. "It's a bit cool out here, don't you think?"

I felt chills race down my arms as the night breeze awoke. Sometimes the summer night air could catch one off guard.

"Are you okay? I'm kind of worried about you, Sage."

I heard genuine concern in his voice. "Why?"

"I mean, it's the middle of the night—or morning. I don't really know which."

I smiled. "That seems like you, a bit clueless."

"Okay, that's rude. I can see you're fine now."

I gave a small laugh. "I'm fine!"

"I know. Well." Elijah looked around. "Goodnight, I guess. Don't stay out here too long. You'll get chilled."

"Leaving?" I called as he sauntered to the hold.

Elijah flapped a hand in response. He then disappeared into the hold.

I began to wonder about Elijah. Why was he such a likeable person, especially back in Elementa? Everyone seemed to flock around him at the Academy. What made his reputation so legendary, and how'd he become so popular? And yet he was close friends with a shadow like Tres. She was genuinely sweet but shy and easily slid into the background. Elijah didn't though. He always seemed to stay in the center of a circle of fans and the leader of any crowd. I was bright and smart and skilled. Why wasn't I as popular?

That's a dumb question and you know it. You're nothing like him. He has better social skills and people just seem to trip over themselves to be his friend.

I sighed and rose to my feet, then retreated to the shelter of the hold. I climbed onto my mattress and rested, but didn't sleep. My thoughts, happily it seemed, rolled over and over. I had finally forgotten about the tragic disaster that plagued my mind until sleep swallowed me.

I was crouched behind a barrel. Tres was at my side, but then she left. I pleaded for her to stay with me, but she refused and insisted that she had to find a key. I wanted to follow her, but I couldn't. When I tried to move, I was trapped. I was pressed between the barrel and a wall. I thrashed about in a panic, but I could not escape the confines of the small space behind the barrel.

Then scraping began. My heart began to pound violently and I felt more and more like a caged animal. I couldn't escape, and a mutation was clawing its way through the barrel.

The barrel was destroyed in a blast of splinters. The mutation towered above me, throwing shadows over me, and the sky was black.

The mutation reared back on its hind legs, getting ready to pounce, to strike, to kill...

I screamed and sat upright, once again. I caught my breath and then shook my head. Two nightmares in the same night. Please let me sleep in peace, I pleaded to my mind. How could I sleep now? There was no way I would let myself fall into the trap of these frightening dreams again. Maybe it was best to stay awake the rest of the night...

I think the looming presence of darkness partially awakened me. Was it the absence of sunlight? Or maybe it was just the feeling that day should be here, but wasn't. When I actually woke up, I felt the edge of day. Night was over thankfully, but why was it still dark?

I sat up on the mattress. Why was it so dark in here? I was shaking, sweating, panting. I fought and thrashed my legs, trying to escape. The sheets were tangled, clinging to my legs. I was trapped like an insect in a spider's web. It's too dark, too dark. *Help!*

I stopped and remained still. My arms and legs were burning from all the panicked movement. I realized my muscles were sore. But sore from what?

I took deep breaths, trying to calm myself. Like a sensible person, I gently untangled my legs from the sheets and tossed them to the side. I stood up and stretched, feeling stiff. *It's time to get up, time to face the world, as much as you don't want to.*

I escaped the bleak darkness of my cabin. The hold was dimly lit by oil lamps attached to the walls. It would be nice to get some real light from the sun. I climbed out of the hold and onto the main deck.

Outside, the morning light hit me like a blow to the face. Sunlight flung itself on my face, warming me like melting butter. I had to squint to block out the harsh rays of the sun. The summer air was hot, but preferable to the sly coolness of dark shadows. This beautiful warmth, the craving warmth that spread on my face, gave life to my green friends. Plants bloomed and prospered because of it. It was now on my face, heating it like a blaze of hungry flame. It was life.

I had let myself think that things would be better, that everything would turn out fine and that my feelings of depression would disappear.

Then I opened my eyes and saw gaping tears in the sails that stretched so high up into the sky and despair began to flood over me again. Yet this sky, this light blue sky with cotton clouds gliding lazily along, continued to stretch on and on without a struggle. The night sky had retired and the sun replaced the moon and the clouds shooed away the stars. The stars were pale eyes that stared without moving but the clouds were warm hugs that welcomed me. I felt like I could float into the sky and join the clouds and never return to my troubles.

A shout jerked me back to the ship. I had been absent once again, letting my spirit drift around while my physical body swayed on the deck.

I looked up. The shout belonged to a sailor. I looked around, seeing very few sailors working on the ship. It seemed that half of them were gone. Did that many perish in the storm of mutations?

Serulean shouted a response, but his words didn't register to me. It seemed that two sailors were talking right in front of me, but I couldn't understand anything they were saying. I felt as if they were speaking in a foreign language. Had I forgotten the common tongue?

"Sage?"

"Wha?"

"What are you staring at?" Korina mumbled through a mouthful of biscuit.

"Uh, nothing," I replied slowly.

Korina squinted and scrunched up her eyebrows to make a questioning expression. "You seem strange. You sick?" She waved a hand in front of my face.

"No, not at all. I feel fine, mostly."

"How's that hand?"

"What hand? Oh! This hand. Not so good, as you can see. But that's natural since it only happened a day ago. I'm sure it'll heal in no time."

Korina raised her eyebrows. "Okay... whatever you say, I guess. Um, you may want to... never mind." She walked away.

What was that? What was I even saying? She looked at me like I had gone mad. Maybe I have.

My gaze returned to the sailors that scurried around with various tools. It seemed that all they did during this voyage was repairs.

Serulean was laboring as well. He hammered nails and made repairs to the mast that I couldn't name. I ambled toward him, a question slowly blooming in my mind like a rose on a drizzling summer day. "Captain, how many did we lose?"

Serulean jerked his head to face me. Sweat dripped off his forehead and around his salt and pepper beard. "Six," he huffed. He panted a bit after he put down a tool. "Unfortunately six. That's half the crew. Sad day, wasn't it? Yes, yes. But we can't let it burden our hearts. They would want us to keep going, keep sailing. And it doesn't stop when we reach our destination—it's only half over. We have the return journey. But for now we make fixes and go. I'm honestly worried that she won't make it to the Islands. But we just got to have faith and keep pushing, don't we? Yes, yes we do. Aw, what's the sad face for? You feeling okay, youngin'?"

Tears collected in the corners of my eyes, threatening to flood over. I knew that my hazel eyes looked glassy. "I'm fine," I sniffed. "Everything was so unfortunate though. We survived so much and then those monsters had to swoop in. I'm not even sure I'm the same person, and it wasn't like there was a war."

"No, but there might be one yet."

"What?" Serulean had murmured softly, and I wasn't sure I had heard right. Did he say there was going to be war?

"Nothing. I must work now. Don't feel bad, girl. Nothing that happened was your fault. It was that sea rat, Devin's fault. With no doubt in my mind, he called those beasts here. I didn't know he was working for them. Well, he won't be working for me anymore. If I ever see him again, he's a goner." He shook his head.

"Thank you," I smiled. "I think I ought to visit Mage Melody and see if she can help me. I feel that the previous day has plagued my mind. I feel heavy and burdened."

"Then I advise you to go. Cheer up, girl. The storm clouds may cover the sun but it's not going to stay that way."

Mage Melody was in her cabin, just as she was when I found her last night.

"Sage, here you are again. Is everything okay?"

"No, that's why I came."

"What's wrong?"

"I feel... different. Different since what happened yesterday."

"How so?"

"I've been absent. I let my mind wander until I'm not thinking at all and I'm just staring and I'm all blank."

"I'm no healer, but I think you're trying to cope with what happened yesterday. You have been traumatized and you're trying to comprehend everything but can't. You want to get away from the tragedy and the heavy feeling of loss, so your mind leaves your body and you fall into a trance. My reasoning is probably flawed because I've never studied human behavior and mental sickness, but that is what I believe."

"But didn't you work at the healer's place, to help heal injuries and such?"

"Yes, physical injuries. But even so, I think I have something that may help you. Healer Rose gave me mixtures and medicines of all sorts for this trip." Melody retrieved a kit and took out a bottle. "Here we go. For the peace of mind." She poured the substance into a spoon and handed it to me.

"Thank you." I took the spoon and gulped down the medicine. It was tangy and sweet and sour all at the same time. I made a face.

"Now, you shouldn't be frightened as easily, or become absent, as you say. You'll still feel a little sad but that's natural. For now I want you to go spend some time with the other students and get your mind off the tragedy that happened yesterday. It's all in the past now."

I followed Mage Melody's advice and joined Korina and Tres on the main deck. I was a little nervous, and hoped that Korina didn't consider me insane.

"Sage! There you are," Tres said, as if she had been looking for me. "We've been worried about you—you've been in your cabin most of the time."

"You shouldn't be worried. I'm fine," I assured, and sneaked a glance at Korina.

"Are you sure? It seemed as if you weren't acting like yourself earlier," Korina stated.

"I'm fine now, honestly. Mage Melody gave me some medicine to calm me down."

"Medicine? Are you sick?" Tres worriedly exclaimed.

That was the wrong thing to say.

"No! Just a little dazed. Last night was a little frightening and depressing."

"I told you we should've stayed out of it," Tres remarked.

I shrugged. "You were probably right."

"It's all done now," Korina pointed out. "Everything is going to be fine now."

"We hope," Tres said. "The ship looks pretty beaten up. And after everything it's been through, I just hope it won't sink."

"I'm sure the crew is taking care of everything," I said, trying to reassure myself.

Korina pulled out a biscuit from a belt pouch on her trousers. "Want some? I snuck an extra one from the kitchen when I went for breakfast." She bit into it.

"I'll take a piece," Tres said, and pulled a crumb off of the biscuit.

Korina thrust the biscuit toward me. I shook my head. I didn't feel hungry at all. She shrugged and took another bite.

Elijah walked up behind Tres. Korina and I looked up, and he motioned for us to be quiet. I smiled while Korina rolled her eyes.

"What?" asked a puzzled Tres.

Elijah shoved his hands down onto Tres's shoulders and shouted. Tres yelped and jumped, startled. Elijah began to laugh and Tres stood up and started to hit him on the shoulder repeatedly.

"How dare you, you tramp! You dumb fluff-brained child!" She began laughing.

"I'm so offended," he said mockingly.

"Shut up!"

I smiled ruefully, a sad feeling stirring inside me. Was I longing for something? I looked at Korina. She wrinkled her nose in disapproval and then buried it into her biscuit. She didn't care for the two's mock quarrel, and probably brushed it away with annoyance. I, on the other hand, seemed to have a different feeling. Did I feel left out?

Elijah was still smiling by the time Tres settled down. Teressia got over the prank immediately and returned her gaze to me and Korina. Elijah sat down in between Tres and Korina. The same feeling returned inside of me.

"So where have you been?" Korina grumbled impassively to Elijah.

"Ah, nowhere."

"I don't believe that for a second," Tres remarked. I sat quietly, waiting for Elijah to respond. I looked at Teressia. She was smiling at him. How come I never cared to notice these kinds of things before?

Elijah gave a short laugh. "No, really. I haven't been anywhere. I've spent most of the morning in my cabin. It's better to stay out of the way of the crew's work."

"The crew," I whispered sadly. I looked down.

"What's with the sad face?" Elijah asked.

"Don't you think it's sad? That half the crew... you know."

Elijah's warm smile vanished. His face turned grave. "Oh, that. It's what happened though and we can't change it. But it makes me feel guilty that they defended us so bravely while we waited in the hold. We should've come out on deck sooner."

"What we should've done is stayed in the hold," Teressia proclaimed. "It wouldn't do anybody any good if one of us had been killed." Her face transformed into a frustrated and pained expression. "If only nobody had died! I—we—shouldn't have witnessed anything like that! My mind keeps rejecting that several sailors are gone, but deep down I know the truth. It's so hard."

"Like Elijah said, it's in the past," Korina said. "We can't change it so we should just accept it. We did all we could, going out on deck to fight. It's none of our faults so we shouldn't blame ourselves. I know it's sad, but we shouldn't dwell on it. I'm tired of hearing whiners."

"Korina," Tres argued. "Whiners? It's natural for people to grieve. You should give them a break and not accuse them of 'whining.'"

Korina rolled her eyes. "Okay whatever."

"We're all going through hard feelings, Korina," I said. "I think it's hard for us to cope with it all."

"I agree. But we shouldn't talk about it all the time. It makes us remember the pain of loss," Korina said.

"Sometimes talking helps," Teressia stated.

"Mage Melody said it would be a good idea to keep my mind on other things," I informed.

"See?" Korina said.

Elijah was staring at the deck, obviously deep in thought. "Elijah?" I questioned.

"Hm?"

"Care to share your thoughts?"

"I was just thinking about Devin."

"What about that imbecile?" Korina demanded harshly.

"Nothing, really. I was just recalling how I saw him in the crew's quarters, hunched over that crystal ball, being all secretive. I was just putting the pieces together. He was contacting some evil force and that's how the mutations knew where we were."

"So it's that scoundrel's fault that people were killed," Korina observed bluntly.

"Basically. But I still wonder what he had locked up in those boxes. I'll never know."

"I don't think you'd want to, anyway. It was probably something real bad," I said.

"He's gone, isn't he?" Elijah guessed. "He ran off with those mutations, right?"

The three of us girls nodded in unison.

"Too bad. I would've given him a good lesson."

Korina startled us all with a burst of hysterical laughter. "You—! Giving him—" She exclaimed in between laughs. When she finally stopped she wiped tears from her eyes. We stared at her with blank expressions, waiting for her to speak again.

"I'm sorry," she sighed, catching her breath. "What would you do, send a little fireball down his trousers?" More laughter. "Elijah, he could probably take you down without any trouble if he works for mutations."

"You have so little faith in me," Elijah joked, shaking his head. "I'd give him a run for his gold coins, that's what I'd do."

"That rat probably doesn't have gold coins. Else he wouldn't be a sailor. I bet you he carried, hm... three, four silver coins in his belt purse," Korina estimated.

"Then I'd give him a run for those four silver coins. Anyway, I'd like to, but I can't."

"Well I'd like to—" Korina paused and jerked her head to the side.

"What is it?" Tres and I asked anxiously.

Korina ignored us and got up from her sitting position. She walked to the rail of the ship and peered over the side. She seemed to be staring at the water below.

"Korina! What are you doing?" Elijah shouted across the deck.

Korina kept her eyes fixed on the water.

"Korina!" I called. She still didn't answer.

"I guess we better go get her," Elijah suggested. The two of us followed Elijah as he strolled to the side of the ship.

"Korina?" Tres gently tapped her on the shoulder.

"Hm? Oh, you."

"Do you see anything?" I asked.

"No, not yet… I just had the strangest feeling. Like there's a disturbance in the water. I could feel it through my magic—I just know something's there."

"I don't see anything," Elijah declared.

"That doesn't surprise me," Korina replied, rolling her eyes. "But I don't either. I guess it was nothing. But still, I can't shake the feeling."

Captain Serulean appeared behind us. "Mage Melody and Mage Isaac want to see you four in my cabin. I think you'll be interested."

"What for?" Korina rudely asked.

"You'll see in a moment if you come. I'm involved as well." Serulean led us to his cabin. It was a typical captain's cabin, with a single porthole and a desk in the center of the room. The desk was littered with stacks of papers and maps and a globe was perched on one corner of it. Two plain chairs were at the desk, but pointed in opposite directions. More papers and scrolls were strewn across the floor as well. His mattress was tucked in the corner of the cabin, and at the foot of his mattress was a large chest.

Captain Serulean ushered us into the cabin and shut the door behind us. Mage Melody and Mage Isaac were already seated, in chairs that they had drawn up to the desk.

"Two of you will have to stand," Serulean informed. He rushed over and swept all the papers and scrolls off the desk into a heap on the floor. He was quite disorganized.

Serulean went to a small bookshelf that lined a wall. He pulled out a slender hand mirror. It was framed in brass and was a decent size. It gave me a shivery feeling when he brought the mirror to the desk.

We were then beckoned to the desk. Elijah kindly motioned for me to have one of the chairs while Korina plopped herself down in the other without the slightest consideration for Teressia.

"What's with the fancy glass?" Korina asked, indicating the mirror.

"It's a mirror, if you hadn't noticed," I informed.

Korina shot me a hard glare and squinted her eyes.

"Actually," began Mage Isaac, "it's a looking-glass. It's like a crystal ball. You can use it to scry—if you're a seer—and communicate with people."

"What are we going to use it for?" Korina wondered.

"I've been getting 'calls,' if you will. Meaning, someone is trying to contact me through it and it seems that this person is from Elementa. Who do you think it would be?"

"Headmaster Ignatia," I concluded.

"Right you are."

"What does she want?" Korina asked in a slightly unkind tone.

"Korina!" Melody scolded.

The mirror flashed, catching everyone's attention and the Headmaster's bronze face appeared. Ignatia's midnight hair ran in neat black waves and was well kempt. Her face was glowing as usual, but dark circles polluted her golden brown eyes. She seemed on edge and anxious.

"Headmaster Ignatia! It's so great to see you. It's been quite a while—"

"Stop flattering, Melody. I have grave news for you all. Is Serulean there? Ah, I see him. What about the children? I see Sage and Korina. Oh! There's Teressia and Elijah. And I see Isaac. Good, you're all here."

"What's the news, Ignatia?" Mage Isaac asked.

A shadow fell upon her face. "You must turn the *Naviganti* around *now*."

"What?" Everyone gawked.

"Yes, yes. You're all in danger—an immense amount of danger! We have discovered, thanks to August, that you will face a threat far greater than any mutations you have encountered."

"Has it been reported to you that we have been attacked by flying mutations?" Serulean asked.

Ignatia's curiosity was piqued. "No, not at all. Were they treacherous?"

"Quite so, Headmaster. We lost six sailors, the rest injured. One of them was a traitor, and called them here with a looking-glass."

"I'm sorry to hear such news. Things aren't going so smoothly over here either. We've had a couple more mutation attacks as well, though none were winged."

"What is the danger?" Elijah asked Ignatia.

"We're not quite sure, Elijah. But it is a force strong enough to destroy you all in a matter of seconds. Imagine the damage it could do to Elementa, let alone several cities. At this point it's better to leave the evil alone, whatever it is."

"But we can't just wait for it to come over here and kill us!" Korina protested.

"Four kids and two mages can't defeat it, Korina. It's best to wait for it to come to us. Then, at least, we would have the capital's forces to help us. But I'm not even sure that would be enough."

"What else is going on in Elementa?" Isaac said.

Ignatia sighed. "We have Gileon trying to destroy the city. Fortis declared war, but then Soror asked us to join them and Oceanus in a civil war against the capital. Like the idiot he is, Gileon agreed. A few days ago he admitted to me that he was in debt with Fortis and was leaving Elementa to join the army. Coward! And he's left me in charge of the city. As if I don't have an Academy to run, students to teach, and the city to protect." Ignatia was livid.

"Rid us of his stupidity," Melody muttered.

"I want you to come back to Elementa. Serulean, turn the ship around. Please, I don't want to be the cause of your deaths. I expect you back in three weeks to a month or so. By fall, you should be home."

"Very well, Headmaster," Isaac said.

"Are you sure, Headmaster?" Serulean questioned. "You want us to cancel the quest?"

"Quite sure, Serulean. Please do not keep sailing onward to the Sacred Islands. I must go now."

Without another word she disappeared.

"Well, it seems as if we have to make a decision now," Serulean announced.

"Please, let us not stop!" Korina protested.

"You wish to go against the Headmaster's orders?" Melody asked calmly.

"But we've come so far!"

"I don't know if the *Naviganti* can handle it, Melody," Serulean said. "She's pretty beaten up and we might have to reach land to make further repairs before we're able to sail back to Elementa. We're almost to the Islands anyway."

"Are you all saying you want to keep sailing?" Melody asked disbelievingly. We nodded. "I think you'll regret it. I advise we turn around now."

The adults lingered in Serulean's cabin to further discuss the situation. Korina looked bored and I had no desire to stay so we left. Elijah and Tres followed us.

Back on the main deck, Korina returned to the rail.

"Do you sense something?" I asked.

She nodded. "I don't know what it could be, but something is definitely different."

The four of us lined up, shoulder to shoulder, and leaned against the rail. Although none of us uttered a word, we were comforted by one another's presence.

A flicker of movement flashed on the horizon. I squinted, trying to make it out. All I could see were two threads of dark green weaving in and out on the surface of the sea.

CHAPTER 27

KORINA

I leaned over the rail with my feet off the deck, staring intently at the Lata Sea. Something was slithering through the magic-poisoned water. Was it the dark magic playing tricks on me? Was it just exhaustion? *I don't want to end up like Serulean, telling stories of fake monsters. Taffy stuffed cloud heads. People like him try to tell a phony story and make it seem ominous and dramatic. Those kind of tales are meant to keep energetic children in bed at night.*

Something was the source of my strange sensations. I felt—I knew—that the sea was disturbed, different in a funny way. Two bodies in the distance moved in the harsh glint of the sun. What were those things, anyway? Animals, creatures of the sea? Was it a monster of dark magic? I quickly glanced at Sage, trying to read her expression in a brief moment. Did she see the same creatures I did?

I raised a hand to my forehead to shield my eyes from the sun's annoying glare. A clear sky with no clouds to blanket the sun was bothersome. Sage was fanatic about the sun, and claimed that it fed all greenery and was life, but to me it was just a bright figure in the sky. I couldn't appreciate the sun, couldn't feel joy from it like Sage. Instead water gave me energy, fuel that made me feel alive. Nothing gave me the same breathtaking feeling I experienced when working with water, when I felt it move through me and my magic within me. It felt so right, the way it streamed through my hands and the way I could command it not with authority, but with amicable benevolence. I would never admit that, never let people know I have a soft side. Maybe people like Sage and Tres or even Elijah had already picked up on my weakness for water.

"Korina? Do you see anything?" Teressia asked with her usual vexing hesitance.

"All I see is two strange figures on the water, way off in the distance," I snapped back, irritated with her soft tone of voice. Would it kill her just to speak up with a bit of confidence? And then there was Sage, who spoke with too much confidence, unconsciously projecting an air of arrogance. And when she became frightened or anxious she sounded ridiculous, like a young child scared by a storm.

"Oh, okay. I was just wondering." Tres seemed ashamed, and sorry that she ever asked. "I thought I saw something, just making sure it wasn't just me."

"Look, I didn't mean to snap, okay? And I'm sure we all see it."

"Still got that strange feeling, Korina?" Sage asked.

"Yes but I'm not sure what's causing it. Or maybe it's just the amount of dark magic floating on the water, since we're so close to the Sacred Islands."

"Finally," Sage announced exasperatedly. "I just want to be on solid earth! I'd do anything just to feel soil on my toes again. I'm tired of all this rolling water."

"I think the water is soothing," I declared.

"We all know that," Elijah chipped in.

"As for me, I just want some rocks that aren't embedded in the seafloor," Tres said.

We all murmured in response. Of course there was something each of us wanted. When did people ever stop wanting things?

I turned my head back to the sea, irritated with the burning heat that I felt from the sun. Summer was officially here, and it brought unwanted weather. What sane person could tolerate the heat of summer? I preferred spring or autumn, when the weather was pleasant: not too hot, not too cold. I certainly despised winter, for in some areas of the country the weather had the ability to freeze water for what seemed like an eternity. Winter was heartless! Freezing water against its own will? I shook my head.

"Well, I'm having ever so much fun," I remarked sarcastically. "I think I'm going to find something else to do before I drop from so much excitement."

"You have no patience, you know. You can't stay in one place for more than a few moments before you're drowning in boredom! Why can't you just stay still and discuss the situation instead of brushing it aside?" Sage huffed.

I narrowed my eyes at her. "Brushing aside the problem? What problem am I 'brushing aside?' Would you care to explain, O Great Knowing One?" I paused, watching Sage's angered face. "I'm going to go where *I* want now, if you'll please excuse me from our little party of four." I stalked off, ignoring Sage's cries of protests.

I *was* filled with boredom. What was so bad about leaving them for an hour? Sage could be so annoying and arrogant at times, like now. And Tres just stood there quietly until she was given an invitation to speak. Was it so bad that I wanted to leave them? I admitted I had flaws as well, but at least I could tolerate myself.

I didn't really know where I wanted to go after I stormed away. All I wanted now was to get away from the nagging Sage, to show her that anywhere away from her was a better alternative. I surveyed the decks, looking for a place to go. Maybe I could sneak off to the kitchen and steal a bite of food. Maybe it would be a good idea to hide in the crow's nest, where no one would bother me. The sailors wouldn't be taking shifts in the crow's nest at this time anyway. They were probably focusing on repairs and there weren't very many of them anymore. I even thought about retiring to my cabin, but quickly dismissed that idea—I would become so bored in that cabin. Besides, it was only noon. I had the whole day ahead of me.

Although I didn't consciously decide on a certain destination, my feet took me to the captain's cabin. Maybe the adults had finally decided to keep sailing. We were almost at the Sacred Islands, so why turn back now? Besides, Ignatia had probably overestimated the strength of whatever evil was there. There was no physical being in the world that could possess as much power as the Headmaster claimed.

I knocked on the door to the captain's cabin once and waited for a brief moment. When no one answered right away, I shoved the door open myself. Why wait on people to do things when I can do them myself?

Mage Melody and Mage Isaac stood by each other, throwing their voices at Serulean. Mage Melody looked at me unexpectedly. "Korina? May we help you?"

"No," I answered crisply. "I mean, I was just wondering if you adults had made up your minds."

"Made up our minds?" Isaac prompted. His voice carried a formal tone. It irritated me when people tried to speak elegantly.

"You know, about sailing on or turning back."

"We were in the middle of that until you so—"

Melody shot Isaac a glare that interrupted his sentence. "We haven't decided yet, dear. How about you return to the other children and we'll report our decision shortly."

I groaned. "I'm not just a child! I've fought against mutations twice, I think I can handle this discussion." Why was she treating me like this all of the sudden? She never acted this way in class.

"Korina," Melody warned sharply. "I expect you to treat us all with respect, and we will do the same in return. I'm sorry if I have offended you, and I know you are a mature young lady. But right now my head is a little cloudy from everything that's happened and is going on right now. So I would appreciate it if you left us."

I stared at her with a protesting look. I could feel my mouth hang open in disbelief.

"Korina, please do as your teacher asks," Isaac said formally.

"Promise you'll tell us right away?"

Melody nodded and motioned for me to leave. As I left, I let the door swing shut with a bang. I cringed when it made the loud noise. Hopefully the adults weren't paying attention to my exit.

The three nuisances stood right outside the cabin, as if they were waiting for me. I paused and stared back at them with a questioning face.

"Oh, stop squinting your eyes at me," Sage barked.

"I'm not squinting at you."

"Yes, you are, Korina."

"Okay, okay, we get it. Calm down before you start clawing each other," Elijah intervened. Sage looked back at him with sparkling hazel eyes. I looked to the side and sighed annoyingly.

"So now you're all better?" I asked Sage. "You were all in a dizzy daze of depression, and oh, the world was so horrible and poof! A visit to Melody and her healing magic makes you all better!"

"What's that have to do with anything?" Sage cried.

"Ah, nothing. I just thought of it suddenly."

"So, Korina!" Tres awkwardly announced. "Did you find out what we're going to do now that the Headmaster has ordered us to go back?"

"No, because apparently I'm just a child that gets in the way!"

"It's all right! I'm sure we'll find out soon enough," Elijah assured. "For now I say we should try to get along for once. Sage, you and Korina need to call a truce. You've been arguing since before we set foot on the *Naviganti*."

"Okay," Sage replied. If *I* had suggested that, she would surely have protested all the way from here to Elementa.

"Fine. I agree to stop arguing with her. But if she starts anything don't expect me to just stand by."

"There are more important things that we need to discuss," Tres remarked. "I think we should try to draw some conclusions about the recent attack, even though we don't want to."

"I'm fine with talking about it," I retorted.

"Sage and I have been affected more deeply than you and Elijah, I think."

"Probably," Sage mused.

I shrugged. "Elijah and I were the first ones to go fight. It's not like we didn't see the same bad things you saw."

"The way we perceive and digest things differs from person to person," Sage reflected.

"Exactly," Tres remarked.

"So, what about the mutation attack?" I prompted, changing the subject.

"First of all, did we all agree that the mutations are from the Sacred Islands?" Tres began. We all nodded our response. "And did we also agree that Devin was the one that contacted the mutations, yes?" More murmurs and nods. "Then we've established two facts. Would anybody like to add anything else?"

"Before we become completely submerged in this conversation, I think that we should go somewhere a bit quieter," Sage whispered. We were still standing in front of the captain's cabin.

"The crow's nest?" I suggested.

"Oh must we?" Sage complained. "It is ever so high, and we could easily go to someone's cabin instead. No one would hear us there."

"Are you scared of heights, Freckles?" Elijah teased. Sage blushed.

"No, I think Korina has a point," Tres said. "Someone could eavesdrop right outside the cabin and we mightn't realize it. There's no wind to carry our words either, so our best bet is the crow's nest."

"But the crew is making repairs on the sails and such, so they'll be near us, and at the same height."

"Nonsense," Elijah stated. "There won't be any sailors close enough to hear. We're wasting time."

I got my way, for once, and the four of us climbed the shrouds to the lookout. I went first, for I was wearing trousers instead of skirts. Elijah followed, then Tres and Sage. Sage was wearing her long olive skirts with a petticoat underneath that billowed in the wind, while Tres wore her usual dark magenta chemise with a gold overdress. I wore one of my plain peasant blouses, with my corset over it. My mother always despised my fashion, and disapproved of me wearing trousers. She claimed it was inappropriate for a lady to wear a man's clothes, and that I should do away with the trousers immediately. My mother had also mentioned that she thought I wore a bodice too often, and had bought an ornate stomacher for me to wear over a dress but I never wore it. I suppose I was too unladylike for my mother.

Elijah smoothed out his sleeveless jerkin that he wore over a buttoned shirt once we had reached the top. Sage shook out her skirts and immediately grasped a wooden beam. She was obviously frightened by heights.

"Scared?" Elijah mocked, echoing my thoughts.

"No, I'm not," Sage denied instantly. "I just need something to help me balance."

I smirked at her and leaned up against the side of the cylindrical lookout. "So continuing our conversation?"

Tres nodded. "I was asking if there was something we might add to our knowledge, I think."

"Let's go over what we know," Sage suggested methodically. "We know the mutations were winged, which was something we had never seen before. The mutations were also more intelligent than the ones in Elementa. They were... different in a way. So those mutations were definitely from the Sacred Islands. So who or what did Devin contact? The evil itself, or someone even higher in command? Do you think we'll see Devin again at the Sacred Islands? The mutations did fly that way."

Elijah, who had been deep in thought, looked up. "There's going to be more mutations on those islands. Think about it. Some or all will be winged and definitely vicious. We need to be prepared. We should train on the ship."

"And damage it even more? I don't think so," Tres said.

I shrugged. "Maybe it's not that bad of an idea. What's the alternative?"

"Dying," Sage breathed. "We can't let them be more powerful than us." She fell into thought before she finally spoke again. "Let's think bigger than mutations. What other creatures or beings might live on the islands? Would they be stronger or weaker than the mutations?"

"You're right, there's bound to be other forces," Elijah commented seriously.

"I think we should train like Elijah said. And you know it must be a wise idea if I agree with Sage and Elijah."

Teressia flapped a hand in the air. "That aside, what could be something so bad that would cause Headmaster Ignatia to order us to go back so urgently?"

"Weren't you listening?" I questioned irritably. "All Ignatia said was that there was a huge threat and some great evil and such."

"Okay, I'm sorry. I was just asking a simple question."

Simple questions from simple minds. "No matter. We know that she was very concerned about something, but think! Ignatia's not even here! She's miles southward, back at Elementa. How could she possibly judge the power of something that's at such a great distance? I think that we should just ignore her little anxiety and continue onward to the islands. I think we're almost there."

"Her 'little anxiety' was a warning, Korina. She was afraid, couldn't you see it?" Tres cried. "Something's definitely wrong and I think we should listen to Headmaster Ignatia."

A faint voice from the deck below interrupted our discussion. I peered over the edge of the crow's nest, seeing Melody on the main deck. Her hands were cupped around her mouth as she called to us.

"Time to go," Elijah announced.

"We just got here!" Sage complained. The four of us clambered down the shrouds, with Sage lagging behind as usual. It took time for a delicate girl like her to negotiate the ropes.

Mage Melody did not look pleased. Her face was flushed and worry was present in her eyes. I couldn't tell if she was more anxious or angered. "We have made our decision in regards of traveling to the Sacred Islands."

"Finally," I murmured under my breath.

Melody cleared her throat. "Apparently we will keep on sailing. Like fools," she added quietly. "The captain has claimed the ship unfit in its current state to sail a great distance, such as the distance required to return to Elementa."

"I thought repairs were being made," Tres whispered.

"They are, but the ship will have to be anchored near land for them to completely mend all of the damage. But what does it matter if we're all dead?"

"What?" Sage asked questioningly. "Did you say we're all going to die?"

"No, forget that nonsense. Listen, children." She looked at me then apologized for calling us children. "We can't expect to just waltz in there and investigate and leave unharmed. I do believe it is worse than we thought. Ignatia is right, I think. I just wish Serulean would acknowledge it. We must prepare ourselves for the worst before we set foot on Divite Island. Understand? We're going to train hard every day. If we return home without you, I don't want to have to explain to your parents how you were killed."

Elijah seemed excited to train, but Sage and Tres looked weary. I was just hesitant to put any more work into training after the seriously demanding lessons we had to endure before the trip. Ignatia was merciless when she trained us, and made sure our mage teachers were the same way. Why should I have to go through that again?

"Okay, I think that's all I wanted to share with you all. Let's see." Mage Melody hummed to herself while she thought. "Nope, there's nothing else you need to know. Carry on, but I want you four to spend some time together. I can see that not all of you are exactly on good terms." She lowered her voice and glared at me. I shrugged at her. "Oh don't look at me like that, Korina. You know what I'm talking about." Melody left and strutted across the deck, disappearing in the captain's cabin again. The four of us stood awkwardly in a line.

"Well... she wants us to stay together," Sage repeated.

"Yeah, no kidding." I crossed my arms and shuffled one foot. "I think I'm going to go spend a few hours in my cabin. There's nothing better to do."

"What? Hey, no! Mage Melody told us to stay together," Sage retorted. "It's not fair if you get to leave."

"Last time we all disobeyed Mage Melody's orders things didn't go so well," Tres reminded.

"But that wasn't our fault!" I protested. "Do all of you follow the rules every day?"

The two girls nodded like I was insane.

"Elijah?"

"Wha? Nah, I follow the rules. Why wouldn't I?"

"You know we can't believe you when you use that tone," I informed.

Tres rolled her eyes. "I know him well enough to tell you he's lying."

"Well, I don't care if you're a real 'rule breaker,' Korina. We are going to do what Mage Melody told us to do," Sage insisted. Her face was reddened. I looked down at her, since she was shorter. It was hard to take her seriously.

"The whole point of us spending time together is so that we can work out our differences and finally start to get along," Elijah said. "How about we stop complaining and go do something. I don't care what we do. Let's just stop standing around."

"Okay, I agree with you Elijah—" Sage was cut off as the ship tilted sharply. We stumbled suddenly, flapping our arms out. The ship seemed to jump, as it crashed to one side and jerked. A loud thud sounded, as if we had hit something in the sea.

The sensation I'd felt before had now returned. It filled my nostrils and burned. My magic screamed in my core and I became light headed. I felt as if something like dark magic was clogging the air. I fell to the deck and tucked my knees to my stomach. My core didn't feel so balanced and I couldn't stand the feeling in my head. What was going on? I felt so paralyzed, unable to think, to move, to stand on my feet.

"Korina?" Tres called.

I felt and heard the wind rise. A spray of water sprinkled the air. The waves were pacing, growing.

"Korina, are you okay, we're worried about you—"

It thundered, as if a sonic sound wave had shot out in the air. The boom turned into a growl, into a roar like a thousand lions, into an ear splitting screech, a siren. *Raaarrrr!*

I covered my ears and screamed. I looked up from the deck, and saw Elijah, Sage, and Tres with their mouths and eyes wide open and breathing hard. They had their eyes fixed on the same thing. I suddenly realized that the sky had darkened. I climbed to my feet slowly, and followed my unmoving friends' gaze.

A green-gray head, three times the size of the helm, stretched as high as the mainmast. Fangs as thick as my waist shot out of a mouth filled with teeth as sharp as jagged cliffs. Four whiskers slithered out of the sides of a revolting head that was covered with wrinkles and horns. Yellow eyes glared at me so hard, I felt as though the very sight of it could kill me. Blue and green scales glittered like diamonds. I froze, remembering.

"The dream," I whispered. "The dream, the dream, it was real. All real."

Another roar as the head thrust forward. The three of us flung our hands over our ears and cringed. The roar vibrated through my bones.

Suddenly, another body exploded from the sea followed by an immense wave that assailed the ship.

A hand on my shoulder made me jump. I yelped and turned to see Melody. "Don't move, don't make a sound," she instructed.

Tres shook like leaves in the wind. "The cave, it's haunting me!"

Another death shriek and the serpents plunged forward and whipped their bodies upward. They crashed into the side of the ship, and it dipped forward. We all screamed.

Wooden boards snapped and the deck began to break apart. Foaming water raced onto the deck and the serpents opened their mouths wide. They roared, their heads only feet above the main deck. Sailors ran in panic, Serulean yelling at them from the helm.

A serpent plucked one of the sailors from the deck with its teeth, and swallowed him whole. Sage shrieked in terror and I looked the other way.

One serpent turned and spotted Serulean. It snaked toward him as quick as light and as swift as a swordsman.

"Serulean watch out!" Melody screeched.

The serpent continued and after a second snapped its jaws in the air. Serulean dove off the helm and tumbled onto the deck. The serpent plunged its head into the deck, creating a hole that it became stuck in. The serpent writhed and wriggled, causing the ship to shake like it was in a storm. The other serpent dove into the sea and vanished. I was thrown off my feet and into the air as the serpent collided with the hull underwater. The serpent that had its head in the deck broke free, and deck boards went flying.

The four of us and Melody had scrambled away in different directions. The serpents were hovering above the deck, snapping their massive jaws. Their roars filled the atmosphere with a horrifying thundering sound.

I sprawled on the deck as a serpent's body floated above me. Its head was elsewhere, creating damage to the ship. Its body smashed into the mainmast. I rolled on my side, and pushed up on my arms, staring at the mast. A loud moan erupted from the mast as wood cracked. The mast leaned forward, then back. I couldn't bring my body to move.

The mainmast snapped, and plummeted down. I jumped to my feet and half crawled away in panic. Half of the mast fell to the deck, smashing the deck into pieces. The hold was now visible from where

I lay. Sails fluttered down and covered half of the deck in a white blanket. Ropes and shrouds dangled in midair. Screams called from all around the deck.

I got to my feet, shaking. For the first time since I had first seen the serpents, I tried to think. These monsters were ruthless, and would try to destroy the ship and eat everyone on it. The two mages and remaining sailors were separated and unorganized. There was nothing we could do to repel the serpents. How likely was it that we would get away from them, alive?

Should I try to attack the serpents? All I could do was send the wrath of water upon them, which would hardly do anything.

I hastily looked around. I couldn't spot Isaac or Melody or my three peers. Then I saw Elijah. He was crouching behind a piece of the fallen mast, his arms and hands outstretched in front of him. A piece of a serpent's snake-like body writhed in front of him. The serpent did not know Elijah was there.

I shook my head and mouthed "no" to Elijah even though I was facing his side and he did not see me. He was going to try his fire magic on the serpent.

A dark flicker of fire sprouted from his hand. Soon, after what seemed like a protracted delay, a thread of flame streamed, growing thick. The threads of fire wrapped around the skin of the serpent. The slimy body jumped and then moved, sliding forward. Elijah shrank back. The serpent twisted and then whipped about to face the deck, its enormous head with frightening horns poised to strike. It screeched at Elijah, staring directly at him. Elijah covered his ears and fell back. The serpent gnashed its teeth together and slowly crept forward. Elijah didn't run, but remained motionless.

"Elijah!" I shouted, and before I knew what I was doing, I sprinted over to him. He was near the bow, at the base of the forecastle. The serpent instinctively turned its head toward me and growled.

"Korina, no!" Elijah protested.

I ignored him and kept running. I skidded to a halt as the serpent rose and slid in front of me. It bared its teeth and growled again. I expected it to plunge down on me and pluck me up, but instead it returned its focus to Elijah. Maybe he looked tastier to the serpent.

I slowly inched forward, ready to send a blast of water onto the serpent if it dared to face me again. I had no other ideas as the serpent opened its mouth ever so slightly and breathed over Elijah, dripping saliva onto his face. Fangs as tall as he was glinted in the light.

"Hey!" I called. The serpent turned around and stared at me. I called on the water around me and sent it gushing onto its hideous face. It shook and snarled. Before it could snap at me I leaped up, and landed on the serpent's rough head. It threw back its head and growled in frustration.

The serpent shot into the air, towering above the deck. I looked down, bile rising in my throat from the unnerving heights. I stood up and began to climb down the serpent's neck. It snapped in the opposite direction very abruptly, throwing me off balance. I flipped over onto my back and dangled head first off of the monster. I quickly tightened my stomach and rose up. The serpent writhed and traveled over the ship, leaving a wide swath of destruction as it tried to hurl me off of it.

I mustered the strength left in me and stood up, fighting all my instincts that screamed for me to sit down and hold on tightly. Once I had found my balance, I swept my arms upward, and the water far below me obeyed my commands. The seawater whirled in a funnel and came to me. I pulled smaller threads of water from the funnel and used them to carry me off of the serpent's body. I nearly dropped myself, causing me to gasp in sudden fear. I safely pulled myself to the top of the funnel and wrapped threads of water around my legs until I was entwined with the column of water. At that instant I broke free from the maelstrom and thrust the waterspout forward.

The serpent quickly discerned what I was doing. It reared up until it matched the height of my waterspout and snapped at me as I hung in the air, its large fangs within inches of my body. I quickly bent the funnel back, causing the serpent to barely miss me. The serpent took advantage of my retreat and swung the other half of its scaly body into the middle of my spout. I lost my magical grip on the water and the funnel collapsed, leaving me hanging in the air once again.

I felt the wind weaving around me as I plunged down. I was silently panicking, and I didn't think to call on the water around me. Blurred sights whizzed past me as my mind dizzied. Within a few seconds I plopped into the sea. Sprays and splatters of water leaped into the air as I tucked into a pocket of the sea and disappeared under the surface. Water gushed into my mouth and eyes and I went blind. I was carried downward by the momentum of my fall. I lost sight of the surface of the water, the surface that the light penetrated and wove into the water.

I felt myself drifting from consciousness as the surface grew distant. I became wide awake and tried to spring upward, but there was nothing to push off of. I was floating in the vast sea, and who knew what creatures it held in its depths?

I called to the water around me and wove it around my legs with circular motions of my arms. Using my magic and the water, I twirled my body and let the water push me up.

I started traveling upward, picking up speed as I rushed toward the surface. Then to my horror, I began to slow. I pushed the water on with my magic, but it refused. I realized my connection with the water was being severed. My lungs felt bloated, and the impulse to breathe was intense—I was running out of air. And it wasn't like I had all the time in the world to reach the surface! *I don't want to die! I can't, not like this! Not by drowning in my own element.* I sounded like Sage, always thinking of dying. *No, I can't think like this. I have to keep going.*

I slowed until I was motionless. The water that I had wrapped around myself dispersed. I blasted the water with one command after another, but it felt as if my magic had been bottled and tightly corked, and I couldn't access it—I couldn't use my magic at all. I panicked, and flailed in the sea. I tried to calm myself, tried to think, but I wasn't good at thinking. Sage was good at thinking, not me.

With no other alternative, I kicked my legs and stroked my arms, attempting to swim to the surface. I almost made it, but I ran out of air and darkness swept over me. Just before I passed out, I felt the warmth of the sun hit my fingertips. I stopped swimming and drifted downward again.

There was a shadow that covered me. My eyes flickered open and I tried to focus on the figure that hovered above me. I was alive, at least. I didn't know how I had gotten wherever I was, but I was grateful.

I tried to move, tried to roll over so that I could stand up. My bones and muscles groaned, but I finally managed to stand up with a bit of struggle. I was still damp, but that was expected and quite frankly a minor nuisance compared to drowning.

I ducked and exited the wooden structure I had been tucked under. I realized that it was a piece of wreckage from the ship. I was on the *Naviganti* again, by some miracle. Or maybe it wasn't a blessing that I had somehow returned to the ship. Those serpents were still prowling about. How much more of this could we take before the ship sank?

My lungs felt tight, and suddenly I felt nauseous and pained. I bent over and coughed up strings of seawater. My mouth was very dry.

I crawled back under the wreckage and poked my head out. I wanted to observe the damage and find everyone before I went back out in the open. As I rested there under the wreckage, surveying the damage, there was one thing I knew for certain—I wasn't afraid of the serpents anymore. In fact, I wanted them to pay for what they had done. *They* will *get away from this ship after I'm through with them.* I clenched my fists and dug my nails into my palms. Rage was boiling inside me.

CHAPTER 28

AUGUST

$\mathcal{T}$he next morning my legs were sore, but I was determined. I had shoved the broom under my bed the previous night, the night I had discovered very large forces were marching straight at us. The army had obviously just crossed the Lux Mountain range, so we had a little bit of time before they reached us. Did anyone else realize that there was an army coming our way, though? The brief period of time before they arrived left no room for chances. I decided to report my sightings to Headmaster Ignatia.

My Academy robe flapped behind me as I rushed to the Headmaster's office. I had been there once and was sure I could find the way back. I took a couple of wrong guesses and entered completely different levels and hallways, but I eventually arrived at Ignatia's office. I instantly recognized the dark engraved wood door and knocked confidently. I stepped back and waited. No answer. I knocked again.

I stood there awkwardly, waiting for her to appear. I decided Ignatia was not there, which was very unfortunate for me. Even if I could navigate through the Academy and somehow find her quarters, I wouldn't be allowed to enter the corridor in which it was located. I was only a young student, and was certainly not authorized to access the most important areas of the large Academy.

I tapped my foot on the lightly colored stone floor. Where could I find Headmaster Ignatia? If she wasn't here, or in her quarters, she could be anywhere. She might not even be in the Academy at all. Should I just wait for her to come to her office? No, that would be ridiculous. It might take hours for her to come, if she came at all.

I turned away and decided to ask one of my teachers. There were no classes today, but most of the teachers and mages would be in the Academy. Other mages would be out in the city, patrolling in place of guards that had left for war.

By the time I had arrived to the student area of the Academy, I was out of breath and feeling out of shape. Currently, I did not have classes dealing with magery, for I had not discovered my magic until recently. The teacher that I sought, Professor Adalardi, specialized in teaching the class of different kinds of magic. She had studied the ways of scrying and using looking-glasses, even though she was not a seer. She had a small amount of magical abilities but was not a mage or wizard.

I had better luck finding her than Ignatia. Professor Adalardi was in her classroom, her dirty blonde hair pulled back in a braid that wrapped around her head. She wore casual skirts instead of a more formal dress, corset, and overdress. The professor usually wore a sheer turquoise veil, symbolizing her social rank. Women of higher rank could wear darker veils that were either royal blue or purple.

"August? Do you have a question about the class?"

"No, professor. I'm trying to find the Headmaster. I have something very important to report to her," I replied.

"I see. With apologies, I do not know where Headmaster Ignatia is. Though, if she isn't in her office, I recommend looking in the Second

Courtyard. She holds private lessons there for select students, such as yourself. I assume you did not have any lessons today?"

"No, today's my day of rest." Ignatia had almost forgotten to give me one day of the week off. But after reminding her about it a number of times, she had finally decided that today would be my day of rest every week.

"Ah, I see. Lucky you then. Us professors seldom get one of those days," she grinned. "Is that all?"

"Yes, Professor Adalardi. Thank you." I left the classroom, heading to the Second Courtyard, the same courtyard that I trained in.

The Headmaster was in the courtyard training a handful of students, just as the professor had suggested. She was instructing combat techniques, combined with elemental magic. She was training student mages.

One of the students, a short blonde girl, clumsily swept a foot out, stirring up a small gust of air in the process. She tried to drop swiftly and roll to the side to finish the well-known move, but lost balance and fell on her rump.

Ignatia scolded her immediately. "No, no, no! You had no balance when you dropped. Why didn't you have any balance?" This was Ignatia's teaching technique, providing hints disguised as questions to help the student figure out how to solve the problem on their own.

"Um, I was worried about the leg that I kicked out too much?"

"No," Ignatia responded bluntly. "Your core is weak. That's where you need to balance when you kick out and drop down. It's a fast, swift motion. You didn't tighten your core and hold it firmly. Instead, you slouched and let your muscles relax. Also, when you kicked out, you didn't have enough momentum to create a powerful gust of air. Your magic comes from your core, and since your 'core form' was sloppy, very little of your magic was actually applied. Plus you were timid, which was also a factor in your inability to create a strong gust of wind with your air magic. Perform the motions as if *you* are the one in control." Ignatia abruptly twirled and gracefully kicked out as she dropped on one foot and then rolled defensively. "Keep practicing that same move."

Ignatia stepped back and observed the student as she began to work on the motions, then glanced at me. "You don't have lessons today, August."

I trotted over to Ignatia. "I know, but I need to tell you something important."

"Well, what is it?" she replied briskly.

"Um, I think it would be best if... others didn't hear." My face warmed as Ignatia stared at me with irritation.

"Must it be right now, August? I'm in the middle of a lesson if you hadn't noticed." She narrowed her eyes slightly.

I knew that my news of the army would have to wait. Headmaster Ignatia would not let me interrupt her lessons. She was a very dedicated teacher. "Yes, Headmaster Ignatia. If it is allowable, I will report the information to you after you are done with your lesson. My apologies, Headmaster."

"Since when did you become so polite, August? After you let loose that whole closet of mops?" she joked and scolded at the same time.

I grew hot with embarrassment again. "I will be waiting just inside the west walls."

Ignatia grunted and then returned to her students as I walked away. She aimed for excellence when teaching combat, academics, and magic, and expected her students to achieve perfection. That explains why she was so picky when it came to the basic principles of the subjects she taught.

I sat looking out the window into the courtyard that was adjacent to the west wall. After the city clock struck the hour of noon, Headmaster Ignatia released her students. To my surprise, she went to the west wall, where I said I would be. I turned around on the bench, ready to present her with the news of the army.

Ignatia strolled inside, wiping her face with a cloth. "Okay, August," she sighed impatiently. "What did you so highly desire to tell me that you wished to disrupt one of my lessons?"

"Last night, I was taking a stroll outside. In front of the Lux Mountains, way off in the distance, I saw an army. It appeared to stretch for miles and was traveling right toward us. Are they going to attack Elementa?" I decided it was best not to let Ignatia know about my flight aboard the broom.

Headmaster Ignatia raised her eyebrows. "An army, did you say? Are you certain, August?"

"Positive, Headmaster."

"And how big was this army?"

"Enormous. I would say it was many times the population of Elementa. They were at the base of the mountains, so I assume they had just crossed through."

"Ah. I don't doubt you on that. And they were coming right at us?"

"I think so. Maybe they're going to Oceanus. Or Soror, though I strongly hope not." Soror was my home. I didn't want it to be plundered and burned by a bunch of soldiers. I knew that we were involved in a war, but I didn't think that Soror should be punished. After all, it was the City of Oceanus that had started the civil war. I planned to return to Soror after I had gotten a good start on my mage training, and I didn't want to return to a wrecked city.

"Hm. I don't know what their plans are, but I'm sure this army is ready to fight. The civil war has officially started."

"Where is this army coming from, Headmaster?"

Ignatia looked at me with a puzzled face. "You mean, you don't know? Come on August, use your head. The civil war is between us, the city states, and the capital—the City of Lux. That army just came from the other side of the mountain range. What is on the opposite side of the mountains? The capital. That huge army is the forces of Lux." She squeezed her eyes shut. "I just pray they decide not to attack Elementa. We have no chance against them, especially without our own forces. The mages can't defend us against them."

"Do you think they'll go to Oceanus?"

"It seems that is the most likely place they will go. But if we look defenseless, I don't know. They may target us."

"Are you going to do anything about it?" I inquired.

"There isn't much that can be done about it, though I'm not Gileon. I refuse to stand by and do nothing, or in his case, cause more damage." Headmaster Ignatia paused and thought for a moment. I said nothing, only waited. "I suppose I can make it seem like we have some line of defense, though I seriously doubt they'll be the least bit intimidated unless we get help."

"What do you mean?"

"The City of Lux knows Elementa has joined the war on the side of Oceanus and Soror. They are smart enough to know that most of our army has gone to join them, but they might be surprised to learn that all of our forces have left the city. Gileon, the idiot," she muttered. "Regardless, it's no secret that our army is small, and that makes us an easy target. So I suspect the capital's first move will be to come and easily wipe us out unless Oceanus and Soror anticipate their plans and send forces back to protect Elementa. Though I doubt it will be our own forces because once Elementa's army arrives at Soror, they'll be separated into different divisions and sent in sundry directions. I'm not familiar with the ways of battle, but I'm certain the commanders won't leave all the armies in the same place. If they do, they're all as stupid as Gileon."

"I am encouraged, however, that Oceanus and Soror have been sending small delegations to other city states to try to get more people to join the war. They'll need all the people they can get if they are to stand a chance against the capital's forces, that's for sure."

"You say 'they,' as if you're not a part of the war at all. Why?"

Ignatia sighed irritably. "Because I *don't* want to be a part of a civil war, August. We're already involved in what seems like an ongoing skirmish with Fortis, and to make matters worse, Gileon accepts the invitation to join this civil war as if it's an invitation to a party."

"So... what is your plan against the capital if they come this way? Something about making it seem like we have a line of defense?"

"Oh, yes! I thought that if I lined the mages up in front of the city, they'll see that we have some sort of defense." Ignatia shook her head and scoffed. "But our three rows of mages will pale against their massive army. Nevertheless, I suppose it's better than nothing. I'm afraid it won't change our fate, though."

"I think you should do it, Headmaster."

For once, Ignatia genuinely smiled at me. "I think I will, August." She brushed a thick strand of wavy hair back. "But maybe it would be wiser if we didn't, giving them the impression that we don't want to pick a fight. Thank you for your support, August."

I smiled back. "Of course, Headmaster."

"Is that all?"

I nodded.

"Then run along, but stay away from closets and mops. Do you think you can handle that, August?"

"Yes, Headmaster Ignatia."

"Good, you learned that it's wiser to agree with me. I must go now and inform all of the mages and others of my plans."

"What others?"

"Don't be ridiculous, August. The Academy contains wizards, a handful of sorcerers, and a few seers. Though..." Ignatia paused. "The seers don't fancy fighting, so I suppose I'll leave them alone." She smiled at the thought of harassing the seers.

"Headmaster Ignatia, if you don't mind me asking..." When Ignatia waited for me to go on, I continued, "You're a mage, aren't you?"

She gave a chuckle. "Yes, of course. Why would you think otherwise?"

"I was just wondering, Headmaster. No one really knows what your element is, beside a few of the mages and professors, but they won't give anything away."

"Hm. That's too bad for curious students, then." She knew that I was basically asking her what her element was, but she refused to admit anything.

"I wonder why the Headmaster keeps it a secret?" I prompted.

Ignatia smiled and shrugged. "I have much to do today, so I will see you tomorrow, August."

* * *

Every night, the time of day when I assumed no one was watching me, I practiced flying on the broom. Maybe it was unnatural for a light mage to do so, since I wasn't a witch, but I still practiced. I mostly did it to keep an eye on the capital's army. Every day they advanced, closer and closer.

My only concern about broom flying was Headmaster Ignatia. If she caught me doing it, there was no telling what would happen to me. I might not be alive long enough to return to Soror if I was caught by the Headmaster.

Ignatia had been watching the army everyday as well. About a week and a half had passed when Ignatia ordered the mages and other magical people to line up in front of the city. The Headmaster had decided the army was too close for her liking. I had learned that she always preferred to be prepared ahead of time.

The next day the army took a turn to the northeast, towards Oceanus. Ignatia had misjudged the Capital's intentions but this was fortunate for Elementa and everyone was able to relax a bit, especially the Headmaster. Nevertheless, she still instructed her people to go out in front of the city every day and keep watch for a certain period of time.

It seemed that the enemy would stay in Oceanus for a little while; I predicted a month at least. I became less tense, but still worried. Not for Elementa, but for Soror. What if the capital decided to send its army there?

Headmaster Ignatia was working the sweat out of me in a lesson. The summer's heat beat down on the courtyard, making me feel as dry and hot as the plains in southeastern Lux.

The clock had just struck the top of the hour when the ground seemed to rumble. Ignatia froze and kneeled on the dusty ground. She leaned even closer to the ground and put her ear next to it.

"Headmaster Ignatia, what's wrong?" I asked worriedly.

"Something's..." she trailed off, listening intently. After a few moments she raised up. "Something's going on right outside of the city. I think we both have an idea of what it is."

I knew instantly. My heart skipped a beat, in fear of the army. It was so large, and now they were here!

Ignatia looked at me and saw my concern. "Don't worry too much, August. By the sounds of it, the whole army isn't here. Let's take a look."

I had to run to keep up with Ignatia. If I had ever wondered how she acted up close when sending out commands, I knew now. She was firm and confident, but very quick. She rushed by several wings of the Academy, calling out the mages and others. Soon Ignatia and I were outside the city with all of the mages, wizards, sorcerers, leftover guards, and whatever else the Academy had, all lined up in three or four rows. There weren't nearly enough of us to stand up for a fight. Maybe there was enough to fight off mutations, but not the capital.

My legs were trembling, but I tried to ignore them. In front of us stood rows and rows of the enemy's forces, but not nearly in the vast numbers I saw in front of the mountains the first night. Most of the army was probably still in Oceanus.

A patrol of several soldiers approached Ignatia and a mage that stood by her. The soldier that led the patrol spoke to Ignatia. "This is the city state of Elementa, governed by Headman Gileon, home of the Magical School and Arts Academy of Elementa, presently administered by Headmaster Ignatia, is it not?"

"You are correct," Ignatia affirmed curtly. She would not allow herself be walked on by these capital soldiers.

"And by the decree of Headman Gileon, the city state of Elementa has officially joined the civil war against the capital—the grand City of Lux, on the city state of Oceanus's side. Is this true as well?"

"Right again," Ignatia replied through slightly gritted teeth. "And what of it? Are you here to attack?"

The soldier actually chuckled. "I appreciate your boldness, Lady...?"

"Headmaster Ignatia," she finished.

"Ah, you are the legendary Headmaster of the Academy. It is quite a pleasure."

"I beg your pardon but I cannot say the same. Why are you here?"

"I have orders to investigate Elementa, to determine whether it has formally joined the civil war against us. With your assistance madam, I have now affirmed the intentions of your city. I also have orders to attack if I must, but I am hoping to return to Oceanus by tomorrow, maybe even tomorrow morning."

"Do you have any more business that requires you to enter the city?" Ignatia asked firmly, holding his gaze.

"Yes, but only to make observations, not to attack. We will then pass through to the Shrouded Forest, and then to the city state of Fortis."

"Very well then. But I will have you watched at all times and have a patrol and myself accompany you through the city. You understand the need for our safety, I presume? And I would advise you not to go near Shrouded Forest. It is unsafe."

"We have had reports of strange activity in the forest. We will investigate whether you advise it or not, Headmaster Ignatia."

"Then your own ignorance will be your demise," Ignatia murmured darkly.

"What's that?"

"Nothing, soldier of the capital."

"Then may we begin our patrol through the city?"

Ignatia nodded. "Of course. But I wouldn't try anything if I were you."

The small patrol of soldiers went through the city, but the rest of them skirted the borders, marching to wait in front of the Shrouded

Forest. I silently feared that they would rouse the mutations, which would lead them to attack the nearly defenseless city.

I followed Ignatia the whole time until the soldiers stopped in front of the forest.

"You may want to stay back, August," Ignatia advised. "These mutations haven't attacked in weeks, and we might be surprised by their strength and astuteness."

"Are the mutations going to come out and attack?" I questioned.

"I would think so."

Ignatia and I stood with a few mages at the west border of the city, watching the capital's soldiers carefully. They poked around at the edge of the forest, but didn't enter it. I wondered if they would. Dark magic was even visible on the grass and plants outside of the forest, so would they take it as an ominous warning?

A howl sent a line of soldiers jumping back. Ignatia smiled with pleasure at the surprise and took it as a cue to approach them. She probably wanted to make sure they acknowledged her earlier warning now. I followed the few mages that trailed behind Ignatia.

"Do you take my advice into consideration now? There is more where that howl came from," Ignatia warned.

The soldier that conversed with her earlier scowled. "It is merely an animal. If it is a monstrosity of so-called dark magic we have been hearing about, we will simply eliminate it. The armies of Lux are known for their great strength and skill. We could easily wipe out something so..." He paused, searching for the right word. "So petty."

"The great army of Lux would be rather surprised," Ignatia muttered under her breath. If the arrogant soldier heard he showed no sign of it.

"We will venture into the forest and investigate. Do not try to stop us," the soldier announced.

"I wouldn't dream of it. We will wait here and watch your patrol from afar." Ignatia calmly folded her arms over her chest. She seemed unaffected by the soldier's decision. Pleased, even. She turned her head slightly to fix an eye on me. "As for you, I want you to leave. It isn't safe."

"Why must I? You're staying."

"Don't argue with me," she snapped. "What if the mutations come charging out of the forest? Worse, what if they recognize you? Soror is expecting you back in a month or so. How would I explain this to them? 'I'm sorry to inform you, but August Primerano isn't coming back. He was eaten by a bunch of monsters!'" She squinted at me, obviously not in the mood for argument.

"Fine, but you have to promise me you'll tell me every—"

A firm snarl erupted from the hungry jaws of a mutation. Its deformed body sprung from a clump of bushes, sending leaves that fluttered like the wings of a bird. More mutations followed, sprinting on all fours toward the mass of soldiers. Solid shapes could be seen in the mutations' bodies, and they looked less like a glob of hardened liquid. It seemed as if their bodies had solidified, as if the mutations had grown and formed hard bones and muscles. I shuddered.

The soldiers unsheathed swords and raised shields. They positioned themselves in a firm stance as the mutations charged toward them. The first mutation leaped and cleared an unbelievable distance. The mutation landed on top of a soldier, who threw up his shield as the mutation plunged onto his shoulders. The mutation swiped the shield away and slapped the man's neck with its paw. The soldier fell to the ground, limp, without time for even a cry.

This happened to a couple of soldiers. Their commander instantly calculated their odds of surviving and barked, "Retreat!"

A larger mutation growled and the others stopped attacking. The mutations sat on their haunches and waited. I stood at the border of the city, ready to run, but the mutations did nothing.

Ignatia had not budged from beside me. "What is going on?" she whispered to herself.

"Why aren't they attacking?" I gazed up at Ignatia in wonder.

She glanced down at me briefly and slowly walked closer to the soldiers. I followed in the same manner. Ignatia swiped an arm in front of my chest, halting me as we neared the mutations and Lux soldiers. "Don't move," she whispered. I obeyed without question.

A mutation bristled. Another one growled. The creatures glared at each other and made low rumbling sounds in their throats. They were communicating. I knew that the mutations could speak though, for I had heard them do it myself. They knew that we could speak in the same language, so the mutations probably warbled in noisy nonsense so that we could not understand them.

In a blink of an eye, five mutations lunged with powerful leg muscles. I yelped in surprise and hopped back, while the mutations leaped onto Ignatia.

I shielded my eyes as the wind picked up and sunlight was yanked from the sky. Threads of sunlight were weaved into the wind. I could barely witness this, for the light was simply blinding.

Some of the mutations whined, while others growled. More mutations flooded toward Ignatia, while the soldiers and even the other mages dumbly watched. I was frozen with surprise and fear, feeling as if I could not move even if I willed myself to.

When the breeze faded, the light was lost. I realized that Headmaster Ignatia had manipulated the sunlight and grabbed and strengthened the wind. Was that her element?

Then the Headmaster pulled hundreds of dancing leaves off the sickened trees of Shrouded Forest. She wrapped them in a storm around her, spinning them fiercely. The mutations reared back in fear, but overcame it and plunged into her vortex. The leaves bit into the mutations and some fell to the ground. Others pushed on and attacked Ignatia.

Once she came into contact with a mutation the leaves dropped. Ignatia resorted to physical combat, jabbing at the mutations, and even kicked one back. As she caught a break from the attacking mutations, Ignatia waved her hands in a series of complicated motions, until a small wispy fog materialized overhead. She pulled her arms gracefully down, as if she was guiding a lost child. A wind came from the fog, which became denser until I realized it was a small cloud. The breeze carried white flakes, snowflakes it seemed. Ignatia had just created snow.

She made the flakes grow bigger, until they appeared as ice daggers. Headmaster Ignatia sent them flying at mutations that neared her. Many mutations retreated. Ignatia was very quick with her magic.

I noticed that the mutations were only attacking Ignatia, no one else. None of the mages were helping Ignatia, until I sprinted toward her with a battle cry. I pulled streams of light from the sun just as Headmaster Ignatia had done, and sent it spiraling toward mutations. Soon all of the mages had joined.

The mages and I rushed to Ignatia, but more and more mutations jumped in front of us. Soon the area in front of the forest was flooded with the monsters, and the soldiers had disappeared silently and unnoticed.

I frantically looked around. The soldiers weren't the only ones that had vanished. Headmaster Ignatia was gone, gone from the band of mutations that had encircled her.

I jerked my head toward the forest, seeing a group of mutations dash away with a body. Tumbling black waves cascaded over the shoulder of the body.

I didn't think. I sprinted as fast as I could toward the mutations. Once they realized I was following them they picked up their pace until they flickered out of sight. The speed at which the mutations ran now surpassed my own ability.

I calmed my racing thoughts, and tried to halt the shakiness and the rush of adrenaline that coursed through me. It was going to be fine. After all, the mutations would take Ignatia back to their nest and I knew where it was. Where else would they go? But why did the mutations take Ignatia? And was she dead or alive?

I shook off troubling ideas and focused on getting to the heart of the forest. The most important thing at the moment was finding Headmaster Ignatia and bringing her back.

I jogged and walked the rest of the way, until I was far into the forest. I stumbled around, searching for the familiar tree that I had been in about a week ago. I had been captured by the mutations myself, and I expected the same thing was happening to Ignatia.

When I finally found it, I stopped at the foot of the looming trunk and craned my neck up at the tree's canopy. It was dark and emitted an ominous feeling. The leaves had wilted into a brown and blackened color, and the color of the trunk was darkening. It was poisoned. The dark magic was so strong, even I could smell it without having the particular element that the magic was contaminating.

I grabbed a sickly vine that crawled silently down the trunk and heaved myself up. Once I had gotten a foothold I climbed upward. I stopped and rested when I was many feet above the forest floor. I could see no mutations.

I continued climbing, and halted once more when I reached a familiar area of the tree. I was in the crook of where several branches met. Leaves were laid methodically on the bark, like a nest. This was where the mutations had brought me when I was unconscious.

The forest was silent except for the eerie hissing of the wind. The slight breeze wove through the leaves and dying trees, disturbing the still plant life. I shivered as it grazed my skin.

I looked around the huge tree, which I was sure was the nest of the mutations. I was sure it was empty. Nothing—no one—was there.

The mutations had seemingly dissolved into thin air. Their nest was abandoned. Where had they gone? Where was Headmaster Ignatia now?

I ambled slowly through the forest once more, keeping an eye out for anything. I flinched at every rustle of a bush, every sound that the wind aroused. There were no animals. Were they dead, or had they all become mutations? Or had some been smart enough to escape?

I spent seemingly hours in the forest. I was sure that all the mutations were completely gone. I shook my head in bewilderment and stumbled noisily to the city. The sun was drowning in the sky, sinking until it met the land.

I couldn't go back to the Academy. Ignatia was still missing and the city needed her and her leadership. It felt wrong to go back without her. But I felt lost, having no idea where she could be, let alone the mutations.

I gave up and went to the Academy, promising myself that I would only stay there to think and to stare at a map.

As soon as I opened the doors of the west side, chaos was running rampant in the halls. Mages and professors dashed with satchels, stacks of papers, looking-glasses, and some with a slender rod that I assumed was a wizard's wand.

People were running over each other, tripping, and dropping things. A mirror crashed to a floor and shattered into a million pieces. The seer gaped in horror at the catastrophe and knelt to the floor.

I hugged a wall and slid past the pandemonium. Other areas of the Academy were no better than the previous scene. I scoffed, questioning the intelligence of the Academy's leadership. Could they not organize themselves without the Headmaster? Who was the next person in charge, anyway?

I isolated myself in my dorm, thinking. I dragged out a map and hastily spread it over my desk. The map showed the northwestern shore of Lux, the tiny bit that showed the tip of the Vast Lake, Elementa, Shrouded Forest, and Fortis.

I ran my finger over the familiar places, thinking rapidly. Where would the mutations go? My eyes darted among the possible destinations, over and over again. Finally, my eyes settled on a peculiar site. My fingertip hovered over the shore of the Vast Lake. In front of the western shore was a bundle of trees. I had learned in Soror of rumors about a cave in the midst of those trees, a cave that tampered with people's minds. Anyone who had dared to wander about in that labyrinth heard things, and saw things in crystals and puddles that weren't really there. Sometimes seers even ventured inside of the cave, searching for visions of the future. People believed that there were magical elements in the cave. I had been scared to even go near that dark place, but now I was desperate. I was convinced that was where the mutations had taken Headmaster Ignatia. I told myself to be brave, that the magical rumors weren't likely to be true anyway, but it didn't help.

* * *

I leaned on a rock that protruded from the entrance to the cave. It was dark and damp inside, and the only lights were from the crystals that jutted out of the rock walls and floors. I wondered how it was possible for the crystals to be glowing, illuminated. Was it really magic, or some trick of reflection?

I took a tentative step forward, wrinkling my nose. The smell was disgusting, as if something had been rotting. Maybe the mutations really were in the cave.

I froze, my foot sinking into cold thick liquid. I slowly pulled it out, the liquid squelching loudly. It felt as if I was yanking my foot out of fresh mud, heavy and viscous. I hesitantly looked down, squinting in the darkness. I could see a darkly colored puddle, but it was too dimly lit in the cave to see it clearly.

I bent over, attempting to get a closer look at the mysterious liquid. But no matter how close I got, it still looked like the same dark mass. I gingerly dabbed a fingertip in the puddle, yanking it back when my finger stung instantly. I sniffed my finger. Mutations.

I trudged along the dank cave and used the moist walls to guide me, cringing when my hands met some slimy object. I stopped, realizing how stupid I was being. I didn't have to stumble blindly around in this maze. I was a light mage, and even though I wasn't an accomplished one, I was sure I could figure out a way to make a light.

I closed my eyes and took several even breaths. I focused on energy that nestled in my core, calling on it just as Ignatia had once instructed during a lesson. Dazzling light flashed and quickly faded into a tiny ember that I nurtured in the palm of my hand. I fed energy to it, running my hands around it to increase its size. I finished with an orb of light that was the size of my fist. It was a perfect sphere, with rays dancing out of it and illuminating the space around me. I was fortunate I didn't have to rely on sunlight to be present. I could conjure light magic any time I wanted, as long as I was well rested and energized.

A soft howl sounded further back in the cave. At that moment I knew the mutations had moved their nest into the stone prison that I was wandering in. Headmaster Ignatia had to be in the cave, had to be there. And I would find her.